A.J.MITCHELL

The Prince of the Dead

First edition

ISBN: 979-8-9905865-1-2

Editing by Katie White
Illustration by BMR Williams
Cover art by Adrian Mitchell
Typesetting by Adrian Mitchell
Proofreading by Sarah Joseph
Proofreading by Ashley Mitchell

I dedicate this book to Ashley Christine Mitchell
Thank you for being the best support that I could ever ask for.
Not only in writing this book but in all aspects of my life.
You challenged me to be better.
I grew as a person because I watched your growth.
I praise God everyday for the blessing He gave me that was you in my life.
I love you. Forever and Always

Chapter 1

The most important thing to remember was that a dead body weighed less than a living body. A dead body does not have the weight of the world bearing down on its shoulders. Ronan repeated this to himself. The iron-fermented air filled his lungs and he gagged. He repeated the mantra again as he struggled to flip over the particularly heavy-set soldier with plate mail armor and a large stab wound in his back. He needed to prove he could do this. His knees sunk into the dew covered, black earth. With one more large heave, the rigor mortis stricken soldier rolled over, revealing a young, mud-covered face, staring up at the endless sky. Ronan wondered if the morbid feeling at seeing corpses would ever dull.

"I am sure that you fought your hardest," Ronan said to the corpse. "I guess it wasn't enough. I understand that."

Ronan searched the man's pockets, finding only two silver coins, a half-eaten biscuit, and a necklace with an engraved pendant. Ronan stood up and inspected the medallion. Finely engraved on its surface was the mantra, 'Forge Through Fire'. Ronan pondered this life motto. He understood the concept; the application was where he struggled. His issue was not a shortage of 'fires'. Ronan was not lacking in tribulations in his life- forced into an orphanage at an early age, turned to a life of stealing in the streets, and admitted into an underground criminal organization at the age of fifteen (just two years ago). However, he struggled to understand the idea of being better through the trials. He had never felt that his troubled life had led him to being refined.

Ronan put the loot into his satchel and moved onto the next body. The

1

thigh high grass brushed against him as he moved. He looked up at the sun to check its position in the sky. It was about halfway to its pinnacle. Its rays cast down onto the Field of Hormáne, illuminating the remnants and carnage of the battlefield. Ronan took out a handkerchief and mopped his sweaty forehead and his short, black, bristled hair.

Ronan stooped down to check another body. Even though this was only his second scavenging mission, he was hoping to find something valuable. He didn't want to let Arkeen down. Arkeen had stuck his neck out for Ronan when he convinced their boss, Mr. Kemin, that Ronan was ready for field work. That he was trained up enough for the real thing. Ronan looked across the field to find his half Elven friend. He caught a glimpse of Arkeen bobbing in and out of some tall grass by a tree. His thin, pointed ears and long, auburn ponytail reminded Ronan of a wild rabbit. Arkeen moved from corpse to corpse at a speed that Ronan could not comprehend. He guessed it came with practice. Arkeen knew exactly what was valuable and didn't waste time with anything that wasn't. Ronan hated how slow he felt as he pulled four silvers from a deceased archer's leather clad pouch. He moved to the next corpse.

This soldier was a young woman, likely no older than Ronan. Four black shafted arrows stuck out of her abdomen. Ronan was saddened by the sight, but the sadness was replaced with anger at the Council. How could the Council recruit people this young into the military ranks of the Zwellian Legion? How could they justify this war? Ronan knew that the nine shadowy leaders of the Council could care less about this girl. He also knew that this girl wouldn't have had much choice. People had two real choices in the Zwellian Empire: join into the military ranks of the Zwellian Legion and fight under the bloody banner of the Council or struggle through life under the oppressive laws, regulations, and taxes of the Council.

"I'm lucky to have a third option," Ronan reminded himself as he checked the girl's pockets. He would never forget the day he had snuck into that winery and shoved a few vintages under his shirt to sell on the streets. Even now, he regretted how poorly he had planned the heist. The elegant Elven owner had caught him red-handed, with three large bottles of crimson wine under his shirt. Ronan remembered how terrified he had been when the man had dragged him into a storeroom. He had been certain he was about to be beaten or killed for his crime. Ronan had known that no one would have heard him scream in this back room. But the man had just smiled at him with his perfect white teeth. Ronan had thought it was a sick joke when the man had introduced himself as Dandrick Kemin and offered him a job.

Ronan felt that he replayed this memory a lot in his head. Who could blame him? It had been his once-in-a-lifetime chance to get off the streets. It had been the difference between him scrounging in trash piles for scraps of food and being paid real money to buy real food. This wasn't like the orphanage, in which the city officials had required all orphaned children be "housed". This wasn't a half empty hay mattress or bowl of vial sludge fed to the boy's morning, noon, and night. Mr. Kemin had offered Ronan a chance to earn respect. How different that had been from being treated like a rabid dog or an asset of the Empire. All Ronan had to do was prove himself. He would never forget what Mr. Kemin had said to him two years ago in that storeroom.

"I can offer you glory and wealth apart from the rule of the Council. No more petty thefts in order to eat. No more nights out in the cold. What I offer is a different life. However, it is not for the faint of heart. It is a one-way ticket. There is no going back. After this point, you're either going to be useful to the Carpenters, or you're going to be making some new friends with the fish in the river. Do you understand what I'm saying?"

As Ronan remembered the subtle threat, he hurried to the next cluster of bodies. From a distance the bodies looked human, but as he approached, he recognized them as UN'kra. The distinguishing differences were the ghostly pale skin that was accented by their dark black lips and the thick black fur that surrounded their face and covered their arms and shoulders. They also all had red eyes, which resembled that of a goat and freaked Ronan out.

"Aww, the sworn enemies of the Council," Ronan mocked. "The savages of the north." He smirked to himself as he quoted the propaganda posters plastered all over. You couldn't go anywhere in the Zwellian Empire without seeing the advertisements. The Council had made it a point for the last seven years to paint the UN'kra in the worst possible light in order to bolster morale behind their war against the supposed savages. It was this war that currently employed Ronan as a scavenger.

Ronan knelt down and inspected the large humanoids. He had to admit, their appearance was unsettling, and he understood why people were easily convinced they were evil and barbaric.

Ronan had never met a living UN'kra. His initial introduction was seeing their corpses on his first scavenge a week ago. Had it not been for his training with the Carpenters, he might have fallen prey to the lies of the Council about the northern dwellers. However, Ronan trusted Mr. Kemin and his teachings more than the Council. Mr. Kemin even claimed to have lived with the UN'kra for a few years.

Ronan shook his head again. He needed to stop daydreaming. He had to prove he could be good at scavenging for he feared what would happen if Mr. Kemin thought he was inept at the task. This week couldn't be a repeat of last week's fiasco when Ronan had only been able to acquire twenty silver worth of valuables despite his vigorous efforts. He checked the UN'kra corpses. Excitement fluttered in his chest as he found a bag of odd coins on one of the bodies. They were not Zwellian silver but maybe they were still valuable. He closely examined one to identify its makeup. Maybe bronze? Copper?

"Those coins are rubbish. Don't get your hopes up." The female voice startled Ronan, making him drop all of the coins onto the ground. He turned around to see Vallia standing behind him. How was she so quiet? Vallia was the third member of their scavenging party. She was a head taller than Ronan with bright blonde hair and a unique blue rune over her right eyebrow.

As usual, Ronan found himself staring at Vallia's hair. While its color was rare in these parts, it was not what always caught Ronan's attention. Vallia's hair flowed in a breeze of its own, even when indoors. Ronan knew this trait was not something that Vallia controlled. Rather, it was a result of her connection with the Ether. It was not as impressive as the wind she could blast out of her hands, but he didn't get to see her do that often.

Ronan shook his head, berating himself for his obsession with the Ether. He needed to focus on his mission. Now was not the time to get lost in thought about the plane of chaotic elemental energy that occasionally interacted with the Prime Plane. Ronan lived on the Prime Plane and couldn't afford to daydream about the elemental energies that occasionally seeped through the planar walls and randomly latched onto developing babies in their mothers' wombs. Idolizing those who were Ether touched in this way was not going to make him an Ethalladros like Vallia.

But despite his efforts, Ronan couldn't quell the excitement that always flashed through his mind when he thought about the Ethalladros' fascinating elemental abnormalities like stone skin or magma for blood or their fantastic elemental powers. *'What would it be like to shoot fire out of my hands, breathe underwater at will, or punch people with gem encrusted knuckles?'*

Vallia snapped her fingers, "Are you listening to me?"

Ronan crashed back to reality and realized Vallia had been talking to him.

She rolled her eyes. "I told Dandrick that you weren't going to make it out here. You're too spacey. As I was saying, Arkeen told you last week, those coins can't be melted down into anything valuable. Unless you are backpacking up north, they are worthless."

Ronan cursed himself for letting his mind wander and forgetting Arkeen's lesson. Ronan tried to save face by lying, "Yeah, I know they weren't valuable, I just wanted to look at them. And I wasn't spacing out, I was trying to think of a way to use the coins so we could make a profit."

"We don't have time for you to reengineer UN'kra economics. We'll have a hard enough time making money on this scavenge. I swear these troops have nothing on them. It's like they were shipped out in a rush or something."

Ronan attempted to prove himself. "I think I have found some good stuff today." He opened his satchel to show her, hoping to confirm the value of what he had collected.

5

Vallia looked into Ronan's pouch and frowned. "Not much but it's better than last time I guess." Her voice was deeper for a woman and had a bit of a harsh inflection indicating she came up from the south. She did not talk about her past, so Ronan only had speculations.

She sighed, "I have not had much luck either. Probably some reserves that were thrown together at the last minute to fight off this UN'kra movement. I found some Centurions near those rocks on the hill." She pointed. "Centurion are the leaders of one hundred Legion soldiers," She explained as if Ronan didn't know.

"I know what a Centurion is," he insisted, rolling his eyes.

She ignored him and elaborated, "They didn't even think to send scouts behind the rocks. As a result, they were ambushed. Rookie mistakes." She shook her head. "Speaking of scouting, can you summon that Ether hawk Arkeen helped you raise, and have it circle overhead to check the surrounding area? I want to make sure we are alone out here."

Ronan nodded, excited for the opportunity to be helpful and kicking himself for not thinking of this before. He whistled through his fingers and looked up at the sky. A few seconds went by. Then a patch of air began to ripple as a large bird materialized straight out of the Ether, accompanied by a popping sound. The hawk circled Ronan's head and landed on his shoulder. The feathers on the hawk's head were a beautiful deep red that transitioned to gray further down his back. The hawk's tail was long and plumed into white feathers that wisped at the tips like a breath on a freezing day.

"Hey Sabastian," Ronan said as he reached up and scratched the hawk's neck. "Hope I didn't wake you from a nap in the Ether. Think you can keep an eye out for us? Make sure we are the only people out here? Keep watch."

The bird nuzzled into the scratches, chirped once, and took flight.

"Sometimes I wish I could just disappear into the Ether like your bird," Vallia voiced as they watched him fly.

Ronan didn't know what to say to this sad comment. He wondered where she would go if she wasn't tied down with the Carpenters. But he was too hesitant to ask.

6

After a moment she directed, "Let's go check in with Arkeen. See if he wants us to keep going or cut our losses."

She walked away without waiting for Ronan. He followed her.

They walked across the field stepping over fallen soldiers and UN'kra warriors. Ronan was nervous to report what he had found to Arkeen. He didn't want to disappoint him.

Arkeen was on a hill, tossing UN'kra black steel weapons behind him as he searched through a group of bodies. Arkeen looked up at them as they neared.

"I hope you're coming here to tell me you found a cart of solid silver ingots just lying around," Arkeen jested. Ronan smiled. He had always appreciated Arkeen's light heartedness mixed with his optimism. While he was older than Ronan by about ten years, this had never hindered their friendship since the first few days of Ronan's recruitment.

"Keep dreaming," Vallia said. She walked up to him and kissed him on the lips. The affection was an unfortunate result of their betrothal. Ronan was happy for them but wished they would tone it down.

Arkeen grinned from ear to ear. "How are we looking? I found some really old stuff. Might be worth a little on the streets if we can con the right old lady. We just need to make up the right story about it." He looked at Ronan. "How is the picking today?"

Ronan shrugged, "I think I am getting the hang of it." He tried to fill his voice with confidence.

Arkeen nodded. "Wonderful. Let's take a looksee." He held out his hand.

Ronan pulled off his satchel and handed it over. He thought he had improved a little from last week. Maybe Arkeen would feel the same. Arkeen rummaged around the bag and then got a surprised look on his face. "Lookie here. Ronan found himself a gem."

Arkeen lifted out a silver ring with a large emerald set into the center. Ronan had never seen the ring in his life. His heart sank as he realized what Arkeen had done. He was trying to make Ronan look better by planting the ring. Arkeen was trying to be helpful, but Ronan didn't want to just be handed success. It was something he wanted to earn. He was about to

7

protest the ring when a screech rang out. The three looked skyward to see Sabastian, swooping up over the hill and circling above. He gave off a second screech and then flew back over the crest of the hill, vanishing from view.

"I think he has spotted something," Ronan warned. "Come on, let's see what it is." The three crouched low in the dried tall grass as they climbed to the top of the hill to see over it.

As Ronan crested the hill, he could see below, a gigantic lumbering figure. The creature easily stood fifteen feet tall even with its curved back. It had no visible neck with the way its head hunched forward, centered between two massive shoulders. Its chin almost touched its chest. Ronan observed the worn, leather-colored skin of the giant was stained with blood down its front. Then he understood that the red coloration was coming from two human bodies draped over the shoulders of the creature like shoulder pads. The bodies were adorned in golden armor which marked them as Legion Centurion. Ronan had a sickening realization that they were not draped but rather impaled in place. The giant had what appeared to be broken shafts of spears stabbed through the critical mass of the bodies into its own thick shoulders.

Vallia hissed, "What kind of giant is that?"

"That's a corpse walker," Arkeen answered enthusiastically. "They are hill giants that have been known to adorn themselves with dead bodies as armor. Looks like this one found the shiniest bodies he could."

Ronan was grateful they had Arkeen with them. Being a nature enthusiast, he spent all his free time reading about all sorts of creatures big and small.

"Look!" Arkeen whispered. "At his hip."

Ronan squinted through the sunlight at the meandering giant and saw a large shape on his side. A cloud covered the sun and Ronan realized it was a large burlap sack overflowing with several shiny things.

Arkeen smiled. Ronan knew this smile; it was the smile his friend got when he was planning on being mischievous. "Oh, this is too perfect. He has already done all our work for us. All we have to do is procure that bag. They are very dumb, and their eyesight is abysmal. I bet you we could sneak up on him no problem."

Vallia whispered, "What's your plan once you sneak up on him? Kill him? There are only the three of us out here and the kid has probably never even drawn his sword."

"I have too," Ronan hissed back. "I started sword training with the Carpenters a few months ago."

Vallia rolled her eyes, "Forgive me. You're a true giant slayer now. I'm sure you could just kill anyone you wanted. We might as well call you Ronan, Prince of the Dead."

"Shut up. Both of you." Arkeen had pulled off his backpack and was quickly rummaging through it. He pulled out a tightly coiled rope. As he started unwinding it, he explained, "We don't need to kill him. We just need to trip him up and tie his ankles together. Once we do that, we steal the sack and run. By the time he breaks free, we will be long gone."

Vallia shook her head and whispered, "That is the stupidest idea you have ever had. He is huge. How are you going to trip him?"

Arkeen grinned even wider. "Love, that's where you come in. You just hit him with a big blast of wind once Ronan and I have wrapped the rope around his ankles. He will come crashing to the ground like a falling tree. I'll tie his ankles, while Ronan gets the sack. It's foolproof."

Ronan agreed with Vallia that the plan was dumb, but Arkeen seemed so confident. Ronan couldn't think of a time when his friend had been wrong about these things. Then Ronan imagined the look on Mr. Kemin's face as they dragged the sack into his office, and he heard how Ronan had helped steal it from a giant. He would never be questioned again for his usefulness.

Ronan looked at Arkeen. "I love this plan. Let's do this."

Vallia was about to protest but before she could, Arkeen kissed her on the cheek and said, "I hope you're there to knock over the giant or this plan is not going to work. Come on Ronan, follow me and stay low."

He handed one end of the rope to Ronan and then took off into the tall grass toward the giant. Ronan looked at Vallia and gave her an apologetic shrug. He then crouched lower and followed Arkeen. They snaked through the grass slowly approaching the giant whose back was turned to them. Ronan's heart was racing. His stomach was tight. From nerves or exhilaration, Ronan couldn't tell.

Arkeen reached a bush about fifty feet from the corpse walker. He looked back at Ronan and nodded. He then checked Vallia's position. She had followed them, but she looked like it was taking everything she had to do so. Arkeen nodded at her. She shook her head and mouthed, "Please no." Arkeen winked at her. He took a big breath. He was about to start running forward when the bush next to him rustled.

Both Ronan and Arkeen looked at the bush. Ronan was able to identify the limp body of a male UN'kra warrior, suspended in the branches of the shrub. It held several crossbow bolts in his chest and blood covered his torso. Suddenly, as if struck by lightning, the UN'kra's red eyes flashed open. The body had not moved before this jolt of adrenaline. Arkeen was not prepared. The UN'kra, once thought dead, now thrust its arm forward and lodged a black, gnarled spear through the center of Arkeen's chest.

Chapter 2

"ARKEEN! NO!" Vallia shrieked, her voice carried across the field. She stood up and began sprinting at the two figures.

Ronan was terror-stricken as he stared into the UN'kra warrior's ferocious eyes. Ronan couldn't process the blood now pouring out of Arkeen's chest or how the UN'kra was not dead. Its wounds should have killed it a day ago. Arkeen's approach must have startled him out of whatever near death coma he had been in.

Arkeen's face was caught in pure astonishment, looking at the warrior. His eyes then trailed down to the spear in his chest and the blood that ran down the shaft onto the hands of the UN'kra. Arkeen then collapsed sideways into the grass.

Vallia, running at full sprint, raised her hand and made a fast, chopping motion through the air, screaming in a rage of pure adrenaline. The air before her suddenly shifted into a curved blast of condensed wind. It looked as if she had just swung a giant scythe at the creature who just killed her husband to be. Despite being fifteen paces from the warrior, the blast traveled forward connecting with the neck of the UN'kra, severing his head from his body.

Ronan stood frozen staring at the gruesome scene before him. Arkeen had just been stabbed and Ronan had not been able to do anything. Tears welled up in his eyes. Arkeen had only come down here because Ronan had agreed to help him. This was all his fault.

The sharp squall of Sabastian brought Ronan to his senses. The UN'kra's

11

spontaneous attack had rendered the thought of the lumbering giant obsolete. Ronan's head jerked to his left and saw the behemoth had in fact noticed them and was thundering forward, directly at Vallia. Each stride shook the ground. Vallia's focus had narrowed to the single target of the UN'kra. She didn't even turn around before she was slammed in the back by the corpse walker's forearm. She flew ten feet in the air, falling into a crumpled pile.

Ronan watched with terror. His heart raced in his chest, pounding away, threatening to burst out of his ribs. He had seen the attack coming, but his throat was not working, and he was unable to warn her. Why did he not warn her? The giant stood over the corpse of Arkeen and the now twice fallen UN'kra warrior. He slowly turned his torso to face Ronan.

Ronan needed to run. He needed to do something. But he couldn't move. Why were his legs not moving?

He couldn't think over the hammering of his heart and a terrible pain that had risen up in his eyes. He needed help. He needed someone to save him. He couldn't fight this thing. He was screaming for help in his mind, but his throat would not work. He was going to die here like his two friends because he was the only living person for miles, and he knew that.

The pain in his eyes started shifting his vision. Everything before him started losing color. The world shifted to a grayscale. No saturation remained, except for an orange aura outlining the hulking giant and what looked to be green fire emanating from the bodies of Arkeen and the UN'kra. The pain behind his eyes was immense, almost enough to make him pass out. Then a voice thundered in his mind. Not his own inner voice, but an unfamiliar one. He heard it command one word: *"**HELP.**"*

As the words reverberated in his head, the pain was pushed out of Ronan's body, as if a pulse of energy exploded outward. The pulse seemed to hit the bodies of Arkeen and the UN'kra because the newly appeared green fire was seemingly blown out.

The giant's form started walking toward Ronan. Seven massive steps away... six... five... Ronan was frozen in fear. His mind screamed at his legs, but they were locked up. With the creature's long strides there was

12

no hope of outrunning the giant. All Ronan had to fight with was the end of the rope, which he still held in his hand, and a short sword he had little experience using. Ronan closed his eyes, preparing for his life to be over.

A thought crossed Ronan's mind. *What was it like to die?*

He held his breath counting the giant's steps as it advanced.

Four... Three...

A guttural howl shattered the air. Ronan opened his eyes. Color had instantaneously returned to the world. The giant was standing before him howling in pain. A figure stood beside its leg, a large black steel scimitar dripped with the giant's blood, having just cut into the tendons of the giant's ankle. Ronan blinked twice. His eyes must be playing more tricks on him. The figure by the leg was armored in a light leather vest. Its shoulders were covered in black fur, but the humanoid stood headless. The UN'kra that Vallia had beheaded now stood brandishing its wicked blade.

The UN'kra took a reverse swing, flexing its large muscles as it tore through the same right tendon of the giant's leg. The giant fell to one knee with a resounding crash.

From behind the giant, another figure appeared. Ronan couldn't believe it. Arkeen came out of nowhere in a full sprint, the spear that had plunged through his chest only moments before now in his hands.

Ronan's heart jumped. How was Arkeen alive? His body was coated in blood. A large hole remained in his chest. There was no way he could have survived the stabbing, but here he was, fighting a giant to save Ronan. Then Ronan had a dark realization. There was no way the UN'kra could be alive without a head on his shoulders. Which meant, if the UN'kra was not alive, neither was Arkeen. If they were both dead, how were they standing and fighting?

Arkeen used the momentum from his sprint to jump off the giant's grounded right heel. This propelled him into the air and onto the giant's back. He drove the spear into the neck at the base of the skull.

The giant bellowed again in pain. This attack had hurt it, but not stopped its ability to react. Its meaty hand rushing up and grasping the body of Arkeen off its back. With one mighty flex of its hand, the giant crushed

Arkeen's bloody body causing several muffled cracks and threw him onto the ground, broken and unmoving.

Ronan stood mere feet from the giant. His vision faded back into the gray world and a pressure built in his skull behind his eyes. Again, he saw the green flame coming off the body. Was that the spirit of Arkeen? It didn't matter what the fire was as long as it kept helping him not die.

Ronan watched the green flame rise from the crushed corpse and coast into the air. Like smoke rising from a campfire, it flew toward the centurion on the left shoulder of the course walker. As that happened the UN'kra's body began slicing at the giant's arms. These attacks were not nearly as effective as the ones on the ankle. The ankle must not have been covered in the thick hide of the upper body.

The giant flailed its arm into the warrior, launching him backwards. With the two assailants seemingly dealt with, the giant shakily rose to its feet. It was careful not to put its full weight on its right leg. Its beady eyes locked onto Ronan.

Rona's legs seemed to suddenly remember how to function, and he was able to move back two steps only to have his foot catch something in the grass. Losing his balance, he fell to the ground. He stuck out his arm, trying to brace himself. As his wrist hit the earth, a sickening crack accompanied an eruption of pain that seared up his arm as his. He screamed and writhed in pain.

The giant rose to its full height and let out a low, loathsome laugh at Ronan's agony and misfortune. Ronan saw triumph in its beady dull eyes, and he knew he was a goner. The assault of the dead bodies had failed. He had no other hope.

The giant was about to advance forward to finish him off when the body of the centurion on its shoulder started to thrash. The body contorted itself and pushed itself up the shaft of the spear that held it to the giant's shoulder.

Ronan couldn't believe it. The spirits had not abandoned him. All he could think was, "Kill the giant. Please save me."

The centurion's body brought its knee under its torso, reached for its boot, and pulled out a hidden knife. The day-old corpse took the blade and thrust it under the double chin of the giant into its windpipe. From any other attack angle, the creature's lack of neck would have prevented this assault. However, from the shoulder, the centurion had a perfect vantage point.

Ronan would have jumped for joy had he not been prone on the ground.

The giant made a gargle as the entire knife blade vanished into its windpipe. It reached up but its oversized fingers could not grab the tiny blade. Blue black blood ran down its chest. A major artery must have been cut because the creature convulsed; its eyes rolled back into its skull. Gravity took hold as the giant lost its balance. Like a massive tree, it tipped forward.

All Ronan saw was the bloodied, bulbous body of the brute toppling forward toward him. He tried to roll out of the way, but his broken wrist thwarted his quick evasion. The giant's body crashed into him.

Ronan's world went black.

Chapter 3

Ronan stood in a familiar two roomed house. The wooden walls and floor were all lightly stained. There was a small, rusted metal stove in the corner of the room with well used pots and pans hanging above. A small table with four gnarled chairs sat in the opposite corner. Ronan looked down at his feet to see a crude wooden rocking horse that he remembered fondly. This was the house he had grown up in before the fire. He remembered the warm meals they would eat at the table, and the games they would play on the floor. His heart yearned to bask in every small detail and savoy in the humble abode.

A deep and gravelly voice echoed through the house, rattling the windows and shaking the pots and pans. The same voice that he had heard in his mind before the spirits came to his aid.

"Ronan."

He looked around frantically but did not see the speaker.

"I know your past. I can see your heart and I know the struggles you have endured. You were too weak to save the lives of your family. Too powerless to stop them from dying."

The room's walls suddenly were engulfed in forest green flames. Ronan backed to the center of the room watching everything burn in the smokeless fire. He watched in horror as his childhood home once again went up in flames. He fell to his knees. "No... no please no," he stammered. The walls were burnt away revealing a different space. He found himself kneeling in a long stone room filled with ten rickety bunk beds. Light drifted through four small grubby windows. Ronan recognized this as the orphanage he

16

had grown up in. He stood next to the miserable excuse for a bed that he had occupied for so many years. He remembered how the bunk would shake through the night as the older boy that slept below fought off his nightmares. The thought produced a deep desire in Ronan to escape this room as fast as possible. There were no happy memories for him here. He stood up and started running for the exit. Then, the bodiless voice echoed through the space.

"You were too weak to stand up against the other children. They stole from you, and they beat you because they knew you were easy prey. You were powerless to garner their respect and their friendship."

Ronan reached the door, but it was locked. He desperately rattled the handle trying to open it.

This room ignited just as the house had. Green flames forced Ronan to back away from the wall. The walls slowly dissolved as the fire engulfed everything.

Ronan no longer stood in a room. He was in a flat field with windswept grass that brushed his knees. Nausea overtook Ronan as he saw dozens of butchered bloodied bodies hidden in the grass. His heart dropped as he recognized the bodies of Arkeen and Vallia among the dead. He couldn't breathe as he looked at them. His friends were dead because of him. He had been unable to save them. Suddenly, Arkeen's head rotated toward Ronan. He screamed and backed away as quickly as he could.

"You were too weak to stop your friend's demise. But that is where your weakness ends. Through my blessing, a giant was slayed at your command." The bodies of both his friends stood up, wreathed in green flames. Other corpses began to stand up all around Ronan until he was surrounded. Then they all bowed to Ronan.

"Who are you?" Ronan demanded the empty space as he turned to see all the bowing bodies.

"Your benefactor. The source behind your powers over spirits. I have graciously given you a great gift to control the spirits of the dead."

17

"Powers? What powers?"

"Think about what you have just witnessed. Your friend was killed. His murderer died immediately after. Then both rose to save you at your plea for help. That was no freak occurrence. That was my blessing. The spirits of the dead are now your servants. Soldiers for your cause."

Ronan thought of the gruesome image of the corpses of Arkeen and the headless UN'kra fighting the giant. He remembered asking for help and then help came. But he didn't understand. Then skepticism filled Ronan. "Why me? Why now? Who are you to give out this power?"

"It has always been you. You were chosen at birth. Selected to become... What was it your friend called you? Ah yes... a Prince of the Dead. How well that title suits your new position. As for my authority to give you powers, that is too far outside of your understanding at the moment. All you need to know is you now have powers beyond your wildest dreams, and I am the one who gave them to you."

Could it be true? Ronan wondered. Had it been the spirits of Arkeen and the UN'kra that animated the bodies to save him? Ronan looked around the scene before him. The bowing bodies had not moved from their positions. He didn't know what to think of any of this. "What is it you want from me?"

"Obedience. As my champion. Now you serve me. Through your obedience, your powers will grow. You will no longer be weak or helpless. Spirits will obey your commands while the living will fear and respect you."

"What if I don't want powers? What if I don't want people to fear me?"

"Then you would be lying to yourself and to me. I know your heart, young Ronan. I know your deepest desires. How often do you dream of power and respect? What would you give up for people to value you? This is what I give you. This is what you have been granted."

Ronan couldn't deny there was truth in what the voice said. He didn't want people to fear him, but respect was a different story. But how could he be a champion? Something was not quite right. This was too good to be true.

"Am I supposed to believe that you gave me these powers out of your benevolence? You must get something from this."

The voice produced a chilling cold laugh. **"You show wisdom in what you say. I do in fact benefit from you. These abilities are an extension of my own. Your development allows me to have influence in your world. My will can be done through you. We both get what we want."**

"And what is it that we want?" Ronan asked cautiously.

"We share a common enemy. We both wish nothing more than to see the group you call the Council to be brought to their knees and for their reign to end."

This surprised Ronan. "You are against the Council? And you want me to help you to stop them?"

"My motives are not too dissimilar from your own. As my champion, I will help you end them forever. In their absence, a void of power will need to be filled. Right now, you are but a prince. One day you could be a king. A commander of armies of the dead. An emperor over the Zwellian Empire. Imagine the respect you would wield. Think of the possibilities that my gift could grant you."

A crown of green flames appeared before Ronan, floating in midair. He stared at it, enthralled. The voice offered lies. There was no way any of this could be true, could it? Ronan didn't even want to be a king or a commander of an army. Or did he?

The voice interrupted his thinking. **"One day soon, I will divulge more about my plans for you. For now, my concern is you and the development of your abilities. Like a muscle, your powers must be flexed. You must learn how to condition these abilities. Days of grandeur await you in the future, but for now, all I ask of you is to grow."**

Ronan was still cautious. Then he thought to himself, all he was being told to do was learn about these supposed powers. That didn't seem so bad. It wasn't like he was being asked to hurt innocent people. The voice wanted him to help stop the Council. How was that any different from the Carpenters who actively opposed the oppression and broke the laws of the Council. There was no question about the Council's corruption, and it was true that ending their reign would help a lot of people. Anyway, hadn't he always wanted powers? Wasn't he always thinking about life as an Ethalladros? If he really did have the abilities the voice spoke of, what harm could come from learning to control them? That seemed like the most responsible thing he could do.

If he didn't have powers and this was all a dream, he would wake up and his friends would still be alive.

For a moment he hoped it wasn't a dream, then guilt washed over him. If that was the case it meant he wished his friends were dead. *No this must be a dream. There is no way I am some champion of the dead. Or was it the chosen, or the...*

Confused, Ronan asked, "What is it that I should call myself?"

"I call you my champion. You will call me your Justice: The Justice of the Dead. As my champion you will be known as another name in your world. They will know you as Eidolon. Eidolon of Death." At this statement, green flames surrounded Ronan and he lost sight of the field, the green crown, and the bowing bodies. The flames closed in, and he found it harder and harder to breathe.

Chapter 4

Smoke filled Ronan's lungs, sending him into a coughing fit. His eyes started to open only to be licked by the heavy smoke that surrounded him. His attempt to roll over was halted. First by something restraining his arm, and then by a sharp pain in his wrist. He remembered his failed attempt to catch himself and the resulting crack he had heard from his limb. Ronan felt a breeze blow away the smoke, and with his good hand rubbed his eyes. This movement made him realize his entire body hurt. His head felt like it was made of stone and his ribs as if they had been kicked by a horse.

He opened his eyes to see an orange sky. Purple clouds drifted above at the edges of his periphery. After a few moments, he slowly arrived at the conclusion that it was dusk. He had been unconscious for several hours, or possibly days.

With gritted teeth to fight the pain, Ronan used his good arm to push himself into a sitting position.

The source of the smoke was a large fire that raged in front of him. The brilliant glow of the inferno gave him an instant headache. The blaze consumed what looked like a large pile of branches. Taking in more of the surroundings, Ronan gathered he was still in the fields of Hormáne, but this was not where he remembered getting knocked out.

'So, the giant attack wasn't a dream. That meant Vallia and Arkeen were...' It was all his fault. His friends were all dead and it was his fault.

"Good, you're awake. You have some explaining to do," Vallia's voice rang out, starting him out of his emotional uprising.

Ronan's heart leapt. He whipped his head around to see Vallia walking up from the direction of the fire.

"You're alive!" Ronan exclaimed.

"Yes, I am alive," Vallia said with a resolute anger in her voice.

As she approached, her body was silhouetted by the inferno behind her. The closer she got, the more detail Ronan could make out. Her eyes were red from what Ronan guessed was hours of crying. Her hair still flowed in its own breeze, but it was dirty and filled with dried grass. She had a hard expression on her face.

"What happened?" he asked, trying to wrap his mind around the current situation.

"You don't get to ask that question. You need to tell me what happened. When that behemoth flung me, I smashed my head into the ground, and I got knocked out. When I came too, the giant was dead, laying on top of you. Arkeen's body..."

At this thought she started to choke up, but her determination won over the sadness. "His body was smashed and was not where he had fallen. That UN'kra monster was lying next to the giant. What happened to Arkeen's body?" She looked down at Ronan with a contorted frown and puffy eyes. He had never seen her this sad.

Ronan didn't even know where to begin. He knew Vallia must be emotionally wrecked. How could he tell her what happened? She would never believe him.

Vallia's face changed to a deadly glare. She lashed out and kicked Ronan's leg. "What happened?" she demanded again with tears in her eyes.

Ronan recoiled as the blow struck him. He felt he deserved much more than a kick from her. He stammered, "You got knocked away. I thought you were dead. I was all alone. I thought for sure I was next, but something happened inside me. I don't know how to explain it, but everything went gray and then I saw green flames by the bodies of Arkeen and the UN'kra you killed. And... and.. I guess I asked them to help me, and they did."

Vallia stared at him. Ronan couldn't read the expression on her face. She said slowly, "What do you mean green fire helped you?"

Ronan contemplated how to answer. If it had not been for the fact that he was currently alive, he would not believe it either.

"I don't understand how, but once you had been knocked away, the giant started coming to squash me like a bug. But then something happened with my eyes, and I was able to see two spirits." He opted to not explain how he knew they were spirits. "I was pleading for help and the spirits responded. They repossessed their bodies and then fought and killed the giant. They are the ones who killed him, not me." As he spoke, he flinched as he realized he sounded absolutely mental.

Vallia hadn't moved. She seemed to be debating whether Ronan was lying or if he had lost his mind.

He insisted, "I'm not lying. Why would I? I wish I could take credit for killing that thing, but you know as well as I do that I didn't single handedly slay a giant."

Vallia furrowed her eyebrows. His confessions of his inability seemed to help her make up her mind. "You just asked the spirits of Arkeen and his murderer to help you? And they did?"

Ronan nodded.

"Then what happened to Arkeen's body?" Her tone directed Ronan to be cautious.

He said in a small voice "His body jumped onto the giant's back. The giant grabbed him and crushed him. He got crushed saving me." At this, Ronan was overwhelmed by the reality of the statement. "I'm so sorry. I am so sorry for everything." Tears began running down Ronan's face. "I shouldn't have agreed to help him trip the corpse walker. I just wanted to prove myself. It's all my fault he went out there." Ronan was racked by a deep guilt at the loss of his friend. Tears ran down his cheeks as his chest seemed to develop an empty void. He would always blame himself for what had happened. The hollowness in his chest would haunt him forever.

He sensed Vallia staring at him. He looked up and saw through blurry eyes, Vallia's expression softening. The anger on her face was lessening. She seemed to lose her momentum. As if deflating, she lowered herself to the ground and sat cross legged across from Ronan.

Vallia shook her head. "No, you should not have told him you would help him." Her tone then softened. "But even if you would have said no, he would have still tried. Once he got something in his head, that was the end of reasoning with him." She let out a long sigh. "How did the knife get stabbed into the giant's neck?"

Ronan sniffled and wiped away the tears. He knew he owed her a full explanation, so he attempted to pull himself together. "Arkeen's spirit possessed the body of the centurion on the giant's shoulder and made it stab the knife into the giant's throat. That's when it fell on top of me. I'm guessing you dragged me out?"

Vallia nodded, "And I fixed up your arm. Your wrist was bent the wrong way, so I set it back in place."

Ronan winced at the imagery and then looked down and inspected the makeshift sling that now hugged his arm to his body. He was grateful he had been unconscious for the hasty treatment.

"Thank you, for helping me," he said earnestly. He paused. There was so much to process that he didn't know which question to ask out of the thousand rattling around in his head. It hurt too much to speak of Arkeen, so he instead asked, "Have you ever heard of someone seeing the spirits of the dead?"

Vallia stared down and drew with her finger in the dirt. She eventually said, "No."

He tried again, "Do you think it could be something to do with the Ether?"

She continued to look at the ground. She shook her head and said, "No." Then, knowing he wanted something more, she said, "You said you saw their life energy? And you spoke to the green fires?"

"I don't know how else to explain what I saw. And I didn't talk to them. I asked them to help. But they must have listened because they didn't do anything until I asked."

Vallia looked at him. "As far as I know, the Ether is a plane of elemental energy. I have never heard of an Ethalladros gaining abilities at your age. Maybe it's possible but even so, I don't think life energies are an element. That is more of, I don't know." She paused to think. "Life energy is more of a fact. It's not a force of nature. Things are alive or they are not. That's just how things are. The Ether is all forces of nature in various forms. Like I'm connected to the wind, but another Ethalladros who is touched by the element of air may have abilities that manifest in a way that resemble storms, or even freezing gusts." She shrugged.

Then she asked, "You said the world changed color?"

"Everything went gray," he confirmed.

"That is similar to what happens when I access my connection with the Ether. But the world becomes more colorful and overly saturated."

Ronan had never really talked with an Ethalladros about what it was like to use their gifts. He sighed, "It was weird. Something definitely changed in me."

Vallia pointedly said, "Not just inside you."

"What do you mean?"

"Your eyes changed. They are bright green now, like emeralds. Look for yourself." She pulled a small pocket mirror out of her satchel.

He glanced into the mirror. The distant bonfire light illuminated his features just enough to see himself in the darkness. Ronan saw his buzzed black hair, his small round nose, his angled jaw that was covered with dark patchy stubble that simply refused to grow consistently. But his irises were no longer brown. They had transitioned into bright green circles that surrounded his pupil.

He really did have powers. It was almost impossible to believe. But between his eyes, the dream, and the reality of the situation, there was little evidence to the contrary. Granted, he didn't understand anything about them, but he had powers.

The two sat on the ground in silence. The only sound that permeated the air was the crackle of the fire, the chirp of crickets, and Vallia's hair as it fluttered about to its own breeze. The tranquility of the moment was interrupted by a popping sound, a familiar flapping, and a pressure on Ronan's shoulder. Ronan felt the warm feathers of Sabastian against his cheek. The bird sensed his troubled emotions and nuzzled into him.

"Hey, buddy." He scratched the Ether hawk under the chin. "You feel warm. Were you hanging out in a fiery part of the Ether?" Sabastian cooed and nuzzled into the pets.

"Do you remember when I got Sabastian?" Ronan asked Vallia. "It was one of my first survival training sessions for the Carpenters. You and Arkeen dragged a few of the new recruits out into the woods in the dead of winter last year."

Vallia nodded as she stared into the inferno. She said, "I remember. It was in the Shemlock Woods." She nodded toward the North. "That was the coldest survival training we ever taught. Arkeen wasn't even phased by the temperature."

Ronan felt weird reminiscing about Arkeen in this way. He had heard other Carpenters share stories of their fallen comrades and guessed this was appropriate. He continued, "I remember all the trees were covered in those horizontal icicles because of the wind. I was convinced I was going to freeze to death. Arkeen laughed when I told him that. He was so confident."

Vallia's eyes welled at the corners. "He always was."

To distract her, Ronan continued the story. "We probably would have frozen if we hadn't stumbled into that flaming grove of trees. Remember how the center of the woods was still burning from the battle that had happened there? All the trees were blasted to pieces or badly scorched."

"Yeah, the wonderful work of Ether Crafters," Vallia said, shaking her head, a dark expression covering her face.

Ronan immediately regretted mentioning the burning grove as he remembered Vallia's hostile view on Ether Crafters. Before Ronan could change the subject, Vallia started into her usual fiery tangent about the Ether Crafters.

"Every one of them is just a wannabe Ethalladros. They weren't pelted by Ether energies in their mother's womb, so they have to teach themselves how to abuse and manipulate the energies of the Ether. And they can't even control what elements they are pulling from the Ether through their stupid little rifts. It's just a roll of the dice whether they are burning down buildings or summoning toxic gases. I hate the Council so much for using those chaotic Ether touched imposters in their war. There is not one crafter among them who isn't under the thumb of the Council."

Ronan had heard this speech countless times, but he did not protest the outburst. He hoped it would help her vent some of her internalized anguish. But as soon as she took a pause he jumped back into his reminiscence about Arkeen and Sabastian to stop her from continuing.

"Arkeen was so excited when we found those smoking Ether meteors with the hollow cavity set into one. He couldn't contain his excitement when we found that porcelain-looking egg in the opening. I don't know how, but he identified it as an Ether hawk egg."

Vallia said, "His entire apartment is filled with books and scrolls about creatures and animals. Anything he could get his hands on from naturalists and biologists. He was always spouting off facts about plants or animals."

"He told me that Ether hawks were impossible to capture because they phased out of any trap. I asked him if he thought the egg would still hatch. He didn't know but he said he would do everything in his power to help it hatch."

Vallia closed her eyes and said, "Didn't Arkeen convince you to keep the egg under your coat until we got back to Shem? He was always elaborate and over the top. I loved that about him. He was never afraid to take risks and he somehow always came out on top." Tears started rolling down her cheeks.

There was a long silence. "I guess his luck finally ran out," she choked. "I thought he could do anything. I knew it was dumb of me, but I thought he was indestructible. He took so many risks, but it always worked out. How did he not see that UN'kra? How could he miss that?"

She hung her head and sobbed. Ronan awkwardly put his hand on her shoulder, not sure if she would shove it off. She didn't.

He said "I thought he could do anything too. I mean he helped me hatch an Ether hawk. There wasn't any proper documentation about them, but he still managed it. He helped me keep it warm and guessed what sort of environment it needed. He wanted it to hatch so badly. The day that the egg started to wobble, I ran with the egg to the Carpenters' headquarters and found him. He blew off a combat training session to watch it hatch."

Ronan reached up his good arm and straightened his index and middle

27

finger, tucking the others in. A sign Arkeen had helped him teach Sabastian. Sabastian fluttered to his forearm and looked at him with his big black eyes. He cooed softly. Ronan's face was wet with his own tears. "When he came out of his egg, he was so little and gray. Arkeen was so excited to watch him hatch. I remember how Sabastian hiccupped as he broke through the shell. He vanished and then reappeared on the table. Arkeen and I spent two hours trying to coax him into our hands. Arkeen stole a bunch of treats from the kitchen to try and figure out what Sebastian ate. Over the next few months, he helped me to train him to do a few things and to respond to my whistle using crackers and little fish."

"Why did you name him Sabastian?" Vallia asked as she raised her head and hand wiped away the tears that clung to her cheeks.

Ronan didn't answer for a moment. He put his forehead to Sabastian's and then thrust his arm into the air. Sabastian took flight, circling their heads twice before popping out of sight in a puff of ethereal mist. "It was the name of my brother," Ronan said.

Vallia took note of the past tense. "How old were you?"

"Five. He was twelve."

Vallia nodded. "I'm sorry."

Ronan nodded, "Yeah, me too. But life hasn't really gotten easier when I look back at my different trials." As he said the words, he remembered the necklace with the pendant that said, 'Forged Through Fire.' Such a stupid saying. He reached into his bag and pulled it out to throw it into the field. As he lifted it up, he saw it was tangled around the emerald ring, Arkeen had slipped into his bag. He stopped and looked at the ring. Arkeen had given him this because he knew how badly Ronan wanted to prove himself to Mr. Kemin. It was probably the most valuable thing Arkeen had found today. And he had given it to Ronan. He took the necklace, removed the pendant, and slid the ring onto the chain. He then put on the necklace and slipped the ring under his shirt.

Neither spoke as neither knew what else to say. Vallia eventually took a deep breath and then stood. "There is nothing left for us in this field. This fire consumed everything that mattered. Everything burned to ash. It's late, we should go. I'd rather face the bandits on the road than sleep here.

Ronan nodded in somber agreement.

"I want to watch this whole field burn. I thought about lighting it all on fire, but I knew that he wouldn't have wanted that."

She walked away and knelt to grab something. Ronan watched her pull a large sack from the ground and slung it over her shoulder. It made a sound of metal scraping against metal and a jingle as smaller objects collided. Ronan realized this sack was the one that had hung on the giant's waist. The one Arkeen had died trying to obtain. Vallia walked past him and started heading for home.

Ronan looked back at the blaze and processed what Vallia said. He suddenly realized what the blaze was, its significance. It was a funeral pyre. Vallia must have built it for Arkeen. An emptiness filled Ronan. He felt for Vallia. He knew the loss she was feeling. This fire brought back another flood of memories.

Adult voices shouting. His brother Sabastian pulling him into the cellar. A reassurance that everything would be alright. His mother's scream, his brother running up the stairs telling him to stay back. The shattering of glass overhead. Heat and light coming from the cracks in the floor above. The smell of smoke. The cacophony of the house above falling in on itself. Several days trapped in the darkness. He blinked away more tears and turned his back on the fire as he followed Vallia.

Chapter 5

The mid-morning sun shone across the clay shingles and red brick smokestacks of the city of Shem. People bustled about the cobblestone streets, peddling wares, guiding carts, and dragging children from one errand to another. Vallia and Ronan had arrived through the north gate after walking through the night.

Traveling at night was usually avoided by most people due to the increase of criminals and creatures at that time, but Vallia had insisted. They themselves were criminals, though not violent like bandits, so operating at night was sometimes part of the job. Ronan was confident that Vallia had been looking for a fight. During their walk back, she had kept her fists clenched and assaulted every noise made by the night with a stare of pure malice, but their travel had gone unhindered.

Ronan spent most of the walk thinking about Arkeen. About all the wilderness survival training that he had instructed and the fetch quests he had drug Ronan along for. Ronan had always loved how Arkeen would get distracted on these missions and climb a tree to see baby birds or follow tracks in the earth to find a new animal. The best part of these memories was Arkeen's investment into Ronan. Ronan had been grateful to have someone pour into him and dedicate time to teaching him and joking with him. In this way, Arkeen had been Ronan's first real friend.

They were able to navigate past the grand marquee, which was full of colorful canvases stretched over wooden stalls that provided the vendors underneath with shade from the sun. Voices called out in a symphony of sales and bargains. Vendors fired their confidence and charisma across the street as if they were archers, targeting the people walking by. Claims of the freshest produce and the best made rugs peppered Ronan and Vallia as they walked down the main thoroughfare. Ronan loved the market, the energy of the people and all the wonderful smells that wafted through the air. Baked goods right out of the ovens, fruits picked that day, and spices in large burlap sacks. On any other day he would have been thrilled, but Ronan did not feel like being surrounded by people at the moment.

They turned down a side street where people only walked to get to and from the market. Another right down an alley and all pedestrian foot traffic ended. They followed the narrow passage making two more turns down empty side streets and alleys, seemingly getting more and more lost in the jungle of buildings surrounding them.

They stopped before a large square multi-story brick building with no windows and only one door. Ronan looked at the shabby building and, as always, was amazed by the cleverness that hid behind these walls. He could never get over the sheer genius Mr. Kemin had displayed by hiding the headquarters of his criminal organization in the basement of the second largest gathering of Legion soldiers in Shem. The building above acted as a makeshift Legion infirmary. It was established after the war began.

When Ronan had asked why the Carpenters operated out of this space, Mr. Kemin had simply explained, "People are coming and going constantly from this place. Who is going to notice a few shady individuals in a large crowd? Plus, easy access to the medics if we need them."

Over the two years, Ronan had picked up on the fact that Mr. Kemin was a large donor to the medical facility. At first this confused Ronan, but now he understood the motive behind his boss's seeming hypocrisy. Mr. Kemin had once explained it to Ronan by saying, "Dead men tell no tales. But wounded men will spill every secret they have to the nice nurses helping them recover. With a few winks and a few coins, the Carpenters learn all those secrets too."

A man in gray rags laid on the ground by the single door, a half empty glass bottle of brown liquid rested in his hand. The man was clearly lame as he had a full cast on each leg.

31

Vallia called out to the grubby man, "Hail and well met Victor. Drinking away the day as always, I see."

The man lifted his head at the call. His eyes were sharp and clear. They were not the eyes of a drunken beggar. Ronan knew that Victor was in fact one of the best lookouts this side of the Zwellian Empire.

While truly lame, he was by no means helpless. Ronan had experienced this truth the first time Mr. Kemin had brought him to the headquarters. When Ronan had first laid eyes on the brick building, he had seen Victor lying in his place. Before Ronan could even pity the man, he had exhaled a dense, blinding, white mist that filled the entire ally in seconds. This is when Ronan understood that Victor was a powerful Ethalladros.

Later Mr. Kemin had informed Ronan, "I wanted you to see Victor's abilities. It's important to understand the utility of those with whom you will be working."

Vallia asked Victor as they got closer, "Have you shot anybody recently?"

"Why ma'am, I surely don't know what ya talkin' about."

Vallia rolled her eyes. "How many times do I need to tell you, you don't have to pretend with us. We know you have a crossbow under your legs ready to shoot... What did you call them? Dumb blind fish in a barrel?"

Victor could not help but grin at her words. Ronan had learned that he was not affected by his own blinding fog and thus, with great enjoyment, was able to shoot intruders lost in his mist.

Victor chuckled, "Na ain't shot nobody this week. But let me tell ya, Imma itchin' to. Nothin' like shootin' a bunch a blind morons lost and confused. All bumpin' into each other. It's the best of fun."

Vallia shook her head and rolled up her sleeve to reveal a tattoo on her right forearm of a red hammer striking a gemstone. The tattoo was a symbol of the Carpenters. All members of the organization had the symbol on one of their arms.

When Ronan was getting his symbol by the Carpenters' personal tattoo artist, he had asked Mr. Kemin why a secretive organization would visibly mark all its members. Mr. Kemin had replied, "It would be odder in our society to not have a tattoo for your current affiliation. This résumé mark is no different from any other occupation. The best way to hide is in plain sight and the best way to lie is to tell most of the truth. So, we proudly represent the mark of the Carpenters. That doesn't mean that people have to know what the symbol means. Our members are trained to give very dull responses when asked what they do for a living. The type of conversation that does not incentivize more questions."

Ronan had asked, "But what if the Legion were to figure out what the symbol stands for? Wouldn't that endanger everyone with this symbol?"

Mr. Kemin had smiled and said, "That would require someone to betray us. It's my professional practice to prevent any backstabbing by stabbing the backs of anyone even thinking of betrayal. You would never think to betray me, would you?" He had raised his eyebrow, and, in a flash, the tattoo artist had held a dagger against Ronan's throat.

The cold steel against his windpipe was when Ronan had learned what type of man Mr. Kemin was. He was a businessman through and through. Ronan had realized back then that Mr. Kemin had seen some potential in him, but he saw Ronan as an asset and nothing more. If Ronan could help him produce profit, then he had nothing to fear and would be happily accepted as a Carpenter. But Mr. Kemin would not have given a second thought about ending Ronan's life if he thought that Ronan was a threat to his organization. This started Ronan's desire to prove himself to the Carpenters and his new boss.

Victor knew who they were but was required to check their tattoos upon entry under Mr. Kemin's insistence on following procedures. Ronan looked down at his sling and his injured right arm. He looked back at Victor. "Can you let me through just this one time? I can't really roll up my sleeve." Victor knew he had the mark on his arm after all.

Victor raised an eyebrow. "Just cus ya injured ya think I should break da rules?"

Ronan protested. "You know I have three résumé marks. They are the same ones I had yesterday morning. The Carpenter symbol is my most recent. Above that I have the one from the Waning Moon Orphanage. You know, the green house with four windows with the crescent moon in the

33

background. On top of that I have my weird smoke skull tattoo. The left half of the skull is normal, and the right half is made of green smoke with the wavy eye. Just like it was yesterday.

Victor sneered, "Ya, I know the one. The one you ain't got no clue where it came from. Says ya had it from when you were just a wee babe."

Ronan regretfully nodded. It was true that his very first résumé mark was a mystery to him. He had no recollection of receiving it or even why. It had been there as long as he could remember. No one had ever been able to identify that symbol. Ronan had once even shown it to a high investigator at the local library, but she had never seen the symbol in all her research.

As Ronan thought about his first résumé mark, a thought occurred. What was it the Justice of Death had said in his dream? '**It has always been you. You were chosen at birth.**' What an odd thing to say. Could the skull have anything to do with the Justice? It seemed too perfect. The spirits had been green just like the smoke on the skull and what better way to represent death. Was this résumé mark always an indicator of being the Eidolon of Death? Ronan had become so lost in this contemplation that Vallia had to punch him to bring him back to reality.

Victor repeated to Ronan, "Ya good to go. Now git."

They entered a familiar scene of the medical facility basement. The space was large and full of crates and shelves forming four aisles that ran the length of the building. The ceiling was just high enough to not warrant claustrophobic vibes.

The basement was broken up into sections where different factions had set up headquarters. Vallia and Ronan walked past a section where four people stood around a model of a house that sat on a table. One of them pointed to the back windows of the house making a comment about a lack of visibility from the street. Another section housed free standing doors where several people raced to pick locks. The group in the next section sat before a table where an instructor showed them crude, but effective first aid for situations where time and delicacy are not available. Ronan assumed this class was where Vallia learned to create the arm sling he currently wore.

They passed by a bulletin board with nine portraits tacked onto it. Five were featureless silhouettes. Four were detailed pencil sketches. Each picture was labeled one through nine and had notes and maps next to them. Some had names with question marks next to them. All the sketched portraits were people with masks. These were the members of the Council. Over half of them had not been identified. The ones that had been seen were only ever sighted with metal masks on their faces. Ronan had never really understood why the Carpenters had bothered to sketch out the masked people. What was the point?

He looked up at the photos and for the first time took notice of something he had never given a second thought to. One of the sketched portraits with the masks had been colored with yellow irises. Ronan had always thought this was just the artist taking liberties or possibly the person depicted was an Ethalladros. He now wondered if those unnatural yellow eyes were similar to his new irregular green irises. He thought about asking Vallia, but they had reached Mr. Kemin's office at the back of the hideout and the thought left his mind. The door to the room was lightly stained wood with an intricate floral scrolling around the edge. Ronan looked at Vallia and asked, "Are you ready?"

"Are you?" Her face was hard and difficult to read.

He nodded somberly. Then he processed what that meant. They were not only going to have to talk about Arkeen, but he was also going to have to explain his powers. What if Mr. Kemin wanted a demonstration? What would Ronan do? If he couldn't prove he had powers, what would Mr. Kemin do to him? Not wanting to let Vallia know about his sudden panic, he nodded his head slightly.

She took a deep breath. Ronan did the same to steady his nerves. Vallia raised her hand to the door, rapping it three times.

"Come in," a male voice called from the other side.

Vallia turned the knob and swung the door open.

The inside of the room was well lit by candles and a fire roaring in the stone fireplace. Paintings hung on the walls that Ronan knew used to belong in various rich houses around Shem. The floor was decorated with a pure white polar bear skin rug. A table sat next to the rug and two men leaned over the table while a third man leaned against the back wall. Upon their arrival, one of the men at the table nodded at the other and said, "We will discuss this when more information arises." He took his leave passing the two in the doorway.

Mr. Kemin looked up from the table and exclaimed, "Ah! If it is not my favorite scavenging crew, back from the fields I see. I was not anticipating that to be an overnight job." Then he saw the large sack that hung over Vallia's shoulder. "But by the look of your haul the overnight expense will be well worth it."

Dandrick Kemin was a full Elven man who dripped with energy and confidence. He was six feet tall, and his well-conditioned muscles were apparent under his freshly pressed white buttoned down shirt. The vest he currently wore was a royal indigo that perfectly accented his plum pants. His brown hair fell around his shoulders like a well-groomed mane. Sticking through his long locks, his elongated ears pointed back from his head, like those of a rabbit but narrower and more decorated with jewelry. All his good looks were accented by his bright blue eyes that glittered cerulean and pierced anyone caught in their path. He had a smile that looked like it was made of polished marble framed with a thin, trimmed goatee. People joked that Mr. Kemin was an Ethalladros with a connection to the element of money or charm. He had both in abundance.

The other man in the room was Blue, Mr. Kemin's personal bodyguard. Blue was a mountain of a man standing as tall as his employer and twice as broad. His chest was the shape of a wheelbarrow, wide on the top and narrowing at his waist. His Ether connection was the most physically dramatic manifestation that Ronan had ever witnessed. His skin was a gray blue color with veins of a blue gemstone spidering along his muscles. His hands looked as though he was wearing brass knuckles with the large blue gemstones jutting pop from the bones at the base of his fingers. He wore a black vest and a short sleeved buttoned shirt, leaving his impressive forearms exposed. Résumé marks covered every surface of his arms, depicting symbols from three separate prison sentences, two military tours, a blacksmithing guild, several taverns, the Carpenters' symbol, and oddly enough, a local horse stable.

Mr. Kemin asked, "Where is Arkeen? I have some good news for him."

Vallia took a deep breath, tears starting to well up in her eyes. "Arkeen is dead," she said, choking back a sob.

Mr. Kemin seemingly heard her statement, but he didn't seem to comprehend her words. A look of confusion crossed his face, and he tilted his head.

"An UN'kra got the jump on him. We all thought it was dead, but it jumped out of a bush and... and... stabbed him through the chest." At this point tears were streaming down her cheeks.

Mr. Kemin seemed to be in a haze, blinking slowly and squinting at Vallia, still not processing what she was saying.

"Arkeen is dead!" Vallia shouted at him, fury filling her with the truth of the statement. Wind blasted forth from her, threatening to extinguish all the candles in the room. "He died trying to get this stupid bag so he could impress you!" She threw the cloth sack that had hung over her shoulder onto the floor in front of Mr. Kemin.

"Your son is dead, Dandrick!"

Chapter 6

Mr. Kemin stumbled backward into a high-backed chair, holding his chest. His bright blue eyes suddenly had a wild look about them. They shifted over to Ronan looking for confirmation from him. Ronan slowly nodded.

Mr. Kemin's perfect composure seemed to crack at that moment. He slowly turned to the fireplace and his eyes glazed over. "Tell me everything." This command was said in a low, almost inaudible voice but Ronan still registered the authority of the statement. Vallia transitioned to the corner of the room to an ornate buffet table. She uncorked an expensive looking liquor and began drinking straight from the bottle.

Ronan took this as a cue that he was going to have to be the one to tell the account. He found himself, for the second time, relaying the events of the day before, about Arkeen's plan to steal from the giant and that plan's execution until the UN'kra attacked. He depicted Vallia's decapitation of the UN'kra and the giant's response. Not knowing how else to address what happened next, Ronan repeated exactly what had transpired with the spirits and how they had responded to his call and killed the giant. He didn't even spare the detail of Arkeen's body being crushed despite his hesitation.

The entire time, Mr. Kemin stared ahead, unmoving, unblinking, unreadable. When Ronan had finished the account, he felt exhausted, like he had just relived the events all over again. By this time Vallia had finished off half the bottle. She swayed back and forth, tears sporadically falling down her face.

The room was silent for a long uncomfortable time. Then Mr. Kemin stood up, walked to the table, and slammed his fists down. He swept

38

everything onto the floor in one violent motion and then flipped the table over. Ronan had never seen this side of him before. He had never seen him mad let alone belligerent. The man had always maintained such an unwavering demeanor.

Mr. Kemin then walked over to Vallia and snatched the drink from her, taking three big swigs before he threw it into the fireplace. The decorative glass shattered, and the fire exploded as the potent alcohol was consumed. Mr. Kemin leaned against a wall and slowly sank to the floor where his rage seemed to dissipate.

Ronan didn't know what to do. How was he supposed to console his boss? Mr. Kemin looked up at Ronan, his gaze hollow. "How long have you been a spirit whisperer?"

Ronan stuttered at the challenge, "I swear... I had no idea that I could... I didn't mean to ask Arkeen to help. It just..."

"It just happened," Mr. Kemin finished his sentence. "Like it just happened that you agreed to help him steal from a giant. Like it just so happened that you didn't see the UN'kra."

"Dandrick!" Vallia interjected. "Don't blame Ronan for this! You were the one who kept trying to incentivize larger payouts. You were the one who pushed Arkeen into this criminal life in the first place. Arkeen died trying to please you. At least Ronan was there for his last moments. You weren't there for any of Arkeen's life. Maybe in presence but never as a father. All he wanted was to make you proud."

Vallia could have easily blamed Ronan as well. The fact she had stood up for him and condemned Mr. Kemin's actions took Ronan by surprise. He had never seen anyone speak to Mr. Kemin like that. It was a bold move fueled by what must be terrible anguish. Her statements also added another layer to his already staggering guilt. Ronan's largest motivator for helping Arkeen was to impress Mr. Kemin and prove himself.

Mr. Kemin glared at Vallia for her statements. His jaw was clenched in a hard line. He then closed his eyes and seemed to process something. Then he spoke in his standard commanding voice. "This development requires a pivot in my priorities. I am recruiting both of you for an emergency mission of utmost importance."

"What are you talking about?" Vallia asked, bewildered. "Arkeen hasn't even been dead for a full day, and you are already thinking about the next mission!"

Ronan agreed that this was a peculiar form of grieving. He was surprised to see the hollow look in Mr. Kemin's eyes had vanished. His boss stood up and began pacing the room, a sign Ronan had learned to mean he was deep in thought.

Mr. Kemin spoke more to himself than to anyone in particular. "Arkeen was to head up this mission but that is not an option. I can no longer wait for more information. We must act immediately."

Vallia stepped forward into Mr. Kemin's path. "Dandrick, what are you talking about? What mission could be so important that you need to prioritize this over grieving for Arkeen?"

He looked her in the eye and said, "The mission is to save my son."

Vallia looked from Mr. Kemin to Ronan who shook his head and shrugged. He had no idea what Mr. Kemin was talking about. He had just torn apart his office over the death of his son and now he wanted to save him.

Vallia said in a slow voice, "There is no saving Arkeen. He is gone. We all have to accept that."

Mr. Kemin sighed and said, "I am not talking about Arkeen. I need to save his brother."

There was a long silence in the room. This was news to Ronan. He had always thought Arkeen was an only child as he had never mentioned a brother. Ronan had thought that he was the brother Arkeen never had.

He looked at Vallia and registered surprise and hurt in her eyes. She obviously didn't know either.

"He has a half-brother," Mr. Kemin explained, also recognizing Vallia's sadness. "They had a falling out when they were young, so it doesn't surprise me that he never talked about him."

"What do you mean by needing to save him?" Ronan inquired.

Mr. Kemin sat in his high-backed chair and put the tips of his fingers together. "I have tried to keep tabs on my son over the years. I lost track of him for the last few, but my spies have found him again. My intel has informed me that he is currently being held in Dur Volgen."

"The maximum security prison?" Ronan blurted out. The astonishment in his voice had not been hidden at all. His knowledge of the prison was minimal and most of what he knew had come from superstition and speculation of the other Carpenters. From what he had heard, Dur Volgen was the Council's most severe form of punishment, next to public executions.

Ronan knew that most of the time, if someone broke a law or acted against the Council, they were shipped off to various labor camps along with their families where they would be worked to death. Dur Volgen was the place where they sent the most dangerous and unyielding prisoners. The ones who were deemed unfit for the labor camps. If Mr. Kemin's son was there, he shuddered to think why. Then Ronan realized what his boss had meant by saving his son.

Vallia had clearly made the same connection. "You want us to initiate a prison break? It's not bad enough you lost your son, now you want to put our necks on the line. If we are caught the best thing we could hope for was a quick death. I can't even imagine the horrors of being trapped in that place."

Mr. Kemin nodded. "I have known his location for several months. The problem has been compiling a functional strategy to extract him."

Vallia threw her hands in the air. Ronan could tell the liquor was getting to her. "Let me get this straight. We came here and informed you of your son's death, and your first reaction is to replace him with your other son who you have not spoken with in years? Was Arkeen that disposable to you? I know you don't have a deep well of emotions, but I expected you to mourn Arkeen for at least a few days before you tried to find a suitable stand in."

Mr. Kemin stood and approached her. He said in a deadly calm voice, "Vallia, I understand that you grieve differently than I do and that you are inebriated, but I will remind you to whom you are speaking."

Vallia gritted her teeth and jutted her finger into Mr. Kemin's chest. "I know exactly who I am talking to. A cold heartless man who has as many emotions as the fancy desk he hides behind. You may think you can just command me to help you on a fool's errand to save your other son, but not this time. I am done helping the Kemin men risk their lives and the lives of those around them with their insane schemes." She stomped to the door. "I can't do it, Dandrick. Not anymore. Not after I have seen what happens when those schemes fail." And with that she left, slamming the door behind her.

At her exit, Ronan looked over to Mr. Kemin. He could not remember ever seeing a more broken person. Not among the homeless of Shem or the boys from the orphanage whose lives were in shambles. He knew he had screwed up in the fields of Hormáne. The weight of Arkeen's death weighed on him more heavily than any other memory and he desperately desired to do something to alleviate the guilt he felt. *'Maybe helping Mr. Kemin to save his son would provide some form of relief?'* There was also the unquestionable desire in Ronan to prove himself to Mr. Kemin. After the events of the day before, he knew this was his only chance.

Ronan made up his mind. He said in a quiet voice, "I will help you save your son."

Mr. Kemin turned to him. "You will?" he asked, a tone of surprise in his voice.

"This is not a task you will be able to do alone," Mr. Kemin informed him.

"I recognize that, sir. I think I may be able to talk to Vallia and convince her that it is what Arkeen would have wanted. But I think we need to give her some time to process in her own way."

Mr. Kemin nodded, accepting this statement. "Then let us talk for a moment about you Mr. Riviera." Ronan was not used to being referred to in such a formal way. Mr. Kemin looked into Ronan's eyes and said, "Your eyes are different. Is this a result of your new command over spirits?"

Ronan shrugged, thinking about the Justice of Death and how he had described Ronan as a commander of spirits. "I guess so. So, you believe me then? About my powers I mean."

Mr. Kemin's eyes stared into the depths of Ronan. "Are you lying to me

Ronan?"

Ronan shook his head in response. "No sir. What I said was the truth."

Mr. Kemin nodded. "I presumed so. The story you told was unimaginably unbelievable, but I know you are not a stupid man, and I don't believe you to be crazy. That leaves me with the only conclusion that you told me the truth."

Ronan was grateful to hear Mr. Kemin believed him.

"Have you ever heard of anything about powers of seeing and commanding spirits?" Ronan asked hopefully.

Mr. Kemin gave it a thought and then shook his head. "No, I have not. I have heard tales of people summoning dark spirits and trying to use them for their own benefits, but that is an unnatural and foolish thing to do, seeking out dark spirits. Everyone has a spirit, I suppose, so there is nothing dark about that. An ability to see the apparitions of a person's life force is not concerning. But I am interested in the idea of them responding to your call. Again, you do not describe it in a dark manner. It was not like you summoned dark spirits. You merely asked the spirits of the recently deceased for help and they helped." This casual talk about the deceased seemed to get to Mr. Kemin as one of them had been his son.

He shook his head as if to clear it and asked, "You know nothing about these powers? You don't know where they came from or how to control them?"

Ronan wondered if he should tell Mr. Kemin about the Justice of Death. Would it seem like a conflict of interest to his boss? The last thing Ronan wanted to do was incite suspicion from Mr. Kemin about Ronan's loyalties. He also didn't know much of anything about the Justice. He decided that it was best to keep all that secret for now. Ronan looked as innocent as possible and said, "No idea."

Mr. Kemin eyed him for a long moment. Had he sensed Ronan's hesitation? Then he gave a small nod and said, "Then I would like to test your abilities and see what all they can do."

Ronan shared a similar desire but had no idea what that looked like. "How do you plan to do that?"

"Well, if we are going to test your abilities to talk to the spirits of the dead, it would stand to reason that we will need some dead people."

Chapter 7

Ronan looked at Mr. Kemin with confusion and concern. Mr. Kemin gestured to the door. "Come on, walk with me." He turned toward the door. "Blue, please get my coat."

Ronan started as the large man in the corner of the room shifted for the first time since they had entered. He had completely forgotten the man was there as he had been as still and silent as a statue. Ronan presumed that was the best thing a bodyguard could do. Stand by and be forgotten until you need to punch someone's lights out.

Blue grabbed Mr. Kemin's deep indigo suitcoat and handed it to him. Mr. Kemin threw the coat on in one elegant motion. The three left the office and traveled to a staircase at the back of the basement. At the top of the stairs, Mr. Kemin put his eye to a peephole in a heavy wooden door. "All clear," he announced and pushed it open. They excited the basement into a white hallway. Blue closed the door behind them, and Ronan saw that it blended perfectly into the wall. You would never know it was there if you were not previously privy to its location.

They walked down the hall and passed several Legion medics who were easy to identify in their crimson hooded robes with blue accents. They paid the group no mind as they passed.

Further down the hallway they passed by a painting of the symbol of the Council: a golden tree with four branches and twin leaves on each branch. Mr. Kemin stopped to stare at the tree.

"Arkeen always enjoyed the Council's symbol." Mr. Kemin reminisced. "I assume it was because it was a tree. As a child, it was all I could do to stop

45

him from climbing trees."

Ronan stood and stared at the symbol. His memories of the emblem were significantly less nostalgic.

As Ronan had been in an imperial orphanage, this tree had been painted in the dormitory wall where he had grown up. He recalled when the painters had come to change the tree from three branches to four. Ronan remembered all the kids standing around the painters and watching them work. They kept bombarding them with questions about why the tree needed a fourth branch. That was the day that Ronan had been told that the High Arbiter of the Council had been killed and replaced by a new High Arbiter. The painters had informed the kids that the fourth branch was to represent the new political arm of the Council that oversaw the military and the future protection of the citizens.

That was when the war had officially entered Ronan's life. After that came the food rationing and the reduction of supplies like extra blankets and wooden toys. That is how he remembered it at least. Now he understood the shortages came from resources being reallocated to fight the UN'kra.

Ronan realized that Mr. Kemin had said something, and he shook himself out of the memories. "Sorry, what?" he asked stupidly.

Mr. Kemin gave him a stern look, non-verbally reprimanding Ronan for not listening. "I said, let's test your knowledge Mr. Riviera. How well do you know our adversaries? What do the four branches of the tree represent?"

Ronan had not been expecting the test. "Uhh, they are the four branches of the Council." He racked his brain for the different branches. "One branch represents the two Legislators in charge of acquisition of raw materials in the Zwellian Empire. One branch is the two Legislators in charge of the laws about the production and sale of goods and trade. One branch is the new military control, and the last branch is the two Legislators in charge of commerce and the production of money. And the trunk represents the High Arbiter." The last part he threw in with the hopes of impressing Mr. Kemin.

"Very good. And do you know why I am so adamant that all Carpenters

46

are aware of these facets of the Council?" Mr. Kemin challenged.

Ronan felt a little deflated. He felt like he should know the answer to this question but did not want to guess and seem dumb. He shook his head.

Mr. Kemin looked up and down the hallway to make sure it was clear. No one was coming from either end. He explained, "Because we actively work against the Council and their oppressive regime. If you do not know who the Council is, then you do not know who you're fighting against. If you do not know who you're fighting, then it is very easy to be deceived. If you are deceived, then you're as good as a traitor against our cause. Ronan, I want to make sure you are aware of whose side you are on."

Ronan was confused and as Mr. Kemin spoke, he grew more concerned. Did he think he was a traitor? Did he think Ronan had done something against the goals of the Carpenters? Was this about Arkeen's death? Was this about his hesitation back in the office?

Mr. Kemin could obviously see the distress on Ronan's face. He said, "I ask the question because I need to know where you stand before we reach our destination. From what you described to me, the powers that manifested inside of you could be very powerful. That is the sort of thing that I would hate to have working against me. So, I ask again whose side are you on?"

Blue flexed his impressive muscles behind Mr. Kemin indicating there was a correct answer.

Ronan was hurt that Mr. Kemin had to question his loyalty. He looked his employer in the face and said, "I serve the Carpenters. I have no love for the Council or the Legion. I have seen what their rule has led to. I would never serve the monsters who sunk me into that orphanage. I answer to you and no one else."

"No one else?" Mr. Kemin repeated, his piercing blue eyes fixed on Ronan.

"No one else," Ronan confirmed. As he said the words he thought again about the Justice of Death and him calling Ronan his champion. An Eidolon. Ronan forced himself not to look away from Mr. Kemin no matter how badly he wanted to.

Mr. Kemin stared into Ronan for what seemed like a terribly long time. He finally nodded and said, "Then let's get to shaking up some spirits."

They rounded the corner of the hall and pushed through two double doors. A troubling scene was laid out before them as they entered. Rows and rows of stretchers lined the space directly inside of the large open room with small windows high on the walls. Almost all the makeshift beds were full; many of the occupants were bandaged or visibly wounded. At a quick glance, there appeared to be no organization among the diverse crowd of injured individuals. Young were next to old and humans lay next to half Elves, men next to women. Ronan surmised that this area was hastily filled with the surviving soldiers as they flowed in.

Glancing around, he saw nurses bustling about. They could be seen walking from bed to bed, checking on their patients and inspecting their dressings. It was not hard to imagine the chaos of this room on the day of a battle, but the energy at the moment was low and quiet.

Mr. Kemin wasted no time as he started walking toward the back end of the room. His strides were long and graceful as he passed by cot after cot. He stared straight ahead not looking at any of the soldiers laying on either side of the aisle. Blue and Ronan followed.

"Why are we here?" Ronan whispered, looking around at the wounded. They made him sad. He remembered the faces of the bodies he had seen in the field. These people were the ones who had gotten to leave, but just barely. He thought about all the faces of the fallen he had scavenged that would stay in the tall grass until they were bones being bleached by the sun. He gritted his teeth and cursed the Council all the more.

Mr. Kemin looked over at Ronan and said, "I see many opportunities with your powers. If you can control them, they could be a vastly effective resource."

Ronan's empty stomach knotted up at the statement. Despite the large room, the isles of wounded soldiers were making him feel claustrophobic.

The temporary beds occupied only the first three quarters of the length of the room. The back quarter was filled with a combination of makeshift offices and privacy rooms made with light blue curtained walls. Glancing in one of the rooms, Ronan saw a metal table on wheels with leather straps and a wooden cart with various medical instruments neatly laid out on top. He looked away as his imagination ran wild with his nerves. Mr. Kemin stopped walking and Ronan ran into him.

Mr. Kemin put a hand on Ronan's shoulder. "You okay?" he asked.

Ronan nodded.

Mr. Kemin looked around, "This spot is as good as any. Let's see what you can do Ronan."

Ronan looked at him. He hated questioning Mr. Kemin but he asked again, "I don't understand. Why bring me here?"

Blue answered for his boss. "Ya don't got any spirits if ya don't have people dying. People die in this room every day." His voice was low and grave. Ronan was not sure if this was part of his Ether connection or because the man never spoke. Thinking back, this was only the third time he had heard Blue speak in two years.

Mr. Kemin nodded in affirmation, continuing to stare at Ronan expectedly.

So, they were in the infirmary to ensure spirits would be present. This made sense to Ronan. He thought about his new sight. About the pressure he had felt behind his eyes. Ronan had an inclination of how to summon his altered vision, but he was not sure it would work. He tightly shut his eyes and willed a pressure behind them.

His eyes started to hurt with his strained effort. This pain was not the right feeling. He lessened the intensity of his closed eyelids and just concentrated on the blackness. He moved his eyes around as if he was looking for something, but kept his eyes closed. He was frustrated because he knew he must look like an idiot.

What had activated them the first time? Fear? Peril? Cowardness? Thinking back to the giant attack, he remembered a strange sensation. It was almost like his eyes had blinked sideways. Like the eye of a lizard. The memory of the sensation activated something in his muscles causing what felt like a second eyelid underneath his first to blink sideways.

He opened his eyes and saw Mr. Kemin was watching him intently. An

49

orange aura pulsed around him, but all other colors were gone. Ronan smiled to himself, having activated his ability intentionally.

"Your eyes are glowing," Mr. Kemin observed. "Does that mean you were able to activate your powers?"

His voice sounded distant to Ronan even though he was standing right next to him. Ronan guessed his eyesight changed so it made sense the rest of his senses did as well.

"Do you see any spirits?" Mr. Kemin inquired. Ronan looked around the room to check.

Surprisingly, Ronan saw two green formless flames floating right behind him. As he looked at them, they began to morph into humanoid shapes. Arms and a head became distinguishable from the flames. Then faces developed in detail on the heads. Ronan's heart stopped when he recognized both faces. He couldn't process what he was seeing. The spirits of Arkeen and the UN'kra that had killed Arkeen were the ones floating next to him.

'Why were they here in the Legion infirmary? *Why were they following me?'* Ronan wondered. Ronan had just assumed they had vanished or floated away or whatever spirits did. Why would they have followed him?

The spirit of Arkeen seemed to recognize his concern. A voice permeated Ronan's mind, speaking to him telepathically.

"You summoned us to help you, so here we are."

Ronan's eyes widened. He said aloud "I can hear you! You... you can talk?" Then Ronan remembered who his audience was. He looked at Mr. Kemin, knowing he would see the fear on his face.

Mr. Kemin smiled at him. "There are spirits here you can talk to? Are they frightening?" He looked around as if he was searching for them. So, his boss could not see his dead son and his murderer floating a foot from him.

Ronan looked at Arkeen and the UN'kra. Should he tell Mr. Kemin? How would he react? Ronan couldn't imagine it would be positive. Ronan opened his mouth to tell Mr. Kemin but he could not bring himself to say the words. Instead, he said, in the most stable voice he could muster, "I am sorry that you are dead."

Arkeen responded in Ronan's head, *"Mate, it was not your fault. I was dumb and I didn't pay attention to my surroundings. That's like the first lesson of scavenging. And if we are going to point fingers, technically it's his fault."* He pointed to the UN'kra.

"You said it yourself, you were dumb," the deep voice of the UN'kra sounded telepathically. *"Mine was an attack of defense. I was awakened by you, and I thought you to be Legion scum."*

"I would say you are the dumb one if you mistook me for a Legion soldier. Clearly, I was not; I was dressed in all black leathers," Arkeen retorted back.

Ronan couldn't believe the fact that there were two spirits floating in front of him, let alone the fact they were arguing about one killing the other. He interrupted their argument to ask, "Why are you still here?" He wondered if he was able to telepathically communicate with them like they did with him.

"You told us to help you and in doing so you tethered us to yourself," the deep voice of the UN'kra permeated his head.

Cautious of what he said in front of Mr. Kemin, he asked, "What do you mean?" Ronan didn't know what the UN'kra meant by tethering the spirits. He had not intended to make the request let alone tie the spirits to himself.

"You may not know what you did, but here we are," Arkeen said, responding to the thoughts in Ronan's head. So, they could hear his thoughts. *"We are not here by choice mate. We are tethered to you."*

"What are they saying? How many are there?" Mr. Kemin inquired. Ronan realized it must be weird just watching a one-sided conversation. Luckily, they were in a medical facility and the assumption of any passerby would be that Ronan was just insane or dealing with post battle trauma.

He responded to his boss, "Just two. They are telling me why they are hanging around."

In his head he asked the spirits, *"What do you mean tethered? How am I able to tether you?"*

"I am uncertain of the answer to your questions, but you are preventing me from resting with my ancestors in the glory of the Great Light. I want to be released for I have helped you as you commanded," the UN'kra stated plainly.

51

Ronan shook his head. "I don't know how to do that. If I did, I would help, but I just discovered I have these powers."

"They are asking for something from you," Mr. Kemin interrupted cautiously. "Don't promise them anything, that could be dangerous." The two different one-way conversations were hurting Ronan's head.

Trying to organize his thoughts he looked around the room. It was only then that he noticed the sea of green flames near the entrance they had passed through. He had been so focused on Arkeen and the UN'kra that he had not noticed all the spirits of the recently dead soldiers slowly floating toward their group. Ronan was not able to distinguish individual spirits from the mass of green. There were too many of them.

He was now aware that the attention of every spirit in the room was being drawn to him like moths to a flame. Activating his ability must have triggered something in the room. Like he was some kind of beacon to the lost spirits. He looked around and saw Blue and Mr. Kemin watching him with puzzled looks. They could tell something had changed.

Mr. Kemin asked, "Is something wrong? You look scared again. What are the spirits asking you to do?"

Ronan then looked back at Arkeen and the UN'kra. They too had noticed the mob moving toward them.

"I think they are coming for you mate. You may want to tell them to stay back. I don't know what they will do to you if they reach you," Arkeen stated as he took a defensive stance.

"Why come for me?" Ronan projected in his mind. Fear was boiling up in his chest. His question was answered as his mind was suddenly assaulted with a cacophony of voices as the spirits got within range to speak to him telepathically. So many voices speaking at once. All echoing inside his mind. He could only comprehend snippets of ideas and thoughts.

"You can see me, please help me..."
    "Tell my family I'm sorr..."
    "Can you bring me back to..."
    "I can't be dead; I just can't be..."

"My son. Who will take care of my..."
"Please have mercy on me, give me another chan..."
"Those UN'kra devils did this to me, make them pay..."
"Help me please…"
"I can sense your power; you call to me..."
"I will not leave this life that eas..."

Ronan fell to his knees; his hands instinctively covered his ears, but the action did nothing to dampen the voices. He screamed at the mass, "Stay back! I can't help any of you." But his statement held no power. Ronan could see faces and hands coalescing from the wall of green flame. His palms pressed flat to the floor; his back arched as he tried to make a mental block from the spirits but there were too many for him to do anything. He felt helpless against the throng of spirits.

They kept drifting closer and closer. Then the spirits in front stopped advancing about ten feet in front of him, seemingly halted in their approach by an invisible curved wall.

The mass of floating fires fanned out, distributing around some form of spiracle barrier that surrounded Ronan. They began to envelop the area where he and his companions stood creating a semicircle of green flame. Pressure began to mount all around his subconscious. He realized that the barrier they were hitting was being created by his mind. The more spirits that pressed against the wall, the more Ronan felt like his head was being crushed in.

Then, spirits began to stretch the barrier with their faces, shoving themselves toward Ronan. As they did so, their visages became clearer and more identifiable. Their features deepened and gained resolution. Ronan looked around at Mr. Kemin and Blue. They were staring at the spirits coming through the barrier, fear clearly visible in both their eyes. They could see the spirits pressing their way through the wall. How were they able to see them? Was Ronan able to make the spirits visible to others somehow? Mr. Kemin had drawn his hidden cane sword from its walking stick sheath and Blue had his fists raised, his gemmed knuckles glittered, ready to defend himself and his boss. Ronan was somehow manifesting the spirits into existence. Or rather the spirits were manifesting themselves using his powers.

This idea infuriated Ronan in a way he didn't understand. He knew he should be terrified, but he only felt anger. These spirits were violating the natural law by manifesting themselves. Ronan didn't know how he knew that, but the feeling could not have been clearer. The natural balance was being infringed upon and it was not permissible. He was the Eidolon of Death. Prince of the Dead. These spirits have the audacity to challenge him?

The rage at the supernatural violation happening before him suddenly boiled over. Despite the debilitating assault on his mind, he shakily stood up and shouted, **"Get back! Obey for I am the Eidolon of Death!"**

It was as if Ronan's mental barrier exploded. A blast of force erupted from the barrier around Ronan, sending a shock wave cascading through the mass of spirits. The green flames were catapulted back, sending beds and soldiers toppling over and the curtained dividers to be torn and flung asunder.

Mr. Kemin and Blue crouched to the ground at the explosion of energy, but remained unhindered as they had been inside the barrier around Ronan.

Ronan suddenly felt drained of all energy as color flooded into his vision; his legs collapsing under his own weight. Blue caught Ronan under the arms. Mr. Kemin didn't miss a beat in his reaction. He sprang to his feet and shouted, "We need to leave now!"

Ronan felt himself being lifted into the air and flung over Blue's massive shoulder. Blue began a dead sprint after Mr. Kemin who was running not to the front of the room where they had entered, but to the back wall. Ronan was facing backward over Blue's shoulder looking at the room's entrance and the mangled beds and sprawled soldiers. He then saw several Legionnaires sprinting after them. Several of the nurses were in pursuit as well.

Mr. Kemin reached the back stone brick wall. "Blue!" he yelled. Blue hunkered down and, without hesitation, lowered his shoulder as he collided with the brick. The masonry was demolished as Blue charged through the wall like it was paper. In all the dust and chaos, Ronan, looking back and saw a young girl in red nurse's robes pursuing them. Her hair was raven black, braided around her head like a crown. Her skin was kissed by a life in the sun. But it was her eyes that really caught Ronan's attention. They glowed purple just as his eyes glowed green.

There was an odd familiarity about her, but he was sure he had never seen her before. Blue continued his charge away from the building, trailing Mr. Kemin who ran into the maze of alleyways.

Ronan bounced along atop the bodyguard, too drained to move or try to fight Blue's grapple. He couldn't even process his surroundings. All he could do was think about the spirits pressing themselves through that barrier. Manifesting themselves into the living world.

Questions flooded his mind. What was that barrier? How did I make the spirits appear to the others? Who was that girl with the purple eyes? Is she like me? Are there other Eidolon?

Chapter 8

Ronan's legs were about to buckle as he leaned against a building. Their retreat had left them weaving through the city for a few minutes, but Ronan might as well have run for a whole day. Even though he had been carried, his mental exhaustion was overwhelming him. Mr. Kemin had constantly been looking over his shoulder to confirm they were not being followed. Blue's fists were still tightly clenched. His breaths were labored and sounded like rocks being ground together.

Ronan took in his surroundings, and discovered they had stopped in a small alleyway between two buildings that were each two stories tall. Ronan turned to Mr. Kemin to start questioning him about what had just happened. He stopped himself as he saw Mr. Kemin with his ear pressed against a stone support wall that the buildings sat upon. He was tapping on different stones to hear their sound. His hand compressed one of the stones into the wall and he grabbed the edge of the adjacent rock. He pulled it toward himself. Without a sound, a section of the stone swung away from the wall, revealing a narrow wooden passageway of stairs leading upward. Mr. Kemin motioned the other two to follow as he began to ascend.

The stairs were dimly lit as the sun peeked through cracks in the exterior wood of the building. The passage topped out onto a landing blocked by a wooden wall. Ronan was attempting and failing to understand where they were. *'Why was this passage here?'* He watched Mr. Kemin knock twice on the wall, pause, and knock four more times. Then there was silence in the cramped narrow stairwell. The door behind them had closed leaving the hidden space very stuffy and warm. Blue was still breathing heavily as he braced himself against the wall while staring at his feet. Ronan was slightly concerned the large man was going to breath up all the usable air. With a scraping sound, the wooden wall in front of them swung open, revealing a very unhappy looking Vallia.

"Someone better be dead, Dandrick," Vallia said as she stared daggers at them.

"Yes, the problem is dead people. Mr. Riviera here summoned a hoard of violent spirits in front of a room full of people and then proceeded to cause a small explosion," Mr. Kemin said. This statement startled Vallia enough to allow Mr. Kemin to push past her without any resistance. She looked confused at Ronan.

"I'm honestly not sure what happened," he said as he also walked past her, thankful to leave the stairwell. He looked around the space and saw a small, well-furnished living room. He assumed that they had just ascended a secret passage into Vallia's home.

Large tapestries depicting seasonal changes hung on opposing walls, serving as a nice pop of color in the room. The floor was covered by a large woven rug of grays and deep blues. The furniture all looked to be old and rustic. The decor matched Vallia's personality well. In the time he had worked with her, she had never extended an invitation to anyone except Arkeen to come to her house. She was definitely a person that kept work and home life separate. Or at least Ronan had thought that prior to ascending the secret staircase in her wall. Ronan figured that she was one of the most senior members of the Carpenters and Mr. Kemin must trust her a lot. Especially considering the fight the two had undergone. This was the first location that Mr. Kemin had thought to bring the group in a moment of panic.

Ronan turned to Mr. Kemin who was sitting in a lounging chair with the tips of his fingers pressed together in front of his mouth. He was in deep thought, but Ronan had to know what was happening.

"I don't know what happened back there and I don't know what you saw, but whatever I did, I didn't mean to do it. I didn't mean to summon those spirits. It honestly felt like they were summoning themselves without my permission," Ronan blurted.

"We, alongside at least fifty other people, who were mostly Legionnaires might I add, just saw a young boy summon flaming apparitions out of the air." Mr. Kemin spoke in a manner that indicated he was processing the information as he said it. "I had a vague understanding of what was transpiring, and I saw it as a serious threat to my own life. I can't imagine what the uninformed people in that room must have thought. It wouldn't be too difficult to draw the conclusion that a terrorist attack was taking place. I would surmise that you just earned us the title of some of the most hunted individuals this side of Celsus."

Ronan's eyes grew wide. He had known the test of his powers had gone badly. He didn't realize how bad it was. Mr. Kemin had brought Ronan there to help understand the potential of his powers. He had let Mr. Kemin down. Ronan had lost control and endangered everyone there as well as put a target on all their backs. He should have been able to command the spirits and stop them before they had attacked. This reinforced what the voice had told him in his dream. He needed to learn how to control these abilities.

"Did anyone get hurt?" Ronan asked dejectedly, as he leaned up against one of the walls and started to nervously fidget with a tassel on the trim of a tapestry.

Mr. Kemin shook his head. "No one was close to us. I think the worst of it was some soldiers getting knocked out of their cots. You sure did a number on the area where we were standing. But it doesn't matter if anyone got hurt. By now the rumors and stories will have already grown more elaborate. People fear what they don't understand Ronan. I guarantee that no one in that room understood what happened with those spirits."

Ronan tried to justify himself. "I didn't know the spirits would all come after me like that. They were so aggressive. All I wanted to do was show you it was not crazy or a liar."

"This is not the time for a pity party. We are past that point. Obviously, I didn't know you were going to summon the whole room to attack us" Mr. Kemin said. A small amount of frustration could be heard in his voice.

"Due to the circumstances, I don't think we have much choice. Ronan, we need to get you out of the city."

This hit Ronan like a punch to the gut. Leave Shem? This had been his home his entire life. It was where his parents had lived and where they had died. Ronan had just started to be getting established with the Carpenters. Now he was being forced to leave. Leave all he had worked so hard to achieve? "Can I just lay low for a while? Keep my head down?"

"Unfortunately, that would make you too much of a liability. We need to get you out of the city but obviously we can't send you alone."

Vallia frowned at the three men. "So let me get this straight. I tell you that I was done dealing with your drama, and less than an hour later, you come here, knocking on my secret stairs because you are on the run from the Legion after attacking the infirmary. Now you are asking me to shuttle Ronan out of the city and take him away?"

Mr. Kemin gave her a startled expression. "I didn't come here to pawn Ronan off on you. I came here because I know I can trust you even when you're mad at me."

"That is a bold-faced lie, and you know it, Dandrick. I know how you operate. I can't believe this. I am going to go make some tea." She exited the room through a swinging door.

Mr. Kemin cursed under his breath. "I will go talk to her." He followed her into the kitchen.

Ronan was left in the room with Blue, who just so happened to be standing directly in front of the secret door. Ronan assumed that was not a coincidence. Were they worried he was a flight risk? This annoyed him, but he was honestly happy to be alone. Or at least as alone as one could be with a large rocky man standing in the corner. Ronan sat in a chair that faced away from Blue and closed his eyes. He sought the lizard-like blink sensation again and felt his powers activate.

Upon opening his eyes, he saw Arkeen and the UN'kra floating there along with the black and white apartment.

He mentally spoke to both, "*I don't need you to follow me. I didn't mean to tether you to myself. Until you said it, I didn't know spirits could be tethered to*

59

someone."

Arkeen looked around the apartment clearly reminiscing about the space. "I think the tethering thing is special to you, my friend. I don't think anyone else can even see us." He floated over to Blue and waved his hand in front of his face.

"Well, you are free to go."

"You say we are free yet here we remain, chained to you in servitude. My family waits for me. The Light waits for me," the UN'kra interjected.

"The last thing I want to do is stop you from resting with your people and your light, whatever that is. Please go, I don't want you here. You killed my friend. The fact you're still here is honestly a sore subject," Ronan projected.

"You speak of my presence as a sore subject, yet you stand in the house of the elemental woman who took my life. You do not see me complaining," the UN'kra droned. Ronan had never talked with an UN'kra before. He was not sure if this was their normal state of communication or if this one in particular was just annoying and very literal.

"Don't worry about him mate. He has been this way the whole time. He won't shut up about being dead," Arkeen chimed in.

The UN'kra scoffed and crossed its arms.

"What about you?" Ronan asked Arkeen. "He literally stabbed you. Doesn't that make you mad or upset or something?"

"Hmm, yeah I guess he did stab me didn't he."

"I would think that would be a large point of contention between you two. I would assume you would be at each other's throats."

Arkeen smiled at this. *"A lot of good that would do, considering all the breathing and swallowing we will be doing."* Even in death Arkeen was still witty. Ronan couldn't help but smile and was glad Blue could not see.

Arkeen's spirit projected, *"I don't feel mad about it. I am not happy that he stabbed me, either. I guess I would say I am indifferent. I don't really feel like it is that important of a distinction to be honest."* As his spirit projected this idea, he seemed to get lost in thought. *"I guess when you're dead the past seems less important, ya know? I mean I can't change the fact that he killed me. I can't change anything about my life. Concerns for the world seem so trivial now."*

60

"What about Vallia?" Ronan asked as he looked at the kitchen door. *"You two loved each other and were about to be married. Does it bother you that you two won't have a future together?"* As he asked the question, Ronan realized if he kept the spirits a secret from Mr. Kemin, he would have to do so with Vallia. This felt like a betrayal of her trust, and he didn't like that. She had defended him in front of Mr. Kemin.

Arkeen floated to the window and looked out. *"I watched her today. I watched her sadness and her anger. I saw her despair and her grieving. But I don't know if I can feel those things now. I truly did love her when I was alive and I believe that I would have been so blessed to marry her, but it didn't happen. It can't happen."* He seemed to struggle finding the next thoughts. *"I think the best way to describe my current state would be with a book. Imagine if every decision and every risk and every memory that you experienced in life was written down in a book. All the details of your time alive, cataloged into a comprehensive tome. Then you die and the final period marks the last sentence on the last page and the book gets put onto a shelf. I feel like I have been given the ability to pick up that book and remember all my life, but all I can do is read it over and over again. I can't change it or rewrite it. That's how I feel right now. Unable to emotionally connect with the life I lived and not sure what death holds for me."* He turned and gave a half smile. *"Death is kinda morbid, isn't it?"*

"If you are not concerned about your life and your family, why is he so worried about his?" Ronan nodded toward the UN'kra.

The UN'kra responded, *"I am not worried as you say. Even in life I understood that it was foolish to store up treasures of the world, to hold the things of this world as valuable. For where your treasure is stored, there also will your heart be. No, I knew that I was a foreigner and an exile in the world. I trusted in the Light and that after my short time in this world, I would be welcomed into the kingdom of the Light for my faith. My 'worry', as you say, comes from knowing that truth. My ancestors have passed into the Glory of the Light and they wait for me to join them. This fool's family is still living."* He gestured to Arkeen. *"The Light calls to me but I am held against the laws of nature to stay here. I know that my actions in life, both good and bad, are not what matters now. I know I lived my life as my ancestors did. Trusting in the Light. Walking along the path of the Light. When you release me, I will go to the Glory of the Light and my ancestors will greet me, and we will celebrate the Light with unending praise."* The UN'kra also floated to the window and looked out into the sky.

Ronan was taken aback by the heartfelt response. Ronan's guilt intensified knowing the UN'kra's accusations were valid. He was deeply upset that the UN'kra had killed Arkeen, but like the spirits said, it was not like that fact could be changed. He figured he would have to continue to deal with the UN'kra spirit until he could figure out how to release them. With this realization, he decided to try and make the best of the situation. *"Do you have a name? I don't know how to release you, but I promise I will try to figure it out."*

"Ha ah ha," the UN'kra spirit's booming laugh filled his head. *"You jest with your promise. This is a good jest, yes. The living have no right to promise anything. Their promises are like flowers of the field. So quick to bloom but then they wilt away with the change of a season. The UN'kra have a saying: Let your yes be a yes and your no be no. As for my name, in life I was called Ta Rhe Vos Hundar."*

Ronan felt like his honor was being challenged. Who was this spirit to question him? It was bad enough he was treated that way by people, but he was supposed to be a commander of the spirits. They shouldn't disrespect him like this. *"Listen, I said I will let you go, and I will! When I figure out how to do it, I will happily send you away. Like I told you, it's not like I want you here. I don't need you questioning my motives or my integrity..."*

The kitchen door swung open and an angry Vallia and a disgruntled Mr. Kemin came back into the living room. Ronan quickly closed his eyes and released the pressure behind them. Opening them again color had returned to the world.

Vallia aggressively pointed a finger at Mr. Kemin and said, "You and I both know that any Carpenter could get him safely out of the city. But you don't just want him to leave the city. You want him to go on your quest to save your son and you want me to go with him. Admit it, Dandrick."

Mr. Kemin pursed his lips at the statement. "I can't lie and say that it has not crossed my mind but..."

"But what?" Vallia demanded.

He continued firmly, "But it's not all about my son. It is also about Ronan. What just transpired with the spirits was a catastrophe, but it also showcased the vast potential of Ronan's abilities. He needs to learn about these powers. He needs to learn to control them. If he doesn't, he is a risk to himself and everyone around him. It will be difficult to control his powers if he doesn't understand where they came from and why they developed now. They do not seem like something connected to the Ether. That takes away almost every scholar I know who could help give him answers."

Ronan listened intently to his boss, not sure how he felt about his statements.

Mr. Kemin looked at Ronan in the chair. "I want the best for him, and he knows that. I also want the best for the Carpenters as a whole and that means we need to hone in on his abilities. There is one man I know of who may be able to help. He is a lead scholar in the field of interdimensional integration or something like that."

Ronan perked up at the statement.

Mr. Kemin continued, "Basically he is one of the smartest minds in the world on the subject of planes crossing into each other. I don't know much about Ronan's powers, but I don't think for a moment that they are coming from this plane."

"I agree that it sounds like Ronan needs to understand his powers. Again, any other Carpenter can bring him to this scholar. I fail to see why you need me to do it?" Vallia demanded.

Ronan's interest began to transition to anger as the adults continued to argue like he wasn't in the room.

Mr. Kemin seemed to choose his words carefully. "I told you; you are the one I trust for this mission. You already know about his powers. For now, the less people that know the better."

Vallia glared. "I don't believe you. That is not why you came to me. What are you not telling me, Dandrick?"

Mr. Kemin tensed up his mouth. He looked at Vallia's determined face. He then sighed. "The scholar's name is Arch Archivist Nimin Osmodius.

I do not know his current whereabouts. Last I heard he was somewhere in Ristiven. I want to clarify this before I say anything else. I don't trust the man any further than Blue could throw him. I do know that if anyone understands what is happening to Ronan, it will be him. Osmodius is funded by the Council, but with the proper motivation and incentivization you might get him to talk."

Vallia crossed her arms. Ronan could tell her patience was running out. Ronan was intrigued to hear about this Osmodius but was also further irked that they were continuing to ignore him.

Mr. Kemin continued. "I have a contact that has worked with Osmodius in the past. They will know where to find him. This is why I came to you, Vallia. You are correct, other people could take Mr. Riviera to Ristiven. However, you are the only person I trust to meet up with my contact." Before Vallia could question him again, Mr. Kemin confirmed, "Yes, the contact who knows where to find Osmodius is my son."

Vallia's eyes grew wide. "I knew it. I knew this had to do with him. You still want me to help you break him out of prison. I told you Dandrick. I am not going to help you replace Arkeen!"

At this, Mr. Kemin's face fell. It was as if Ronan could see his composure crack. Mr. Kemin said in a weak, small voice. "I am not trying to replace Arkeen. I lost one of my sons yesterday. I can't lose another one. I learned where Leo was and now all I can think about is getting him out of Dur Volgen. But I promise you, I also want to help Ronan. And I know Leo can help him get answers. He can help him reach his full potential."

"You know I am right here, right?" Ronan blurted, unable to contain himself any longer. He was used to people treating him like a child, and not respecting his opinions, but this was his life they were arguing about. "You are talking about me like I am not in the room. Why do you keep saying that my gift could have a lot of potential? Do you see me as some weapon to be used or some power to harness? If that is the case, count me out. Also, I have never even agreed to be ushered out of the city. I don't have any of my possessions. I don't have Sabastian. I trust you Mr. Kemin, I do, but I am not going to stand here silently while you two decide my fate."

Mr. Kemin looked at Ronan with his piercing blue eyes at the outburst. Ronan immediately wondered if he had overstepped his rank. But Mr. Kemin's expression showed mostly surprise. Ronan had never been one to question what he was told and was not the type to stand up for himself like he just had.

"I didn't mean to cut you out of the conversation, Ronan, but you truly cannot stay here. What you did back in the medical facility will make you a large target. I know you are not incompetent and that you are an adult who can make his own choices. As for your powers, I can't tell you how they will be helpful when I don't understand their capabilities. You are no more a weapon to me than Vallia or Blue or any other Ethalladros I employ. But that doesn't mean that I don't look for value in all my employees. You need to understand your abilities, or they will tear you apart. You have great potential. You always have. That is why I brought you on board in the first place. I am sorry for treating you like a child, which was wrong of me."

Ronan had never heard his mentor apologize for anything. Nor had he ever been told he had potential. Ronan's face grew hot, and he knew he was blushing. He nodded and said, "I didn't mean to explode like that. I am sorry."

Vallia seemed to lose part of her hard edge as Mr. Kemin spoke as if his genuine words were breaking through her emotional wall. She said, "You really think your son is going to be the one who is able to help Ronan get answers?"

Mr. Kemin nodded. "Yes, I do, and I would be lying if I said I did not have selfish, personal motives for retrieving my boy, but I do truly believe Osmodius will have answers. The only way I know how to find him is through Leo." He looked between the two of them. "I lost Arkeen, I can't lose Leo as well. Not when I have a chance to save him from the nightmares of Dur Volgen. Will you two please help me?"

Ronan had never heard Mr. Kemin plead for anything. He was always in command and his authority was so rarely questioned. Ronan could see Vallia's emotional wall breaking down. The hint of a tear formed in the corner of her eye. She gritted her teeth, looked away from the group, and sighed. "Fine, I will help, but only if you are able to offer up an unbelievable plan as to how we are supposed to break your son out of the highest security prison in the Zwellian Empire."

Mr. Kemin's bright blue eyes sparked. He sat in an armchair and pulled out a notebook from his vest pocket. This is where he thrived. This is why the Carpenters had become such a strong presence despite the oppressive oversight of the Council. Mr. Kemin was a mastermind when it came to hatching schemes.

Mr. Kemin began explaining with a sudden, uncharacteristic excitement, "I have given this a fair bit of thought. You need to get into the prison without bringing attention to yourselves. The question is, who is allowed to enter the prison unhindered?"

Ronan and Vallia looked at each other, not sure if their boss wanted them to answer.

Mr. Kemin exclaimed, "The answer is criminals and the guards of the prison. Obviously, we cannot get you inside as prisoners. You would never be able to escape. So, we have to get you in as guards. I have some spies set up at the Dancing Bear Inn, about a day's journey south of the prison. My spies have confirmed that the bar is a common stopping point for prison guards who are on leave. I need you to go to the inn, meet up with the spies, and with their help, incapacitate some prison guards. You don't have to kill them," he clarified, seeing Ronan's expression, "Just knock them out and the spies will take them to a…"

He paused to pick the right phrase. "To a safe place where they won't interfere with our operation. With their armor you will have access into the prison. From there you will need to locate Leo. It may take a couple of days so you both will have to play the part of guards. I don't mean just playing dress up. I am talking about full immersion. If a prisoner is to be punished, you have to be willing to punish them. If you are told to clean the latrine, you do it no question. It may not be pretty, but it is the only way to avoid suspicion. My intel has told me that some of the experienced guards have been carted away in the war effort and some of their replacements are pretty young. This is good for us because that will help Ronan blend in."

"That gets us in but what gets us out?" Vallia asked doggedly.

Mr. Kemin smiled at the question. "Every week the prison gets a shipment of food. It comes in four large wooden crates in the early hours of the morning. Not that they feed the prisoners much, but when you have a few hundred people the food can add up. The crates are large enough to hide someone in. All you have to do is make sure you both are scheduled for the early morning shift the day the food comes. On your patrol, you will be able to break Leo out of his holding cell and help him to the kitchen. All you have to do is get him and yourselves into the crates and my spies will take care of the rest. The normal delivery wagon will undoubtedly experience a tragic bandit attack on the way to the prison that morning. The whole convoy will be replaced by Carpenters. They will pick you up and bring you to a safe location. We will figure out details from that point and assess our situation. Then we can figure out the next step of talking with Archivist Osmodius."

Ronan was captivated by the entire plan. He had never been involved in something so intricate and elaborate. The thought of playing the guards was troubling, but he knew Mr. Kemin was right. They would have to sell the act. He couldn't believe he was going to be trusted to do something of this level. Vallia seemed to have been thinking the same thing.

"You want me and Ronan to infiltrate Dur Volgen. Why Ronan? He does not have any experience with infiltration or subterfuge."

Ronan's soaring emotions crashed as she said these words. What she said was true, but he knew he could do this. He was about to voice this when Mr. Kemin replied. "Ronan was not my first pick for this mission, this is true. To be honest, I was going to send you and Arkeen." He paused to compose himself and then continued. "But that is not an option." He looked at Ronan. "While you do not have the experience that I would normally require for a mission of this caliber, you do have a set of skills that could be very useful if you are able to control these powers of yours. If my plan was to go badly or if someone was to identify you or see through our ruse, well if things get violent, you would not have to leave a trail of bodies behind you. Your new powers mean the difference between a guard finding a body and raising the alarm and there not being a body to find. You can command a dead guard to stand up and follow you. You can command them to help you break out Leo. But you can only do that if you can control your powers."

Ronan looked back at Mr. Kemin. He now realized how large of expectations Mr. Kemin had for his powers. He gulped. Would he be able to live up to those expectations?

Mr. Kemin looked at Vallia. "What do you say? Is this plan up to your standards? Will you help me with this?"

Vallia looked out the window and let out a long sigh. She began to pace around the room, wringing her hands and she walked. As she did this, she looked down at her engagement ring. A simple silver band. She stared at it for a moment and then slowly nodded. "I will do this mission," she held up her finger. "But I am not doing it for you or Leo. I am doing this for Arkeen. I believe this is what he would want me to do. And after this mission I demand a paid sabbatical. Do you hear me?"

Mr. Kemin looked at Ronan. "I know you are new to this, and it may seem daunting..."

"I'm in," Ronan said before Mr. Kemin could finish. He was determined to prove himself in this mission. If he could pull this off, he would for sure earn the respect of Mr. Kemin, Vallia, and hopefully Arkeen's brother. For Leo was the key that opened the door to a tantalizing promise of meeting this Arch Archivist. Then Ronan considered how this could aid him in the eyes of the Justice of Death who wanted Ronan to grow in his understanding of his powers. What better way to do that than real world application?

Then Ronan remembered he had zero supplies. "But I am going to need my stuff from my house. My sword, my traveling pack, and Sabastian."

As he said the name, a pop sounded up above him. In the rafters of the ceiling, Sabastian appeared. He shimmered in the light from a small attic window as he flew in a circle and landed on Ronan's shoulder. The bird's long wisping tail feathers rested halfway down Ronan's back. Sabastian nuzzled Ronan's cheek. Ronan never understood the bird's ability to come when beckoned, but he was grateful to have his friend with him after the morning he had been through.

"Well, that is one less thing to remember to grab," Mr. Kemin said, standing to his full height with his signature half-smile shifting his face. "Blue, can you please go to Mr. Riviera's apartment and grab some necessary supplies? I will draw up a map for these two and get them ready to go. Vallia, you will want to pack a new bag. This trip is going to be a little longer than your recent journeys."

It amazed Ronan at how fast Mr. Kemin went from a broken man to being a commanding leader, assigning tasks for his troops to complete.

Blue stood from the chair that had been sagging under his hefty weight. "Good thing ya bird showed up cause I don't mess with no birds. They think I'm a statue or something. I'll get ya stuff. Anything else ya need, spirit man?"

Chapter 9

The three sat around Vallia's living room while they waited for Blue to return. Ronan recounted in more detail the events of the morning. Vallia listened with the occasional distressed fidget. Ronan didn't know if it was his account or if her anxiety was a result of the mission she had just agreed to go on. Mr. Kemin remained quiet for the duration of Ronan's explanation. He sat in a high-backed chair against the wall, deeply engrossed with writing in a journal he had produced. Ronan would have liked to be freer with information and wished to hear Vallia's thoughts on his circumstance, but thought that now was not a good time with Mr. Kemin sitting five feet away.

Ronan stopped talking when the secret knocks resonated behind the wall. Vallia stood and walked to the wall. She grabbed a piece of trim that ran through the middle of the wall and rotated it. The hidden lever opened the secret door with a creak. Blue filled the opening, holding a potato sack slung over his shoulder. He lumbered into the room and placed the sack by Ronan's feet. He then took a small pouch off his belt and threw it to Vallia. Coins jingled together as she caught it.

"That's ya fund for ya travel, plus a little extra for our interruption," Blue said.

Mr. Kemin stood up and tore two papers out of his journal, handing one of them to Vallia. "My field operatives will be notified that you are setting out today. You should be able to make it there in three days' travel. I will send this via message falcon to them. They will wait for you at the Dancing Bear Inn. It is on the southern road, across the river. The prison of Dur

70

Volgen is about twenty miles northwest of the inn. When you get to the inn, look for the usual meeting markers. The spies will inform you about the prison and everything they know. And to squelch your disdain for a lack of information, I don't have any more. Messages are not as secure as they once were. The Council has been making a habit of shooting falcons out of the sky to intercept communications. I have not felt comfortable sending or receiving any messages that contain more than a minimal encrypted note. I'm lucky I got the information about my son when I did. Now, you better go pack."

Vallia glanced over the paper and then folded it twice. She turned and walked down her tight hallway, disappearing into a room.

Mr. Kemin nodded, seemingly checking off a mental list as he went. He turned to Ronan and said in a low voice, which was barely audible. "Ronan, I have a job for you as well. I need you to deliver this to my son." He handed Ronan the other paper. It was folded into a tight square, with its edges tucked into itself. "This will hopefully help you convince Leo to aid you. It has been a few years since I have spoken to him, but I am optimistic that he will agree. That is the type of person he is, altruistic and open hearted." He saw the look that flashed across Ronan's face and added, "He gets that from his mother."

Mr. Kemin then produced a small cloth pouch and also handed it to Ronan. Something hard with curves and bumps was inside. "This will prove to him that it is I that gave you that letter. He will know what it is."

Ronan nodded and pocketed the items. "I will make sure he gets both."

Mr. Kemin leaned in and gave Ronan a hug. Ronan was taken aback at the odd show of affection. He then understood as he heard Mr. Kemin whisper into his ear, "Vallia will most certainly despise Leo for all that he is. Keep her from killing him." He leaned away and said at his regular volume. "Now Ronan, keep practicing with your powers if you can. Work on finding a way to control them. They may save your life in the prison."

Before Ronan had time to process Mr. Kemin's warning Vallia exited her room with a backpack that was filled to the brim. She walked over to the main entryway and pulled an elegant looking bow from hooks on the wall. The bow was made of dark wood with silver bands on the tips. At its unstrung length, Ronan guessed it would have been about as tall as he was. She slung it onto her shoulder. Reaching over to a side table by the front door, she grabbed a mahogany quiver and affixed it to her belt. She looked at Ronan. "You ready to flee the city?"

Ronan nodded. He had pulled his own backpack from the sack Blue had given him. Blue had not grabbed everything that Ronan would have preferred, but he had the essentials. His tent, bed roll, and travel necessities were all accounted for.

He hosted his backpack onto his back with a little difficulty due to his sling. Sabastian squawked in protest as he had to flutter off Ronan's shoulder for a second to let the strap slide into place. The overlapping sling strap and backpack were less than comfortable. Blue helped Ronan fasten his sword to his belt. As he did, he remembered it had been Arkeen that had given him this sword on their first scavenge together. He had pulled it from the body of a centurion and said, 'If it is good enough to kill a centurion, it is good enough for you.' He patted the sheath and thought about the spirits probably still floating in this room. If he was going to say something about them, now was the only chance. If he didn't say anything now, how could he bring it up later?

Fear filled his chest. What if Mr. Kemin was furious with him about Arkeen's spirit? What if his boss didn't let him go with Vallia? What if Vallia was so mad that she shot him right on the spot? He could not bring himself to confess the secret of the spirits.

Instead, he remained silent and went to stand beside Vallia. He looked back at his mentor, expecting him and Blue to follow them. They, however, moved back to the wall with the secret door. "Everyone saw you with me during the spirit attack. Are you staying in the city? Won't you be wanted as well?"

Mr. Kemin smiled, showing all of his perfectly spaced white teeth. "I cannot leave the city Ronan. Not right now at least. I have too much work to do. Don't you worry about me. I do not plan to make any public appearances any time soon. Once we get back to the headquarters, that is where we will stay for a little while. When we eventually stick our heads out of hiding, I will make sure to inform people about the black haired, emerald eyed boy who possessed me and my bodyguard with evil spirits and forced me to help him escape the medical facility."

Ronan frowned at this. "If that is your story, then that means…"

"It means you will not be returning to Shem for a while." Mr. Kemin completed the sentence for him. "It is just not safe. When you have secured Leo, you will need to correspond with me. We will figure out the next steps after that. Likely, we will need to find a way to get you into Ristiven." He pulled the wooden trim piece and the wooden wall swung open with a creak.

"Vallia, there is no point to a secret entrance if it announces itself to the whole neighborhood when it is opened," Mr. Kemin called out as he and Blue began to descend the stairs. "I will have one of my men come by and fix that while you are gone. Good luck to you both and stay safe." Blue looked back as he closed the door. He nodded wordlessly at the two and the wall closed behind them.

"I don't understand how he does it," Vallia said, shaking her head. She then looked at Ronan who was not trying to hide his sadness. "What is wrong with you? Are you upset you won't be able to come back to Shem?"

That is exactly what he was upset about. Shem had always been his home. Sometimes it had not been a safe home, or a welcoming home, but it was still his home. Mr. Kemin had warned him when he first joined the Carpenters that relocations happened and that he should not get too attached. He had never thought that a relocation would happen so suddenly without his input. He had finally felt like he was going to be able to grow and become important in the Carpenters and believed that his powers would help him get respect and a higher position than that of a scavenger, but that notion seemed to be further out of reach than ever.

He shrugged at Vallia and said, "I'm just tired and life is not working out how I thought it was going to, that is all."

She nodded somberly. "It so rarely does." After an awkward pause she asked, "Are you ready? Once we leave here there is no turning back. We have to keep our heads down and get out of the city."

Ronan took a deep breath and pushed his feeling of displacement to the back of his thoughts. "I'm ready".

She nodded and walked to her front door and exited the apartment. Ronan followed her, closing the door behind him. The two of them merged into a crowd of pedestrians making their way to the eastern gate.

As they strolled down the street, Ronan became nervous about encountering any guards. He was sure that word would have spread about him by this point to all the guard posts in the city. He wanted to pull his hood over his head but knew that would draw more attention.

"How are we going to get through the security check at the gate?" He murmured to Vallia as they walked.

"We are not leaving through the gate. That would be suicide. We are going to use one of Dandrick's smugglers' tunnels."

Ronan should not have been surprised by this statement but couldn't help but be amazed at the vast infrastructure that Mr. Kemin had established in the city. "There always seems to be more secrets and surprises the longer I am in the Carpenter's," he mused.

"Unfortunately, that never changes, regardless of how long you have been with them," Vallia expressed. She seemed to get lost in thought about this truth and began to subconsciously make small wind blades in her hands.

"Have you always been able to make those air blades?" Ronan asked curiously.

"No," she said, realizing what she was doing with her hands and shoved them in her pockets. "I didn't know I could do that until yesterday. I just have to compress it and accelerate it. In the fields, I was so angry I just imagined the air being smashed into a blade and it followed my instructions." She stopped talking and they walked in silence. Ronan assumed she was reliving the beheading of the UN'kra Ta Rhe because that was what he was doing. The thought that the spirit was following them at that moment, possibly reading Ronan's thoughts, unnerved him. He was relieved to hear Vallia say, "We're here."

The structure, if you could call it that, was a one-story building with boards falling off the facade and a sign that hung crookedly from two metal rings that read *Knik Knacks*. Vallia pushed open the door, setting off the bell that hung just inside. The sign did not misrepresent the store. Shelves were piled high with small figurines, antique decorations, and miscellaneous pieces of bent and formed metal. The smell of dust was heavily present in the air.

Vallia walked to the back counter that was covered with piles of mismatched shoes. A short man poked his head out from behind the counter. His white bushy mustache completely covered his mouth. It was the only hair on his head. Without saying a word, Vallia lifted her sleeve and showed the man her Carpenter tattoo. It was the only one on her right arm indicating it was either the only place she had ever been officially connected to or her other arm was completely covered. Ronan knew she had entered into the Carpenters young but found it hard to believe it was her only résumé mark. Ronan respected Vallia's privacy and knew not to inquire.

The small man whistled through a gap in his teeth in approval and motioned them to follow him. He went into the back room and started to push a large bookshelf full of tiny glass objects. All of the objects rattled dangerously as the bookcase rolled away. Behind was a small hole in the wall with a tunnel descending into the ground. The hole was just large enough for a grown man to go down. Vallia nodded to the man, crouched down, and vanished into the secret passage. Ronan watched her disappear into the lightless space. He looked at the shopkeeper and smiled awkwardly. The man looked unimpressed. Ronan let his smile die and followed Vallia into the darkness.

Chapter 10

They stumbled out of the dark tunnel twenty minutes later. The bright sun attacked Ronan's eyes. The passage had been narrow and they had used the close walls to guide themselves along.

He fought his way past the clinging branches that hid the entrance of the tunnel, blindly bumping into Vallia's back.

She caught him by the front of his tunic, so he did not fall over and pushed him upright. After several attempts he was able to slowly squint his eyes open.

He saw the greens of leaves and heard the sounds of birds calling from above. They were on a hilltop at the edge of a small forest. Ronan turned around. Down in the valley about a mile away, he could make out the outer wall of Shem. He turned back to see Vallia was already walking away toward the western road. Looking again at Shem, his heart sank. He had no idea when he would see the city again if he ever came back. What did life hold for him? What adventures awaited him? He wished he knew. He wished he could see a glimpse of the future. For now, all he could do was follow his friend. He accepted this truth and walked after Vallia.

After making it to the main eastern road they walked for five hours. Ronan forced his feet to keep moving despite his exhaustion. His eyes burned from lack of sleep and his legs were heavy like lead. He barely noticed when the colorful bands of travelers passed them on the road. He did take notice of one group that consisted of eight older men with peppered beards. They wore turbans and exotic travelers' silks. The group joked and laughed with jovial energy as they passed. Ronan profiled the men as a primary target for road bandits. Then he noticed the pair of double-edged scimitars that hung at each man's belt. Ronan did not know the origin of the men but knew that it took a skilled swordsman to dual wield weapons of that nature.

After they had passed, Vallia stated without prompting "Mají." Ronan looked at her curiously. "Those men," she nodded backwards. "They're Mají. Nomads from the Ishan Deval Desert. I have heard they are masters with their blades and that their fighting style is like a deadly dance."

"Wow, that sounds intense. Have you ever traveled that far south?" Ronan asked, testing the conversation to see if he could learn more about Vallia and her past.

"Yes. I used to sail out of Golgotha. Never spent much time on the land."

"You sailed in the south? Where did you sail to? What did you do on the boat?" Ronan had heard some crazy stories about the rough and tumble sailors from Golgotha.

She gave him a side glance with a wondering expression as if she was considering whether or not to answer.

"When I was about your age, yeah," she said as she faced forward. "I was part of a merchant crew that traveled all over."

"What kind of merchants?"

"The kind that procures goods from less fortunate merchants and sells them for profit,"

Ronan's eyes grew large. "You were a pirate!"

Vallia looked at him once again and shook her head at his excitement. "We work for a criminal organization that focuses on theft, trade, and movement of stolen goods. That is your life. But when I tell you that I stole, moved, and sold stolen goods on the high seas, that gets you all pumped up?"

Ronan shrugged sheepishly. "I don't know, it just seems more exciting, you know, with the boat and the open sea. Nothing holding you back. Pirates can go anywhere and do anything. Everyone knows and fears pirates. The Carpenters are all secretive. I can't just go around telling people I am part of the Carpenters, but pirates always boast of their adventures and spoils."

He thought for a moment. He now understood her analogy of being a ship pushed by the wind. "It makes sense. You would be very helpful on a ship with your connection to the wind. It seems kind of like the perfect place for you. Why did you stop?"

"Because life did what it always does," she said as her eyes glazed over in a distant memory. "It changed unexpectedly and violently in a different direction. So, I left everything behind without looking back."

Ronan considered the statement. He thought about Arkeen falling to the giant and how it must have affected Vallia. He had been so focused on himself that he had not given Vallia much thought. If it wasn't for this mission, she may have done what she did in the past. Left everything behind and started anew. Then he looked around at his surroundings and realized that, in a way, they were both doing exactly that. They were on a mission to a foreign place with little opportunity to return. He was grateful Vallia was the one with him. While he had never been very close to her, he had spent a decent amount of time with her and Arkeen together.

His thoughts then wandered to what he was leaving behind. If he was honest with himself, he didn't have much in Shem to leave behind. No family to miss him. His guardians from the orphanage had only ever seen the boys as a burden with tax benefits. They had never even tried to follow up with Ronan once he ran away. He didn't have any friends. While he was friendly with many of the Carpenters, they were merely his co-workers. Besides the street vendors he bought his food from, he really didn't interact with anyone else in the city. As his mind wandered through these thoughts, he realized his life had made him a perfect candidate for being on the run, for being a wanted criminal with no place to call home.

Ronan was shaken out of his reflection on his life when Vallia pointed to a road sign and said, "In about an hour we will be reaching the edge of the Breant Forest. It is about a day's travel through the trees and that is not a place that I want to traverse at night. It's full of lowlife thugs and dangerous animals. There is a camping area about a half mile from the forest line where we can set up for the night. Hopefully Blue grabbed all your camping stuff because you are not about to share with me."

Ronan smiled at her bluntness and nodded. He had checked before leaving Vallia's home and took inventory of his go bag. He had enough dry rations to last him four days and his tent and stakes had all been accounted for. The tent on his back and his rolled-up bed roll were two of the nicer possessions he owned thanks to Mr. Kemin. The man insisted that sleep was one of the most important tools in life. He had always told his employees, "If you are not getting the best sleep you can, then you are working tired. If you are working tired, you are working sloppily. If you're working sloppily, then you're not working for me." He had invested the money to get all his employees' nice beds in their houses and nice camping supplies for when they were out on the road. He called it a sign on bonus for joining the Carpenters.

The two walked the last hour in silence, taking in the changing landscape around them. The typography around Shem was mostly flat moss covered, rocky stretches with grass poking through the spider web cracks in the stone. As they traveled east, the land transitioned into grassy fields full of tall purple and yellow flowers. Individual trees stuck up here and there. They looked like torches, blowing in the wind as their bright fall colors were at their peak.

The road crested another hill and in the distance the sea of browns, golds, and reds that made up the Breant Forrest came into view. A stone ridge jutted out of the ground in between the hill they stood on and the edge of the tree line. Ronan could make out several wagons accompanied by tents and the small shapes of people along the base of the outcropping. This made sense as a good spot to camp before going into the forest. The cliff provided protection from the North and the site had a clear view of the road in both directions.

Vallia sighed at the site of the other travelers and said, "I was hoping that we would be alone here. We can set up on the southeastern side of the cliff away from the wagons. Come on."

She started the trek down the hill.

At the base of the cliff, Vallia put down her pack next to a large boulder that provided visual cover from the wagons. She picked up a small stick and snapped it into two unequal parts, rubbing the two between her hands. Then she held out a clenched fist with the two sticks poking out the top. "Shortest stick has to set up both the tents, longest stick has to go and talk to the yahoos and see if they have any wood or supplies we can buy."

Ronan looked at the sticks and frowned. It was a fair way to divide the equally unappealing tasks and he knew that. He grabbed one and pulled. Holding it out to compare it to the remaining. Vallia smiled as her stick was an inch shorter than Ronan's. He reluctantly handed her his pack and caught the money pouch Vallia threw at him. He guessed this was probably for the best with his injured arm.

The wagons were owned by a rowdy lot. As Ronan approached, he could hear their elevated voices from a way away. It was very apparent that the group had already downed one bottle of wine and seemed to be working on the second. It took Ronan far longer than he would have liked to convince the drunken men that he did not want to join them but rather that he was hoping to buy some supplies from them. He finally got a short man with a bushy gray beard and a mustache soaked with wine to get up and go to the wagon. He had to tell the man three times that he was not interested in buying an ornate tea set before he was able to convince him to sell some wood logs. The man asked for five silvers for a bundle. The price was outrageous, but Ronan paid it to put an end to the conversation and to get away from his fermented breath.

Ronan shook his head as he walked back, holding the twine that tied the bundle together with his good hand. He was preparing to tell Vallia that she owed him and was ready to fend off a snide remark about how long he had taken when he heard lowered voices from the other side of the boulder. Confused, he quickened his step and rounded the rock to see Vallia standing with her back to him. Her shoulders and back muscles were tensed as she held her bow fully drawn, an arrow nocked. Ronan looked aghast as he saw the arrow pointed at a young girl, her hands raised up near her braided raven black hair. Her purple eyes locked onto him as he came into view.

Chapter 11

Vallia, sensing Ronan's return, called out in a cool, calm voice, "She says she is here for the emerald-eyed boy and the girl with hair that is always in the breeze. Judging by her robes, she followed you all the way from the medical facility. Do you know this girl?"

Ronan could not overcome a feeling of familiarity with this girl. He blinked and said, "I saw her at the infirmary as we were fleeing, but no, I don't know her."

Vallia called to the girl, "Did you come here to collect some sort of bounty? How did you follow us? Did you bribe the shopkeeper to show you the tunnel?"

The girl had a steeled look in her eyes as she looked between Vallia and Ronan. "We need to talk." Her voice was soft but held some authority. "I need your help. I am supposed to find the emerald eyed boy and the woman with flowing hair."

"I haven't shot you in the trachea yet, so as of right now there is nothing stopping you from talking," Vallia threatened.

Ronan called out, "Who are you and what do you want?"

"Open your eyes and see for yourself," the girl called out, her confidence seemingly growing.

Her words caught Ronan by surprise. His interest in this girl immediately peaked. Did she know about his powers? She surely saw the display in the infirmary with the spirits, but how could she have known about his abilities? Maybe this was a trap. His curiosity was winning out over his caution. He inhaled to bring forth words, his mind raced to make sense of all his thoughts that were flying around in his head. But he was not able to consolidate his thoughts into sounds before the girl shifted her weight. She had been standing still but her feet had been perched on small loose rocks. At that moment her constitution broke and she moved her foot to better her stance.

The small rocks slid under her feet causing her to almost lose her balance. Her foot moved forward to catch herself. Vallia's battle hardened reflexes kicked in. Her tense, defensive state loosed the arrow she had been aiming directly at the girl's critical mass.

Ronan watched the scene from a distance, horrified.

He saw the girl's foot begin to slide, and a flash of purple in her eyes. Ronan watched as Vallia released the tension of her bow string. The arrow flew through the air as the girl's other foot also began to slide back. Her whole body shifted with it, threading her torso sideways to reduce her visible surface area. The arrow accelerated forward, destroying the sting clasp of the girl's robe but never touching her clavicle. The girl used her backwards momentum to pivot into a full rotation.

Vallia had another arrow nocked before the girl had finished her spin. It was clear she was working on muscle memory and adrenaline at this point. Ronan panicked as Vallia had clearly not processed the first movement as a loss of balance. She must have seen it as an offensive action. He watched helplessly as she drew her bow and fired again.

The girl had been able to advance two steps before the second arrow was let loose. Both her hands rose before the arrow left the string. The projectile would have hit its mark if it had not been for the girl's left hand closing around the arrow shaft just behind the head. The momentum of the arrow continued the missile forward, but the girl's fingers were able to fully close, paralyzing the trajectory in its path, catching the arrow midair. Her right hand lifted across her body and grabbed onto her robe. In one continuous motion, she pulled the robe forward, causing the whole garment to come loose without the clasp to stop it. She whipped her arm forward launching the silky scarlet cloak at Vallia and covering her face for a second.

That second was all the girl needed to close the eight steps between the two. In a flash of black leathers, she advanced forward and ducked low, throwing her full weight into a shoulder tackle. But Vallia was a head and a half taller than her and double her weight. To counter the weight differential, the girl jammed the feathered fletching of the arrow still gripped in her left hand into the inside curve of Vallia's knee.

Vallia screamed through gritted teeth. The blow buckled the knee, dropping her into a kneeling position.

Ronan couldn't fathom the girl's amazing reflexes. They were inhumanly fast.

The girl had managed to knock Vallia down but didn't seem to have a follow up maneuver. Vallia saw this and took the opportunity to punch the girl square in the nose, displacing it with a wet *crack*. She then used her kneeling position to straighten her good leg driving her shoulder into the girl's chin, sending her toppling over onto her rear.

Vallia steadied herself as she rose to her full height. She grabbed another arrow from her quiver at her side and lifted it to the string for a point blank shot.

"Stop!" Ronan yelled as he grabbed Vallia's wrist before the arrow made contact with the string. Vallia's eyes flashed to Ronan with a furious intensity. "If she knows about my powers. I need to talk with her. I need to at least hear her out." He didn't know if the girl was lying but he needed to know.

Vallia's arm tensed in his grasp. He was preventing her from bringing the arrow home. Preventing her from extinguishing what may be his only chance at understanding his powers. For a moment the two battled in a strength contest to determine the fate of the arrow and the girl. After a moment, Vallia jerked her arm away. Her eyes shot back to the girl still on the ground. The girl had not made a move. She watched the two standing over her with eyes that seemed too large for her head. Vallia slammed the arrow back into her quiver. She took three steps back and glared. Her hand never left the top of the arrow.

Ronan turned down to look at the girl. He blinked his eyes and then ethereally blinked again. Like snuffing out a candle, the world turned gray.

The girl before him glowed with a bright orange energy. However, her eyes remained purple. Then her eyes flashed violet as if they had been lit on fire, like dried leaves touched by a flame. Purple energy began radiating from her, creating an orange and purple aura around her. He did not understand his powers, but he could feel a kinship in their energies. She stared back at him with a look of wonder that mirrored how he felt. Her gaze transitioned down and behind him. He turned his head and saw the green figures of Arkeen and Ta Rhe wreathed in flame. He looked back at her. She seemed surprised and slightly scared. But she was definitely looking directly at spirits.

"What are you two doing?!" Vallia's voice called out, muffled from the transition of Ronan's senses. He closed off the pressure behind his eyes. "You wanted to talk with this psychopath and now you're just staring longingly into her eyes. If you don't start talking to her and figure out who she is, I'm going to fill you both full of arrows."

"She is like me, I can... I don't know, sense it," Ronan said. He had not looked away from the girl. Was she also a champion of the Justice of Death? Her powers didn't seem to have anything to do with death. Were there other Eidolon that were different than he was? He asked, "What is your name?"

"Maya Alitha," she replied. Her eyes stopped glowing.

Ronan continued, "You said you wanted to find the emerald eyed boy and the girl with windblown hair. Who told you to come and find us and why did they send you?"

Maya looked at Vallia and slowly moved her hand to her belt. Vallia watched intently, her grip tightening on her arrow. Maya slowly pulled out a cloth from her belt and wrapped it around her hand which was bleeding. She said, "I saw you in a vision."

Vallia scoffed, "Great, she is a charlatan."

Maya shook her head. "I have the ability to see the potential energy in the world around me. You saw me fight. I saw what you were going to do before you even acted. I caught your arrow out of the air."

"You got lucky and that is all that happened," Vallia said, lifting her hand from the arrow and pointing at Maya.

"Sometimes my powers go beyond just seeing potential energies," Maya continued, ignoring the comment. "Sometimes the energies of the world intersect and collide together with such force and purpose that they create a blazing trail of possibility. That trail is made up of current events and choices and tragedies that all interconnect and correlate to become a specific probability of something to come. My ability inadvertently picks up on that trail of macro events and I am sometimes given visions of things that can and will occur."

"And what did you see in this 'vision' of us?" Vallia asked, her tone overflowing with sarcasm and disbelief.

Maya looked at her with a stale, solemn expression and said, "I saw three figures standing before a massive fissure of light. Both of you were there. The girl whose hair is always blowing in the breeze and the boy with glowing emerald eyes. The third figure was an UN'kra man who was soaking wet but who was summoning fire from floating, glowing fissures. Somehow, I knew you were standing in front of the Ether Scar up north. Behind you was a raging battle. Then the ground began to shake and crack. My vision shifted to a masked man riding a black horse through the battle. With one swing of his sword, I watched him turn a whole army to dust. His eyes blazed yellow behind his onyx mask as he jumped into the Scar, stabbing his sword into the ground next to a river of energy. The energy began to crack like glass. He was trying to break the energy loose from its invisible bonds and set it free. From the little I know about the Scar; it serves as a form of dam preventing the chaotic elemental energies of the Ether Plane from getting loose and devastating our world. I believe the vision showed me the near future where the masked man will try to destroy that dam and unleash devastating chaos. I don't know why, but you two seem to be directly involved with trying to stop him from destroying our world."

Chapter 12

"That is the stupidest thing I have ever heard," Vallia belted out after a moment of stunned silence. Maya's statement had surprised both Vallia and Ronan, but Vallia was quick to cover her shock with skepticism.

"Give me one good reason to trust any of that useless divination nonsense," Vallia demanded.

Maya looked pleadingly up at her. "I don't know what I can say to gain your trust. You think I came here to attack and kill you and then steal him and bring him back to Shem. What do you think my master plan was? Take you out and then knock him unconscious only to have to drag him back to Shem on a sled made of bark? You might have missed it when I defended myself, but I chose to hit you with the back of the arrow and not stab you through the knee with it."

"Oh, how generous of you," Vallia quickly retorted. "The only reason you were holding my arrow in the first place was because you moved to attack me first."

"My foot slipped and you know it," Maya declared as her temper rose. "And I was holding your arrow because you weren't good enough at shooting to even hit me." She pushed herself to her feet in one quick motion. Vallia pulled the arrow free from the quiver.

"Let's see how well that vision of yours works when I shove an arrow through your eye."

"Show us your résumé marks!" Ronan said loudly, catching both the women off guard and stopping the escalating tension before things got bloody. They both glared at him with adrenaline filled breaths. "Show us your résumé marks on your arm. Let's see where your allegiances lie."

Maya scowled at the request.

"What, you don't want to show us your mark of the assassin?" Vallia taunted.

Maya rolled her eyes and scoffed, "What idiot would put the mark of a secret group like an assassins' guild on your arm?"

Vallia and Ronan shot each other a glance. "Show us your arms or I'll make you," Vallia said with a smile. Ronan assumed she would rather Maya resist at this point.

Maya sighed knowing defiance would only cause more problems. She pulled off her black leather gloves, revealing her small but surprisingly well-worn hands. Dirt under her fingernails, calluses on her palms; her hands looked rougher than Ronan's. She unlaced the leather ties of her sleeves up to her elbow bending back the leather to show off her inner arm. Three marks were visible on her right arm. The very first mark depicted a black triangle pointing down toward her hand. On top of the flat part of the triangle, were three phases of the moon. A purple full moon in the center with mirrored crescent moons on either side. This mark was unfamiliar to Ronan.

The second mark was not a tattoo but rather the remnants of a scar from a brand. The brand had two capital letters 'HT'.

"You are a traitor to the Council?" Vallia inquired in a surprised voice. Ronan knew the brand and had even watched it be applied to several people when he was younger. It stood for High Traitor. It was reserved for people who were actively trying to overthrow the government or at least people that the Council considered threats. Those declared as rebels had two fates: execution or internment into a labor camp. If someone like Mr. Kemin were to ever be caught, it would certainly mean his death. But a small pawn like Ronan would likely get deported to a labor camp, where he would spend his life sentence mining for precious metals or building weapons for the Legion.

The third mark on Maya's arm explained her fate. The last mark was six brown wooden logs stacked on top of each other in a pyramid. Each log had an L on the end. The symbol for the labor camp, Camp Latis.

"What was your crime against the Council?" Vallia prompted.

Maya's face grew very somber. "My mother could not afford the additional taxes the Council was imposing to support their bloody war. A cruel tax collector came to our house. My mother was not able to tell him who my father was, and he took that to mean she was hiding information and was insubordinate for not paying the tax. He had both my mom and I detained and taken to Camp Latis. I was twelve." Tears were starting to form in the corners of her eyes.

"We are no friends to the Council," Ronan said in an attempt to reassure her. Vallia shot him a dirty look.

"What is the other mark? Your first résumé mark," Vallia asked, cutting short Ronan's attempted sincerity.

Maya shook her head and shrugged her shoulders. "I don't know. I have had that mark as long as I can remember, but I don't know what it is from. No one knows it seems."

"Right, you just happen to share that trait with Ronan. Yeah, that's not suspicious at all," Vallia challenged.

Maya looked at Ronan with her eyebrows raised. She spoke and her voice was higher pitched in excitement. "Do you have this mark too?"

Ronan shook his head. It felt odd to him to divulge personal information like this, but he was filled with a hope that they could help each other learn about their powers and their backgrounds. "Mine does not look like a triangle. Mine is a skull." Ronan had not told Vallia that he had a better understanding of where the mark had come from. He had not told anyone about his dream because he didn't want people to think he was crazy or that his allegiance was not to the Carpenters. Ronan wanted to ask Maya if she had talked to a Justice that was different from his own but knew now was not the time. He wondered why her mark was different.

Ronan knew that this girl could be important for his goals. If he was going to have a chance to talk to her about it, he would need to convince Vallia. He looked to Vallia and said, "Can we have a sidebar, just for a moment?"

Vallia watched Maya with a distrustful disdain. She took a few steps back and Ronan followed her, letting his back be the one tuned so Vallia could maintain a visual on Maya. "Are you going to try to convince me she is a valuable asset and that I should not judge on first appearances?" Vallia asked with a stale tone.

Ronan blinked a few times, caught off guard. She had in fact said exactly what he was going to say.

Vallia sighed, "You're young and naïve. I get that. But you can't honestly tell me you trust this girl. You don't really believe she had some vision about us fighting some masked jerk who was trying to unleash the Ether into our world? Do you believe that the space energies lined up just perfectly to allow her insight into the future?"

"When you put it like that, yeah it sounds mental. Then again, a week ago I would have said the same about commanding the spirits of the dead to kill a giant for you. Look, I don't trust her. But I know that she is like me. I feel a connection to her through my powers. Mr. Kemin told me to get a grasp on these powers. I don't know how to do that; but maybe she can help me." He was desperate to convince her, and she knew it.

"Mr. Kemin once told me that an enemy is only an enemy while they are working for their own motives. If an enemy can be convinced to pursue your objectives, then they can be convinced to become an ally."

Vallia stared unblinkingly at Maya and shifted her lips from side to side. "Ronan, you are one of few people I trust. Mostly because I know I could overpower you if I needed to and you have never struck me as a serious threat to myself... But also, because you were Arkeen's friend. He trusted you from the start." She paused for a few moments and thought some more. "If you have to, talk with this girl about your powers. See what she can tell you. Find out more information about who she is and what she wants. Give her as little information as you can. And get her goals to align with ours. Oh, and if she kills you in your sleep, stay dead. If you come back as a spirit, I will find a way to lock you in a jar so I can tell you 'I told you so' every day until I die."

She walked away. As she passed Maya, Vallia stopped and whispered something Ronan could not hear. Maya's face revealed no hint as to what was said. Vallia continued forward and stooped down to grab the logs Ronan had dropped on the ground. She walked to a flat rock fifty paces away and crouched down to build a fire. Ronan gathered his thoughts and approached Maya.

Chapter 13

"Would you like to sit?" Ronan asked, motioning to a large rock.

Maya nodded and walked to pick up her discarded crimson robe. She then sat on the rock. Ronan sat about seven feet away. He knew that blind trust was a bad idea and hoped the distance would help him see an attack coming if she made a move, but he suspected she would not. She seemed as interested in him as he was in her. She wrapped herself in the robe and tucked her feet underneath her.

"So, I guess the obvious question is, what do you know about what we are?" Ronan started.

Maya seemed to be sizing him up. "Something tells me you know the answer to that question. What would you say that we are?"

Ronan contemplated how to answer. "I would say we are champions."

"Champions of what?" Maya asked.

Ronan did not like her asking the question. "I am not sure yet." He answered truthfully. "Do you know anything about a Justice of Death?" he attempted.

Maya raised her eyebrows. "I don't know anything about a Justice of Death, but I do know about a different Justice," she replied coyly.

Ronan frowned at the vague answer. They were both playing a game of who can share the littlest amount of information. This frustrated Ronan. "Would you say after getting your powers you were given a mission?"

"I told you; my vision showed me you and Miss Crazy Arrow over there. I don't know why but I knew I had to find you." She then gave Ronan a sideways glance. "Are you on some mission?"

91

Ronan bobbed his head back and forth, debating how to answer. "I would say I'm on several missions. Some for my Justice and some for others. Mostly I am working on learning more about my powers. Figuring them out, you know. I have not had them for very long. Have you?"

Maya said, "I will tell you about my powers if you tell me about yours. This whole beating around the bush thing is not going to get us anywhere."

"That seems like a fair trade." Ronan affirmed. "Well, my powers showed up yesterday. As far as I can tell, I have the ability to speak with and command the spirits of the dead. They developed when a giant was about to squash me. I summoned some spirits, and they killed the giant." Ronan internationally was vague. He thought she would judge him if she knew he had been scavenging dead bodies.

Maya nodded, looking over to the spot she had seen Arkeen and Ta Rhe. "And then you attacked the infirmary with your spirits?"

Ronan blushed. "I didn't mean to do that. It was a test of my abilities. The spirits came at me. I didn't tell them to do that." Feeling embarrassed he asked, "What about you?"

Maya eyed him for a moment. He could tell she did not trust his answer, but she did not push further. Rather, she began to explain, "My powers developed in Camp Latis. They are the only reason I escaped."

Ronan knew about Camp Latis. It was one of the topics covered in the Carpenters training about the inner workings of the Council. If he remembered correctly. Latis was the largest lumber producing internment camp under the control of the Council. He knew that the foundation of the labor camps came just after the Council grew from seven to nine members. Reports had come to the people about a deal that had been struck between the Zwellian Empire and Neshunhile, the capital of the Elven territory in the west.

Ronan recalled the story of Neshunhile to himself. Legends spoke of a great city that floated atop a lake, clear as glass. The city was said to be constructed entirely of trees whose roots were so numerous and so spread out that they created a natural raft underneath. The Neshunites were rumored to be a very selective and reclusive people. They were nationalists

92

in their own right, refusing to let any other nation or people group into their "sacred forest" called Ithitka. The forest was legendary for its plentiful production of produce. The forest was said to have the ability to supply the whole continent with fresh fruit. Until seven years ago no one else had access to the forest. The Elves guarded it with a deadly passion.

If he remembered the story correctly, when the Council officially declared war on the UN'kra to the north, the political segregation of the Neshunites changed. They refused to participate in the war regarding supplying troops, but they made an agreement with the Council that the Zwellian Empire could have full access to 2,000 acres of Ithitka. They could utilize the forest as they saw fit. Take the lumber to make defenses and weapons or war machines. The Council took the deal as a two-sided coin. They received access to the timber they needed, and they developed a perfect place to send their unwanted or 'dangerous' civilians. Thus, Camp Latis was born.

"How did your abilities manifest? All at once or over time?" Ronan asked.

"They just developed in a moment of extreme stress. They appeared without notice or me having any prior knowledge of them." She paused. Ronan guessed she was weighing the information as Ronan had done, identifying how much to reveal.

She slowly let her breath out through her nose. "About one year ago, we were working in a new section of the forest. The trees in this area were older than the ones we had previously cut down. They all had a strange gray moss covering their bases. We, my mother, and I," she clarified, "had the job of trimming off the smaller branches to make the trunk easier to transport. We had small hatchets and clippers we would use to trim. We had to wear long thick sleeves regardless of the temperature because if we didn't, our arms would be shredded to pieces on the sharp bark. Once the branches were removed, we would gather them up in a bundle and carry them to the ox sled."

Maya furthered, "There was a foreman in this area that did not like my mother or myself. He had made this incessantly clear to us any time he saw us."

"Why?" Ronan asked.

93

"Because he was a stupid misogynist." She shrugged and continued, "An accident happened on site one day where one of the old mossy trees fell the wrong way. My mother and I were close to the tree when it fell. Luckily, we were not in its path, but a guard on site was not as fortunate. It came crashing down. The guard was smashed by the tree and impaled by a broken limb. There was no hope for him."

At this thought she paused. Her mouth thinned at the memory. She blinked and continued the story. "The crushed guard was a close friend of the foreman. When he saw the tree fall, the foreman came running immediately. One of the men who had cut down the tree bolted into the woods when he saw the wicked man approaching." Maya paused again, struggling to proceed.

Ronan listened intently, transfixed by the account. He was hooked but didn't want to push her to continue if it was uncomfortable.

Maya took a long look at Ronan. He realized that she was gauging whether it was worth it to finish the story. He was a complete stranger to her. Her story was a catalyst for trust between the two of them and they both knew it.

"When the foreman reached the fallen tree, he saw the guard's face sticking out from underneath, staring up to the night sky. The remaining lumberjack approached and tried to explain what happened. He only got three words out before the foreman ran his sword through the man's chest. The man coughed up blood and fell to the ground gurgling. Then the foreman turned to us. His eyes were filled with pure hatred. My mother put herself between me and the man. He started yelling about how we had distracted the men cutting down the tree. About how he knew women should never have been on his work site. He began approaching the two of us, continuing to yell. It was at this point that my eyes started hurting and color started fading from the world."

Ronan nodded, relating to the account.

"I watched as the foreman raised his sword to strike down my mother. But the world seemed to slow down. I saw the black and white foreman. I also saw a flickering purple projection of his figure. His body seemed to

94

be moving at half his speed, but the flickering clone moved much faster. As each of his muscles tensed or loosened, the purple figure flickered into a forecast of his movement. I didn't understand it at the time, but now I know I was seeing his potential energy, and my powers were presenting a visualization of how that energy would be used and the exact path it would take. My brain was doing math that I couldn't even understand. I could have told you how fast his sword would swing and how much force it would have come down with. It's like my powers show me the world as if it were made of numbers and only I understand how to read those numbers."

Ronan attempted to process this statement. He had never thought about energy having math that it was based on. It hurt his head to contemplate this reality.

Maya continued, "Without thinking, I lifted up the small hatchet that was still in my hand. I raised it to match the purple rendition of the foreman's swing and a second later, I felt the ax in my hand catch the steel of his sword. Without understanding it, I used the downward momentum of his sword to rotate his wrist the wrong way, causing him to lose grip on his hilt. His sword went flying ten paces away burying itself eight inches into the ground."

Ronan thought back to the fight with Vallia and could visualize the account well.

"My mother didn't miss a beat. She had always been a survivor. She elbowed the man square in his chest knocking the wind out of him and then she chopped his trachea to keep him from sucking air back in. She then sprinted in the other direction holding my hand, dragging me along. I saw my mother's purple outline predicting her every step. Every spring of her foot as it launched off the ground."

Ronan felt the adrenaline of the moment as she painted the picture of what happened. He didn't dare interrupt despite his many questions.

"I glanced back, and I saw the recovering foreman. He was starting to run after us holding his throat with one of his hands and a long knife in the other. My eyes were still searing with pain and my powers were still muting the colors of the world. I knew he would catch us quickly. His legs were seven and a quarter inches longer than my mother's, meaning he would have caught us in twenty-two and a half long strides. My brain pulled my attention to the weight of the ax still in my hand. It told me exactly what I needed to do to stop him. I knew it was just a matter of force applied to a top-heavy object that weighed six pounds. I didn't even think about the man chasing after us. All I saw was the math. I continued to run forward as I slipped my hand free from my mother's and spun around. I threw the ax end over end. Eleven perfect spirals..."

Ronan realized he had not been actively breathing as the story was laid before him. He took a deep breath, which he immediately realized seemed like a gasp. Maya's reaction reflected this. She seemed offended that he would be surprised at her action.

He tried to hastily explain, "No, no, no, I totally get it, sometimes you just have to kill someone. I mean not that you killed him. I don't mean to assume you just murdered someone. But if you did, I would totally get it, that scum had it coming. Not to say anyone deserves to die but sometimes..." he trailed off knowing he was just digging a hole deeper and deeper. "I'm sorry I didn't mean to interrupt your story. Please finish, I want to know what happened."

"I split his skull with a hand ax from eighteen paces" Maya replied, scowling at him for his demeanor and comments.

"I didn't mean about the foreman, sorry. No, I mean what happened to you and your mom?" Ronan knew he was blushing and wished she would activate her eyes to spare him the embarrassment of her seeing how red he must be. He was kicking himself. The goal was to learn about her and not make a fool of himself.

"My powers see movement and how things will play out and the path things will take," Maya said. "They don't work so well at seeing things that are stationary. Things like the five other guards who were standing watching the scene play out. I didn't notice them standing off to the side, watching me execute a ranking official. At that moment, the adrenaline or whatever it was wore off and so did my vision. I saw the five guards and my mother with her hand over her mouth. Then I saw the motionless body of the foreman. My mother looked at me with tears streaming down her cheeks. She told me to run, and I did. Straight for the tree line. I didn't look back. That's the last thing my mother said to me. 'Run...' I don't know what happened to her. She must have stopped the guards from pursuing me because they didn't catch me."

By this point, tears were streaming down Maya's cheeks. Her shoulders were hunched, and she curled into her robe, pulling it tightly around her. Ronan sat quietly, taking in all the information she had just laid out. He listened and heard the distant crackle of Vallia's campfire. He checked on her. She had not moved from her spot on the ground.

He looked back at Maya and saw her staring into him with her deep purple eyes.

"Who are your flaming bodyguards?" she asked as she wiped her eyes on the robe. "What's their story?" She looked over to the patch of dirt where Arkeen and Ta Rhe had been standing during the earlier altercation. Her eyes flashed purple. She looked back at Ronan.

"Shhhh, keep your voice down," Ronan said, glancing over at Vallia. He was not convinced that she had just given up on trusting Ronan and Maya alone. She had not moved and that made Ronan even more suspicious. "So, you can see them?"

Maya nodded, lowering her voice at his behest. "You said they are spirits, and you command them?"

Ronan shrugged, "That is the conclusion I have come to. They are the ones who saved me from the giant. I kind of trapped them unintentionally. They are now tethered to me." He felt dumb saying this. Maya had been so elegant with her own understanding of what she could do. Ronan knew he could command them and tether them and apparently pull the attention of every spirit in a room. He reminded himself that he had only had a day with his abilities, and she had over a year.

He ethereally blinked his eyes to make the spirits appear. "Can you hear them?" he asked.

Maya shook her head. "Do they talk?" She seemed put off by the idea.

Arkeen pointed at Maya and said telepathically in Ronan's head, *"I can't talk to her. I have been trying but she can't hear me. Not sure if she is just dense or if it's only a you thing."*

"Why is he pointing at me?" Maya said, sounding more concerned.

"He is just saying he can't communicate with you. Don't worry, I am pretty sure they are harmless."

Maya scowled at him. "The ones in the infirmary didn't seem so harmless."

Ta Rhe projected, *"I would not say we are harmless. We slew the giant for you. If you remember, we did it on your orders. When not prompted, it is true we would not harm anyone. Under your influence, however, we can become quite deadly. It all depends on you."*

Ronan blinked back to the colored reality to shut the spirit up. But Ta Rhe's words clung to Ronan's thoughts like a bad aftertaste. The spirits would do anything he said. He had a lot of control which made his powers potentially dangerous.

Ronan explained to Maya, "The ones in the medical facility saw my power and flooded to me. They wanted me to help them. Then they got violent and started forcing themselves on me. I guess I made some sort of mental shield. That stopped them from getting to me, but they started trying to break through. I commanded them all to get away and that caused the explosion you saw. We had to flee after that. That is when I saw you. What were you doing at the infirmary? Are you actually a medic?"

She shook her head, "No, this is just a disguise, but I am digging the style. I was at the infirmary because I was looking for you. I had a different vision that led me to believe that is where I would find you."

"How often do you get these visions?" he asked curiously. He wondered to himself what it would be like to see the future.

She shrugged. "In the last year, I have only gotten a few. Most have been in the last month. Those have all been about you, windbag over there and the masked man dissolving armies and unleashing the Ether."

"Vallia doesn't believe you, but I think you're telling the truth," he assured her. He didn't know why but he felt a kinship with Maya that he could not explain.

"So, her name is Vallia?" Maya inclined. "What's yours?"

Ronan was confused for a moment but realized he had not introduced himself. Pleasantries had not been exchanged. "My name is Ronan Riviera. Some have called me Prince of the Dead." He added the last part in an attempt to add some levity to their conversation.

"Well, Prince of the Dead," Vallia's voice rang out over his shoulder, startling Ronan, "We need to sleep so we can get through the forest tomorrow." He had not heard her rise or her approach. "I am going to take the first watch. I'll wake you up when it's your turn. You need to sleep; you look like one of your own corpses. What is the story with little miss fortune teller over here? Is she going to teach you all about controlling the dead and the history of your powers?"

Ronan sighed, glancing apologetically at Maya. "I think she can be very helpful with our mission. Plus, I think she needs to talk to the archivist as well. Look, I will vouch for her."

Vallia looked displeased with his answer. She eyed Maya. "Did you follow us completely unprepared? No bag, no bedding?"

Maya shook her head. "My pack is on the other side of this cliff. I dropped it before I came and tried to talk to you two."

"Go get it," Vallia said after seemingly calculating which was the best option. Letting her out of her sight or going to get it herself and leaving Maya alone with Ronan.

Maya nodded and stood quickly pulling her robe on and jogging to get her things. When she turned the corner, Vallia looked at Ronan with a questioning glance.

"I think she is being more honest than we are," Ronan began justifying. "I don't think she is a threat."

Vallia sighed. "I don't trust her. I don't know what it is, but something seems wrong."

"To be fair, I don't know of anyone you really trust," Ronan pointed out. "She can predict how people or things are going to move. If we can get her on our side, that could be extremely useful for infiltrating a prison. Between that and her being like me, I think she could be vastly helpful." Ronan was really hoping to convince Vallia. The Justice of Death from his dream had told him to learn about his power. Maybe Maya could be a teacher of sorts. She also seemed to not have a love for the Council so that could help with the Justice's long-term plans.

Vallia bit her lip and rolled her eyes. "Fine. If you say she can help you learn about your powers, she can stay. But she better be useful. Keep one eye open, maybe set your hawk to watch her. And don't tell her any information that you don't need to. Okay?"

Ronan nodded. Vallia walked away to check the perimeter. Ronan whistled through his teeth. The shrill sound was met with a pop and a flutter of wings. He caught Sabastian on his forearm and scratched his beak. "Can you watch out for us tonight buddy? It's been a long couple of days, and I need to rest. I trust you. You'll keep us safe, won't you? Who's a good boy?" Sabastian puffed his chest and ruffled his feathers. He took off and flew into the sky.

Ronan laid down in his tent that Vallia had set up for him. He removed his sling and tested his wrist with small movements. It hurt a lot, but it was not a blinding pain. He hoped that was a sign of improvement. He cleaned his arm with a rag and some water. It felt gross after being in the sling all day. He re-wrapped it so as to not hurt it while sleeping. Outside the tent, he heard the rusting of Maya returning and setting up a tent. He took a deep breath and closed his eyes.

He drifted off into a deep sleep.

Chapter 14

Ronan stood in the middle of a dense forest. The area around him was illuminated but he could not see past the trees that surrounded him. He heard the low growls and shifting of large animals in the darkness beyond his vision. He turned and started running in the other direction to avoid being attacked and devoured.

Out of nowhere, he ran into a shadowy figure and fell backwards. As he looked up, he recognized it was Maya. He was relieved for a second until he realized her eyes were pure black.

Then he heard the deep voice of the Justice of Death echo from the darkness.

"Hello Ronan."

Ronan looked around to find the source of the voice but couldn't see anything except Maya.

"You have met another Eidolon I see." Ronan watched as the shadowy version of Maya began walking toward him.

Ronan began to crawl backwards and called out to the darkness, "Why didn't you tell me there were others?"

"Of course there are others. This girl is my sister's champion. She is caught up in her web of foresight and perception. She is the Eidolon of Kinetic Energy." The shadowy Maya halted her advance. She struggled against something holding her back. Ronan realized she was caught in a spider web. **"She does not do my bidding, at least not on my command. But if you can convince her, she could be a valuable asset. She could also be a liability."** The shadowy Maya was wrapped in webs and hoisted into the air suspended over the forest floor. The apparition thrashed to no avail. **"She surely has her own motivations and that makes her dangerous. My sister will most certainly have plans for her. I do not appreciate those plans involving you."**

Ronan watched the suspended Maya struggle with a mix of horror and concern as he considered the Justice's warning. He needed more information, but he did not know what question he needed to ask. The last thing he wanted was to upset the Justice of Death. "How do I know if she is an asset or a liability if I do not know what your plan is?"

"I have told you before, I will reveal more to you when the time is right. Although the girl has already proven useful on that front. It would seem that there is a meeting in your future of a man in a metal mask. How tantalizing."

The suspended Maya vanished to Ronan's relief. Then a shadowy figure materialized in front of him with glowing yellow eyes. Ronan felt apprehension grow in his stomach.

Ronan asked, "Maya said the masked man had the ability to destroy barriers between the Ether into the Prime Plane. Is he another Eidolon? How many of us are there?"

The Justice of Death chuckled, **"Too many. Yes, he is undoubtedly an Eidolon. The Eidolon of Entropy by the description of his powers. Master of decay and dissolver of all order. If she truly did have this vision, and I surmise she did, you are in desperate need to grow in your power."**

Ronan could have sworn he felt his heart stop beating as he stared at the yellow-eyed figure. *'How am I supposed to fight someone like that? I have only been an Eidolon for a day!'* He didn't want to be a warrior and fight some crazy maniac who could turn an entire army to dust. There was suddenly a desperation to meet the Arch Archivist Mr. Kemin had sent him to find. He was supposed to have information that would help Ronan get stronger. But he could only do that if he somehow was able to save Leo from the most secure prison in Celcus. Panic rose in his chest as he imagined the possibility of not being able to save Leo or meet the Archivist. Overwhelming dread filled his tightening chest as a solitary question ravaged his thoughts. What would it be like to be dissolved into ash?

The Justice's voice jolted him out of his spiraling dread. **"The fact he is an Eidolon is not the most intriguing information the girl told you. Does the description of a masked man mean nothing to you?"**

"How could that possibly matter more than his powers? Ronan asked incredulously.

"Believe me it matters. Think about it."

Ronan tried to calm his frantic emotions to think. After a moment, he managed to say, "He wants to hide his identity?"

"Obviously." There was a hint of impatience in the voice. **"Who do you know who wears masks to hide their identity?"**

Ronan pondered the statement for another moment and then exclaimed, "He must be one of the Legislators of the Council. One of the Council members is an Eidolon?"

"Very Good"

Eight other shadowy figures appeared on the outskirts of Ronan's vision. Metal masks coalesced their faces. **"Eidolon are naturally drawn to positions of power. This should not be a surprise to you. This man has power from politics alongside the blessings from his Justice."** The masked figure with yellow eyes stretched out his hand and the trees around him began to decay. Before Ronan's eyes, the trees lost all their leaves and then began to twist and curl in on themselves until they fell to pieces. **"This is the man you are seemingly destined to face. You must prepare yourself for your meeting. You must grow stronger so that when the time comes, you can put an end to him."**

The yellow-eyed figure was violently hoisted into the air by a rope around his neck. He hung suspended before Ronan.

Ronan winced, "You want me to kill this Legislator?"

"Not only this Legislator. But we can start with him. Did you not hear the girl? He is trying to destroy everything." The hung figure was lowered back to the ground. The rope disintegrated and the shadowy figure began walking toward Ronan slowly. **"What more motivation do**

you need to stop this man?"

Ronan defensively drew his sword as the figure started to menacingly circle around him. He agreed that this man's plan was insane and that it needed to be stopped. But he was not the one to do the job. Ronan was trying to figure out what the Justice was planning. What did he mean by 'not only this legislator?'

"If you're in charge of death, wouldn't you want this man to destroy everything? Wouldn't that kill thousands of people?"

"Boy, you know nothing of what I want." The tone became inflicted with a snarl for a second before it returned to its normal deep gravel. **"There is nothing that your people do better than kill each other. I have no shortage of death at my fingertips. My plans do not involve the masses dying. No. What I desire is to remove those who know about you."**

The shadowy figure of the masked man suddenly ran at Ronan. Ronan was not able to swing his sword up fast enough. Before the man could strike him, a green flame erupted next to him, and a spirit cut the man down. **"I desire to protect you. The only way to do that is to remove the Legislators from the picture."**

Ronan backed up at the appearance of the spirit. He was trying to process what just happened while struggling with the answer the Justice presented. "What are you talking about?" he demanded.

"There are few left in your world that know about the Eidolon. The Legislators of the Council are among those few."

Ronan wondered how many knew. How few was the number who understood what he was? "How do they know about the Eidolon? I never knew before you? Wait, why does it matter if they know about me?"

"I don't have the time or patience to get into the how. As for why it matters, I will tell you this. Anyone who knows about you, also knows about me. That is dangerous information. I operate in the shadows. That is where I am most effective." Two of the eight shadowy figures surrounding Ronan were snatched back into darkness, disappearing from view. **"Out of sight, out of mind."**

Ronan took a sharp breath as the two more of the figures seemed to be grabbed by the ankles and were dragged back into the darkness. **"If these Council members know about me, they will do everything in their power to stop me from rising to power. Which means they will do everything to stop you from rising to power. In this, we are bound together."** Two more of the figures were impaled from behind. Ronan cringed at the sight as they collapsed onto the ground convulsing, only to be sucked back into the blackness. Ronan found his attention pulled to the last two figures with fear and a morbid anticipation. **"In order for you to rise to your promised position of power, I must be anonymous."** The remaining two figures lurched forward and seemed to shrink in size. They were being sucked into the ground. They clawed at the roots to try and stop themselves from being pulled under, but they both vanished into the black soil. Nine flaming green spirits appeared where the nine shadowy masked figures had been standing.

"I need you to be ready when the time comes. Ready to take up your command of the spirits. Ready to put a stop to the Council. I need you to be stronger. So let me ask you, are you up for the task Ronan?"

"Ronan?"

"Ronan!"

Ronan's eyes shot open.

"Ronan come on, get up, it's your turn to watch." Vallia's voice cut through his sleeping state.

He frantically looked around and saw Vallia with her head in his tent flap. She was kicking his boot. After taking several breaths to calm his racing heart, he got to his knees. It had only been a dream. Or was it something more? He grabbed his sword belt and struggled to fasten it with one hand before exiting his tent. He blinked a few times, letting his eyes adjust.

He could see the faintest orange of the sun on the horizon, but the cool morning air still chilled his sweat stained clothes. The night had been turning dark as he had gone to bed. Vallia must have been on watch for more than half the night. She would only get about an hour or two of sleep before the day broke and they would be moving again. She must be exhausted from not having slept for two nights. Then Ronan wondered if her insomnia was due to the loss of Arkeen. He again felt looming guilt of keeping Arkeen's spirit a secret, but suppressed the thought, not willing to focus on Vallia as well as the dream he had just had.

He forced himself to walk the perimeter of their campsite, checking the surroundings and the tree line in the distance. He kept running over the dream in his head. He was expected to kill another Eidolon. To kill a member of the Council. Ronan could not fathom this idea. Mulling this over, he did not have an issue with any of the Council dying. They were all corrupt to their core and he knew that. They did not care for the common people or their wellbeing, nor were they good leaders or good people in general. Ronan brooded on the implementation of the ruthless tax officers that ravaged the common folk for all they had and lamented at the atrocious public punishments he had witnessed at their hands. But the idea of him killing one of them, let alone nine? He was not an assassin. He was not even a common thief. By trade, he was a scavenger of trinkets from corpses. How was he supposed to kill the powerful yellow eyed masked man? He had never been in a real sword fight or even killed an animal on a hunt. He felt hopelessness wash over him.

The dread he now felt led him to unsheathe his sword to practice some of the forms and stances that Arkeen had been teaching him before... He felt his stomach sink at the second thought about his lost friend this morning. It seemed he could not escape the guilt.

"Wait," Ronan thought to himself. *"Arkeen is not gone."* Ronan blinked and there he was. Standing, watching Ronan.

Arkeen chastised, *"Your left foot is too far back mate. If you swing your sword like that, you will fall on your face."*

Ronan smiled at the heckle. It was such a relief to see his friend after the morning he had been through. *"Do you remember how to fight?"*

Arkeen gave a sly grin and retorted, *"I'm dead, not useless. I remember how to fight."*

Ta Rhe let out a deep laugh. *"You are better to learn how to fight from a weeping willow than from this weakling. Your kind can't even hold a sword until*

106

your voices drop and your chin hairs grow. My people learn to wield a sword when they learn to walk."

"Do you remember which one of us was dead in the field and which one of us was looting the bodies of the fallen?" Arkeen retorted.

Ta Rhe shook his head on his thick neck. *"The memory is not lost to me. I remember after I was done with you, you were the one lying in the dirt dying."*

Arkeen smiled. *"Touché, big man. But you did stab me in a surprise attack. Human toddlers can jump out of the tall grass and get the jump on someone. That does not mean they are superior fighters."*

Ta Rhe mouth curled upward in a smirk. *"Just tactical."*

Ronan cut in, *"Listen, you're both dead. One of you is not less dead than the other one. You're as equal as you can get. But I am still alive, and I think I need to learn how to use a sword better. According to my new friend, and my nightmares, my future involves me fighting. I know some basics and that is about it. I don't know if you can teach me in your current state. If you can give me pointers though, that would be better than nothing."*

Ta Rhe versed, *"One cannot simply tell an apple to fall from the tree. One must pull the apple off themselves if they wish to taste its sweet flavor."*

"What does that even mean?" Ronan asked, bewildered, and possibly offended.

"Manifest me and I will show you. Do as you did to the spirits in the tent and make me corporeal," Ta Rhe replied.

Ronan thought about it, knowing that if he asked how, the response would be negative and unhelpful. He focused his gaze at Ta Rhe as he breathed deeply and searched for the pressure behind his eyes. Without too much effort he located it and attempted to harness the outward force. His sense of touch felt like it was leaving his body and extending beyond himself. He could feel the presence of Ta Rhe before him. It was as if he could sense the spirit's form and shape but did not know what to do with it.

He considered what Maya had said about seeing the energy of objects and understanding how that energy would play out. Watching Ta Rhe's flame, he saw the energy of the spirit pushing out from its form. Concentrating on that pulse from the spirit, Ronan willed the energy to coalesce around the spirit like a suit of armor. He watched the fire die down and seemingly crystallize. Ta Rhe's body was like an emerald dazzling in the sunlight. His sculpted form flexed its fingers and inspected its arms.

Arkeen, still wrapped in flames, clapped his hands without making a sound. *"That's a fancy trick. But did it actually do anything, or did it just make the big man more shiny?"*

Without a word, Ta Rhe swung his fist in an upper cut into Ronan's gut. The fist connected with the force of a donkey's kick. Ronan doubled over falling to his knees.

"Defend yourself," Ta Rhe said in a steady voice.

Ronan was filled with anger at the attack. He gripped his sword and swung at Ta Rhe. Ta Rhe caught Ronan's wrist and applied intense pressure to a nerve on the joint. With his other fist, the UN'kra punched Ronan's forearm. Ronan lost all grip on the sword and it clattered to the ground. It took a lot of concentration to not let his focus on the solid spirit fail. Ronan stumbled backwards when he was released. Ta Rhe bent down and picked up Ronan's sword. Fear flashed over Ronan. Was this the UN'kra's plan? Get Ronan to manifest him so he could stab him through?

"Relax yourself boy, I am tethered to you. I serve you until you release me to the Great Light. Then I will serve the Light. I will not kill you. Had I been in my flesh it is true that I would have dismembered you for what your people have done to mine. But as I have told you, the draws of the flesh hold no sway over the dead." He handed the sword back to Ronan hilt first. Ronan took it.

Ta Rhe instructed, *"Come at me again. This time, leave behind the recklessness. This is the only way to learn."*

The two continued to spar. Arkeen would call out moves and attacks from the sideline while Ta Rhe continued his abrasive teaching method. They continued until Ronan could no longer maintain the manifestation. He let the spirits fade and sat on the ground panting covered in sweat. The cool crisp atmosphere filled his burning lungs. The sun had begun its climb in the heavens, dousing the nearby forest with a spectrum of reds and oranges.

In the morning light Ronan could see the details of Maya's tent. It was small and gray with a red and white sun on the side. It was the tent of a field medic. Ronan felt for the girl. Her robe and tent must have been stolen from the medical tent in Shem. She probably didn't have anything to her name. It's hard to get hired or make any money when you're branded as an enemy of the state.

Ronan felt the need to give her an opportunity to gather her belongings to avoid any further conflict with Vallia. Slapping the canvas side a few times, he said, "Get up, we will be leaving soon." He heard her startle awake and mumble something about getting ready.

She had stated that she didn't have dreams about her powers. Ronan wondered if that was true. Then he wondered if she was being honest about her intentions.

Ronan roused Vallia a few minutes later and the three were ready to travel by the time the sun was halfway over the tree line.

The trio walked in silence toward the trees. They met up with the road that wound its way through the Breant Forest. The thick sprawling branches of the trees blocked most of the morning light, leaving only a dim path forward.

Vallia cautioned, "Be careful and keep your eyes peeled. It's about a day's journey through the trees. There is a path all the way through but there is a lot of nasty stuff in these woods. Look tough and carry yourselves with confidence, which may at least sway some of the human folk from messing with us. Now that Maya is with us, we have someone we can push into the mouth of a starving beast so we can escape so we are good there too.

Maya scoffed and muttered something about liking to see her try.

Ronan looked at his two companions with trepidation. *'We may not have to worry about the forest,'* he thought. *'These two are going to kill each other before we can make it through.'*

Chapter 15

The walk in the trees was filled with a cacophony of bird calls as the sun peeked through the leaves. Little wrens fluttered from branch to branch while colorful finches watched in large groups as the newcomers to the forest journeyed on.

Occasionally Sabastian would pop into clusters of the little birds, sending them all scattering in a mad panic. Ronan laughed at his hawk's sudden appearances. He asked Maya, "Can you predict where the birds are going to fly next?"

She said, "No. Way too many moving objects. Way too much potential energy. That would give me an instant migraine."

They did not see any other wildlife larger than a squirrel as they walked. Eventually Maya voiced up, "I know I am not exactly trusted, but I was wondering if any information could be shared with me. Like where we are heading or maybe a general goal we have? Just a little direction."

"You don't know where we are going?" Vallia taunted. "What, you can't see the paths we are walking and predict where those steps will lead us?"

Maya rolled her eyes at the comment. "I assumed you were heading up north based on my vision, but the Breant Forest is an odd way to go from Shem to the Scar. Something tells me you are not heading to the Scar."

Ronan made eye contact with Vallia. She narrowed her gaze ever so slightly back at him. He got the message that he needed to be careful.

"No, we are not heading to the Scar. We are on a bit of a rescue mission," Ronan said, starting off vaguely.

Vallia shook her head. "Before we do any rescuing, we need to get information first."

Maya pushed her luck. "What sort of information?"

"We are looking to get information about a man who has been missing for a while but has recently appeared." Ronan wanted to give more information but knew Vallia would not approve.

Maya bit her lower lip clearly wanting to ask more.

Vallia sighed after a while seeing the face Maya was still making. "Dur Volgen."

Maya looked taken aback. "What?"

"Dur Volgen, that's where we are going. I tell you this now because if you are not up for what we are doing, I don't want you here."

"Your man is a prisoner?"

"Yes, he is a prisoner!"

Ronan heard the sharp inflection of her tone and was reminded of how intensely Vallia was not on board with their mission.

"What did he do to be put into prison?" Maya curiously questioned.

Vallia looked at her. "I don't know, but does it matter? For someone wrongly accused and sent to a labor camp, you seem pretty judgmental about us saving a prisoner."

Maya blushed. Then she asked, "So this is some kind of jail break situation?"

"That is a long-term goal. First, we need to go to the Dancing Bear Inn and meet up with some contacts to learn what we will be getting ourselves into at the prison." Vallia seemed irritated. Ronan assumed it stemmed from more than just Maya. The lack of information they had was definitely a factor as well.

Ronan noticed that Maya had stopped walking and turned. Maya was frozen in place, her head turned to the side, her mouth agape and her eyes pure purple. She twitched and her body convulsed. She looked around making jagged movements.

"What's she doing?" Vallia asked cautiously.

Ronan responded, "I have no idea. It looks like she is looking for something." He ethereally blinked and saw Maya surrounded by an inferno of purple flames. Colorful movement in the air caught his attention and he saw tiny rays of purple energy gravitate toward Maya. They hit her and appeared to be absorbed by her body. Then the rays stopped, and she fell to the ground, the purple fire fading into a normal orange glow. Ronan blinked again and ran to her side. He propped her up and asked, "Are you okay? What was that? What just happened?"

Maya opened her eyes and looked frightened. She pushed Ronan off of her and stumbled to her feet. "We need to get to the prison. We don't have time to go to the Dancing Bear Inn."

Vallia scowled, "Was that supposed to be one of your visions?"

Maya nodded and began speaking in a rushed voice, "I saw the prison. I saw people in jail cells. Then I saw one of its walls explode. Something is going to happen at the prison tomorrow at sunset. We don't have time to go to the Dancing Bear. If we stop there, we will miss it."

"What's going to happen?" Ronan anxiously demanded.

"I don't know. I didn't see why the wall exploded. It's not like I can pick what I see. I just get flashes and glimpses and vague understandings. I know whatever is happening, its happening tomorrow evening, and we need to be there when it happens."

Vallia still did not look impressed. "Why would we want to be present if there is going to be an explosion? How do we even know this is going to happen?"

Maya stopped herself from snapping at Vallia. "Think of it this way. If I'm wrong, we spend the extra day and get eyes on the prison before we talk to your contacts. I don't understand why but I know we need to be there. If we miss the explosion, you're not going to be able to do anything after tomorrow. That place is going to be flooded with guards after the event I saw. This is your best chance to break your friend out. I can't explain it. I just know this is an opportunity we need to take advantage of."

Vallia shook her head. "We have a plan. We are not about to sacrifice that based on some weird seizure you had."

Ronan pursed his lips at her attitude. He asked, "How sure are you that something is going to happen? I thought you said that you saw possible futures, not guaranteed ones?"

Maya nodded. "The way the energies work, they show me what seems very likely to happen. It is difficult to explain but that's how it is. Every vision I have had has come true in one way or another."

Vallia gave Ronan a threatening look. She slowly said, "We are not going to go to the prison first. We need to talk with our contacts at the inn. That is the plan."

Ronan knew that improvisation was Vallia's and Mr. Kemin's least favorite thing. They both believed that plans were safe and calculated. Ronan was worried that Maya was right. If the prison did have an explosion, the number of guards at the prison would double overnight.

Ronan looked at Vallia and asked, "What is the harm of observing the prison from a distance one day before we go and talk to our spies? We don't have to get close. All we have to do is see if anything happens tomorrow evening. If nothing explodes, we sneak away and go to the inn and follow the plan."

Vallia gave him a reproachful glare, "And what if something does happen? What if there is an explosion? Are you just supposed to run into the chaos and hope for the best? No plan? No information?"

Ronan saw something in her eyes as she spoke. She must be thinking about Arkeen. This is the exact sort of thing Arkeen would have done. Ronan felt for her. He said, "Then let's make a plan. We have a few more hours of walking through this forest. There is only one path through. We don't need to decide until we are out of the forest. If we can come up with a solid plan in case of a prison explosion, would you feel more comfortable just going to take a look?"

Vallia looked at him. "Why are you pushing this so much? What is wrong with the original plan of taking the time and learning what we can?"

Ronan thought about her challenge. He didn't want to lose an opportunity to save Leo and let Mr. Kemin down. Selfishly, he also desired an audience with the Archivist because he was one of the few people who could help answer some of his questions about his powers, the Eidolon, and the Justices. The guilt he felt over Arkeen's death also surfaced in his mind as a factor.

That part of him didn't want to be burdened by the guilt of letting something happen to Arkeen's brother. He decided to capitalize on that thought process, hoping Vallia shared a similar sense of responsibility.

He said, "I know you're doing this mission for Arkeen. I know that if it were not for him, you would not be here. We are not responsible for Leo being in prison. However, somehow, we have become responsible for getting him out. If there is an opportunity tomorrow to get Arkeen's brother out, shouldn't we at least make an effort? At best, we get eyes on the target. At worst, we implement our plan that we will come up with in the next few hours."

Vallia intently focused on him and then scowled at Maya. She glanced back at Ronan. He could tell she was struggling. She finally looked up the road in the direction they had been heading and then back the way they came. She gritted her teeth, and then punched the air sending a blast of wind into the canopy of leaves. Birds scattered as yellow and brown leaves fell from the sky. She said in a strained voice, "We can go to the prison first, but we will have a plan ready for when everything goes wrong. If we are doing this, if we are going to the prison first, we should at least try to get word out to our contacts at the inn. I am sure they are expecting us soon. Can you send your bird to them with a note?"

"Sabastian is not a carrier pigeon!" Ronan firmly stated. "He is a wonderful lookout but he isn't going to demean himself and carry a letter. Not only does he not know where the inn is, but he won't approach anyone except me."

Maya looked at him perplexed, "Who is Sabastian?"

Ronan whistled and moments later, Sabastian landed on his outstretched arm.

Maya backed up a few steps and looked stunned. "Is that an Ether hawk? How did you capture it?"

Ronan shook his head. "I didn't. I raised him and trained him." He looked back at Vallia. "The spies will just have to wait. If they don't hear from us, they will follow protocols. We need to get going based on what Maya said. If we get there and there is no prison break, you know she is a liar."

Ronan was taking a large leap of faith trusting in Maya. He was curious how accurate her visions were. If her vision of the prison came true, would the vision of the yellow eyed masked man also come true?

He began walking in an attempt to show dominance in the situation. He was not willing to walk too far ahead due to his concern about the reputation of this forest. Fortunately, he heard the two girls continue behind him. Sabastian gave him a look that Ronan pretended was approval.

They continued to walk under the general din of the forest's wildlife. The dirt path before them was mostly flattened earth, with minimal vegetation on the trail due to consistent foot traffic. The occasional root deviated from the sides of the path and stuck into the walkway.

Maya spontaneously chimed, "So you mentioned that you were meeting up with spies... that's pretty interesting. What is it exactly that you two do?"

Without warning, Vallia's hand smacked Ronan on the back of the head. "What did I tell you about watching what you say? We don't need inquisitive minds asking questions."

Ronan rubbed his head and shrugged. "I haven't told her anything." He looked at Maya. "You have to stop asking questions if this is going to work. Trust me that if you keep going, we will both end up with arrows in our backs hidden behind one of these big trees."

Maya shrugged, her red cloak bunching at her chin. "I'll try to quell my curiosity about you two and your mysterious mission."

The hours passed by as the road snaked through the trees. The three worked out some faint details of a plan in case Maya's vision did come true. A majority of the plan revolved around Ronan finding dead guards from the explosion and commanding their spirits to raise up their bodies. The idea was that they could pretend to be escorted into the depths of Dur Volgen with the dead guards. Ronan was concerned that dead bodies from an explosion would be charred and not be convincing as an escort, but he did not voice this opinion. He also worried about being able to successfully talk to the spirits and command them to tell him where Leo was being held.

Ronan noticed that the trees began to grow sparser and the ground began to incline in a gradual slope. He was relieved when Vallia informed the group that they were almost out of the woods. The sun had started its descent casting long shadows through the canopy. They broke through the tree line just as dusk hit.

The landscape on this side of the forest was strikingly flat. In the distance, numerous torch lights caught Ronan's eye. They were all clustered together. He was able to hear a faint twang of music in the evening air. This confused him as he knew that there should not be a city this close to the forest. The number of lights indicated otherwise.

They moved toward the lights until the shapes of structures became visible. Large wagons were silhouetted by campfires and torches. Ronan realized the settlement must be the Apollymi people.

Ronan was sure the Apollymi had been mentioned in one of his lessons. He thought hard, fairly confident these people were a band of traveling sojourners who prided themselves on entertaining and storytelling. There had also been some explanation about them being superb smugglers. If he remembered correctly, the Carpenters had worked with the Apollymi in the past to transport goods until the two groups had a falling out.

"They are blocking the best campsite," Vallia said. "This landscape is a flatland for miles. The ground they are camped around has some caves where the ceiling has fallen in. It makes for a great spot to sleep. Now that option is off the table."

Maya asked. "Why don't we just camp with them? I have heard that as long as you guard your coin purse, the Apollymi are wonderful people."

Vallia looked at her. "I have heard that if you sleep in the Apollymi camp, you wake up with no tent, no money, no shoes, and your hair shaved off. They will take you for everything you own."

Ronan asked, "What are our other options? We can't really stay out in the plains. If we light a fire out there, it would be a beacon to beasts and bandits alike. We could go back into the forest I guess, but I would rather take my chances where there are fires and food." He knew it was selfish of him, but a fire and a warm meal sounded nice.

Vallia was making the same face she made when calculating a long

116

distance shot with her bow. She knew he was right but was trying to find another solution.

"They don't know who we are. They don't know who we are with," Ronan reassured.

Maya cocked one of her eyebrows at him but remained silent.

Vallia exhaled sharply, causing a puff of wind to kick up dust on the trail. "Fine, we can go stay in their camp. But if we get robbed, it is both of your faults." She began walking toward the camp and stopped. "Also, no spirit shenanigans and no future seeing, energy channeling nonsense. We are going to lay low. Do you both understand me?"

Chapter 16

"I bet you twenty Zwell that my friend here can catch an arrow with her bare hands!" Vallia shouted over the cheers of the crowd that surrounded her.

She was very drunk, barefoot, and definitely not laying low. Ronan sat on a bench nearby with her boots between his feet.

They had entered quietly and found the center of the camp to be full of merry making and music. It appeared they were not the only travelers among the Apollymi. Visitors in the camp were not hard to pick out. All the camp residents wore lavishly colorful, flowing outfits. It was a spectacle to see the intricate embroidery work that populated all their garments. Ronan had also never observed so much jewelry in his life. Countless bracelets jingled while audacious rings and excessive earrings shimmered in the fire light. He was able to guess that some people here had a past as citizens of the empire based on their visible résumé marks. They must have left their old lives behind and joined the sojourners. Others had grown up in the camp and had oddly bare forearms.

One of the Apollymi had handed Vallia a drink and it had gone downhill from there. She had first refused to drink it out of protest of the situation. After a little time around the fire, she had apparently forgotten her stance and began sipping the beverage. It turned out the Apollymi made their drinks very strong because it was not long before Vallia had lost most of her inhibitions. She began humming and even dancing with the crowd, which was a complete surprise to Ronan. It was kind of nice to see her relaxed and enjoying herself. It was also kind of off putting because he had never seen her let loose like this.

Maya had been shy at first staying to herself until a few of the Apollymi children had come to her and started unbraiding her hair and then braiding it again with bright ribbons that contrasted her dark locks. She had started braiding another girl's hair. Eventually there was a chain of five girls all braiding and laughing.

Ronan smiled to himself as he watched his companions enjoying themselves. He was sitting on a makeshift bench drinking a hot apple cider. Drinking or dancing were not really his thing. He was content to just watch the festivities.

He was zoning out and swaying to the music and almost didn't notice the elderly Ethalladros woman that sat down next to him. When he registered the Ether touched the woman, he jumped. Ash drifted off her as she slowly moved. Small cracks in her skin glowed a deep red.

"Hello," Ronan said in a startled voice. "How are you?"

She nodded and raised her wrinkled hand, pointing at his right arm in the sling.

He looked down and said, "Oh I fell and hurt my arm."

She nodded again and gestured again.

He was confused but said louder, "I fell! I hurt my arm when I fell!"

She reached out to touch his right hand. He pulled it away for a moment not sure what she wanted. She kept her arm extended. He moved his arm back and cautiously let her touch his palm. A twinge of pain pricked his arm and then a warm feeling spread up to his shoulder. She reached out with her other hand quicker than Ronan could react and grasped his wrist. Both of her hands glowed and his arm seared with pain as if it had been lit on fire. He tried to pull his arm away, but her grip was iron, and he couldn't escape. Instinctively, fear caused his eyes to flash and the gray world embraced him.

Just as this happened, she let go. She smiled and nodded. His anger turned to confusion. Behind her, Ronan saw Arkeen and Ta Rhe standing defensively ready to act on Ronan's command. He looked down at his arm expecting to see it burned or charred. But rather, his sling had fallen off and his hand was unscathed. It was also fully functional and had no residual pain. He flexed his fingers and then gingerly moved his arm. His elbow bent without a hint of pain. He looked at the woman and dropped his powers.

"What did you do? Who are you?"

She smiled and in a frail voice she wheezed, "Come, Eidolon." She rose and began walking away.

He was stunned for a second, processing what she had just said. He blinked and called out, "Wait! Wait! Who are you? What do you know about me? How do you know about the Eidolon?"

She vanished as she went behind one of the wagons. Ronan stood up and ran after her, skidding around the corner. He saw the woman one hundred paces away entering into a dark wagon. He had no idea how she had moved so fast but sprinted after her. He got to the steps of the carriage and pulled aside a curtain that acted as a door. He knew this was foolish to run away from the crowd, but he didn't care. If this woman could give him information about the Eidolon, it would be worth it.

One fresh candle flickered on a table casting the whole interior in dancing shadows. The silhouette of the woman moved around the cramped wagon. She gestured to him to sit on one of two low wooden stools. He did so wordlessly and watched her with sheer curiosity and apprehension. She grabbed a kettle and dipped it into an open barrel of water to fill it. She then seized the sides of the kettle and her hands glowed again. Seconds later, it started to whistle. She poured out the water into two cups and then added tea bags. She then sat and stared at Ronan with a wild intensity.

Ronan looked at the tea and then at his wrist. "Thank you... for healing me. I don't know how to repay you."

The old woman shook her head and cackled, which resulted in a coughing fit. Ash puffed out of her mouth with each cough. The candlelight accentuated the lines and wrinkles of her skin. Her eyes looked hallow and deep.

She gestured for him to drink and he did. He figured if she had an intention of poisoning him, she would not have healed his arm. She then

120

reached into a bag and pulled out a leather tube. She popped the cap off and slid out an old rolled up paper tied with a red ribbon. She slipped the ribbon off ever so carefully and unfurled the scroll revealing an old yellowing map.

Ronan had seen a lot of maps growing up. One of the only books in the orphanage was an almanac that the kids had passed around telling fantastical stories about the different locations. This was one of the methods they implemented to escape the walls of the building and cope with their situation. He had never seen a map that was this old. He grabbed the candle and held it over the paper, cupping his hand underneath to prevent any wax from dripping. As his eyes took in all the typographical information, they stopped on a small symbol that he recognized near a cave at the edge of the Ishan Deval Desert. It was a triangle pointing down with two crescent moons mirroring a full moon. The symbol Maya bore on her arm. It seemed to be burnt into the paper.

Ronan searched the map for a legend to identify the symbol but found none. He pointed to it and asked the woman, "What is this symbol? My friend has this symbol on her arm."

The old woman nodded and said in a quiet voice, "Eidolon."

"Please tell me what you know of the Eidolon!" Ronan raised his voice more than he intended to. He tempered his rising emotions. "I know that I am an Eidolon. I had a dream, and I was told that is what I am, I just don't know what that means. Can you please tell me what you know?"

She pondered the question. Her eyes darted up and down Ronan, as if searching for something. He had received this look when he had haggled in the marketplace in Shem. He knew she was gauging what he possessed. She wanted to make a trade. This was only fair. She had already healed his arm for free. He asked, "Is there something I can trade you for the information? I can get coin if that is what you want."

The older woman cackled, and ash puffed from her mouth with each breath. She shook her head slowly.

Ronan was growing a little more desperate. Why had she asked him to come if she was not going to help him? "What about a favor?" he asked.

121

"Something you need done?"

The voice of Mr. Kemin floated in Ronan's head, *'Never make a deal or a promise without having all the paperwork signed.'* Ronan knew that offering an open-ended trade could be dangerous. It could result in him having to do something he did not want to with little guarantee of a return worth the effort. He didn't know what else to do. He needed to know about the Eidolon and if this woman could tell him, he was willing to take the risk.

At the mention of a favor, the woman's eyes lit up. She stood up quickly and moved to the back of the wagon where she started frantically looking for something. After a moment, she found her quarry and brought a small wooden box back to the table. Its lid was covered in a runic language that Ronan did not recognize. The old Apollymi woman opened the box to reveal a small knife. Its blade was about five inches and was made of a translucent, red gemstone that cast crimson fractals on the inside of the box. The hilt was cast silver. Both Ronan and the woman stared at the blade. Her face was just as full of wonder as his. She then gingerly picked up the knife as if it could break at the lightest touch. She placed the blade on top of the map.

Ronan looked at the blade. "What do you want me to do with this?" Was she going to ask him to kill someone for her? Or was she going to perform some sort of sacrifice or weird ritual? Ronan had heard rumors about the UN'kra sacrificing animals, however, he did not know if this was true of the Apollymi people.

The woman smiled wide, showing several missing molars. She pointed to Ronan, then pointed to the knife. She then put her finger onto the map next to the Rustafar mountain range in the north. Her bony finger rested just above a large black jagged line that extended from the middle most mountain heading south.

"The Ether Scar?" Ronan said, confused. "You want me to take this knife to the Ether scar?"

She nodded. Her lack of verbal communication was frustrating, but at this point, he had to adapt.

"If I promise to take this to the Scar, will you tell me what I want to know about Eidolon?" He was not sure how she would convey the information. He was also not sure how she would enforce the promise. Not that he planned to lie to her. He thought about Maya's first vision. If she was right, he might end up by the Scar anyway.

"What do I do with the knife when I am at the Scar?" he asked.

With blinding speed, a woman swept the knife from the table and stabbed it through the map into the wood below. Ronan wasn't even able to finish his gasp by the time the blade had landed.

"So, you want me to stab the knife into something. Into the ground?"

She shook her head.

"Into the Scar?"

She nodded.

He thought for a second, debating his options. The potential information the woman offered called to him from the depths of his desires. Every part of his upbringing was telling him to flee from this wagon and this woman's deal. But he found that he could not leave his chair. He needed to know more, and this may be his only chance. *What was the harm in making this promise? If I say yes, I will take the knife and try to get it to the Scar at some point. I also may be able to outsource the job if I am lucky.*' He convinced himself that the information was worth the unknown risks. "I'll do it. I'll take your knife to the Ether Scar if you give me information on Eidolon."

At his words, her smile returned. She stuck out her hand to shake on it.

Despite his instincts' dire opposition, he reached out and gently took her small bony hand in his. Her eyes flicked to her other hand that still clutched the knife in the table. That hand glowed red and the knife grew veins of heat in the handle and the blade. As the vines of heat touched the map, thin black lines began to be burned into the old parchment. They twisted and split and formed a new addition to the map. The tip of the dagger was now stabbed through the burned lines that formed the image of a cave northwest of the capital. Above the image of the cave hung a symbol of a goblet with seven spider legs radiating out from the center.

Ronan stared in amazement at the parchment. He then saw the woman's other hand that held his own glow. He once again felt the searing pain of intense heat course through his body. It felt like he could not breathe with the agonizing burning and pain. He was not even able to focus enough to activate his eyes. The burning was more intense than before and didn't seem to end. He had closed his eyes as he tried to shut out everything but even when closed his vision was white. The pain gradually subsided. The woman had let go.

After a few moments of deep breathing, Ronan squinted his eyes open. He sat alone in the wagon. The single candle was now burnt to a melted stub. It continued to cast its haunting shadows. The old woman was gone. The knife still stood where she had left it. His left arm then pulsed with a tingling sensation. He rolled up the sleeve of his newly healed arm. Before his eyes, a symbol appeared on his bare forearm. It was the size of a résumé mark, but it was on the wrong arm. The symbol was a flame emblem surrounded by four runes that Ronan did not know. As he watched, the symbol shimmered with a red glow.

Chapter 17

Ronan sat staring at the dagger and the cave that had been seared into the map. He was not sure what had just happened. The encounter with the old woman felt as if he had imagined the whole thing. He had lost track of everything else: his friends, his mission, his safety. All he had wanted was information from the woman. All he had received was a glowing mark that concerned him, a strange dagger tethered to him with a strange promise, and a map marked by a symbol of a cup with legs but no explanation as to what it meant or how it helped.

He rubbed the flame on his arm. It was warm to the touch.

"How could I be so stupid?" he mumbled to himself. He slid his sleeve down and stood up. He yanked the dagger out of the table and examined it.

It did not look like any smithing he had ever seen. Between the seamless silver hilt and the ruby blade, it was quite elegant. He pulled his own knife from his belt and replaced it with the ruby blade. It was a loose fit in the sheath, but it would work. He then carefully rolled up the map and placed it back in its protective tube. As he placed the cap on it, he noticed it had a wax ring on the inside. The case must have been waterproof.

Ronan stood up to leave the wagon. As he walked toward the door, a green wisp caught his eye. He stopped and looked around. Before his eyes, more green wisps began to fly together, coalescing in the wagon doorway into an emerald green crystalline figure. Ronan thought at first it was Arkeen, but how could that be? Ronan had not activated his powers or even thought about Arkeen. Was he doing this by accident?

The humanoid figure fully materialized and locked eyes with Ronan. Its eyes were black flames. Ronan had not seen a spirit like this before. The form of the solid spirit flickered. Then the crystalline man balled up his fist and punched Ronan across the face. Ronan's jaw throbbed where the attack made contact as he stumbled backward into a cabinet. The impact made him arch his back as he heard a cracking that he desperately hoped was wood. The figure advanced with two more punches. One to his gut knocking the wind out of him and another to his jaw that rattled his senses. Then the solid green hand rose up and grabbed Ronan around the throat. He was lifted off the floor, desperately choking as his feet frantically kicked.

Then he heard the cold deep voice of the Justice of Death coming telepathically from the spirit.

"Is my blessing not good enough for you? I give you everything from power to guidance and it is still not enough for you? You felt the need to make a deal with a being of the Ether?"

Ronan activated his powers, and his world grew gray. He saw the assailing spirit and looked desperately around for Arkeen or Ta Rhe. He saw them just outside the tent. Something was wrong with them. To Ronan's horror he saw their flames were not flickering. They looked as if they were green ice sculptures with elegant flames carved all around them. Something was stopping them from moving at all.

Ronan struggled and kicked at the spirit holding him by his throat. His foot made contact and Ronan cried out in pain. It felt like kicking a statue.

The voice boomed from the solid spirit before him. *"Whom do you serve?"* The spirit pulled its arm back and slammed Ronan into the cabinets, splintering the wood. *"Where do your allegiances lie?"*

Ronan's vision was starting to fade. He choked out the words, "With… you…" The spirit stared into Ronan. Then he was pulled away from the wall and thrown into the small table. It shattered under his weight. The single candle went clattering across the room. Ronan gasped for air on the floor, trying to push himself up. He wanted to get into a fighting position, but his legs felt like jelly. The spirit walked over, throwing the remains of the table aside. It flickered twice and flames began to appear on its shoulders, as if it was losing its solid form. It then delivered a kick to his ribs, driving the previous air he had just regained out again. He collapsed on the floor. The taste of salty iron filled his mouth. As he coughed, flecks of blood covered the wooden floor.

The spirit leaned down. *"Do not forget that fact."* The voice was deep and ominously low, causing Ronan to recoil. The eyes of the spirit lost their black flame and the crystallization faded.

An old Apollymi man floated before Ronan looked down at him. The spirit said in Ronan's head, *"Are you okay friend? You look like you had a tough night."* It was as if this same spirit had not just destroyed the inside of the caravan with Ronan's body.

Ta Rhe appeared through the door followed closely by Arkeen. They looked from the old man's spirit to Ronan.

"What happened, mate?" Arkeen asked, floating over to Ronan. *"How did you tick this guy off?"*

Ronan slowly rolled over. Then pushed himself into a sitting position. He felt his chest. It hurt but he didn't think the assault had broken any ribs. *"I didn't tick off this guy. I ticked off the guy that gave me my powers. He apparently felt that I should not have made a deal with that old Ethalladros woman. What happened to you two? You froze outside. You looked like sculptures."*

Arkeen shook his spectral head. *"I don't know what happened. One minute, we were floating there minding our own business, and then everything froze. We knew you were in danger, but we couldn't do anything no matter what we did."*

Ronan looked at the old man. *"How did you die?"* He knew the question might be insensitive, but he wanted to know if the Justice had killed the old man to use his spirit.

The old spirit shrugged and projected, *"I got bitten by a snake yesterday and had been feeling miserable ever since. Then I woke up and I guess I was dead because I was floating and made of fire. I don't think I was dead for long though. I remember hearing a voice..."* The spirit paused, thinking. *"Then I guess I was here. Not sure what happened."* The spirit looked around at the other two green fires. *"I am new to this whole dead thing. What do I do now?"*

Ronan felt sorry for the old man. He was trying to sympathize but was finding it hard over his self-loathing. Why had he done nothing to stop the

127

spirit from attacking? Why hadn't he tried to command him and tell him to stop? Ronan wondered if he would have even stood a chance in a battle of wills against the Justice of Death.

The old man looked at Arkeen and Ta Rhe again. *"Do you two have any advice for me? Looks like we are in the same situation."*

Ta Rhe floated forward. *"No, our situation is not the same."* At this he gave Ronan a stern look.

Ronan broke eye contact looking around at the damaged caravan. Freeing the spirits was the last thing he wanted to talk about right now.

He heard Ta Rhe explain to the old spirit, *"Leave this world behind. There is nothing here for you anymore. Go and receive your verdict. May the Light find your name in the book life for your faith while you lived."*

The old spirit seemed to contemplate this statement. Before he seemed to reach a conclusion about the farewell, his flames began to evaporate. With a final wave to the three, he vanished.

Ronan looked around. *"What did you do to him?"*

Ta Rhe responded, *"I did nothing. I merely told him the truth about what is next for him. He has gone off to the Light."*

Ronan pushed himself off the floor and stood leaning against the wall. *"How do you know he went to this Light?"*

Ta Rhe tilted his head at the question. *"It is the fate of every person. It is what awaits us,"* he pointed to himself and Arkeen, *"when we are done serving you."* Then in a more mocking tone, Ta Rhe asked, *"Have you made any progress on the front of releasing us? I believe you gave me your human promise that you would 'figure it out.'"*

Guilt welled up in Ronan knowing this was coming. He had made this promise. He had even been angry at Ta Rhe for questioning his integrity. Despite the long walk over the last few days, Ronan had not given it any thought at all. Even now, Ronan realized how much he felt he needed the spirits. How quickly he had sought their help just moments ago. How could he let them go? What if he needed them again? *"I will figure it out. I told you that,"* he said and let his powers fade to avoid any further discussion about the topic.

Ronan proceeded to hobble out of the wagon. He didn't want any more trouble. The last thing he needed right now was for an Apollymi to see what had happened in the caravan and blame him for the destruction. As he wandered back to the central campfire, he thought about the attack and his benefactor.

The attack made Ronan apprehensive. He now knew the jealousy of the Justice and he had learned the Justice could act upon that jealousy. If Ronan deviated from his mission, another attack could come. He wondered if the voice would kill him. Then Ronan thought back to his first dream with the Justice. His benefactor had said, "Your development allows me to have influence in your world. My will can be done through you." Ronan wondered if the Justice needed Ronan more than he was willing to admit. That left the question, how much did Ronan need the Justice?

Chapter 18

Ronan arrived back in the central camp. The party had not slowed down in the slightest. He was eager to find his friends knowing he should not have left them. Why had he been so stupid? If he had stuck around the campfire, nothing would have gone wrong. Looking around desperately, he did not see Maya or Vallia among the revelry. He spotted one of the young girls whose hair Maya had braided. He anxiously approached her and asked where his friends had gone. She shrugged and winked at him. Her deep brown eyes and round cheeks completed her innocent expression. Ronan knew better. He pulled out a silver that he had left over from getting his cider and tossed it to her. She smiled and pointed out of the camp to the west. Then she skipped away.

On the outskirts of the camp Ronan saw Maya's crimson tent. He approached and saw a peculiar scene. Vallia was leaning over a boxed planter that hung off the back of a wagon. She was vomiting into the plants. Maya was holding her flowing hair and patting her on the back. She caught Ronan out of the corner of her eye and said to him, "Queen windstorm here keeps claiming the Apollymi poisoned her. I keep telling her that she poisoned herself with whatever she kept drinking. Where did you run off to? One minute you were close by and the next you were gone. Did you go to a spirit party or something?" she jested.

"They took my boots, Ronan. The Apollymi took my boots. I told you they would." Vallia said, pulling herself out of the planter.

"Your boots are in your tent hun, I told you that" Maya said comfortingly as she patted Vallia on the shoulder. "Why don't we put you where your boots are. In your tent."

Ronan smiled at the empathy that Maya was showing Vallia. Despite her outward persona, Ronan could tell she had a tender heart. He got under Vallia's arm and with Maya's help, led her to her tent and laid her down in it. She was out as soon as she hit the bed roll.

Maya looked Ronan over and registered his condition. "What happened to you?" She pulled some wood splinters off his shirt and then looked at his chin which Ronan assumed was bruised. "Did you get into a fight?"

Ronan didn't want to get into the details of the fight with Maya right now. He needed some time to think about what had happened. He did, however, want to discuss the map with her. He felt now was the best time while Vallia was unconscious. "Never mind what happened to me. I got some information I need to show you."

She looked skeptically at him. He was worried she would keep asking questions, so he pulled out the map and laid it on the ground. He then pointed to the triangular symbol that matched the mark on Maya's arm. Maya immediately became engrossed with the map, just as Ronan had hoped for.

"What is this?" Maya asked as she pulled it close. "Where did you get this?"

Ronan told her about the old woman and the deal he had made with her. He pointed to the cave with the legged cup.

"She made this symbol appear on the map. Have you ever seen something like that?"

Maya pursed her lips "No I have not. Why do you think my symbol is marked?"

Ronan shrugged, "I don't know. I think it has something to do with people like us. I asked for information about Eidolon, and this is what she gave me."

At the mention of Eidolon, Maya's eyes darted to Ronan for a fraction of a second. She had recognized the word. That much he knew. If he had blinked, he would have missed the reaction. Maya started tracing the cliff side that stood next to the triangular symbol.

Ronan wanted to ask Maya about the Justice of Death and about her own benefactor but could not bring himself to do it. If he brought up his Justice now, he would be required to tell her about the spirit that had just beaten him up and he didn't want to get into that. He didn't want to have to explain how he had not defended himself at all from a spirit. That was the sort of thing that would make her question his ability to control spirits. He wanted her to think he had some level of control over his powers. He looked back at the map and said, "I am hoping Osmodius will be able to shed some light on the symbols."

"Who?" Maya asked with a raised eyebrow.

Ronan cursed under his breath. He had forgotten that he had not told her about Osmodius. He sighed. "You know the guy we are getting from the prison?"

Maya nodded.

"He is going to help us get in contact with some Arch Archivist in Ristiven. He is some sort of expert in planar energies or something. We are hoping he will have some answers about me. About us." he corrected.

Maya's eyes grew excited in the dim light. "Why didn't you tell me about this?"

"Mostly because Vallia didn't want me to. She doesn't trust you. You know, for the whole attacking her thing and the general lack of distrust of people. Don't tell her I told you."

Maya scowled at the response, obviously hurt by his lack of trust. "You guys are into keeping secrets, which is fine. But keeping secrets doesn't make friends," she said after a moment.

Ronan felt bad for excluding her but knew Vallia was right about information sharing. In hopes of helping her mood he said, "You can take the second watch. I think Vallia will need the sleep. I'll wake you up in a few hours. For now, you should rest. Something tells me that tomorrow is going to be a crazy day. You know, with the whole prison break thing."

Maya nodded in recognition of his effort. She asked, "Why don't you have them watch for us?" Her eyes lit up purple and she nodded behind Ronan.

132

He activated his powers and looked at the spirits. He had not considered having them keep watch. *"Do you two sleep?"* he asked in his mind.

Arkeen shook his spectral head, *"No mate, we just kind of stare at you while you sleep. Sometimes we whisper things into your mind to see if you react. Nah, I'm just messing with you. Well, about the whispering thing. We do kinda stare at you at night."*

This was off putting but Ronan decided to ignore it. What else did they really have to do besides argue with each other? Ronan asked, *"Could you take watch for us as we sleep and wake me if there is a problem?"* Ronan asked.

"This has been my plan from the beginning." Ta Rhe confirmed. *"We will carry on doing what we have been doing."*

Ronan nodded. *"Let's plan on that then. You two keep watch and wake me if there is trouble."* He knew he was in charge of the spirits, but he was not very confident when giving them orders. He tried again with more confidence. *"We are going to sleep. You two keep watch and wake me if there is danger."*

"Yeah, we get it mate. We know what keep watch means. We're dead, not thick-headed. Do you want to manifest one of us tonight so we can beat you up while pretending it's training?" Arkeen goaded.

Ronan glanced over at Vallia's tent. She had told him not to use his powers while near the camp. He respected her opinion and agreed it could be dangerous. He had already pushed his luck with the old woman and the spirit attack. *"No, I don't want to spar tonight."*

Arkeen leaned over and elbowed Ta Rhe. *"He doesn't want to be seen playing with his imaginary friends."*

Ta Rha looked at Arkeen and stated, *"We are not imaginary. We are the energy and soul of those who once lived. We are very much real. Though our bodies will return to dust, our spirits will live on. We may rely on this child to make us physical, but physicality is not a requirement to exist..."*

"Don't you dare make an analogy about the wind not being physical, I swear," Arkeen cut him off.

"If you know about the wind and its existence..."

Ronan cut off his connection with his energy, not wanting to listen to the rest of the argument. He looked back at Maya. She was biting the nail

133

on her thumb. She acknowledged his look. "You zone out hard when you talk to them." She pointed out. "I don't know if you knew that. Like you get all glassy eyed and you don't blink. Are they going to take watch?"

He shrugged slightly embarrassed "I guess it just takes a lot of concentration. Yeah, they said they would wake me if anything happens."

She grinned at him, "Well don't concentrate on them too hard. We have a prison break to deal with tomorrow. Come on, we need to sleep. I trust your creepy dead friends to keep us safe."

Ronan smiled at Maya; glad she had joined their crew. He then haphazardly set up his tent and clambered inside. He was concerned that the distant rabble would keep him awake. However, the voices and music seemed to have the opposite effect. He found he couldn't keep his eyes open as he laid on his bed roll and was lulled to sleep by the distant sounds of music.

That night Ronan did not dream of the Justice or of his childhood.

Instead, he dreamt he was exploring a chaotic burning landscape. Ronan found himself walking along a floating helix of burning rocks and molten metals. Smoking columns of lava and fire floated through a sea of stars and gasses up above him. Occasionally, super heated rocks would float overhead and collide into each other, exploding into hundreds of tiny flaming meteors. He did not fear the extreme heat or the fire of the mystifying landscape. The limited gravity did not feel unusual to him. Instead, it felt like home. Like this is where he belonged. But he also didn't feel like himself. It was odd. Like he was watching some else's life through their eyes.

The walk was pleasant as he passed by a bubbling lake of lava with flaming fish breaching the surface. Then something appeared in front of him. It was a glimmering, golden slit in the air. As if the space before him had been sliced open with a knife. He felt cautious and recognized the cut as unnatural. There was no explanation as to how this was any less natural than his radical surroundings, but he knew it was off.

He could hear noises coming through the slice, but he could not identify them. Should he flee or investigate? His indecisiveness lasted too long however, and a terrible force began sucking everything nearby toward the shimmering slice in the air. Lava flew from the lake and rocks from the sky. Ronan reached out and grabbed onto the rocky ground to prevent himself from being drawn in.

The arms Ronan saw were not fleshy scrawny appendages, but rather large muscular arms made of fire and smoke. His flaming clawed hands held tight to the ground, but they would not hold on for long.

The fracture in the air pulled more and more through it. It seemed to grow in gluttony, and it consumed more. Ronan's grip began to slip from the rocks. To help stabilize himself, he reached back with one hand and grabbed his knife to plunge it into the rock to hold himself better. His knife was a beautiful weapon with a silver handle and ruby blade. The blade glowed white hot and sank into the rock before him with no effort. It held fast, but the sucking golden slice was too strong. The knife slowly slipped out of the ground and Ronan's flaming clawed hand lost its grip. Ronan went flying, not able to stop himself.

The flaming landscape around him vanished only to be replaced by a cold environment filled with white powder and towering brown sticks covered in tiny green pins. Ronan knew them to be pine trees, but his dream form didn't recognize them. Small creatures that stood on two legs surrounded Ronan Some glinted with metal that covered their small fleshy bodies. Some had hair on their arms and faces. Again, Ronan knew these to be Legion and UN'kra but his foreign body was oblivious to this information. The metal covered fleshlings were seemingly fighting the hairy fleshlings. Suddenly, Ronan understood what the cut in the air had been. It was a rift, from the Ether to the Prime Plane. He had been summoned through the rift to help in this pitiful battle.

Rage filled Ronan at the prospect that he had been ripped from his home. That the metal covered fleshlings who seemed to be controlling the rift, thought they could tamper with the power of the Ether. The arrogance of the fleshlings for believing they could control the unstoppable force of fire was pathetic and laughable. Ronan would show them what it meant to control fire. They would pay for their selfish abuse of his home. Ronan extended out both of his arms and let forth a blast of heat from his flaming core. The blast incinerated every unsuspecting fleshling; both the metal covered ones and the hairy ones. Flames exploded outward and upward, engulfing the tall brown sticks, and catching them ablaze. When Ronan put his arms down there was nothing left but charred remains of the landscape. No other life survived.

The anger in Ronan then gradually subsided, transitioning into sorrow. In his rage he had killed the fleshling that had conjured the rift, causing it to close. He experienced a sickening sensation as the being he was occupying knew its only way home was gone.

Chapter 19

Ronan woke to a sharp pain in his forehead. Sabastian was sitting at his pillow, pecking at his head. When the bird saw he was awake, he reached next to his feathered body and produced a rodent-like creature with translucent skin. Sabastian would occasionally bring Ronan small animals from the Ether as gifts. They were always strange and often made Ronan wonder what terrible environment the animal lived in on the other side.

He thought back to his dream. About the flaming environment that he had walked in and then been removed from. Was that the Ether? Or was it all just a weird concoction of his mind? He didn't think he was that creative to conjure up a place like that. 'It had felt so real,' he thought. It still felt real: more like a memory than a dream.

He heard some flutes in the distance and assumed that the Apollymi were starting their morning festivities. It seemed that every part of their life was a giant party.

He rose and gathered his things as he exited his tent. Vallia was awake. She had started a small fire that she was using to cook some eggs. Ronan assumed she acquired them from the Apollymi.

"No one was on watch when I got up," she said with a side eye. "Are we just throwing all caution to the wind?"

He wanted to make a snarky remark about her behavior last night but held his tongue.

"I commanded some spirits that were hanging around to keep watch." He said it as a half-truth.

Vallia shook her head, "I can't believe you would trust our safety to random spirits you just found floating around."

"As far as I can tell, it's not like they can tell me no," as he said the words, he immediately regretted them.

"Oh, so you have this whole prince of the dead act all figured out? That's so great to hear. Why don't you get your dead friends and miss foresight and go and find this Leo clown and rescue him. I'll stay here and just take a vacation with the Apollymi. I'll just drink my troubles away." She frowned at the eggs. In her anger, she had smashed one of the sunny side up yokes and it was leaking into the fire. She closed her eyes, sighed, and said, "I'm sorry, it's not just you I am mad at. I am mad with you, don't get me wrong. But I have not been sleeping great and I have a massive migraine."

Ronan sat next to her. He confessed, "I didn't intend to let you get that drunk last night. I thought it would be good for you to blow off some steam, but I underestimated the drinks they were giving you. I want you to know that I could not do this without you. You have no idea how much it means to me that you are helping me. You could have told Mr. Kemin no and kicked us out of your house. Heck you could have led us off the path in the forest and gotten me eaten by a scorpion bear or something."

Sentimental emotions were normally Vallia's least favorite. Ronan made a habit of avoiding them around her. However, this morning she did not protest his statements. She nodded and said, "I am helping you because Arkeen would have helped you. I am trying to honor his memory. I just feel like my sails are at half mast. Like my driving force in life has been cut to a small breeze. If I was not helping you, I don't know what I would be doing. Then again, if I wasn't here, who would stop you from getting arrested, eaten up, or possessed by spirits or something." She went to punch his right arm but stopped. "Why are you not wearing your sling? You're going to damage your arm."

He winced at the question and her impeccable perception. Taking a large breath, he quickly explained, "Well you see, while you were partying, I met a kind old woman, who healed my wrist with some sort of Ether fire powers but she alluded to knowing about my powers so I followed her into her wagon, where she made me tea and I asked her what she knew about my powers but she didn't really talk except for like three words but she showed me a dagger and I made a deal with her to take a dagger to the Ether scar in exchange for information so she gave me a map and gave me the location of a cave but then she branded me and vanished."

Vallia blinked three times and then punched Ronan's jaw as hard as she could. She then grabbed his sleeve and yanked it up. As soon as she saw the mark, she grimaced, closed her eyes, and planted her face into her hand.

Ronan yelled, "What was that for? Why did you do that?"

Vallia responded with a matched anger and something that resembled fear in her eyes. "Do you have any idea what that mark is? Do you have any idea what you have done to yourself?"

Ronan's anger wavered as he recognized the concern in Vallia's voice. She clearly knew something he didn't. It took a lot to spook Vallia. He cautiously asked, "What is this mark? What does it mean?"

"You idiot. It's the binding mark of a Kitmazi."

Ronan stared at her blankly.

"That 'kind old woman' was an incredibly powerful being from the Ether. She was just disguised as a human because her regular massive flaming visage would have burnt down this whole encampment."

At her words, Ronan remembered his dream and how his arms had been made of fire. How he had towered over the humans and UN'kra in the place with trees. How he had burnt everything to ash. The dream had felt like a memory. Maybe it was a memory. Maybe he was now somehow bonded with the old woman's fire spirit, and it was her memory of how she got to the Prime Plane.

"What does the mark mean?" he asked again.

Vallia looked disbelievingly at him. "You seriously have no idea? That mark on your arm is a binding seal. That is the Ether equivalent of a legally binding contract. Except if you break the Ether contract, you don't just go to jail. That seal ensures you fulfill your end of the bargain. If you don't, it will slowly burn you to a chard crisp from the inside out. But it won't kill you. No, that seal will keep you alive until you finish your task. It will burn away your body and your ambitions until you are a walking piece of charcoal with the sole purpose of completing your bargain. Planar beings love to make deals with beings from the Prime Plane. Did you not have any fairy tales in the orphanage?"

Ronan felt a deep pit in his stomach. "No, I didn't have fairy tales. I barely learned how to read. Will I actually be burnt to a crisp or is that just some lie used to scare children?"

Vallia threw her hands in the air. "How am I supposed to know? I have never been dumb enough to make a deal with an Ether being. There is always some kind of truth behind those stories. The writers got the idea from somewhere."

Ronan tried to reassure himself. Vallia didn't know he would be burnt from the inside out. That must be an exaggeration. The mark on his arm felt weirdly warm. He realized he was sweating profusely. "Well, how do I get rid of the seal? There has to be a way, right? So, I don't burn up."

Vallia looked at him incredulously "Yeah, if you complete the contract, whatever it was. What did you say, something about a dagger and the Ether Scar? Do you have any idea where the Ether Scar is? Seriously Ronan, what have you done?"

He said apologetically "I just wanted information about the Eidolon. The woman knew what that word meant. I didn't think she would bind me into a contract or something. I mean she healed my arm out of generosity."

Maya's voice chimed in, "Was it generosity? Or was she just setting you up for failure? Enticing you to make a mistake." Vallia glowered at her for the interruption. Maya put her hands up and said, "Sorry, I didn't know if you thought this was a private conversation. I wanted to point out that several of the Apollymi have been intently listening the whole time. Which is not hard when you two are both shouting." She pointed at a flock of colorfully dressed people, fifty feet away, that started to slink away upon being noticed.

Vallia cursed, "Pack the tents. We need to get out of here. Ronan, we will talk about this later." Vallia ran off and knocked her tent down and quickly started folding up the fabric. Ronan didn't have to ask why. He may not know anything about Ether beings, but he did remember his lessons about the Apollymi. The Carpenters had been taught that they were highly superstitious people. This led to somewhat of an obsession in acquiring Ether artifacts and relics. If they had heard about his connection to the Kitmazi, they may try to capture him or worse.

Ronan kicked his tent over and hastily shoved the components into their bag. The girls did the same and he joined them as they jogged away before the eavesdroppers could relay any information to the others.

Chapter 20

As they traveled, Vallia hardly said a word except to remind Ronan and Maya to keep vigilant.

"Stay sharp and keep up." she kept repeating.

Ronan knew there were Legion scouts and patrols all over this area. The closer they got to Ristiven, the more likely they were to get spotted. That was the last thing anyone wanted. If Legionnaires got close enough, it would not take much for them to recognize himself and Maya as wanted fugitives. He knew at minimum his face would have been sketched up and sent out by messenger falcon to all the surrounding outposts. If they were spotted, they would either have to run or fight.

Out of trepidation, Ronan sent Sabastian into the air to keep an eye out. If there was a Legion platoon, Sabastian had been trained to steal their flag and bring it to Ronan as a warning. Ronan thought back to the time Arkeen had helped teach Sabastian this trick. They had trained him by playing fetch with a Legion flag. Sabastian would get treats when he brought it to them. This did not help with scouts or small bands of soldiers, but it was better than nothing.

Vallia brought him out of the memory as she called out, "We will be reaching the bridge of the Krown River soon. There are bound to be guards posted there. We have papers that will pass any initial inspection. But we are going to need to keep them from being too inquisitive." She looked over at Maya and her medical robe and smiled, "You are going to be surprisingly helpful with this. Did your jacket come with one of their masks?"

Maya nodded and reached into one of her pockets. She withdrew a scarlet bandana with the tree of the Council embroidered on it. Vallia knelt on the ground and withdrew a small leather box from her backpack. She opened it to reveal three small glass vials, two spiky dried fruits and some tweezers. Ronan frowned at the fruit. He knew it was necessary. He just hated what was coming next.

Vallia picked up one of the fruits with the tweezers and poured the contents of one of the glass bottles onto it. It began to swell slightly as it was re-hydrated. She quickly stood and poked Ronan in the face in four areas with the fruit's spines. He could have sworn she did it with a grin on her face. The pricked areas stung. Then the stinging quickly changed to a hot irritation. He knew better than to scratch it. Vallia then took the third glass bottle that was capped with a dropper and placed four droplets onto the poked areas of Ronan's face. The irritation flared.

Ronan proceeded to do the same with Vallia. Maya leaned in with wide eyes as they worked. After several minutes, both Ronan's and Vallia's faces had puffed up in the pricked areas, looking blotchy and oily. They were almost entirely unrecognizable. Ronan was not fond of the Carpenter researchers that had recently developed this chemical disguise. Mr. Kemin had loved the idea. Ronan knew the effects usually only lasted about an hour but that did not encourage him much. Several people had experienced an allergic reaction during initial testing, which had resulted in a few individuals needing immediate medical attention.

Mr. Kemin had reassured the Carpenters, "It's good that the nurses see a few of these cases. It will help the stories and rumors spread about an unknown illness in the Zwellian Empire."

Vallia told Maya to put on her bandanna and hide her now ribbon-filled hair in her hood. Maya obeyed without question. One of Ronan's eyes had swelled shut by now. By the time they reached the point where they could hear the river his vision was almost entirely obscured between the swelling and sweat. He saw the suspension bridge in the distance and its accompanying guard post and tower. His heartbeat quickened, though he was not sure if it was nerves or the inflammation of his face.

Two armored guards stood blocking the bridge. Ronan knew several more were positioned inside the outpost building just before the bridge.

Maya introduced herself as "Clericess Androgen Mestona" which surprised Ronan as this was not something Vallia had told her to say. Maya handed the guard the document Vallia had given her that explained the rare condition of her two companions. The note detailed something about a highly contagious disease with terrifying effects.

There were a lot of holes in the story like why Maya was not infected, but the hope was that the guard's fear would outweigh the suspicion. This plan seemed to work as the guards looked suspicious but stepped back a few paces.

One of the two said "Show me your Résumé marks you two."

Ronan's heart leapt to his throat. He saw Vallia tense at the request.

Maya quickly cautioned, "I would not recommend that, the arms are where the puss sores form."

One of the guards gagged. The other guard narrowed her eyes. Maya matched her gaze with a nonchalant expression. She shrugged and began reaching for Ronan's sleeve. The female guard said "Wait, are you serious about the sores?" Maya gave her a sympathetic look and nodded. The guard frowned and bobbed her head back and forth, obviously debating protocol and her aversion to Ronan and Vallia. The guard asked, "Why don't we just kill them and stop the disease right now?" She reached for her sword.

Maya made a tisk tisk sound and said, "You don't want to be doing that. If you get any of their blood on you, you're infected for sure. I need to get these two to Neshunhile to see the Elves. We are hoping they can create a cure to stop this from spreading further."

Ronan was impressed by how quickly she was able to come up with these lies. She must have a lot of practice.

The male guard said, "Just let 'em go. We don't need 'em getting puss or something on the bridge."

The female guard was clearly torn. She released her sword and growled, "Carry on. Get these two far away from here. And stay away from others. We don't want this to spread any more."

Maya curtsied and said, "Peace for the Zwellian Empire and all her people."

Vallia, Ronan, began to amble forward followed by Maya. The guards stepped back as they passed. The three crossed the bridge and passed the guard post on the other end. The troops gave them terrified looks as they passed. Ronan just nodded at the guards and carried on. Once they had walked a few minutes past the bridge Ronan let out a large sigh. "That was incredible," he praised. "You almost made that guard throw up."

Vallia gave Maya an odd swollen head nod and said, "You handled yourself well back there. I am surprised."

Ronan saw Maya's bandana rise up as she beamed. He heard the flapping of wings and a weight on his shoulder. He looked over to see Sabastian clutching the remnants of a Legion flag that he must have gotten from the outpost. Ronan smiled. Not only were the guards tricked but they were robbed by a bird.

They kept their pace quick as they traveled. Maya had said that the prison break was happening at sunset. The sun was at its apex and starting to fall. They had about six hours to get to Dur Volgen.

Ronan was grateful when the swelling from the fruit began to dissipate. The puffiness went away leaving only a slight tingling. The researchers had encouraged minimal exposure to the fruits. They feared repeated applications could have adverse effects.

The landscape was no longer flat, but hilly and rocky. They followed the river instead of the main path. Maya had said that if they followed the road to the Dancing Bear inn, they would miss the action.

As they walked Ronan approached the rushing river. He took in the peaceful environment as he assumed it would not last long.

After a long stretch of beautiful scenery, Vallia spoke up, "The prison is close. May I remind you; we are going in blind. We don't know the layout; we don't know the guard presence. We have no information. So, we have to play this safe. We will stay at a distance and wait to see if anything actually happens. If something does, you two follow my lead. Is that understood?" Both Ronan and Maya nodded.

They eventually crested a hill bringing into view a distant stone fortress that was Dur Volgen. Ronan took in the large, diamond shaped structure that melded out of the rocky ground. The building was set into a natural rock basin. Stone cliffs rose forty feet on either side of the intimidating structure.

The closest corner of the building was barred by a massive iron portcullis that connected the two cliffs. The furthest corner butted up to a particularly violent section of the Krown River. Ronan devised that this design created one way in and one way out. No one would have been able to scale those cliffs before being sniped by the many archers that patrolled the top. And swimming that river was the same as a death sentence.

Ronan then took in the three tall towers that rose from the furthest three corners of the building. Even at this distance, he could make out three large creatures at the tops of the towers. They all seemed to be pacing back and forth. Their bodies were a deep gray pigment. Bat-like wings erupted out of their backs and folded behind them as they walked on four legs.

"See, this is why we should have talked to the spies," Vallia said through gritted teeth. "Then we would have known that the prison was protected by gargoyles."

Ronan thought back to the time he had seen the shattered remains of a gargoyle while on a survival training mission south of Shem. Arkeen had told him that before the Council gained two new members, the practice of creating gargoyles had been frowned upon. The new militarily focused Legislators saw fit to re-invest in the practice. Arkeen had explained that creating one of the creatures required an Ether Crafter to summon Ether energies of earth and of air. They then forced the energies together creating a violent anomaly that was sealed inside of a hollow statue. The energies mutated the statue, allowing it to move and even fly. The Crafter was then tasked with controlling the volatile amalgamation. Ronan had heard this taboo process was usually accomplished with mixed successes.

"We need to get closer, but we have to be careful," Maya cautioned. "We cannot get spotted by those riders."

"What do you mean get closer?" Vallia demanded. "We are not getting any closer. We can watch from a safe distance and see if anything is going to happen. Remember we are here as a way of validating your so-called vision. When nothing happens, we will sneak away and go to the inn."

Maya scowled. "When the wall explodes, if we are way back here, we will be too far away to do anything. I thought you wanted an opportunity to get into the prison."

Vallia pointed to the large portcullis. "Unless your kinetic powers can suddenly smash through that iron gate, we have no way of even getting into the courtyard, let alone the building."

Maya retorted, "You knew it was a prison before getting here. What was your plan for sneaking past the gate and guards before?"

Ronan explained, "We were going to do it dressed as prison guards. Steal their outfits and sneak in that way. I don't think that is an option now." He hated saying it because he knew Maya was right. If the wall exploded, and he trusted her that it would, they needed to be closer. He also knew Vallia would be starkly against this. This may be his only opportunity to save Leo, which meant this was his only opportunity to get an audience with Arch Archivist Osmodius. His attempt to learn about his powers at the caravan had backfired. The archivist seemed like his last hope. Ronan thought about the spirit in the wagon and felt the growing desire to become stronger. He would never be that vulnerable again. They just needed to get through that gate. But how?

Vallia and Maya kept debating but Ronan tuned them out. He was trying to come up with a plan.

The iron gate would be heavy. He was assuming that several people had to raise and lower it. Maybe with the three of them and the spirits of Arkeen and Ta Rhe, they could lift it. That still left the half dozen guards at the gate to deal with.

He looked around for inspiration. He saw the gargoyles on the towers. They reminded him of giant ugly birds perched on the roof. His mind jumped to Sabastian and then remembered the Legion flag now in his backpack. Now he was glad he had kept it. Ronan looked at Maya and her scarlet medical robes. Definitely helpful. His mind jumped around as he tried to piece something together. The wind picked up and began forming a small dust devil on the path in front of them. It had not rained in a while and the dirt was dry and loose. Ronan looked back to the girls arguing and saw Vallia's hair flowing in its own breeze. Ronan smiled as a plan clicked into his head.

He interrupted the two girls. "What if the old plan was still the new plan?"

They both scowled at him with annoyed looks. Obviously neither was in the mood for cryptic messages.

Ronan elaborated, "Why don't we sneak through the gates dressed as prison guards?"

Vallia rolled her eyes. "Oh right, sorry, I forgot we packed three sets of Legion guard armor. We can just walk right in."

Ronan smiled and summoned his best Mr. Kemin impression. "Trust me, I have a plan."

Chapter 21

Vallia chewed on her lip thinking.

Maya seemed to be deep in thought.

Ronan looked at them both, waiting for their thoughts.

He had just finished explaining his plan for getting into the prison. He really had tried to sell it. Not only was this the opportunity he needed to save Leo and as a result, gain an opportunity to learn about his powers. This was also his first time where he was the one with the plan. Arkeen, Mr. Kemin, or even Vallia were always the ones to come up with wild schemes. Ronan was excited that he was able to contribute in this way for once. In the past, there were numerous times he thought up with ideas, but never felt anyone would have listened to him. He was also nervous because if they accepted and his plan failed, he knew it would be the last time he would ever be trusted as a leader. That was assuming they lived.

Vallia eventually said, "I get that this may be the only opportunity we get to save Leo. I understand that. It's just..." she seemed reluctant to express what she was thinking. "Are we really wanting to risk our lives for this guy? For a man who we own nothing and who doesn't even know we exist?"

Ronan thought about what she said. She had a point. None of them owed Leo anything. Ronan knew his plan would be dangerous. He also knew that if they saved Leo, he would owe them and that was very beneficial for Ronan. Ronan assumed that Maya would also be benefited by meeting the Archivist. However, Maya was not the one he felt he had to convince.

Ronan chose his words carefully. "No, we don't owe Leo anything. But I honestly don't know if I would be standing here if it was not for Mr. Kemin."

He had given up the secrecy about Mr. Kemin in front of Maya to Vallia's obvious displeasure based on her glare. "I don't know if you would be either Vallia. If nothing else, I feel we owe him this. We have a solid opportunity to get into that prison without it being an all-out assault. I don't want to die any more than you do. I feel like for once in my life, these powers of mine have given me potential to be someone I never could have been before. I don't want to throw that away. If I want to embrace my powers, I need Leo. To save Leo, I need you both on my side. So will you help me save Arkeen's brother?"

Ronan felt a little shady using Arkeen as leverage, especially with him probably floating several feet away. He also knew that Vallia would not likely bend to any other incentive. Ronan subconsciously fiddled with the emerald ring on the chain around his neck that Arkeen had given him.

Vallia looked first to the prison, next to the rushing Krown River, and then back to Ronan. Her mouth curled down, but her face was not sad. It was distant and troubling. Ronan wondered if he had pushed too much referencing Arkeen.

With a sigh, she said, "Fine. Let's do this. Before I change my mind. It's not like I have much to lose, right?"

"Well, with that depressing note, I'm in as well," Maya confirmed.

Ronan let out the breath he had been holding. "I owe you both."

Vallia somberly nodded, "I know. Don't think I will forget it either."

Ronan nodded, immensely relieved, and then he started giving orders. He handed Maya the Legion flag. "Remember, when I give you the signal, run forward waving this flag upside down. Look as helpless as you possibly can. This will indicate to the guards on the walls that you are in distress. Vallia you will be in position over there." He pointed to a large rock by the road.

She nodded and said, "You want a giant dust devil to obscure all visuals, right?"

Ronan nodded. He had developed the idea based on the Carpenter's lookout, Victor, and his fog cloud. The only difference was they would also be hindered by the dust, unlike the Carpenters lame sentry. Ronan figured that the spirits would be helpful in this. They didn't have fleshy eyes susceptible to dust like his friends and himself.

They all got into position. Ronan took shelter behind another rock across from Vallia. He had informed his companions that two spirits happened to be lingering around. If it was not for the chaos, he was worried Vallia would start getting suspicious. He had pretended that they were prisoners who had recently died. Maya had played along with this without any telling reactions. Ronan would tell Vallia at some point about Arkeen and Ta Rhe. He knew he had to. It was only fair. But today was not that day.

He gave the signal to Maya, and she started limping forward waving the flag and screaming for help. It was unsettling how good she was at this. He felt like he needed to help her even though he knew nothing was wrong.

Ronan peered over the rock and watched intently. The guards definitely had noticed the flag and the girl in the medical robes who was waiving it. This was the part that made him nervous. The prison guard's reaction would be crucial to the success of his plan. He was banking that they would only send a few guards to investigate. If they responded with too many, the plan would surely fail.

The iron portcullis rose up and three guards came out on the backs of black horses. Ronan zealously watched as they approached. Three was doable. He could make three work. He held up his hand to give Vallia the signal. She stood, breathing deeply. Preparing herself to summon the cyclone of wind.

Ronan blinked to activate his powers. The world grew quiet. The blazing orange life energies of the three guards glowed as they thundered closer. Ronan could feel the presence of Arkeen and Ta Rhe. He focused on their energies and willed them both to be condensed and solid. Both green flames transformed into the featureless crystalline forms. Ronan immediately felt his eye twitch and a physical strain in his neck. Solidifying just Ta Rhe had not been too taxing. Focusing on two separate spirits was significantly more demanding. Ronan breathed and whispered to himself "I can do this. I need to do this." He couldn't let his friends down when they had agreed to follow his plan.

151

The horsemen were almost upon Maya. Ronan signaled Vallia. She began to twirl her arms in large circles. Dirt began to fly into the sky. It encircled Vallia creating a towering dust devil. Vallia then began to move forward, bringing the cyclone with her. The guards galloped right into the dust storm.

Ronan thought at Arkeen, *"You get the horses."* Then to Ta Rhe, *"You get the men."*

The two spirits charged forward into the dust storm. Ronan pulled up a bandanna around his mouth and nose and followed them. If it were not for his ability to see life energies, he would have been blinded by the swirling dust. He saw the spirit of Ta Rhe hoist a guard off his horse and smash him into the ground. Then he watched the orange and purple outline of Maya's energy, as she kicked off a rock and landed behind another mounted guard. She aggressively wrapped her arms around the woman from behind and put the guard into a choke hold. The woman tried to fight her off without avail.

Arkeen's solid spirit grabbed the reins of the horse Maya was atop as well as the now riderless one. Both horses were frantic, trying to escape, but the spirit held them fast. The third horse bolted from the conflict. Before it could exit the dust storm, Maya, with one arm still wrapped around the throat of the guard, whipped her free hand through the air. Ronan saw a glint of metal and then watched the third guard fall off his horse and collapse onto the ground. Maya then heaved the female guard off her horse. The guard was unconscious and fell next to her comrade.

Ronan looked at the guard Maya had stuck with a throwing knife. The orange flames of the guard were dissipating quickly and changing to green. Ronan cursed under his breath. The plan was to knock the guards out. He had not wished to kill them. He had no desire to murder random Legion soldiers and now there would be blood all over the armor. The death of this guard was a possible failure point in his plan. Ronan couldn't let his first plan fail. The others would never forgive him. Why had it not occurred to him that the horses would become skittish? Ronan was annoyed at his lack of foresight. He couldn't dwell on it now though. They needed to change into guard armor quickly to alleviate suspicion from the guards watching on the wall. The dust devil would only insure the scuffle for so long.

Ronan focused on the green flames of the newly dead guard. **"Stand up, take an unconscious guard and follow me."** The command almost made Ronan collapse. He was already strained by the solidification of Arkeen and Ta Rhe. The command had pushed his limitations.

Ta Rhe picked up both unconscious bodies and the whole group moved behind a large rock that would obscure them from the guards on the wall and on the towers.

When everyone was behind the large rock, Vallia dropped the windstorm and the dust began to settle. She panted, putting her hands on her knees to catch her breath.

Maya quickly dismounted and began to help Ronan remove the armor from the two unconscious guards.

She said to Ronan, "Sorry about the dead guy. He was getting away and I panicked. I know you said not to kill them. Sometimes my reflexes are faster than my brain."

"What's done is done." Ronan attempted to stifle his anger. "It's fine, we just need to hurry and clean up his..." he was about to say blood, when he looked up at the guard. He didn't see crimson on the armor. He looked closer and didn't even see where the knife had stabbed him.

"I smashed in his temple with the handle of the throwing knife," Maya said to Ronan as she pulled off the last bit of metal armor from the unconscious man. "You said you didn't want any blood on the armor."

Ronan was amazed by her precision as much as her observance of his request. He was about to say so when Vallia, having recovered enough to don the woman's armor, threw the chest plate at Ronan. "Get dressed. What are you doing?"

Ronan cleared his head and quickly put on the armor. It was slightly too big for him in the chest and shin guards. He figured if he puffed up his chest, it may not be noticeable. They didn't need to look perfect. They just needed to be convincing at first glance.

When fully dressed, he looked at Arkeen and Ta Rhe. In an attempt to

153

regain some control over the almost disastrous plan, Ronan pointed toward the cliff near the bank of the river. **"Take the bodies and hide them."** This command was too taxing. The strain he had felt in his neck shifted to his stomach. Vomit burned up his throat, but he managed to choke it back down. He couldn't let this sign of weakness show. Not now, not when his plan had already almost failed.

With gritted teeth to fight the strain, he watched the spirits obey his orders. Both crystalline figures took an unconscious guard and began dragging them away. Ronan couldn't lie, there was a level of ascendancy that came with watching the spirits do what they were told.

Ronan shook his head, needing to focus on the mission at hand. He put on the metal helmet and clambered onto the back of one of the horses Arkeen had wrangled. They were calmer now that the fighting and dust were done. He wondered to himself how Legionnaires did anything in this armor. It was heavy and cumbersome. It also was causing Ronan to sweat despite the cool fall air.

Vallia mounted the other horse. She looked at Maya and said, "Get on." Maya looked surprised at the request.

Ronan was also surprised but pleased to see the two cooperating. That was until Valia looked at the dead guard standing amongst them and said, "Better you than the walking corpse."

Chapter 22

The two horses approached the iron portcullises. It was larger than Ronan had realized, easily standing twenty feet tall. He was glad he had not gone with the plan to raise the gate. It must take eight men to lift it.

Ronan felt the eyes of the guards from atop the gate. One of the guards yelled down. "What in the Ether happened out there? We saw you ride out and then you were swallowed in a dust cloud."

Vallia called back in a deep voice, "Don't know what happened. One minute there was nothing and the next second we couldn't see anything. We lost one of the horses. No idea where it ran off to."

The guard up above called down, "Who's the medic? What is she doing out here?"

Ronan answered, "She said she was with a band of medics. They were transporting supplies from Golgotha to Shem when her group was attacked by a savage platoon of UN'kra. She said all her companions were brutally killed. She just barely escaped and ran all the way here."

The guard up above scoffed at them. "UN'kra? This far south? No way they got past the Legion line. Even if a few snuck by, they'd never make it over the bridge. She's gone loopy from the sun. Probably got attacked by some hairy bandits."

Ronan was annoyed but attempted to match their harassment to play the part. "Ya I told her that it was probably just a couple of bears, am I right?

The guards up above bellowed with laughter. "Maybe it was bears. Hey medic, did you get attacked by a group of walking bears?"

Another voice called out, "Did they have little hats and vests?"

155

They all laughed.

Ronan couldn't believe the ridiculous nature of the situation. He never would have thought that the hardest part of infiltrating a prison would be dealing with idiots at the gate. "Oye," Ronan called up. "Open the bloody gate. We're covered in dust and the girl needs medical attention."

The gate guard called down, "Keep your trousers on. We're opening the gate. Ruddy newbs. Can't have any fun."

Another guard yelled down, "When you get the bear victim situated, you better go and find that missing horse. I don't care if it takes you all night. You find it and bring it back or don't bother coming back yourself."

With a clanging groan, the gate began to rise up. Ronan realized the guards were hazing them. He recognized it from when he joined the Carpenters. It's what veteran recruits did to new people. It would make sense for the new recruits to be the ones that got sent out on a mission to investigate a frantic civilian. Ronan felt a pang of guilt about the guard whose body was sitting behind him on his horse. He looked back at the corpse. His face was young with a well-groomed goatee. He couldn't have been older than twenty. This man had just been trying to make a living. And Ronan's plan had resulted in this man dying.

The gate hit its pinnacle with a clang. Ronan forced himself to push the guilt aside. He had to remind himself that no matter how old the guard was, he was part of the Zwellian Legion. That meant he signed up to oppress the people and enforce the corrupt rules of the Council. He would have arrested Ronan on the spot if he had the chance. He had not failed. If anything, he had salvaged the plan with his powers. If it were not for him, this mission would have already been foiled.

Ronan didn't know if any of that was true, but it's what he told himself to help focus on the mission at hand.

The two horses trotted forward, and the gate began to close behind them. The courtyard they entered was narrow and mostly empty. The occasional pair of guards could be seen walking along the grounds. There were no visible barracks, or housing for the guards. Ronan assumed they all must sleep somewhere in the prison. There was also no evidence that the prisoners were ever allowed outside the high stone walls. No sign of life or occupation. Ronan looked to the rear of the prison and saw it was not surrounded by the towering cliffs that encircled most of the fort. It was open and unprotected. He was able to look out at one of the widest, most choppy sections of the Krown River. There was no need for guards or walls. The river was the only deterrent anyone would need.

Ronan looked up. He could see the tall towers rising high in the sky. From down here, the gargoyles were not visible. If only this encouraged him. If anything, it made him feel vertigo as he looked up.

He pulled his horse up beside Vallia's and asked Maya, "We got in the gate, now what?"

As if answering his question, distant bells started ringing from deep inside the prison. Then they echoed throughout the stone basin that the prison sat in.

The guards that were roaming the courtyard responded to the alarm. They all began to run toward the front gate of the prison. The guards on the gate all turned and pointed their crossbows at the building.

Ronan jumped off the horse. He mentally instructed the dead guard to do the same. At this point he released the solidification of Arkeen and Ta Rhe. They should have had plenty of time to hide the bodies and would be faster as floating spirits to return. The mental strain immediately was reduced as he let the spirits regain their fiery forms. Commanding one spirit occupying a body was barely any strain at all.

"Come on. We need to get inside," he instructed.

Maya dismounted as well and told him, "No I don't think we do need to go inside. I saw the people in the cells but in my vision, I never saw us inside. I watched the wall explode from the outside. I don't know how to explain it, I just feel like we need to stay outside."

Vallia hopped off the horse and asked, "Do you know which wall is supposed to explode?" This was the first time she had admitted that Maya may have been correct. The alarm bells seemed to indicate something was going on. Ronan looked up and observed the warm colors of the sky informing him that it was sunset, just as Maya had predicted.

157

Maya looked up at the wall nearest to them. "These walls all look the same to me, but if I had to bet, I would put my money on this one." She pointed up at the nearest tower.

Ronan and Vallia inclined their heads to look where she was pointing. The tower of stone rose before them as a solid wall except for one small oval window near the very top. The stonework around the window was unusually dark, as if it had gotten wet. As Ronan watched, the dark spot grew. Water began to flow over the windowsill. The water fell all the way to the ground where it splashed against the cobblestones. To Ronan's bewilderment, the amount of water cascading down doubled in a matter of seconds.

The air was filled with the sound of crashing water. Then the sound of cracking mortar intermixed with the splashing. Small fissures formed in the split block exterior of the wall and quickly began to spread.

Maya's eyes flashed purple as she looked up at the wall. "We need to move. Now!" She started backpedaling away from the wall. Vallia and Ronan did not need to be told twice. The two horses seemed to have a similar sense of danger as they both bolted away. Ronan and Vallia followed Maya's retreat to the base of the high wall. The reanimated corpse was not as quick to respond. An instant later, a large chunk of masonry separated from the wall and fell directly onto the standing corpse. Ronan lost all connection to the spirit. He felt another pang of guilt before he remembered the body was already dead.

Water erupted out of the new hole in the wall. Another section broke off followed by another explosive torrent of water. Ronan's nostrils were filled with the smell of salt water. This didn't make any sense. Then again neither did the water gushing from the wall.

Maya, with her eyes still glowing, covered her ears. Ronan took the hint and mimicked her. The wall before them shuddered. Then with a ground-shaking crash, the entire wall exploded outward. What was once stone became a cascading wall of frothy water filled with rocks and dust that dropped in elevation forming a violent waterfall. This wild phenomenon escalated as deafening cracking filled the prison courtyard as the remnants of the wall gave way in the shape of a massive wave. Ronan could barely move fast enough to shelter behind a large stone next to Vallia and Maya. The water impacted the rock with an unimaginable force and immediately enveloped it. Ronan was soaked to the bone as he desperately clung to the slate gray stone. The aftermath of the wave came up to his knees. Vallia's hair was plastered around her face, too waterlogged to blow in its invisible breeze.

Ronan rubbed his eyes which stung from the salt water. He looked around the rock to see what remained of the tower. One quarter of the structure still stood; its innards exposed the world. What remained of a spiral staircase jutted out from the remnants. Then Ronan saw a soaking wet man trudging through the water on the ground. He wore an orange tunic and matching pants. He had long, dark hair that was draped over his shoulders. The tips of pointed ears stuck out from the tangled mess. He was broad shouldered, tall, and muscular with pale skin and dark lips. Blood dripped down one of his arms as he sloshed forward. Then Ronan's breath caught in his through as he saw the man's piercing blue eyes. Ronan knew exactly who this man was.

Ronan yelled "Leo Kemin?"

Leo looked at Ronan. For a second, he stared at him with an avid curiosity. Then he chopped his hand through the air. Next to Ronan, a floating shimmering line appeared. It looked like a tear in the air. Ronan recognized the glimmering line, though he could not remember why. Then the tear exploded with a blast of salt water that knocked Ronan, Vallia and Maya down into the sanding water. Ronan pushed himself out of the salt water and stood back up. He spluttered and hacked up water he had swallowed.

Ronan remembered his dream of the world of fire. That is where he had witnessed the glowing tear. It was a rift in the Ether. This was only accomplished by...

"An Ether Crafter!" Vallia yelled. "He is a bloody Ether Crafter? I'm going to kill Dandrick. I'm going to ring his stupid, rich neck."

Ronan was also surprised but knew this didn't change the mission. He had to convince Leo that they were here to help him. Looking around to find Leo, he saw him sloshing towards the back of the prison courtyard. Ronan wondered why he was heading toward the river. It was out of view from the guards at the gate, but there was no way out.

"Come on," Ronan instructed his drenched companions. "That is Leo. We need to convince him we are on his side."

Vallia said through gritted teeth, "He attacked us. He can drown in the river for all I care."

"We didn't come this far to not save him," Ronan retorted.

"It doesn't seem like he needs our help," Maya pointed out.

At that moment Ronan heard a terrifying sound of large beating wings. Ronan looked up as he saw one of the gargoyles circling overhead. Then it tilted in the air and quickly began descending toward Leo.

Chapter 23

The gargoyle and its hooded rider descended from the sky like a falling stone, directly toward Leo. The fact that the creature could fly defied the laws of nature, but its ability to move so swiftly was unfathomable.

Leo, having spotted the gargoyle, raised his non-injured arm, and closed his eyes as if accepting his fate. Ronan activated his powers to command the spirits to do something. He saw the orange energy of Leo dancing about and watched as Leo's energy dimed and then coalesced into his outstretched hand. It looks as if Leo was channeling his life force into a small, focused point in his hand before he swept his arm down in an arch. In the air, just above Leo, Ronan saw another rift appear. It burned with a white energy. The gargoyle that was about to collide into Leo was blasted out of the sky by a jet of pressured water. The airborne creature was hit with such force that it was knocked back thirty feet where it tumbled end over end as it struck the ground. Its rider was flung off and splashed into the water. Leo's life energy surrounded him once more. Ronan swore that it looked a little dimmer but couldn't be sure.

"That's my brother for you," Arkeen's voice sounded in Ronan's head. *"Always showing off and making a mess of things."*

Ronan acknowledged the return of Arkeen and Ta Rhe and was grateful.

Ronan dropped his powers and yelled, "Leo, we are here to save you. We are friends of your brother Arkeen and your father Dandrick Kemin."

Leo's face portrayed confusion, clearly not understanding how a guard would know the details that Ronan was talking about.

Ronan remembered Mr. Kemin had given him something in Vallia's

161

apartment to gain Leo's trust. He pulled off his backpack and opened up one of the side pouches. Digging inside he found the little object that was wrapped in cloth. Untying the twine, he shook a signet ring into his hand. It was small and ornate, with four amethysts set around the perimeter of a scrolling silver K.

"Your father sent us to rescue you!" Ronan shouted again. He held up the ring and tossed it to Leo. He caught it and looked at it. Ronan watched the creases of his face break into a smile. He placed the ring on his middle finger.

Behind Ronan, a splashing sound indicated that the gargoyle was trying to right itself. Ronan was grateful to see one of its wings was broken off and it was missing one of its legs. It tried to stand and toppled to the ground again.

"We need to cross the river," Leo called to Ronan in a deep baritone voice.

"How do you plan to do that?" Vallia challenged as she fired an arrow at the wounded rider who was struggling to stand. The arrow sunk into the man's clavicle, and he collapsed again. "This is the roughest part of the river. Dur Volgen was built here for that exact reason. There is nowhere to cross."

Leo began moving through the now ankle high water that was settling on the ground.

Ronan heard more flapping wings and turned to see the other two gargoyles above the prison heading their way. Ronan started to follow Leo, toward the rocky shoreline. Vallia drew her bow and knocked another arrow. Without a better direction, she followed after the two, not taking her eyes off the enemies of the sky. Maya pulled out two daggers and sloshed after Vallia.

They reached the shore of the river where all the standing water was emptying into. Ronan stared across the three hundred feet of terrifying, deadly rapids to the other side. It seemed nauseatingly far. How would they ever cross this?

A guttural shriek echoed from behind him. Turning his head, his heart forgot to beat as he saw the larger of the two riders pointed to his party

162

standing by the river, calling them out to his companion. Ronan could now clearly make out the black robes of the riders that billowed behind them and the large goggles that covered their eyes.

"They are coming!" Vallia warned. "We are not going to be able to get across this river. We need to take shelter. We need to get back inside the prison. There is nowhere else to go."

Leo looked at the river and then back at the prison. "I am no longer a prisoner. I was not delivered from the depths of imprisonment only to go back into its embrace. We will cross the river to freedom."

Maya asked, "Is your plan to kill yourself in the river? We are here to save you; not let you drown."

Leo watched the circling gargoyles. The riders were obviously cautious given their fellow riders' demise. Leo then looked again at the river and said, "I have no reason to believe we will die today. Fear not, stand firm, and see the salvation granted to us. Hold back the gargoyles. I will see about our deliverance."

"What does that even mean?" Vallia shouted over the rushing water. "How are we supposed to hold them back? I don't know if you noticed but they are flying rock monsters with Ether Crafters on their backs."

Leo ignored the question and started to slow his breathing. He knelt down and put his bloody hand in the river, to wash it clean. Ronan heard Leo say in a quiet voice, "Great Light, let your path be clear before us. Deliver us from this trial. Give me the faith to trust in you." He then stood and began to move his hands up and down with the sound of the river.

Ronan watched Vallia turn to him for direction. Flustered by the sudden appeal, he found himself frustratingly silent. When Maya proved to also be unhelpful, Vallia cursed and braced herself against a rock and drew her bow back. The gargoyles continued to circle overhead. Maya's eyes flashed and she started watching the two predators as they moved.

Ronan blinked as well. *"Can you fly?"* He thought to the spirits.

Ta Rhe responded, *"We do not have wings like the rock creatures, nor are we tied to the ground."*

"Is that a yes?" Ronan asked Arkeen.

163

"I mean we can get up there, sure," Arkeen confirmed. *"We can't do anything to the gargoyles or the riders while we are all ghosty. If you make us solid, I feel like we would drop out of the sky."*

Ronan looked up and saw the orange flames of both riders. What if the attack came from one of the riders, he thought to himself. "Vallia, if you can take one out, I think I can deal with the other."

Maya looked at Vallia. "Let me help guide your shot." Vallia looked at Maya as if she had asked for Vallia's first child. "Do you want to be killed by flying rock monsters?"

Vallia actually seemed to weigh the options of letting Maya touch her bow and being killed.

"Vallia! Really!?" Ronan called.

She gritted her teeth and said, "Fine."

Vallia looked down the shaft of the arrow and allowed Maya to grab the lower section of her bow. Maya kept looking up. She made several small adjustments to the bow's position. Ronan could see the intensity on her face. Thinking about the math she must have been doing made Ronan's head spin.

Maya called out, "Banking left." Almost as if following her command the smaller rider steered their gargoyle to bank left and started a dive. Vallia noted Maya's command. Together they moved the bow, trailing the rider. Releasing the arrow, it rocketed through the air, skimming the front shoulder of the gargoyle, and found its mark in the chest of the rider. The shot was unbelievable. One hundred feet to a moving target in the middle of the air. The rider clutched the shaft and slumped forward in their saddle. The rider's legs were strapped in to prevent deadly falls so the body hung limply in the saddle. This was beneficial for Ronan and his plan.

Ronan focused on the energy of the limp rider as the gargoyle continued its plummet. The life force was transitioning from a burning orange to a soft green glow. Ronan steadied his breathing and found the pressure behind his eyes. Forcing it outward, he telepathically commanded ***"STOP!"***

The green energy got sucked into the body and it obeyed without hesitation. The body sat up and pulled back the reins. The gargoyle adjusted the slant of its wings and flew just overhead in a directional correcting arch.

"Protect us. Defend us." Ronan focused the command on the remaining enemy gargoyle. He felt his power faltering as he made the command, but he reinforced his will and maintained the connection. The body of the rider yanked the reins and flew the gargoyle higher. The spirit seemed to retain its ability and knowledge of how to control the stone monstrosity. With its massive talons outstretched, it collided with the remaining gargoyle and living rider. The two creatures clawed and bit each other. They smashed their tails against the other's sides and spiraled sideways.

"Do what you have to do, the gargoyles are distracted," Vallia shouted at Leo. She looked back over at the prison. Her face grew concerned. "And do it as fast as you can!"

Ronan followed her gaze and saw at least twenty guards stumbling out of the hole in the wall where the tower had been. They must have navigated through the prison and found that their quarry was no longer behind the walls. The armored guards began running toward them. Some held torches while others brandished swords and maces. Ronan felt a sense of being trapped with his back to the water and no hope of escape. He looked over to Leo, hoping to see the deliverance he had muttered about.

Leo pushed his left hand forward in a fluid motion. A clear shimmering light appeared on the shore of the bank they stood on. It shimmered and shifted in the fading sunlight. The thin rift then expanded forward atop the surface of the water, traveling all the way across to the other bank. Leo made the same motion with his right hand. Another similar thin rift appeared and then expanded out to the opposite shore. They extended like two ropes, stretching out from one shore to the other. He then raised his hands to the sky and both rifts grew downwards, creating two shimmering walls that sank into the water. Ronan saw veins in Leo's neck as he strenuously began to spread his arms apart until they fully extended. As his hands separated, so did the water. Leo was breathing heavily, the muscles in his arms straining with the immense effort he was putting in.

Ronan watched in amazement as the murky bottom of the river became exposed. The two shimmering rifts formed the walls of a water corridor that stretched across the river. A large crashing wave smashed into the right rift and vanished suddenly exiting the left rift without passing through the center.

Leo said through gritted teeth, "The Light will let us cross on solid ground."

He stumbled down the small cliff, reached the bottom and began slowly walking forward, along the muddy bottom. The water walls around him were more than double his height. The rushing water could be seen through the clear shimmering energy vanishing into one end and appearing on the other side. Ronan stared wide eyed at the scene before him.

Maya followed Leo with wide eyes, looking up at the miraculous scene.

Vallia gave Ronan a concerned look and yelled over the sound of the river. "You know I don't trust this Crafter stuff."

Ronan anxiously looked over his shoulder at guards that were almost upon them. "I know. I don't trust it either, but I don't think we have much choice," he offered. "We will go together."

Vallia nodded reluctantly. Together they advanced forward, following Leo and Maya. The ground they stepped onto was a murky sludge that attempted to steal their boots with every step. The translucent glistening rifts displayed all the detail of the water passing through them. One could reach out and touch either side of the channel. Fish could be seen swimming into the rift and appearing on the other side.

Ronan could see the strain of this feat on Leo and knew he could not hold on long. His life energy was ebbing away. Ronan was mostly focused on his concentration on the spirit of the rider, but he managed to warn, "We need to move fast. I can't focus on the rider forever and Leo looks like he is about to pass out."

They somehow made it to the opposite bank. Vallia helped pull Ronan onto the solid rocks. Then she spun around and pointed her bow at the squadron of guards. They had all stopped, not willing to enter into the valley of water to pursue the escaping convict and his new allies. Ronan could see fear in their eyes.

Just then, Ronan lost connection with the spirit rider on the gargoyle.

Moments later, the remaining gargoyle landed in the middle of the channel of water they had just crossed; damaged and clawed. Its body was covered in cracks. The head of the other gargoyle was held aloft in its jaw. It had seemingly won the air duel. The rider on its back had sustained some damage, but not enough to incapacitate them. The guards on the shore were bolstered by the presence of the gargoyle. They shouted a battle cry and started running forward. The gargoyle began bounding towards the four.

Leo somberly said, "May the Light deal kindly with you." He slapped his palms together. The rifts stopped shimmering. The barriers fell and the waters came crashing together, engulfing the guards and the gargoyle in an avalanche of water. The river consumed everything and returned to its previous state as a seamless body of rushing water. Leo shuddered and lost consciousness.

Chapter 24

Ronan, Vallia, Maya, and the unconscious body of Leo all crowded around a large fire. Vallia and Ronan had removed their prison guard armor and piled it up next to their camp site. They had debated if it would be useful to keep. Ronan was just starting to feel the warmth back in his fingers and his clothes were beginning to dry.

Three hours had passed from the river crossing and the sky was now peppered with stars. Vallia had insisted that they fled the riverbank and got as far as possible from it. They had carried Leo away by his arms and legs. He was too big for just one of them to carry and Ronan's mental fatigue prevented him from solidifying one of the spirits in order to carry his body. Not far from the shore they had been fortunate enough to find an old dead hollow tree. Vallia and Maya had been able to break off a large section of the trunk with wind blades and some applied leverage. They had placed Leo's body in the makeshift sled and attached ropes to the front. This made dragging the large man significantly easier.

When they had traveled to the point of exhaustion, they had set up camp. Now that they had the fire going, they removed Leo's obvious orange prison clothes and set him next to the fire to warm up. Upon removing his shirt, Ronan noticed several things.

He saw his four résumé marks on his arm. He had the red hammer striking a gemstone of the Carpenters. This had a significant white scar through the center, indicating that Leo had cut ties with that organization and denounced them. It was against the law in the Zwellian Empire to cover a résumé mark. Ronan knew that if someone wished to denounce and disconnect with a former organization, oftentimes they would cut through the mark with a white-hot knife. He guessed that the scar was from a long time ago. Leo's second mark surprised Ronan. His forearm bore the golden tree of the Council. It was the old version with three branches instead of four and only six leaves instead of eight. This mark was reserved for officials of the government. High ranking tax collectors, city governors, and people who worked directly with the Council. Puzzled, Ronan looked closer at it and saw the golden tree had a similar scar as the Carpenter's. Ronan thought that Mr. Kemin had told them that Leo had no affiliation with the Council. Why would he have lied about that? Did he even know about it?

Below the tree, Leo had the HT brand of a high traitor and then, below that, an orange diamond with a wavy black line above it. This was the mark of Dur Volgen.

The résumé marks were not the most interesting thing about Leo's torso. Even the many scars and burns were not the thing that grabbed Ronan's attention. The tops of his shoulders and his back were covered in thick dark fur like hair. The hair was oddly absent from his chest. Ronan had a feeling that Leo was not simply an unusually hairy person. Alongside the pale skin, dark lips, and thick tangled hair on his head, Ronan wondered if he was part UN'kra. He knew Leo was half Elven based on Mr. Kemin being his father.

Vallia clearly had the same thought. "He is a Council dog, an Ether Crafter, and part UN'kra to boot," Vallia seethed. "Give me one reason I should not slit his throat right now."

Ronan grew defensive and knew he had to convince her quickly. He couldn't come this close to meeting Osmodius and gaining valuable insight into his powers only for Vallia's prejudices to get in the way. "Because Mr. Kemin sent us to save him, and we could have easily died doing so. Let's not waste our efforts and kill him now. We will talk to him when he wakes up and we will ask him a lot of questions. By the looks of it, he has removed himself from both the Carpenters and the Council. We don't know his story and we at least owe Mr. Kemin and Arkeen enough to talk to him."

Vallia shook her head and haphazardly threw a blanket over him. "You keep saying that Ronan. Some time soon, there is going to be a time when I don't owe either of them anything. You can talk to him. But I make no promises that I won't shoot him." She looked back into the fire with misty eyes.

Ronan was upset at first at her attitude. Then he remembered the warning Mr. Kemin had given him in Vallia's apartment. He had said, 'Vallia will most certainly despise Leo for all that he is. Keep her from killing him.' He thought about this. Not only was this man an Ether Crafter, which she despised for some undisclosed reason; he looked similar to Arkeen while also resembling an UN'kra. Leo must be a brutal reminder of her betrothed and his killer. This had to be unbelievably hard for her. Ronan knew that he would have to work hard to convince her that Leo was worth keeping. That is, if Leo proved to be worth it, he thought. Mr. Kemin had kept a lot from them. Had he lied about knowing the Archivist? If so, what was the point in saving Leo? Ronan had to shake the thought from his head. That was incredibly selfish thinking.

Maya interrupted his pondering as she said, "This is the UN'kra that I saw in my vision. The dripping wet UN'kra. Or I guess half UN'kra. Now I see the Elven ears, but this was definitely him."

Ronan looked at the unconscious body of Leo. "Now that you have found the three of us, what was the next part of the vision?"

Maya gave him an odd look that he could not place. Was it fear? Or was it something she was concealing?

"I think the Ether Scar and the yellow eyed masked man are the next looming thing from the vision. There were a lot of flashes that I didn't understand. Things are not always crystal clear. Kind of like a dream, you know?"

Ronan nodded somberly, "I guess with my deal with the Kitmazi, and your vision, I don't have much choice." Even the mention of the Kitmazi made his arm tingle. He wondered how much time he had to accomplish his mission to the scar. How long before he became a walking charcoal shell of himself. Why had he made that deal? All it had done was anger his

Justice and put a timer on his life. All to get the stupid map that put him no closer to his goal. Ronan pulled out the map and was pleased to find the waterproof seal on the canister had kept the map dry. He looked over the details of the typography and then at the symbol of the chalice surrounded by the spider legs. All he had wanted to do was learn about his powers. Then he thought to himself about what he had done with his powers over the last few hours.

It was no small statement to say he had grown in his understanding of his abilities. He had been able to successfully solidify two spirits and have them fight for him. He had commanded a spirit to follow him without any major issues. That is, if getting the corpse smashed by a falling section of wall didn't count. He had even been able to command the spirit of the Ether Crafter rider which saved all their lives. Sure, he was feeling the effects of this now with a massive headache and physical exhaustion throughout his body. But, he was proud of the strides he had been able to make. The thought of talking to Leo about the Arch Archivist also encouraged him. If he did know this Osmodius, then Ronan would get what he needed. Leo owed him that much for helping save his life. Ronan smiled to himself when he looked back at the day.

They sat around the fire and ate a small meal. Leo did not stir. Ronan periodically checked on Leo's life force to make sure Leo did not enter into shock or start to fade. After the river, he barely had any energy coming out of him and his breathing was shallow. After warming up, his orange life force seemed to burn stronger.

"He blew up an entire warehouse once," the voice of Arkeen stated in Ronan's mind as he checked on Leo. *"We were young and dumb. We were being chased by hired goons after making the stupid mistake of pickpocketing some noble bloke in the market. We didn't know he had hired hands guarding him. They watched us nick something from the noble and then chased us for blocks."*

Ronan envisioned a younger Arkeen and Leo working the streets.

"We hid in a warehouse, hoping they would not find us... They did. They surrounded us and they started to beat us up. Kicking us in the stomachs and the head. Leo had been taught some rudimentary Ether manipulation from his

mother. He opened up a rift trying to blast the men back. The rift was much larger than he wanted, and he couldn't contain the explosive inferno that erupted. He was able to divert the energy around us, but the men and the building were not so fortunate. I was mortified at what he did."

Ronan pictured the dark scene. A brother risking it all to save a brother. Ronan thought back to his own brother. He thought about Sabastian vanishing up the cellar stairs to save their mom. Ronan suppressed the memory and asked, *"Wasn't Leo just trying to save you?"*

Arkeen nodded. *"Looking back, I know he saved my life, I was just so scared of him after what I had watched him do. I said some terrible things to him, and he ran away. I haven't spoken to him since."*

Ronan inquired, *"Did you know he worked for the Council?"*

Arkeen shook his spectral head. *"No, I had no idea."*

"Why do you think he was in prison?"

"It seems like he denounced the Council. That never goes over well. I am amazed they didn't kill him. Can't imagine they would have just let a rogue Ether Crafter be locked away. I would assume they did not know about his abilities. If they did, they would have brainwashed him into fighting for them or hung him for refusing. I could be wrong though. I don't know what his life has looked like for the last fifteen years. Maybe he is a mass murderer for all I know."

At that moment, Leo stirred and bolted upright and jumped to his feet, startling the other three. He was wild eyed as he frantically looked around.

Ronan dropped his powers. Vallia had her bow drawn in a flash and Maya had produced three throwing knives from her belt.

Ronan called out, "Whoa, whoa, whoa, everyone calm down or everyone is going to get hurt. We are all friends here."

Leo slowly recognized the three. He said, "You are the ones from Dur Volgen. The ones who helped me fight the winged devils. Who are you? Where did you get my father's ring?" He looked down and noticed he was standing in only his britches. "Where are my clothes?"

Ronan slowly stood, putting himself between Leo and Vallia's arrow. "We're friends of your father. I have proof. He wrote you a letter. It's in my bag. I'm going to grab it. Everyone just put your weapons down and let's not open any elemental holes." After a few seconds of contemplating Leo slowly sat down and wrapped himself in his blanket and nodded at Ronan. Maya lowered her knives and Vallia loosened the tension on her bow. She did not remove the arrow from the string.

Ronan picked up his bag. He pulled out the note from a leather pouch of his backpack. The note seemed to have survived getting soaked through. The edges were wet, but it was not destroyed.

He handed the folded slip of paper to Leo and sat down, watching intently as Leo read the flamboyant writing.

"This is indeed from my father. He sent you to save me from the prison? Why would he risk so much to save me?"

"Well, he is your father." Ronan said. "He does care about you, in his own way."

Leo chuckled. "If you have met my father, then you know that his world revolves around business transactions. Everything is a cost-benefit analysis. I have not seen my father in fifteen years. Now he comes and seeks me out? Why would he do that?"

Leo looked back down at the note and his mouth curled into a frown. He blinked a few times as tears began to fall from his eyes. He didn't try to hide them or wipe them away. "The note says that my brother has died? What fate has befallen him?"

Vallia spoke up, "He was killed by an UN'kra warrior on a battlefield. She had said it with a lot of malice as if she blamed Leo for Arkeen's death.

Leo looked surprised at her statement. "My brother was not a man of war. How can this be?"

Vallia shook her head. "He was not fighting. He was scavenging on your father's orders. The UN'kra attacked him out of nowhere."

Leo gave her a long look. "You were close to Arkeen? You cared about him?"

Vallia narrowed her eyes. "I was closer to him than you were. But I am not here to discuss my personal life. I want to know why you were in prison. Does it have something to do with your affiliation with the Council? Does Dandrick even know about that?"

Leo's face grew sadder at her words about his relationship with Arkeen. Then he looked confused when she mentioned the Council. He looked down at his arm and realized where she had gotten this information. "You have seen my tattoos. Then you have also seen my scars. I am not affiliated with the Council. Not anymore. Which is the reason I was in Dur Volgen."

Vallia scowled. Ronan stiffened as she put some tension on the bow string she still held. "I am not in the mood for vagueness. Tell us your whole story. I want to know everything."

Leo looked at Vallia and her arrow. "I have nothing to hide. I will tell you everything. Please sit and listen."

Maya and Ronan sat. Vallia stayed standing behind them.

Leo took a long breath to center himself. He still seemed shaken by the news about Arkeen, but he steeled himself and began, "Many years ago, I ran away from the care of my father. I was a teenager, probably just a little younger than you are now." He pointed to Ronan. "I did not agree with my father and how he was running his organization. Then Arkeen and I got into some trouble, and I made it significantly worse. That is when I ran away."

Ronan nodded as he talked. This matched what Arkeen had just told him.

Leo explained, "I wandered about for a while without direction. Performed odd jobs to make a living. Then I found my way up north to an UN'kra settlement. Not with my mother's tribe, as I have been exiled from them." He must have recognized the surprised look on Ronan's face at this statement and elaborated, "My powers of Ether manipulation came in when I was very young, and I was exiled as I was deemed too dangerous without proper control of my abilities. That is why I was originally with my father in Shem."

Ronan felt for Leo and all the rejection he had been through. It was almost tragic how much he could relate to not having a place to truly call home. The yearning to feel accepted and wanted. Respect and validation were not just handed out in this world.

Leo continued his story, "I found safety with a sister UN'kra tribe where I was able to learn to better control my powers. Then that tribe was attacked by militants of the Council. Mind you, this was twelve years ago. Before the Council increased to nine, before the formation of the Legion, and war was declared against the UN'kra people. The settlement was attacked and many of the women and children were killed. A number of the men, including myself, were captured and taken to Ristiven. There we were forced into servitude of the Council and their government."

Ronan's anger at the Council was renewed by Leo's account. He knew of the abuses in the cities, but Leo made it clear the corruption had existed before the new High Arbiter. If he had the power, things would be different.

Leo explained, "We were given three years of training to learn about the culture and the language. Having lived with my father, I already knew much about both. I excelled in the training and found favor with the trainer. He respected me and my knowledge. As a result, he elevated me into a high position directly serving the members of the Council."

Maya asked, "Why would you bow to the Council? Why would you serve them and do their will? They have been killing your mother's people for years. You could have done us all a favor by opening up a rift and killing the lot of them."

Ronan thought this was a good question.

Leo smiled at Maya. "I never bowed my knee to the Council. I served them, yes, but I never bowed. There is but one whom I bow to. The Light. As for killing them all, while the thought did cross my mind, it was a temptation that should not have been pursued. I was taught, out of reverent fear of the Light, to submit myself to my masters, not only to those who are good and considerate, but also to those who are harsh. For it is commendable if someone bears up under the pain of unjust suffering because they are conscious of the Light."

"Did the Council know about your powers?" Ronan asked, not sure what to make of Leo's attitude or his perspective on his service.

Leo replied, "No. If they would have, I am sure they would not have locked me away in Dur Volgen."

Vallia asked, "If you were too high and mighty to bow before the Council, why did they keep you around? And if you didn't try to kill them, why did they lock you away?"

Leo considered the questions. "I was a good servant, I guess. The old High Arbiter of the Council was fond of me and enjoyed our discussions. I found myself working under him fairly often. He was by far the most kind of the members. He was still politically corrupt and had no issue oppressing the citizens with his delegations, but he was kind to me. I still vividly remember the night that he was warned about the coup. I was helping him in his study when one of his maids came in and told him that there was a plot to kill him that very night. Apparently, she had overheard his chief advisor planning the attack with several Legislators. It seems like they had been getting restless and were not happy with how the old High Arbiter was presiding against going to war. They had developed a way to get the war they wanted, and it involved murdering the old High Arbiter."

'The corruption never ceases,' Ronan brooded. He was amazed that even among the members of the Council, violence and cruelty was not out of the question.

Leo highlighted the events of the night of the coup. "I offered to cover for him and protect him. I told him I would help him escape and I did. When the assassins came into his chambers later that night, they did not find the High Arbiter. Instead, they found me and a fiery rift of retribution. After I had dealt with them, I too fled. I was on the run for years after that. That is until about six months ago when I put my trust in the wrong person, and they betrayed me. They turned me over to the Legion and I was locked up."

Vallia challenged, "If you knew that the High Arbiter survived and was not killed, that would make you a liability. The Council would not want that information getting out. Why would the Council leave you alive and lock you away?"

Leo replied, "Because they wanted to know information about his current whereabouts. They thought I knew something that I didn't. I was regularly tortured in Dur Volgen for the information that I was not able to give."

Ronan thought of the scars and shuddered at what this man had been through. "You were in Dur Volgen, for six months?" Ronan asked. "Why did it take you so long to break out?"

176

Leo shrugged, "I had to hide my Ether Crafting until the right moment. Had they known of my powers, they would have killed me for sure. A lot of the time was planning and waiting on the Ether."

Ronan, not understanding asked, "What do you mean?"

"The Ether is a fluid force. Crafters are able to pull the Ether into this plane, but we do not get to choose what comes through. I can't just say water and have water pour through my rift. Crafters can only access what is closest to us at any given time in the other plane. We just have to learn to use what we get."

A silence fell over the group. Ronan was processing everything Leo had said. It seemed the others were doing the same. It was a lot to take in. The old High Arbiter of the Council being alive would surely be a concern of the current Legislators. He would be considered a treacherous liability. That would mean he could also be a powerful ally if he could be found.

Leo looked back at Mr. Kemin's note still in his hand. "This note says that I am to help Ronan," he looked at Ronan to confirm his name. Ronan nodded at Leo. Leo asked, "What is it that I am to help you with? What motivation could you possibly have to sign up on a mission to break a complete stranger out of jail?"

This was Ronan's opportunity. His chance to get some direction in his mission to know more about his powers.

Ronan began to elaborate, "We have been told that you have a connection with an individual who has the knowledge to help me with my powers." He looked at Maya and corrected himself. "Our powers."

Leo eyed him up and down. "Powers? Are you Ether Crafters?"

Ronan shook his head. He found himself hesitant and cautious about giving information out to a total stranger. He also knew that he would have to explain a lot for Leo to understand.

"He can command the dead," Maya interjected. "He can control them and make them follow him. That is what he did to the gargoyle rider."

Ronan gave her a sideways glance.

"You beat around the bush too much. Something tells me this guy is a pretty straight shooter."

She turned back to Leo. "Hi, my name is Maya. I have powers of a similar breed as Ronan, but I don't control the dead. I can see the energy of moving objects and predict how their potential motion will play out. Sometimes, I can even predict how future events will play out. For example, I saw you breaking out of the prison. That is how we knew to be there when we were."

"Well hello Maya, my name is Leo Fa Kemin. I suspect you knew that." He blinked a few times processing the rest of the summary. "If you're not Ether Crafters, or Ethalladros, what are you?"

Ronan thought he would take a chance with Leo. "Have you ever heard of the Eidolon?"

Leo thought for a moment. "I have heard that word, yes."

Ronan's heart jumped into his chest. "You have? What does it mean? What is an Eidolon?"

"I see I have gotten your hopes up. I apologize. I know the word from an old legend that my mother's mother told many years ago. When I was very small, I remember her telling me a story about the legends of the Eidolon. They were powerful people with gifts not granted by the Ether. They were few in number but great in stature and standing. She described them as being blessed with great abilities but corrupted by a ravenous desire to gain more power."

Ronan raised his eyebrows. His legacy was built around being unbelievably powerful and seeking more power?

"Do you remember any of the powers?" Maya asked, fully engaged.

Leo seemed to struggle to recall the details. "She spoke of one that used their power to hoist an entire city off the ground so that it flew through the air," Leo recalled. "She also spoke of another that could stop the trajectory of five hundred arrows mid flight, dropping them to the ground. No soldier could attack them, no blade could touch them because they could halt any sort of movement. He looked at Ronan. "I want to say that she did tell me about one Eidolon that commanded an army of puppeteered corpses."

Ronan was enthralled by the account. "Did she know how they got so strong? What gave them their abilities?"

178

Leo shrugged, "I was maybe six summers old when she told me the tales. At the time I was not focused on the details. I apologize."

Maya inquired, "Did you believe the stories were real?"

Leo responded, "UN'kra do not tell wise tales like the Elves and humans. The world we live in has enough wonders that they don't see the need to exaggerate reality."

Ronan wondered how these stories were not more well known. Why would an old UN'kra woman know about a flying city but no record hall he knew of held any recollection of these legends?

Leo looked troubled. "Are you telling me that you three are these Eidolon?"

Vallia scoffed. "Don't put me in that group. I am just a normal Ethalladros. I am here because I cared about Arkeen and saving your sorry butt from prison was my way of honoring his death. These two want your help. I don't want anything from you. All I want to do is wash my hands of this."

Leo looked back to Ronan and Maya. "Who is it that you think I can introduce you to that my father couldn't?"

"Arch Archivist Nimin Osmodius. We have been told he is an expert in planar interactions. Mr. Kemin thinks he may have some knowledge about Eidolon."

At this name, Leo grew a dark expression on his face. "So, you seek the snake that broke my trust and sent me to prison?"

Ronan stared into Leo's sky-blue eyes. He saw anger or maybe remorse and realized what he was asking of Leo. To take them to the man who had been the cause of much pain and suffering. "I guess we are asking that, yes." Ronan said, solemnly. "We don't know who else would have more information about the Eidolon. Unless your grandmother is still around."

Leo shook his head and sighed. "You are correct that he would be the one that would have the information. That seems exactly the sort of knowledge Osmodius would have. But that information will come at a great cost to you. That man is conniving and selfish. Trust me when I tell you that you must consider the value of this."

"So, you do know where he is?" Ronan asked.

"He is not a man of mystery in that area. His laboratory is in Ristiven, but my father would have known that as well. He must have thought that I had a better relationship with him than I do."

Ronan didn't like the sound of Leo's confidence. "Will you be able to make an introduction for us?"

Leo put his fist under his chin and thought. "Yes, I could make an introduction. That does not mean it will be a warm one. It may require a little physical coercion or some form of bargain." He thought some more. "I feel like I owe you for your assistance in my escape. You were willing to risk your lives for mine. Who am I to refuse you a simple meeting? I can take you to Osmodius, but I want to know what you hope to get from him."

Ronan stated, "I want to know more about my powers and where they come from."

Leo analyzed Ronan with his piercing blue eyes. "I mean more than that. What do you gain from Osmodius? Do you simply seek power like the Eidolon of the past? Or is there more?"

Ronan contemplated this question and his personal goals. He did seek power. But he did not want power for power's sake. He needed to be more powerful to complete his mission from the Justice. If he was going to remove the corruption of the Council from the Zwellian Empire, he needed to become more powerful. They had to be removed from their seats of power. If he failed in that mission, they would surely kill him and continue to bleed the Empire dry. But he couldn't fight the whole Council right away. He needed to start with the yellow eyed masked man from Maya's vision. According to her, their paths were going to cross soon. She had been right about Leo's breakout. That did not bode well for meeting the masked man.

Maya spoke up as if on the same wavelength as Ronan. "The power we seek is not for our own benefit. I had a vision of another Eidolon that is trying to unleash the powers of the Ether into the Prime Plane. He was dissolving the barriers between the two at the Ether Scar. I also saw you, Vallia, and Ronan fighting the masked man. If I am not mistaken, he is a member of the Council. He wore a mask just like the ones the Council wear. You know the Council and its members. Did one of the Council legislators have yellow eyes?"

Leo looked grave at this account. "No, when I was there, none of the Legislators had yellow eyes." He paused, a shadow crossing over his face as he said this. "Although... Now that you mention it, I do remember an individual with yellow eyes. He was not a Legislator, but the son of the High Arbiter's chief advisor. The advisor who hatched the plot to kill the Arbiter. If the Advisor was a bloodthirsty man willing to do anything for power, his son was cut from the same cloth. I only saw the boy in passing but I remember the other UN'kra servants whispering stories about the young man's cruelty. He could not have been any older than fifteen summers old at the time," he pointed at Ronan.

"What sort of cruelty?" Ronan inquired, feeling a familiar tightness in his chest as he asked the question.

"I was not part of their gossip, but I definitely overheard accounts of him personally administering beatings and assigning unjustified punishments. His father's position had granted him authority and he definitely abused it. I also remember a few of the others who had angered the young master with patches of gray withered skin on their arms. I thought they were burns at the time, but they were like no burns I had ever seen. It was as if life had been drained from the branded areas."

Ronan's stomach churned at the description. It definitely sounded like the sort of individual who would come up with a scheme to cause mass destruction. It was even more off putting that his eyes had been yellow back then. Ronan's eyes had turned green when his powers originally activated. That meant that the man had at least nine years of experience with his powers. He found himself gritting his teeth at the thought. Why had his Justice waited so long to activate his own powers? How was he supposed to compete with someone with a decade of experience under their belt? This settled it. There was no option to wait. He needed to talk to the Arch Archivist, and he needed to do it tomorrow.

Ronan locked eyes with Leo. "It sounds like the young man received a significant promotion when the coup happened. If his father was elevated to the position of High Arbiter after the coup, I would bet the son was established as one of the Legislators of war. He sounds like the type that would thrive in the role of overseer of bloodshed. If he was cruel to the UN'kra as a boy, killing them in masses would fit him perfectly. We need to stop this man from killing unfathomable numbers. And to do that, I need to talk to the Arch Archivist Osmodius. We can't wait."

Ronan looked at Vallia and was surprised when she did not object. Her face was grave and deep in thought. He could tell she was not happy by hard-set frown, but she must understand the stakes.

Leo looked around the group "Your goal is ambitious to stop something of this nature. If we are to do this, I do believe we will need all the help we can get. Unfortunately, it sounds like seeing the Arch Archivist may be necessary." He grew silent for a long while. Eventually he asked, "You said you were friends of Arkeen?"

Vallia and Ronan nodded.

Leo smiled. "Then let us honor the memory of Arkeen and take on a crazy adventure. Tomorrow we go to Ristiven. We should be able to get there before the sun starts its descent in the afternoon."

Vallia looked at Ronan and said in a low voice, "Dandrick told us that we need to meet up with him before we go to Ristiven. Are we just going to go without checking in with him?"

Ronan remembered Mr. Kemin's instructions to contact him once Leo was safe. But that plan had revolved around the Carpenters rescuing them in food crates. Leo's stunt with the prison wall and the parting of the river had nullified that rescue. There was no time to wait and tell Mr. Kemin. He would only delay things further.

If he was being honest with himself, contacting Mr. Kemin was very low on his priorities right now. Obviously, he would reach out to his boss about Leo's safety, but there didn't seem to be a good way to do that now that didn't postpone the meeting with Osmodius by days if not weeks. To Ronan, that was simply not an option. Answers to all his questions were a day's journey away. Mr. Kemin could wait one more day to hear about his son being safe. It had been years since their last meeting after all.

This ambition led him to say, "We are less than a day's journey from

Ristiven. I think we should go to the city. We can send word to Mr. Kemin from there. We will let him know that Leo is safe. That is what was most important to him. He doesn't care when we meet the Archivist."

Vallia did not look convinced.

"Look Vallia. If we could just go home and keep living out our old lives, I would love that. But I am a fugitive, who just helped a man break out of imperial prison. I can't go back." The truthful statement hurt him to admit. "And even if I could, everything we have been through over the last few days is pointing us up north. I don't want to fight the yellow eyed masked man. But if we don't, think of what will happen. I am in no shape right now to fight anyone let alone this lunatic. That is why I need to talk to this Osmodius. But I can't do this alone. I need your help. I need you with me. We are in this together. I know it is a lot to ask but please, I need your help.

She stared at Ronan, giving him a strange look. Oddly it reminded him of how his brother Sabastian had looked at him when he was protecting Ronan. She gave him the smallest of nods.

Ronan felt a deep gratitude towards her at the moment.

Leo, watching this exchange, asked, "So tomorrow?"

Ronan nodded.

"Then tomorrow we will meet with the snake Osmodius and see if we can get anything out of him. Before we get to that though, do you have an extra pair of clothes I could borrow? I should not enter the city in only my underwear or in my prison garb."

Ronan offered. "You can have a set of my clothes, but they will be a little small on you."

Leo laid down and pulled the blanket over himself. "I'll warn you; you may not get them back. Things tend to catch on fire or explode around me."

Chapter 25

Ronan dreamt that night of the realm of fire again. It was not the same dream, but again, he felt safe and familiar with the crazy environment. There was an innate desire inside him to return to the land of flaming earth and flying magma. The feeling borderlined on homesickness.

Ronan walked along a stone path with glowing embers on either side of him. Then flames grew from the coals. They rose up taller than his head and curled over him forming a hallway of fire. He heard the voice of the old Apollymi woman come through the walls of fire that surrounded him.

"*Eidolon... REMEMBER.*"

The flames engulfed Ronan and he woke with a start. There was a searing pain coming from his arm. Ronan rolled up the sleeve to find the Kitmazi's mark on his right arm glowing red hot. He watched in horror as the area around the red symbol grew black. Before he could process this, the mark stopped burning and the pain went away. Heart pounding, Ronan gingerly touched the apple sized blackened area. It did not hurt to be touched. Rather, it was less sensitive than it should have been. Looking closely at the spot, he understood. Charcoal. There was no other word for the new texture of his skin.

He remembered Vallia's warning about becoming a walking charcoal shell of himself. With an expanding concern, Ronan realized there was truth behind the children's stories Vallia had referenced. He pulled his sleeve down not wanting to look at the mark. There was no denying it now. He had to get to the Ether Scar, and he needed to do it soon.

It was early morning but there was no way he was going to be able to sleep any more. Ronan got up and packed his tent. Vallia had taken the last watch of the night and was off at a distance stretching and bending. Ronan wondered if those exercises helped her calm her mind. He sure could use something to calm his own.

Ronan was distracted from his immediate concerns as Leo arose. Despite not having a tent Leo appeared to have slept well under the stars with only one blanket. The chilled fall night did not seem to bother him. Ronan wondered if he shared Arkeen's love of nature or if it had been Leo who taught Arkeen to love the outdoors.

Once Maya was woken up, they were all ready to depart after a breakfast of dried beef and oats. Ronan shared his food with Leo as he had no supplies. As he handed over the dried meat, Leo closed his eyes and bent his head forward. After a moment of Ronan wondering if he was okay, Leo looked up and began to eat. Not sure what to make of that, Ronan finished his food. As they left their camp, they decided to leave the guard armor.

Vallia was quiet and stoic the entire time they walked. Ronan tried to talk to her a few times, but she remained silent. This was frustrating, but Ronan did not want to push her too much. To be honest with himself, he was amazed she was still with the party after the events of the prison and now with Leo being who he was. He was not fully convinced that it was his persuasive efforts that had kept her from leaving. There was no question that he needed her help and was grateful to have her. He just hoped she didn't feel trapped. *'Once we meet with Osmodius, she can go off as she pleases. Just one more day.'* He reassured himself.

As they walked, Ronan caught Leo up on the events of the last few days. Leo responded by telling some stories of his past. He didn't mention Arkeen or his father. He mostly spoke about his time away from the Carpenters with the Council.

After a while Ronan's curiosity won over him and he asked, "You're a victim of the Council's oppression and corruption as much as any of us are, but you loyally served them? How does that work?"

Leo stared at Ronan for a moment. "The Council is corrupt because they are people of this world. Men and women focused on the things of this world. Any government or body run by people focused in this way will result in corrupt and selfish decisions. You ask a fair question about how I dealt with it. The answer comes from my understanding of the hierarchy of the world and about the Great Light. Have you heard of the Light?"

The only time Ronan had heard the name was from Ta Rhe. He assumed it was an UN'kra thing. Ronan nodded. "I have heard about it once before. From an UN'kra."

Leo looked surprised. "It is good to hear you have spoken with UN'kra. That is a rare feat among most humans. Do you know much about the Light?"

Ronan shook his head.

Leo nodded, "That is okay. I did not know much either when I was younger. My mother's people taught about the Light, but I was a foolish child and was not concerned with such things. I was fortunate to learn more about the Light when I found myself with the UN'kra before we were captured. It was not until this second teaching of the Light that my life was truly changed. The Light is the answer to your question. The Light created everything in this world from the air we breathe to the trees and animals and even us. Naturally, if the Light created everything, then the Light is the ultimate authority. All those of this world in any position of authority have been installed in power by the Light. Does that make sense?"

Ronan did not understand what Leo was talking about. Leo must have observed this on Ronan's face as he explained, "I was able to obey and serve the Council because I know that there is a greater sovereign authority over them. An authority who's plans will not be foiled by the folly or corruption of men. For some reason unknown to me or probably anyone else at this time, the Light has given authority to the Council. Who am I to question that?"

Ronan processed Leo's response. He had been born a true child of the Empire, into poverty and fear. His whole life had been devoted to surviving in the bleak world that the Council had sculpted through brutality and tyranny. He had never pondered the idea of some greater power allowing the establishment of the Council. His thoughts were interrupted by Maya as she exclaimed, "Look! It's Ristiven."

As they crested a hill, they were all able to see the capital city. It was an intimidating citadel to say the least. The capital was surrounded by a massive, thick wall thirty feet tall at its shortest. Ronan guessed that at least six chariots could be ridden side by side along the top rampart. This validated the folklore that the city had never been infiltrated by an invading army.

Within the walls, the buildings were all tall, multileveled structures. Ronan noticed that the architecture amongst the buildings progressed in sophistication throughout the cityscape. The buildings in close proximity to the walls were more modest structures made out of wood, and finally cut stones. As the buildings radiated toward the center, they became more audacious in make and design. Some had golden domes on the roofs while others were made of marble.

At the very heart of the city was a white marble castle structure with one tall thick tower stretching up several hundred feet, dwarfing every other building with its unmatched spiraling block masonry. The top of the tower was crowned with an immense dodecahedron structure made from triangular pieces of tinted glass. Ronan had heard stories of this tower from the Carpenters. It was known as the Watch Tower, the official meeting location of the Council.

As far as Ronan was aware, the Council was only in the Watch Tower when a conclave had been called. Normally the Legislators of the Council did their own thing, in their own undisclosed locations; running the various branches set under them.

Ronan turned his attention to the nearest gate. He saw that the gate was guarded by twelve soldiers, six on either side of the solid wooden doors. The soldiers were checking every person and cart that came through. Ronan did not know if the number of guards was normal or if it was due to the recent prison break last night. Did the Legion expect Leo to run directly into the heart of the Zwellian Empire immediately after escaping Dur Volgen?

Ronan was surprised when Vallia began to lead them away from the main gate. She walked toward the northeast, maintaining a few hundred feet from the wall.

She instructed everyone, "When I give the signal, everyone take shelter behind those bushes." They all nodded. She watched the wall in the distance.

Ronan saw the distant guards pacing along the top. Just as two guards passed behind a large Legion flag, Vallia hissed, "Now!"

He ducked and followed her to the bushes.

"Okay," Vallia explained, "These bushes will get us within about fifty feet of the wall if they haven't removed any shrubs. It's been a while since I had to use this entrance. From there we can sprint to the wall and be completely out of sight. That will take us to the main aqueduct. We can enter the city through a secret gate that Mr. Kemin requisitioned years ago."

Ronan raised his eyebrows. He had known his boss had a far reach of influence. He had not realized that the man had the ability to requisition a passage into the heavily fortified capital city.

Maya asked, "How did this Mr. Kemin manage that?"

Vallia glared at her for asking the question.

Leo responded, "He bought the company that was repairing the aqueduct. That was back when I was still talking to my father."

Vallia shot Leo with an equally malicious look. "Regardless of how he did it," she continued, "it exists. We just need to get up against that wall without being spotted."

Maya nodded. Her eyes flashed purple. "Leave that up to me. I can tell you when we have an opening."

Ronan crouched in the bushes next to everyone else as they edged forward. He felt his pulse rise as he anticipated running to the wall. While the bushes had in fact gotten them close there was still the ominous open section they had to cover. If they were spotted, he was certain that the patrolling guards would not hesitate to fill them full of bolts and leave their bodies for the vultures.

Maya stared up at the patrols. "Why are there so many soldiers here? I can't see any gaps in their pattern. We may need some sort of distraction."

Ronan also watched the guards. He determined that it wouldn't matter if there were ten guards if they were all looking up at the sky. "Leave that to me," Ronan said with a grin as he ruminated on a solution. He gave a small whistle with his two fingers, hoping it was loud enough. The soft popping sound confirmed Sabastian had heard him. The bird landed on his shoulder. Ronan stroked the bird's plumage and pointed to one of the Legion soldiers. "Distract."

Sabastian took off with a flap of his wings and soared up to the top of the wall. With his talons glinting in the sun, he snatched the helmet right off one of the patrolling guard's heads. The guard shouted and launched a crossbow bolt at Sabastian, who swerved to the left and avoided the missile with grace. Sabastian elegantly circled in the air and angled back down flying back at the helmetless man. Another crossbow bolt whizzed by his outstretched wing, narrowly missing. Ronan bit his lip at the close call. Sabastian flapped back up and then dove back down. Just before he was about to collide with the helmetless guard, Sabastian vanished in a puff of mist. The helmet he had been holding continued flying forward and collided with the man's face.

As the helmet hit, Maya whispered, "Now!" They all took off at a sprint for the wall until they reached the cool stone. Ronan could hear the swearing of the guard high above. A wave of relief flooded over him as he saw the parapet above obscure them. They were safe and out of sight.

Vallia quietly led the group along the wall until they reached the aqueduct. It was a large wooden structure that reached out from the wall to the edge of the nearby North River. The wood smelt of rot and mold.

To Ronan, this area did not look like any more of an entrance than the stone wall they leaned against. He watched in fascination as Vallia crouched down and felt the base of the aqueduct where wooden supports had been placed to hold the weight. Vallia grabbed something and with a precise yank, opened a secret door. Ronan couldn't believe it. The support was built entirely for show. Underneath the aqueduct was a low tunnel, about the width of a wheelbarrow and just tall enough for a hunched grown man. Ronan looked at the others and registered the same surprise he felt.

The four entered the hole without a word. Vallia closed the door behind them. The dank tunnel ran all the way through the thick wall and emerged on the other side, exiting out of a disheveled wooden shed pressed up against the inner wall. Ronan was captivated by the brilliance of this. It was very similar to the tunnel out of Shem. However Shem was not known to be impenetrable.

Ronan whistled again and Sabastian popped next to him. He flew down onto Ronan's arm. "Who's a smart boy? Who is going to get some crackers? Thank you, buddy."

Leo looked at him with surprise. "Is that your Ether hawk? How did you train him?"

Ronan replied, "With Arkeen's help. His name is Sabastian."

"Who else could tame an Ether hawk but my brother." Leo cooed and reached out to let the bird see his hand. Sabastian inspected it. He playfully nipped at Leo's fingers and then allowed him to stroke his head. The image of Arkeen doing the exact same thing flashed in Ronan's mind. A cold emptiness developed in his chest. The desire to complete their mission accompanied it. Ronan needed to know about his powers. He needed to be able to prevent what happened to Arkeen from happening to others.

"Where do we find the Arch Archivist?" Vallia asked impatiently. She was clearly all business and had no time for bird enthusiasm.

"He lives in his laboratory. It is in the shadow of the Watch Tower. We need to get to the center of the city."

Vallia nodded in recognition. She threw Leo a scarf from her bag. "Hide your stupid wanted face. Stay casual and stick to the back alleys. If we get separated, we will meet at the Golden Axe. It is a small dive bar on the west end of the city. Dandrick owns the property. If you get captured by the guards..." She paused. "Well don't get captured by the guards."

Ronan swallowed at this. It was nerve racking being in the middle of the hornets' nest of the Legion.

They moved forward through mud covered alleys, crossing red brick streets when necessary. Leo led the group. Ronan presumed Leo did know the exact path, but he had a good sense of direction. The progress was maddeningly slow going but Ronan knew it was safer than walking straight through the city. There were many haggard beggars and grimy children playing in the side streets. It was depressing to see the impoverished conditions of the people close to the wall. Even in the capital city, the people were struggling.

As they walked Ronan registered several notice boards with posters and announcements. He was disheartened to see his own illustrated face looking back at him from a wall of criminals. There was also an odd exhilaration at being recognized as a "most wanted" fugitive. Especially when he saw the amount of silver offered for his capture. For a brief second, he contemplated a plan to have the party turn him. They could receive the reward and then break him out of the Council's detainment. If they split the reward, they would be set for life. Then reality of the present danger fizzled the idea. He put up his hood and put his head down.

Eventually, the four came to the mouth of an alley, maybe two blocks from the outside east wall of the marble castle that supported the Watch Tower. A sun-faded, white, wooden building stood before them. The building had a large glass window on the second floor that faced the main thoroughfare. Ronan could see the sky reflected in the tinted glass. The roof was adorned with several curious long metal structures that Ronan presumed to be strange lightning rods. Several of the structures had components that spun in the wind. Ronan did not see any posted guard.

"That is his lab," Leo confirmed. "I think it would be most wise if I approach alone. Osmodius is skittish during his best times. I think if we all approached, he would have the guards on us before we were able to tantalize him with the idea of two Eidolon."

Vallia frowned at Leo. "Oh, is that the wisest plan? You go in by yourself and what? Sell us out to this guy? Was the whole story about him betraying you just a ruse?"

Leo looked at her with a sad expression on his face. "I understand you do not trust me. I have to remind you that you are the ones who asked me to come here. I have no kinship with the Archivist."

"How do we know you are not going to go in there and kill the man?" Vallia challenged. "You said this man betrayed you and sent you to prison. If it were me, I would have a vendetta against him."

191

Leo gave her a small smile. "I have no desire to kill this man. My mother's people have a teaching of wisdom. It goes like this, 'Everyone should be quick to listen, slow to speak and slow to become angry, because human anger does not produce the righteousness that Light desires.'"

Ronan contemplated the statement. He thought that anger could accomplish a lot. A few days ago, he had watched Vallia's anger decapitate an UN'kra warrior. But Ronan didn't know about anger producing righteousness.

Vallia did not seem enlightened by the phrase.

Leo restated, "I will not kill this man. I have enough blood on my hands as it is. But if you do not trust me, by all means come with me. But it should not be more than the two of us. I would strongly advise Ronan and Maya to stay out here until we can convince Osmodius that you are Eidolon. We will give you a signal from the window when it is safe to come in."

"What if he attacks you or something?" Maya asked.

Vallia gave a small laugh as if the idea was humorous. "Then I will fill him full of arrows and Ronan can talk to his spirit."

Ronan thought of the wanted posters again. He did not like the idea of being left outside. Hadn't he proven himself when he came up with a plan to save Leo? He wanted to protest the idea, but he also didn't want to blow this opportunity to meet with the Archivist. "Yeah, we can stay out here," he said flatly. "But don't take too long. I'm a wanted fugitive and Maya is not exactly on good terms with the Legion. If guards come down this road, we are toast."

Vallia did not seem to be thrilled with her role either, but it seemed to be more palatable than letting Leo go in alone. She nodded at Ronan's remark. Then she turned and walked across the street with Leo following her. Ronan watched her knock aggressively on the door.

After a few seconds, he saw a small, older Ethalladros man answer. Half of his face was made of ice and his frosty breath puffed out as he spoke. Ronan guessed he was a butler by the way he dressed. The old man looked startled when he saw Leo. Ronan wondered what their last encounter had been like. He watched the three proceed to have a small conversation. It drove him crazy not being able to hear. The old man seemed reluctant as he shook his head. Ronan was about to leave the ally they were hiding in when the old man stepped aside, admitting Vallia and Leo inside. The door closed behind them, leaving the street empty again.

Chapter 26

Ronan felt anxious at being left behind. He watched the window with a sense of longing and anticipation, waiting for Leo to appear. Occasionally, he glanced up and down the street to confirm no guards were coming. He swore for a second that he saw someone on a nearby roof but checked again and saw nothing.

Just when Ronan was getting antsy, Maya voiced, "I feel like something has gone wrong. How long does it take to tell an old book worm that he has visitors. I think we need to get inside."

Ronan replied, "I was thinking the same thing. Do we knock and hope the butler answers?"

Maya shook her head. "If something has happened, the butler will not just open the door. We need to get in without him. Do you know how to pick a lock?"

Ronan shrugged. He had in fact been through lock picking classes with the Carpenters, however the skill was not one that he had mastered. The last tumbler never seemed to stick for him, or he would apply too much pressure and snap the pick. He looked around for another solution.

He activated his powers and looked at Arkeen. *"Can you walk through walls?"*

Arkeen gave the question some thought. *"Not sure,"* he said. *"Never tried."* He then tried to walk through the wall Ronan had been leaning against. He smacked into the solid brick. *"Guess not."*

"What about squeezing through the gap under a door? Are you stuck in this form or are you able to flatten?"

Arkeen smiled. *"I like the way you think. Let me try."* The spirit floated across the road to the wooden door of the laboratory. His form became less distinct. Ronan watched as the green fire pressed up against the door and dissipated. The flames licked around the door, vanishing between the gaps on the sides and bottom. Ronan concentrated on the spirit behind the door and solidified just his hands. A second later, the door swung open.

Ronan heard Arkeen in his head, *"Welcome, master Riviera. Please, do come inside."*

Ronan smiled at his friend. Then he looked up and down the street. The coast was clear, so he quickly walked across, followed by Maya.

They entered into a narrow hallway covered in dark wood paneling. It was sparsely decorated with one small table and a vase of dead flowers. The hallway continued before them. A staircase to the right ascended to the second level. Ronan quietly drew his sword. Maya produced two small throwing daggers and gripped them, one in each fist.

Ronan slowly crept up the stairs. At the top of the landing was a larger double door with brass handles. Muffled voices could be heard coming through the door. He quietly put his ear to the door to listen. He heard Leo give a shout and then heard glass shatter.

Ronan gave Maya a concerned look. Then he tried the doorknob. It was unlocked. He put up three fingers. Maya nodded. Ronan put one finger down. He focused and solidified both Arkeen and Ta Rhe into their featureless crystalline forms. He put the second finger down. Maya tightened her grip on her daggers and breathed slowly, her eyes flashing purple. Ronan put the last finger down and he wrenched open the door.

As the door flew open, Ronan saw a brief glimpse of a laboratory before identifying his friends. Confusion crossed over Ronan as he saw Leo sitting in a wooden chair at an ornate desk. Vallia was standing behind him. Neither seemed to be in peril. But as the door opened, Vallia spun around, drawn bow in hand. Without hesitation, Vallia launched an arrow at the intruders. The arrow was headed straight for Ronan. A glint of steel flashed in front of him. It took Ronan a second to realize that he had not in fact been shot but rather Maya had thrown a knife defecting the arrow away.

His heart raced and his mind struggled to make sense of the scene.

Vallia recognized Ronan and anger crossed over her face. Leo, who was slower on the uptake, turned around and looked at Ronan. Ronan now saw an older man sitting on the other side of the desk, facing the door.

The man sat up straight in his high-backed chair. He was dressed in a forest green overcoat. His hair was long, silver, and pulled back into a ponytail. He wore golden spectacles that magnified his gray eyes.

The man surveyed the intruders before him. A smile grew across his face. "Come in, little Eidolon. Welcome to my laboratory."

Ronan dropped his powers and watched the solid green spirits fade away. He looked at Vallia and then at Leo.

Vallia hissed through gritted teeth, "I thought you were going to wait outside."

Ronan's heart was still pounding from the adrenaline, but his mind was foggy. "You were taking a long… We thought something… I heard glass break," he stammered.

Leo frowned at him. "It takes a minute to negotiate. As for the glass, the Archivists cat jumped onto my lap and startled me. I dropped my glass of water. You didn't need to barge in here."

The silver haired man stood up and walked around the desk. "Please Leo, do not be so rude. Of course they are welcome. Come, come. Have a seat. My name is Arch Archivist Nimin Osmodius. Today is truly a special day."

Ronan looked at Maya. She shrugged and put her remaining dagger back into her belt. He sheathed his sword. They both walked forward and sat one on either side of Leo. Ronan could feel Vallia's glare as he looked around the room.

The laboratory had a tall ceiling that he had to crane his neck to see. The space was well lit thanks to the large window that took up the majority of one wall. The other three walls were covered with bookcases and black chalk boards. Symbols and formulas were chalked all over boards along with drawings of creatures and people. Had it not been for the awkward tension, Ronan would have thoroughly enjoyed exploring the space. He saw at several large wooden tables, atop which were glass vials, crystals, and fascinating instruments that Ronan did not recognize or understand.

Osmodius took his seat across from them and stared intently at Ronan and Maya.

"The Eidolon of Death and the Eidolon of Kinetic Energy. What a pleasure." He looked at Ronan, "I see you travel with spirits. Already protecting yourself. Very smart." He then looked at Maya. "And how you deflected that arrow out of midair. Stunning. Truly stunning. What magnificent specimens you are."

Ronan did not like how Osmodius talked to them as if he were admiring pieces of art.

Osmodius gave his four visitors a wide smile. Ronan noticed several gold teeth twinkling in his mouth. "We were just discussing the terms in which I will be giving you any information. I am glad you joined when you did. I dislike repeating myself."

"Terms?" Roan asked after no one else said anything.

"Yes, my green-eyed friend. Terms." Osmodius continued to smile. "My dear friend Leo here has told me that you are interested in gaining information about the Eidolon. You have come to the right place. I have more information about the Eidolon than anyone else in Celcus. But this information is not free." The Archivist stared at Ronan.

Ronan averted his gaze pretending to examine the leather mat atop the desk. "And what is it that you are wanting in exchange for the information," he asked.

"See, that is where I found a bit of resistance from your friends. I am hoping that your craving for an understanding will result in a more productive exchange."

Vallia cut in, "He wants to study you two. He wants to make you test subjects and do experiments on you. We told him that is not an option."

Ronan raised his eyebrows. He was expecting the Archivist to ask for their help in stealing something or possibly for them to go and acquire something rare for his research. He desperately wanted to know about his powers, but he was not willing to be subjected to various experiments. Maya shared a similar look of distaste to the idea.

"Do not worry," Osmodius said. "I will not be cutting you up and looking at your insides. Although, if you were to die for any reason, I would fully expect all rights to do an autopsy. But at least while you are currently breathing, I don't plan to open you up."

Vallia gave a forced laugh. "We told you, you're insane. There is no way we are going to let you do anything to them. Ronan, I say we just take him out now and you can force his spirit to talk to you about what you want to know."

Ronan did not want to be an experiment. He also did not want to kill this man. The man who held so much knowledge about who he was and about where his power came from.

"What about a different trade?" Ronan asked hopefully. "Something other than experimentation."

Osmodius' eyes twinkled at Ronan. "You are not going to be able to buy me off if that is what you are thinking. No amount of money is worth the knowledge that I could gain from the two of you."

Ronan contemplated his other options. This man was an Arch Archivist. He thrived off knowledge. What if they could give him knowledge he did not have. Ronan cursed the lack of information he had to share. 'If only I had gotten any information from the stupid Kitmazi.' This thought of the Ether being led his mind to think of the map.

"What if I could give you more information than you will ever be able to get by running your tests on us?" He proposed.

Osmodius chuckled at the idea. "Your friends have already let it slip that you are new to your powers. I know you do not possess any knowledge that I don't already know."

Ronan sat up straight in his chair. Rallying as much confidence as he could, he said, "No, I don't know more than you. But I do have a map that is marked with a specific location that relates to the Eidolon and their power."

At this, Osmodius narrowed his eyes. "Are you telling me you have a map to a bridge point? Where would a child who just discovered their powers obtain such an item?"

Ronan took a chance. He rolled up his sleeve to show off the Kitmazi's glowing symbol on his arm and the surrounding burnt skin. "I made a deal with a Kitmazi. I am guessing you recognize this mark?"

Osmodius stared at the symbol with awe. "Show me the map!" He demanded.

Ronan smiled as he acknowledged the position of power he was in. "Let's negotiate first. If my map happened to have two different bridge points marked, what would that get us in terms of information?" Ronan had no idea what a bridge point was. Maybe it was the symbols displayed on the map. Maybe they were something completely different. Regardless, he knew that Osmodius valued them, whatever they were. Mr. Kemin had taught Ronan that the easiest way to sell anything was to let the customer convince themselves the item was valuable. That was his plan.

Ronan watched the Archivist process the offer. He saw a ferocity in the older man's eyes as he spoke. Based on his eagerness to see the map and his interest in himself and Maya, he assumed the Eidolon was a kind of obsession to Osmodius.

"If you have a map with two bridge points on it, I will tell you about the history of the Eidolon as well as where your powers come from."

Ronan felt the excitement rise in his chest. He put on a thinking face and looked at Maya.

Her natural affinity for lying kicked in. She frowned at Ronan. "A history lesson? That's it? I think the old geezer misheard you, Ronan. Let me say it again. The map has two bridge points. Two uncharted, previously unrecorded bridge points. Think of the academic possibilities of one. Let alone two? Woo wee, you better be willing to stretch your offer beyond a dusty old history lesson or we'll find another scholar to make a deal with.

Ronan forced himself not to grin at her brilliance. He watched Osmodius' smile twitch at the corner of his mouth. "I will also share with you a section from the journal of the first Eidolon of Death."

Ronan turned his head so fast that he kinked his neck. This definitely caught Osmodius' eye. The older man grinned. Ronan cursed himself for failing to hide his excitement.

Osmodius extended his hand to shake Ronan's. "Do we have a deal?"

Ronan flashed back to the Kitmazi, extending out her hand to make him a deal. His back twinged with phantom pain as he remembered the Justice's spirit that had demolished the wagon using Ronan's body. But this was different. Osmodius was just a human man with intimate knowledge that Ronan needed. If the Justice was not going to divulge information, he needed to get it somehow. If a spirit did come, this time he would be more prepared.

Ronan looked back at Vallia, hoping to get some support from her. She refused to look at him. Ronan looked at Leo, who gave the Archivist a somber look. Maya was the only one to offer any guidance as she nodded in affirmation.

Ronan extended his hand and shook with the Arch Archivist.

"It's a deal."

Chapter 27

Osmodius gestured at the desk. "The map first."

Ronan produced the sealed tube from his backpack and popped the top off. He carefully slid the map out and then gently laid it out on the desk, facing Osmodius.

The Archivist stared at the map in wonder. He mumbled as his fingers circled the goblet with the legs. Then he tapped the triangle with the moon phases on top. He began to look at other details of the map. "This is genuine," he said to himself more than anyone else. He leaned closer to the map to inspect further. Ronan pulled the map off the desk and rolled it up. He placed it back into its tube and closed the cap.

"You get it back when you fulfill your end of the bargain," Ronan instructed with as much authority as he could.

Osmodius gave Ronan a crazed look but calmed his emotions. "Fair enough," he said with a strained smile. "How much do you know? Where do you want me to begin?"

Ronan looked to Maya for assistance in what to ask for. Maya said, "Let's start from the beginning and see if your understanding matches ours. We'll stop you if there is a discrepancy."

Ronan didn't know what he would have done without her. Her duplicitous mind was a true wonder to behold. She made it seem like they knew what they were doing.

Osmodius considered her statement. "I suppose the best place to start is the rudimentary information. I'll try and keep it simple for you." He stood up and walked over one of the chalk boards on the wall. He slid up one board that seemed to be covered in sea charts to reveal a clean board.

Osmodius began to write and lecture. "Some two hundred years ago, the first Eidolon lived and ruled. They seemingly appeared out of nowhere, and quickly used their powers to smash all opposition and conquer the area we now know as the Zwellian Empire. Despite the fact that there were only seven of them, no nation or tribe could stop them or their advances. The seven individuals claimed land for themselves through brutality and bloodshed. If people did not bow before them, they would lay broken at their feet."

Ronan had not expected the 'rudimentary information' to be so full of violence. Leo had made it seem like the Eidolon of the past were great heroes. Not bloodthirsty conquerors. Was this really Ronan's legacy to live up to?

Osmodius continued, "The Eidolon split up the land into territories that neighbored each other. Naturally this led to conflict. In an attempt to maintain peace between their regions, they formed a unified council to address the issues of the land. They would come together to discuss solutions and cooperate with each other when necessary. This was the creation of the first High Council. Are you tracking with me so far?"

Ronan frowned at the question. Osmodius was obviously implying that they were simple and slow. He glanced at Maya. She seemed to not have noticed the insult. Her face showed her a deep contemplation of the information they had just received.

Ronan asked, "Why is this information not common knowledge?"

Ronan felt his ears grow warm from annoyance when Osmodius sighed at the question, as if it was taxing on him to answer. "The proceeding High Councils have all but erased the existence of the Eidolon in an effort to protect their position of power. They obviously figured that the populace would not approve of the foundation of the empire being built with blood-stained hands. So they changed the history books and outlawed talking about the Eidolon until everyone had all but forgotten."

Ronan's annoyance transformed into anger. Of course this was the history of the Council. Bloody hands built an empire that was now soaked through with crimson. Drowning in a sea of blood of the destitute populace. Ronan would bet every silver he owned that more people had died from starvation, poverty, or imperial malevolence than were ever killed by the Eidolon. Conquest of land was one brutal reality. However, Ronan could understand that to a point. But life sentences into labor camps for tax evasion declared against the impoverished... Public whippings and brandings for petty offenses... Requisition of ludicrous percentages of harvests to feed a bloody war... These acts were a completely different, darker beast. This was the enemy that Ronan faced. This is why Ronan needed to become more powerful. To stop the masked monsters who masqueraded around as benevolent leaders.

"What happened to the Eidolon?" Maya asked, startling Ronan out of his thoughts.

"They all died of course," Osmodius said irritably. "Most of them killed each other off. Their powers were unparalleled but so was their pride and arrogance. It does not seem like much has changed in that regard." He gave Ronan a distinct look.

Ronan gripped the arms of his chair turning his knuckles white. This old man didn't know anything about him. He was not some loose cannon, power hungry, tyrant. If it were not for the information that Osmodius possessed, Ronan would have half a mind to have his spirits beat the gold teeth out of this man's head.

Osmodius began writing names and tiles on the board. "The original council divided over issues of policies, power, and control. Some fought each other, while others took what they had and fled. For example, Quazilandon, also known as The Anchor, took his capital city and lifted it into the sky. He was the Eidolon of Gravity. It seemed to be a solid plan until Ritovenda, known as The Great Wall, assassinated him over a lover's quarrel. She was the Eidolon of Rest. So much power wasted on such petty things." Osmodius shook his head as if he couldn't understand how a lover's quarrel could lead to such a response. "When she stabbed him in the back, the city came crashing to the ground with her in it. You may know it today as the Thembrala Marshes."

Ronan looked at the names and titles that Osmodius was writing as he talked. Osmodius continued explaining how the other Eidolon perished but Ronan did not listen. He was too captivated by the seven names and their titles. Titles which stretched his imagination with gripping fantasies.

Ritovenda- (AKA The Great Wall)- Eidolon of Rest
 Quazilandon- (AKA The Anchor)- Eidolon of Gravity
 Sanessa- (AKA The Siren) Eidolon of Resonance
 Hom- (AKA The Ungraspable) Eidolon of Resistance
 Elergiah- (AKA The Future Walker) Eidolon of Kinetic Energy
 Finra- (AKA The Dust Bringer) Eidolon of Entropy
 Nizomotus- (AKA The Lord of the Dead) Eidolon of Death

The last two names were the ones that stood out to Ronan. He stared at the name, 'The Dust Bringer,' remembering Maya's description of her vision. The masked man had turned an entire army to dust. This was who Ronan was supposedly destined to fight. Not only an Eidolon with a vast familiarity of his powers, but a Legislator of War with the entire Zwellian Legion under his command. Then he looked at the last name. Nizomotus - lord of the dead. Ronan was by no means a lord over the dead. Calling himself the prince of the dead felt laughable at this point. Sure, he had grown in his powers but he was still no match for a man who could wither trees and dissolve blades. Someone powerful enough to unleash the Ether from its primordial restraints. What were a few spirits going to do against that kind of power? What he needed was the power to control an army of spirits like the legends of the old Eidolon of Death. He bit his tongue. There was no use focusing on that right now. What he needed at the moment was to learn more about this Eidolon of Entropy.

Suddenly he refocused on Osmodius in a moment of clarification. This repulsive old man worked for the Council. Surely, he knew one of them was an Eidolon.

"One of the Legislators of war is the Eidolon of Entropy. Did you know that?" he blurted out, hoping to catch the Archivist off guard to see how he reacted.

Osmodius stopped his lecture he had been giving with wide eyes of concern at the question.

"How do you…" He stopped himself before he revealed more, but it was too late.

Ronan had gotten the information he had wanted. He gave Vallia a triumphant smile but found her eyes wide and skin pale. Maya had a similar expression but she quickly took a breath and hid her concern. Ronan felt his smile fade as anxious shivers crept up his back. Had he given too much away?

Osmodius narrowed his eyes at Ronan. "It would be suicide for me to tell you anything about my employers. Especially the Legislator you speak of. My discussions with him are not part of this negotiation. Although I am very curious how you know about him and his gifts."

Ronan swallowed hard, cursing his own stupidity. Of course the leading expert on planar interactions would know that his boss was an Eidolon. Why had he even questioned that? Osmodius could very well be in on Legislator's plan with the Ether Scar. He had probably been the one that the Eidolon of Entropy had sought out for information about the Scar. If the Archivist knew they were trying to stop the Eidolon of Entropy and his plans, He would surely summon every guard in the city. He needed to distract the Archivist.

"I saw one of the Legislators of War when I was in Camp Latis." Maya cut in. "He made a visit to inspect the camp. I was hiding in some bushes and saw him disintegrate one of the laborers who had been suspected of leading a revolt against the camp guards. He didn't know I was there. At the time, I thought he was an Ethalladros but once my powers activated, I remembered his yellow eyes and made the connection."

For a moment, Ronan was upset at Maya that she had not told him this when she had told him of her time in the camp. Then he realized she was laying down a masterful lie to distract the Arch Archivist. Ronan could have kissed her for her saving his neck. This odd thought came at a terribly awkward time and Ronan immediately chastised himself for thinking it.

He shoved down the notion and hoped his cheeks had not turned red.

Osmodius narrowed his eyes at Maya.

She shrugged in an unbelievably nonchalant way. "We are looking for information about the Eidolon and wanted to ask you about the Legislator. We thought we could maybe meet him."

At this Osmodius genuinely laughed and visibly relaxed. "If you thought that I would introduce you to the Legislator of War, you must be drunk. Although, legends say the old Eidolon of Kinetic Energy was driven mad by visions she had of the future. Have you had any visions, my dear?"

Ronan was amazed. Maya had not only distracted Osmodius, but she had gotten him to divulge this information so effortlessly. She was so smooth and perceptive about people. She knew just what to say and how to say it. He wondered if this trait was a residual effect of her powers or if a difficult life had just necessitated an adeptness for deception.

"Let's finish our current business and then we can negotiate the discussion of our powers in more depth." Maya directed. "Where do the Eidolon get their powers from? How did they become so strong?"

"And how do we know your information is authentic?" Ronan challenge.

Osmodius' gray eyes flashed to Ronan. "I have spent my entire life researching planar interactions and their impact on our world. That is how I know what I know. This is my life's ambition. You came to me for information and now you question my legitimacy? What I am telling you is the most accurate historical information that I know. Most of which comes straight from the journal of Nizomotus."

Ronan truly did not like the Archivist. He understood why Leo called him a snake. Between him having some level of involvement with the Legislator of War's plan and his general demeanor, the man was dangerous. All he wanted was to hear about the journal of Nizomotus and the origin of his powers and he would be content to never speak to the man again. But in the moment, he had to keep a level head. He had already put their negotiation at risk. Challenging the Archivist was not the way to get information. Ronan desperately wanted to see the journal of Nizomotus. He again fantasized about the idea of commanding an army of spirits against the Eidolon of

Entropy. That was the type of information he needed to know. But if he was going to get his eyes on that journal, he knew he had to be careful with showing his desperation. If Osmodius recognized any additional indication of how badly he wanted the journal, Ronan would lose all negotiating power.

"Where did you get the Journal?" Ronan asked as casually as he could.

Osmodius smiled, a wide wicked grin. Ronan got the impression that the Archivist could sense his desire. "Where I got it does not matter for the purposes of this deal. What matters is that I have it. Let me tell you, the information that I have learned from it about the Nether has been truly invaluable."

"What is the Nether?" Ronan asked far too quickly for it to be nonchalant.

Osmodius sneered at the question. "Aren't you just the cutest baby Eidolon? The Nether is where your powers come from." He turned back to the chalk board and raised the chalk. At that moment, the building shook slightly. Ronan noticed ripples in the colorful liquids that occupied various glass containers on the nearby desk of liquid. Osmodius lowered the chalk and looked around. The building shook again. Osmodius glanced around with an evident caginess.

Ronan didn't have the patience for this old man's games. Why was he stalling? It was just a carriage or something driving down the road outside. "What is the Nether?" he asked again more forcefully.

Osmodius took a moment and then shrugged, turning back to the board.

Without warning, the entire wall with the large glass window exploded outward, toward the street. Glass and wood showered the thoroughfare below and dust filled the laboratory.

Ronan's ears were ringing from the deafening noise of splintering wood and shattering glass. He haphazardly ducked below the desk placing his back against the wood. He peeked around a corner of the desk to look at the hole where the window had been moments before. Through the haze of falling shrapnel, he saw a lone figure floating in the middle of the vast opening.

As Ronan blinked away the dust, he was able to make out that the figure was a man. A behemoth of a man covered in black studded armor. He had

207

a grizzled black beard that hung to the middle of his chest. Then Ronan saw his eyes. They were glowing with a flaming bright blue energy.

Chapter 28

The man floated forward, hovering just above the broken wooden floor. Ronan could see that he was wearing golden greaves that went up to the bottom of his knees. As the man softly landed on the floor, his bulk became more apparent. He was easily six and a half feet tall and an excess of three hundred pounds of well-toned muscle.

The figure called out to the destroyed room, "I am here to detain the Eidolon of Death and collect the bounty placed upon him. The High Council has demanded his capture." He brandished a wanted poster with Ronan's face sketched onto it. "Anyone who stands in my way will be treated as hostile and dealt with by me as such."

Vallia stood up from behind the table that she had flipped to create makeshift cover. With her bow drawn back, she said in a strong, clear voice, "I don't know who you think you are, but you are not taking the Eidolon of Death anywhere. I am going to give you until the count of three to float your fancy boots back out of that hole and glide away from this."

Osmodius, while cowering in the corner, choked out, "Take this outside you savages. This is a place of knowledge, not a bar for brawling." His pleas fell on deaf ears.

The floating man smiled at Vallia and opened his arms as if to receive a hug. "Give me your best shot, Ether scum."

Vallia's eyes narrowed. "One," she called out.

Maya jumped up onto a table, her eyes glowing purple.

"Two…"

209

Leo stood in a fighting stance, ready to open a rift.

Ronan flashed on his powers to solidify Arkeen and Ta Rhe. As he did so he saw the intruder's orange life energy mixed with bright blue flames. It dawned on Ronan who this man must be. The way his life energy mixed with the blue that matched his eyes, just like Maya's energy was mixed with purple. Between that and the fact he had floated into the room...This man must be the new Eidolon of Gravity. This realization came to him a second too late.

"Three," Vallia called out.

She released her arrow. It soared straight for the man's chest, then suddenly changed course, and drastically decelerated. When it was only a foot away, the arrow's speed had been reduced to a causal drift. The projectile slowly floated through the air and began to orbit the man's chest. He looked at Vallia and smiled.

"Nice try, Ethalladros. But your puny arrows don't stand a chance against me. Gravity is my servant. It bows to my every whim. Let me show you." He flexed his fingers. Vallia flew straight up and smacked into the ceiling high above, where she stayed suspended, sprawled flat against the wooden slats of the roof. The Eidolon of Gravity then caught sight of Ronan. "There you are spirit boy. If you come with me quietly, I won't have to kill all your friends."

"Fat chance," Maya called out, before Ronan could say anything. She jumped from her table to another where she scooped up several glass beakers full of different liquids and threw them at the Eidolon. These too began to orbit around the man.

Osmodius called out, "Those are proprietary!"

Maya ignored the Archivist. "That's a cool trick," she jested. "Let me show you mine." She whipped three daggers through the air and shattered the three beakers causing the chemicals to mix midair. They began to sizzle and smoke.

The Eidolon of Gravity tilted his head and said, "Another Eidolon? Wonder what the Council will pay for you and spirit boy." He flexed his hand again and Maya too went flying up into the air, but after seeing Vallia's ascent, she seemed to have been expecting it. With the grace of a cat, falling in reverse, Maya landed on a wooden rafter and began running along the beam toward the Eidolon of Gravity. Ronan watched with exhilaration as she did a cartwheel off the board and launched herself back down, her foot extended toward the man's head. The smoking chemicals must have obscured his view as he did not see her assault coming. Her foot connected with his chin with crack. Ronan gave a silent cheer; however it died as he saw Maya's success had been limited.

She did not descend to the ground. Rather, she floated there, foot extended next to his head. The Eidolon of Gravity smiled and reached up, grabbing her ankle. He held her up like she was made of paper. Then he threw her toward the back wall. Ronan winced as she fell horizontally through the air and smacked into a blackboard. The Eidolon of Gravity used his powers to crush her against the wall. She kept struggling to push herself up and kept falling back against the wall.

Ronan watched her struggle in shock. This Eidolon was powerful and knew what he was doing. Ronan needed to find a weak point in the man's defenses. He saw Leo look at Maya and then back to the Eidolon.

"What's your party trick?" The Eidolon of Gravity challenged Leo. "Or are you going to let me take the Eidolon of Death without a fight?"

Leo shook his head. "My party trick, as you say, is a faith in Light. The Light has delivered me from my darkness and from my imprisonment. The Light will surely deliver me from you. Please friend, have wisdom and choose peace. Your aggression and greed are sins not worth dying over."

The Eidolon of Gravity laughed. "Maybe you didn't see how many zeros they put on the spirit boys wanted posters. Trust me, the money is well worth the hassle."

Leo sighed and said, "I guess we are doing this the hard way." He proceeded to put his fingers together and then slowly pull them apart. Ronan saw Leo's life energy once again coalesce in his hands. A shimmering tear in midair opened just next to the Eidolon of Gravity. The Eidolon looked surprised before a wave of glowing magma fell sideways out of the rift and collided with an invisible domed barrier that surrounded the

Eidolon. Ronan flashed back to a similar dome he had created around himself in the Legion infirmary. *'Some kind of gravity shield,'* Ronan wondered.

The large man braced himself against the flow of magma that spilled from the rift. He held out both his hands trying to prevent the torrent of lava. He was able to hold it back but not stop it completely. The molten rock began to divide around the Eidolon in a semicircle. Ronan, from his angle, saw that while the lava was not touching him, he had no ability to stop the heat from affecting him. Beads of sweat appeared on his brow. A concerned look crossed his face. The lava was pooling on the ground around the man. The wood that the lava touched scorched and burst into flame at the extreme heat.

Then Ronan watched as the magma connected with the floating chemicals Maya had thrown. When combined with the extreme heat, some kind of violent reaction occurred. The floating liquids exploded. Molten rock was launched all over the laboratory. It splattered over wooden tables and caught books and papers on fire. Vallia fell from the ceiling and Maya slid off the wall. The Eidolon seemed to have been dazed by the explosion and lost his concentration.

Osmodius cried, "My research!" and left his hiding place. He ran to try and put out the flames.

The Eidolon of Gravity, in his daze, saw Osmodius running and clearly thought he was another attacker. He clapped his hands together and several large heavy tables and chairs were all sucked toward the Archivist as he became the center of gravity in the room. The furniture collided with the older man, and he fell to the ground bleeding from his head.

"No!" Ronan called out. Osmodius had the knowledge needed. He had not told them what the Nether was. Ronan was filled with a sudden desperation. He had to know what other information the man had. In his anger, he pointed at the Eidolon of Gravity and commanded, **"Stop him."**

The solidified spirits sprinted straight at the Eidolon. The large man saw the two solid spirits running at him. He shook his head while he put his hands forward and pulled them into his chest. The two spirits went from running at the man to slipping and sliding past him. They flew out the opening in the wall and collided with the building across the street. As the spirits smashed into the stonework, Ronan felt like he himself had taken the hit. He lost focus on solidifying them and fell to his knees. He remembered at this moment when Arkeen had told him that if they were made solid while in the air, the spirits would fall. *'They must be affected by gravity when they are solid'*, he told himself. If he didn't stop this man, his friends and Osmodius would surely die. "Get back up here," he thought to Arkeen and Ta Rhe. *"I need you."*

Vallia angrily stood up from the floor and limped forward.

The Eidolon of Gravity saw Vallia's slow approach and called out, "You're stubborn, aren't you? Ready for round two?"

Vallia took in a large breath as if to retort. Instead of speaking, she braced her stance and punched her fists forward. A constant blast of air blew from her fists. The Eidolon of Gravity had to brace himself against the gail. He began to slide back toward the opening in the wall. He braced himself and his eyes flashed blue. He seemed to be using his powers to help ground himself. Vallia's wind kicked up dust, flaming papers, and soot from the now burning furniture that all began to swirl around the man. Ronan realized what she was doing. She was not trying to push him out of the window. She was filling his gravitational shield with debris and dust to obscure his vision.

Leo seemed to also grasp her intent as he created another rift that spewed more molten rock. The lava began to encase the man again.

The Eidolon of Gravity pushed his hands forward and Vallia and Leo went skidding backwards. They both maintained their assaults on the man.

Ronan saw the spirits of Arkeen and Ta Rhe float back through the opening. *"Hang behind him. Don't let him see you,"* he instructed mentally. If he could solidify them at just the right moment... He looked over at Maya. She had gotten to her feet and was eagerly watching Vallia and Leo. She held three more daggers in her hand, ready to throw at a moment's notice. Ronan instructed the spirits in his mind, *"He will have to drop that gravity shield any second. Get ready to hold his arms and give Maya a clear shot."*

Just as Ronan thought this, the Eidolon of Gravity gave out a scream of anger and a blast of force erupted from him. Tables went flying, flaming chairs smashed against the walls. The beams of the rafters cracked above them causing more debris to fall. Ronan and his friends were all violently thrown back. The man stood at the center of the ring of destruction. Lava steamed around him, and flames rose on all sides.

This was clearly not the easy snatch and grab he had anticipated. Now his anger rose off him in waves. He held up his hand, palm up, and Leo, Vallia, and Maya all floated into the air. He then lifted Ronan into the air with his other hand. Maya, Leo, and Vallia all clutched their chests and screamed and thrashed in pain. Ronan, while floating as if weightless, watched in horror.

The Eidolon of Gravity looked at Ronan and said, "Eidolon of Death, I'm going to make you watch as I crush your friends' rib cages in. You'll get to see as spirits leave their collapsed bodies. Then you and I are going straight to the Watch Tower. And there is nothing you can do about it." He had not noticed the spirits floating just behind him. He had been too focused on the living adversaries.

Ronan was boiling with anger at the man. He yelled, "**Hold him!**" as he solidified the spirits again. Each one grabbed one of the man's wrists and wrenched his arms apart. Ronan grabbed his ruby dagger from belt and threw it at the large man. He was nowhere near as accurate as Maya, but he got close enough for the knife to get caught up in the gravitational shield. Just as it began to orbit the man, Ronan commanded, "**End him!**"

Arkeen's spirit grabbed the floating dagger out of the air and plunged it into the man's chest. His eyes grew wide and he looked down at the blade, then at Arkeen, then to Ronan. He coughed up blood and his eyes stopped glowing blue. Vallia, Leo, Maya, all fell to the ground in heaps. Ronan landed and ran to them. Their life energies were all still burning though they were faint.

The Eidolon of Gravity went limp, held up by the two solid spirits that supported him. They dropped him and he fell to the ground.

214

Chapter 29

Everything seemed to slow down, including the dust falling through the air. Ronan felt his heartbeat in his ears. He stared at the body of the Eidolon that he had just put to death. At his command, Arkeen had stabbed the knife into the man's chest. Like a soldier following the command of a general. No hesitation. No questioning whether it was right. Unequivocal obedience.

A dark thought arose in Ronan's mind. He had total control of these spirits. If Ronan commanded it, Arkeen would have killed an innocent person just as fast as he killed this attacker.

This dark thought made Ronan realize he had the power to be judge, jury, and executioner. *'Then again, technically everyone has that power'*, he tried to reassure himself. This did little to fill the empty feeling inside of him. He knew that anyone in the world could choose to commit murder and be an executioner. But very few people had the authority to command an executioner to murder for them without hesitation.

As Ronan stared at the body, he saw green flames begin to emerge. The spirit of the Eidolon rose up to float before him. All traces of the blue energy were gone. Only green spirit energy remained. Ronan contemplated the implication of this. Death was truly an equalizer. No matter what power one had when they lived, that power did not transition with them into death.

The spirit looked at Ronan and then back at his body. His voice penetrated Ronan's mind. *"You have bested me, Eidolon of Death. Now it seems that I am to join the ranks of your spirit army."* He nodded his head toward Arkeen and

Ta Rhe. *"Is that my punishment for trying to capture you?"*

Ronan did not want another spirit following him. But he needed to talk to this Eidolon, and he figured he did not have much time now. He was amazed that the town guards were not already breaking down the laboratory door.

Ronan thought to the spirit, *"This could have ended differently. But you made your choice when you attacked my friends. I didn't want to kill you, but I had no choice. I need you to come with me. I have too many questions to let you go just yet."*

Ronan closed his eyes and felt the presence of the spirit. He wanted to tether this spirit to himself. The first time he had done this, it was an accident, so he was not confident about recreating the effect. He guessed it had something to do with his own spirit. Focusing on himself he could sense his own life energy.

The sensation was odd, as if he had a second layer of skin that was fluctuating and floating three inches above his own flesh. As he examined his own orange energy, he registered two thin, string-like extensions that ran to Arkeen and Ta Rhe. This must be the tethers. That made sense why he had felt the impact when they had slammed into the building. His life energy was directly connected with theirs. Focusing on the Eidolon's spirit energy, he willed his own life essence to make a connection. A stretching of his energy accompanied his concentration, and he felt a new, thin string latch onto the Eidolon and tighten, tethering him to Ronan's life force. Ronan examined the bond and wondered how many spirits he could have connected to him. Did it affect the spirits? Did it affect him? When the spirits had taken damage, he had felt it too. Was he putting himself at more risk?

Ta Rhe floated forward and asked, *"When is it that you will be done with us exactly? To me, it appears that your heart is set on gaining power. Building an army like your predecessor."* He pointed to the chalk board where Osmodius had written the names.

Ronan looked at the chalkboard. The name of Nizomotus was on the bottom of the list. He felt guilty as he remembered the spirits could hear his thoughts and probably feel his desires. He didn't know what to say.

Just then he felt a hand on his shoulder that shook him. He took the opportunity to drop his powers and look to his left. Vallia was next to him holding his shoulder. She looked rough but determined.

"We need to go. Listen."

Ronan perked his ears up and registered a high pitch alternating sound that seemed to turn on and off. It took him a second to recognize the noise as a warning bell. The city guards had been alerted just as he assumed. He gathered his bearings and looked around the room.

Maya was standing by the opening in the wall keeping watch on the street below. Leo was surveying the laboratory that was now covered in patches of fire and smoldering wood. Osmodius was lying at Leo's feet. Ronan registered that the old man was still breathing. The attack had not taken his life as well. This was good. Ronan still needed him.

Maya called out, "I have a carriage incoming. Does not look like a guard chariot. Might be our best chance to get out of here."

Vallia asked, "Think you can secure it?"

Maya cracked her neck and nodded. "Yeah, give me a moment. You guys better get ready to jump on." Her eyes flashed purple and she jumped out of the opening. Several shouts followed as Maya presumably landed on the back of the carriage. More cries followed with several loud thuds. Then there was silence.

Vallia moved to the window as if to follow Maya. She looked back at Ronan. "What are you doing? We need to go!"

"I need to take him with us." He pointed at Osmodius.

"What?" Vallia hissed in disbelief.

"I need to know about the journal of Nizomotus. He has read it. It has probably already gone up in smoke. I didn't come here to get a history lesson. I came to learn about my power. Osmodius is the only one who has the information that I need. If we don't take him with us, this mission will have been pointless."

Vallia was about to protest, but Leo interjected. "Vallia, we don't have time. I'll grab the Archivist. We'll take the snake with us." He bent down

217

and lifted the older man's body onto his broad shoulders and proceeded to the vast hole in the wall. "Now are you coming?" he asked Ronan.

Ronan nodded, having no desire to stay here, and be arrested or killed by the guards. He walked to the edge of the opening in the wall. A black covered carriage with large wooden wheels stood directly below the window. He saw three finely dressed individuals slumped against the building's base. He desperately hoped they were just knocked out. Maya sat at the helm, holding the reigns of the four gray horses that were all linked together.

Vallia jumped down and sat in the passenger seat. Leo dropped down with a heavy thud and then jumped to the ground. He offloaded Osmodius into the carriage and then jumped onto the back. They all looked up at Ronan. He gave one look over his shoulder at the body of the Eidolon and the fire that was now consuming the laboratory. Knowing he had ended this man's life, he also jumped onto the carriage with a heavy heart.

Maya wasted no time whipping the reigns and launching the carriage forward. As they rattled down the cobblestone street, Ronan felt a sudden surge of pain in his arm. The same burning sensation he had experienced when he had woken that morning. Ronan looked down and was terrified to see flames appear in his hand. With a flash, the Kitmazi's ruby dagger appeared, grasped in his fingers. He had completely forgotten to grab the dagger from the corpse of the Eidolon of Gravity's chest.

"If you don't have the dagger, you can't uphold your end of the bargain," Vallia told him as she looked over her shoulder at his cry of pain. Ronan nodded as he cursed himself for this ignorance.

Vallia said, "I saw your burnt spot when you showed the Archivist. Has it been getting worse?" Ronan nodded but offered no other information. He looked at the dagger that had suddenly materialized in his hand. He wanted nothing more than to chuck it into the gutter, although it appeared that the dagger would not so easily be left behind. He wondered how much larger the burn on his arm had grown as punishment for forgetting the blade.

They rode in silence all the way to the north city gate. There was an unspoken mutual agreement amongst the four that they needed to leave the city. Setting one building on fire in the heart of the capital seemed to be as good an indicator as any that they needed to leave. They passed through the gate without so much as a second glance. News of the fire thankfully had not reached the gates yet. Ronan was grateful that the Legion were pompous enough to think their security checks coming into the city were good enough that they didn't have to check people who left.

After about one hour, Maya pulled the carriage off to the side of the road into an open field. She turned in her seat and asked, "What other crimes are we looking to commit?" She started ticking them off on her fingers, "We have successfully broken a man out of prison. We did a beautiful job of arson and destruction of government property. We have kidnapped a government official. Murdered a man, shout out to Ronan for killing that prick before he crushed us by the way. Oh, and now we have stolen a carriage."

Vallia stood up to straighten her legs. She looked at Ronan. "Yeah, for once I have to agree with Miss Foresight here. When does this end Ronan?"

Ronan felt his face flush with anger. "Do you think that I wanted to be attacked by the Eidolon of Gravity? Do you think I wanted to kill him? I just wanted information."

Vallia scowled. "Now that you have that, can we stop this mad quest? Oh wait, no, we can't because you insisted on bringing the Archivist with us."

"He barely told us anything," Ronan protested. "I wasn't looking for a list of names of a bunch of dead people. I wanted to know where my powers came from. He was about to tell us when the Eidolon attacked. We just need a little more time with him."

At this, Maya apparently gathered the argument was only going to get worse. She walked up to Leo and grabbed him by the arm. "Come on. Help me with the horses."

He gave her a confused look not understanding her hint. She pulled on his arm, and he begrudgingly followed. They walked off to the front of the carriage away from Vallia and Ronan.

Vallia watched them go. She had been inflating as she did when she argued, her hair blowing more aggressively in its own breeze. But she let out a breath and gave Ronan a sad look. "Ronan when we started this mission, I thought you were just a confused kid wanting to understand a traumatic event in your life. You had just lost your best friend, and trust me, I know how that feels. But now you are possessed by this idea of gaining knowledge. It has overwhelmed you. You are angry and conceited. You don't even appear to be phased by the fact you just killed a man. That is a heavy weight to carry on your shoulders."

Ronan had been preparing for an all-out shouting match. He had not expected this drastic change in Vallia's demeanor. His retort shriveled up in his throat.

Vallia stated in a quiet voice, "Maybe death doesn't bother you as much now you have this whole prince of the dead thing figured out. Is that it?"

Ronan was baffled by this assumption. What did she mean that death didn't bother him? He was devastated by Arkeen's death. He was about to make a sarcastic remark when he gave her words a second thought.

Did death have as much of an impact on him? Yes, he had been devastated by the loss of Arkeen, until he realized that Arkeen was not gone. Not gone like he was to everyone else anyway. To Ronan, his fun-loving, joke-cracking friend was still with him. Guilt filled Ronan's thoughts. He realized how it must look to Vallia. How cold he must seem. It hadn't even been long enough to plan a proper funeral for most people. Here he was acting like nothing was wrong. He knew in his heart that the time for secrets was over. He couldn't keep lying to her. She deserved better than that.

"I'm guessing you noticed the two spirits that I kicked down the laboratory door with. And that helped us stop the Eidolon of Gravity?"

Vallia nodded. "Yeah, that was another thing I was going to ask about. What is up with those? Are you important enough now that you need bodyguards?"

He took a steadying breath and said, "Those two spirits have been with me from the time my powers activated."

Vallia gave him a raised eyebrow but said nothing.

Ronan continued, "I told you that I asked Arkeen and the UN'kra to help me fight the giant. What I didn't realize at the time was that I did something when I made that request. Something I didn't understand how I had done it. I linked their spirits with mine. The two spirits that you saw today..." he felt his stomach tighten. "Those spirits are Arkeen and the UN'kra. They have been following me since they helped me kill the giant." He watched her face as she made out what he had said. "I didn't know what I was doing at the..."

"You enslaved Arkeen and his murderer into your servitude!" Vallia shouted with a gale of wind erupting from her. "And you are still dragging them around with you to protect your pathetic hide?"

Ronan immediately regretted not telling Vallia upfront about Arkeen Ta Rhe. Vallia's hair was now blowing as intensely as he had ever seen it. Vallia grabbed Ronan by his shirt and lifted him into the air. He felt his powers attempt to activate to protect him, but he restrained them.

Vallia had tears in her eyes. "You let him go right now, or I will beat you with my bare hands until your spirit floats off with his."

Still being held up by her, Ronan said, "Vallia, you of all people must understand why I haven't let him go. I was given a second chance to hold onto him. If I let him go it will be like losing him twice. I can't do that." These words poured from Ronan's mouth without him even contemplating them, as if this idea had been dwelling inside of Ronan, waiting to escape. Ronan realized that this had been a fear that had been lying dormant in his mind. He stared down at Vallia.

Vallia stared back up at him, her knuckles turning white in his balled-up shirt in her hand as she held him up. She blinked several times, her breaths heavy and quick.

Ronan took the opportunity. "When I first tethered him to myself, it was an accident. I didn't mean to do it. I will set him free, but I can't right now. Not yet. I need him in my life for just a little longer."

Vallia said in an almost incomprehensible whisper, "Do you think I was ready to let him go? We were about to be married." Her voice began to rise. "He was my world and then he was snatched away from me. So don't you tell me that you can't let him go. That is just the way life is. Sometimes you have to let people go. Every part of that hurts, but there is nothing we can do about it. You know as well as I do that this isn't what he would have wanted. He would have hated being shackled to you, unable to control himself. He was a free spirit, Ronan. So set him free." A single tear rolled down her cheek. "I can't stand by you. Not if you are going to be this power hungry, selfish child." She dropped him and he fell backward landing on the ground. She turned and started to walk away.

Ronan processed her words as she walked away. Of course she was right. Arkeen had hated to be cooped up or confined. But Arkeen didn't seem too upset, Ronan tried to justify. His conscience countered that thought by asking: Was that because Ronan had forced Arkeen into this? He shook his head. Ronan couldn't worry about any of that. Vallia was walking away from the carriage. She was leaving and he couldn't lose another friend. Not right now. He needed her. Needed her help with his mission.

Ronan then felt a prod in the back of his mind. He activated his powers to see Arkeen floating over him. *"Let me talk to her,"* he projected.

"I don't know how," Ronan stated hopelessly.

"Do what you did in the Infirmary with the other spirits. Bring me over to your side."

A tiny glimmer of hope rose in Ronan's chest. He called to Vallia, "Wait! He wants to talk to you."

Vallia stopped dead in her tracks. She didn't move or turn around. She stood still as a statue. "You mean you want him to speak to me?" she said coldly.

"No, he asked me to talk to you. By his own free will he wants to speak to you."

"How do I know it is him and not you?" she asked, still not facing him.

"Talk to him. You will know if it is me or if it is truly him. There is no way I could fake his personality. Not to you." Vallia remained motionless. Ronan knew what she was currently processing. As a child, if someone, even one of the bullies from the orphanage, had promised him an opportunity to speak with his mother again, or his brother, how could he have refused?

Vallia continued to stand still so Ronan focused on Arkeen's energy and

222

its separation from his own. Ronan knew he did not want to solidify Arkeen. Rather he needed to bring him fully to the Prime Plane and not in the in-between space he currently occupied. Trying to recall what had happened in the infirmary, Ronan breathed in and willed the energy to cross the planar barrier.

He knew it was working the second he attempted the planar transfer. It felt like pulling a boot that had sunk deep into the mud. At first Arkee's spirit resisted, but it slowly transitioned.

Vallia, who had glanced over her shoulder, slowly turned around. She was staring at the space where Arkeen was currently floating. Ronan was not sure what it looked like to her, but to him, Arkeen was shrinking and expanding, rippling into the Prime Plane. Within seconds of performing this feat, Ronan recognized that this action took a lot of effort. Much more than he had anticipated.

Condensing the energy into a solid mass took a lot less concentration. This was different. It felt like the difference between a rock sinking into a river and pulling a floating wooden plank under the water and holding it there.

Vallia stared forward, looking at the apparition. The spirit stopped shimmering. Ronan was hoping the sucking feeling would go away, but it remained. Something in his mind told him that what he was doing was forbidden by the laws of nature. He didn't know what that meant, but he definitely knew it. He then realized that he could not do this for very long. But he would attempt to hold this transfer as long as he physically could for Vallia.

Vallia cautiously approached Arkeen. She instinctively reached up to touch his face. Her hand passed through his incorporeal head.

She jumped back in surprise. She looked at Ronan and back at Arkeen. He assumed that Arkeen had just made the mental connection to talk to her. This was the same reaction he had when this first had happened to him. Ronan could not hear the conversation between the two. He was grateful for their privacy and also didn't think he could have listened to the conversation and maintained this apparition.

Ronan was straining through a massive headache that seemed to be building at the front of his skull. He felt grateful that Arkeen and Vallia were able to communicate and braced himself against the ground to try and give them the time they needed. He told himself he was doing this for Vallia. Even if she didn't stay, he owed her this much. He looked up at her face. Tears freely flowed down her cheeks. She smiled and nodded at Arkeen.

The silent conversation continued. Arkeen looked at Ronan. The spirit extended its hand, palm out, facing Vallia. Ronan understood. Arkeen was asking for Vallia's trust. This was his way of reassuring her when he was living. If Vallia had been hesitant about something or didn't have faith in Arkeen's knowledge or abilities, he would extend his hand and ask her to trust him.

Ronan gritted his teeth and focused on Arkeen's hand, solidifying it up to the wrist. Immediately spots started appearing in Ronan vision from the mental strain.

Vallia slowly reached out and interlocked her fingers with Arkeen's. She smiled.

Ronan's vision was becoming more and more dark around the edges. He could not do this much longer. Spirits obviously could not exist like this in the Prime Plane.

He reluctantly released the energy that was making Arkeen appear to Vallia. Color ebbed back into Ronan's vision. He saw their two hands woven together. One fading away leaving the other, outstretched, fingers limp, holding nothing. Empty.

Ronan's heart wrenched as he watched. *'If she can let him go, how can I keep holding onto him?'* Ronan questioned.

Vallia fell to her knees looking up at the empty air. Ronan laid back onto the ground, looking up at the sky. They both wept.

Chapter 30

Once Ronan felt the wave of emotion begin to subside, he sat up. For the first time, he took in the field they had parked next to. It appeared to be free from the disturbance of man. In the light of the fading sun, Ronan saw wildflowers growing in abundance in a full spectrum of colors. He looked back to the carriage. The horses were munching on the grass at their leisure. Maya and Leo were sitting at the helm chatting. They noticed he was looking at them and they jumped off the wagon.

Maya looked at Vallia, "So, are you staying?"

Vallia's face had returned to her normal passive scowl.

"For now." she said.

Maya nodded her head. "Good. Thought you were out for a minute there. I was worried that we were going to have to find another prodigious windy Ethalladros with flowing hair and a kick butt attitude." She gave Vallia a sly smile. Ronan could have sworn that Vallia gave her a small smile back.

Ronan was pleasantly surprised and bewildered at the positive exchange between the two women. He was happy Maya was also wanting to keep Vallia around.

"So, are we heading up to the scar in this stolen wagon?" Maya asked Ronan.

Ronan felt like he was in no position to decide where they were to go. He was surprised to see the other three looking at him, expectantly. It then registered that they were all there because of him. Now they all looked at him as if he had the answers. He knew what he wanted to do. The question was whether it was the best course of action. Not knowing what else to say,

225

he looked back at the carriage. "Well, we did not get all the information from Osmodius that we came for. Before we make any decisions about what is next, I think we need to have another chat with our Archivist friend."

No one raised any objections to Ronan's claim. They followed him as walked over to the carriage and opened the door. The interior was finely decorated. Red velvet, buttoned seats faced forward and backward. Osmodius lay sprawled half on the floor, half on the seat. Ronan hopped in and with Leo's help, lifted the Archivist into a sitting position. He looked at Maya and Vallia. "Come in, I don't think we will want to have this conversation out in the open. He will probably try to escape."

Maya grimaced, "Do we have to? It smells like bad cologne."

Vallia showed her shared displeasure at the idea as she suggested, "We can talk out here and if he runs, it gives me an excuse to shoot him."

With neither complaint winning Ronan over, they both gave in, clambered into the carriage, and closed the door.

Ronan sat across from Osmodius next to Vallia. Maya and Leo sat on either side of the Archivist.

"Vallia, can you wake him up?" Ronan asked.

Vallia put her hand in front of Osmodius' face and expelled a blast of air. The older man woke up with a start. He took in the surrounding people and immediately started screaming, "My laboratory, you destroyed my laboratory!" He looked around and realized he was in a small space with all exits blocked. "Help! I have been kidnapped! Please, someone help!"

Ronan pulled out his ruby knife and pointed it at Osmodius, who stopped shouting immediately.

"I don't know how the Eidolon of Gravity found us. I will figure that out later. Right now, I want to finish our negotiations. You were about to tell us about the Nether. What is the Nether?" He spoke in a calm, steady voice, never breaking eye contact with the Archivist.

Osmodius weighed his situation. His eyes darted to everyone in the carriage and back to Ronan's knife. "You destroyed my laboratory. Years of hard work and research and you destroyed it. Now you expect me to give you more information?"

"We did not destroy your lab. The Eidolon of Gravity did that," Ronan stated.

Osmodius gave a sharp laugh. "Yes, but only because you had a bounty on your head. Now the research about the Nether is all gone because of you."

Ronan frowned as the bounty was brought back up. He was definitely over the infamy of his face on wanted posters.

"Now, that is not true, is it? If anything, we saved the most important part of that research. You. I know you're getting up there in years, but something tells me that your mind is just as sharp as it ever was. Which means that you have all the research stored up there." He touched the tip of his knife to Osmodius' forehead. "You are going to tell us what you know about the Nether."

Osmodius' eyes dashed around looking for help. Then something flashed across his face. "The Bridge Point. The one up north."

Ronan narrowed his eyes. "What about it?"

"You will take me to the Bridge Point, or I will not tell you anything about the Nether."

Maya chuckled. "You are not exactly in a position to negotiate. It's five to one."

Osmodius' eyes lit up at this. "I may be outnumbered, but I hold all the power in this negotiation. I am the one that has read the Journal of Nizomotus, which I am guessing has gone up in flames due to your antics. I am the only one who has the information you need."

Ronan glowered at the man. He felt a deep loathing as he recognized that the Archivist was right. He was the only one who could give him the information that he needed. What other options did Ronan have?

'I could always kill him and force him to tell me about the journal,' Ronan thought to himself. This idea came to Ronan as a small nagging at the back of his mind. 'One more spirit to add to the ranks.'

Ronan shook his head. Where had that come from? He couldn't think like that. Vallia had been right. He couldn't let this new desire for power remove his conscience and morals. This man was alive, and Ronan could

227

not simply ignore that fact and kill him just because he wanted something the Archivist had. Spirits were more than his playthings. They were the result of a living person dying.

Ronan looked at everyone else in the cramped space. He could tell that none of them were pleased with the idea of taking the Archivist with them.

Maya spoke up first. "You are just looking for a chance to escape. The second you get your opportunity; you are going to slither away and report us to the nearest guards you can find."

Ronan inspected Osmodius, "I am not too worried about that. He wants to see the Bridge Point just as much as I do. He is not going to pass up the opportunity to have an armed escort with a map to the Bridge Point. I would be more concerned with him trying to kill us once we got there. Anyway, if he does try to run, I have no problem sending a spirit after him." He looked directly into Osmodius' eyes. "You should know that they don't eat or sleep. If I tell them to hunt you down, they will never stop searching for you until you are dead. Then they will bring your spirit back to me and I will get the information I need."

This statement was entirely a bluff. Ronan had no inclination if he could actually sick a spirit on someone. He was taking a chance in hopes to scare Osmodius. Staring into his eyes, Ronan thought he saw the slightest twitch of his face at the threat. Ronan smiled and said, "At the Bridge Point, you will tell us everything about the Nether, or you will die. Is that clear?"

Osmodius looked as if he would like nothing better to strangle Ronan but knew he would never win in a physical altercation. "I will tell you everything I know about the Nether, once we reach the Bridge Point." Ronan could feel the anger in his voice.

Ronan nodded, mostly satisfied. "We'll camp here tonight. Osmodius, you will sleep in the carriage. We will be blocking the doors so don't try and escape."

"You're just going to leave me in here? With no food or water? What if I need to pee in the middle of the night?" The Archivist sounded like he had never been treated so poorly.

Ronan sheathed his ruby knife and pulled his backpack off. He pulled out some dried meat and threw it at the archivist along with his own water skin. "If you need to pee, knock on the door. I'll have one of my spirits escort you to the tree line."

Osmodius gave him a disgusted look. "Like some common animal?"

Ronan shook his head in disbelief at this man that had clearly lived a pampered life in the heart of the Empire. What luxuries he must have known if he thought relieving himself in the woods was dehumanizing. He scooched out of the carriage followed by the other three. He found some springy weeds and tied them around the handles of the carriage doors to keep them shut. When he was done, he noticed everyone was watching him.

"What?" he asked.

Vallia said sullenly, "So we are keeping prisoners now? I guess that is on par for you now. And I guess we are going to the Bridge Point?"

Ronan flushed at the statement. Not wanting to start another all-out shouting match, he elected to ignore the prisoners comment. He defended himself, "Ten minutes ago you were all looking at me to decide what to do next. I assumed you wanted me to make a decision. Look, what other option do we have? If we let him go now, we'll have Legionnaires encircling our camp by midnight. The Bridge Point is about a three-day journey. We'll suffer through hauling the Archivist up there and then figure out what to do with him. Do you have a better idea?" He didn't love the plan, but he disliked being questioned about his decision even more. If they were going to look to him for direction, they better not complain when he gave it.

Everyone looked at each other and then back to Ronan. No one said anything.

Ronan shrugged and gestured to the ground. "If no one has a better idea, let's make camp."

They silently obliged. Maya and Vallia set up their tents while Leo took long grass and began weaving it together. His deft hands worked quickly and within the hour, he had made a decent sized mat of weeds and grass. Ronan started a fire and they all sat around it. Leo, who seemed the least bothered by their current situation, eventually began asking about Mr.

Kemin, Blue, and some other long-standing Carpenters. Vallia gave him short responses, not willing to divulge too much information. After that conversation died, everyone decided it was time to sleep.

Ronan offered to take the first watch. Despite his tired eyes, sore body, anxious energy, and emotional exhaustion, he couldn't sleep. Not until he interrogated the spirit of the Eidolon of Gravity.

Chapter 31

Ronan activated his connection to the Nether. He didn't know what that meant but that is where Osmodius said his powers came from. With the limited information he had gotten, and based on the Archivist's main focus of planar research, he assumed the Nether was another plane like the Ether and Prime Plane. While this basic information was something that Ronan could have guessed, it was nice to put a name to the plane if nothing else.

Three spirits floated before him in the black and white world. Arkeen, Ta Rhe, and the Eidolon of Gravity. Ronan focused on the Eidolon.

"Who are you?" his mind directed at the figure of green flame.

"My name is Mishkawl. I was the Eidolon of Gravity. Before you killed me, I was the best bounty hunter in the Zwellian Empire."

Ronan thought back to his time at the Carpenters. He had heard of Mishkawl. While Mr. Kemin did not condone the practice of bounty hunting (mostly because the Council were the main group placing bounties), he occasionally needed someone found. Ronan remembered one occasion where Mr. Kemin had requested a falcon be sent to Mishkawl because of his ability to trap slippery targets. With his powers of gravity manipulation, this made sense.

"How did you get your powers?" Ronan asked.

Mishkawl replied, *"I used to help my father in collecting bounties. He was small-time, mostly petty criminal. While chasing two Ethalladros, we were tricked into a trap. We ran into an alleyway where several of their gang were waiting. They forced me to the ground and made me watch as they killed my father. Something awakened in me at that moment. A primal rage. I crushed in the chests of the men holding me with just a thought. Then I sent the men who had killed my father flying into the air. They begged for mercy, but gravity is not a forgiving force. It affects everyone the same."*

"But how did you learn about who you were? Did you hear a voice when you dreamt?" Ronan was growing excited. He finally had someone to talk to about the voice from his dreams.

"Do you mean the Justice?"

"So, you have one too? Tell me about your Justice."

Mishkawl replied, *"That's just what she called herself. The Justice of Gravity."*

"She?" Ronan asked, surprised.

"Yeah, I would occasionally hear the voice of a woman in my dreams. She was the one who told me who I was and what I could become. She explained to me that she had chosen me as her champion and gave me my influence over the force of gravity. That it was a great honor to be chosen as an Eidolon. Then she gave me some tasks to train me and make me stronger."

Upon hearing this, Ronan felt his annoyance against his benefactor grow. He had received zero training. The Justice of Death had been cryptic and mysterious but had obviously not thought that Ronan was worth putting in the effort to give him proper training. Ronan made a mental note to challenge the Justice on this point.

"What sort of tasks would she give you? Was there a larger goal behind them?" Ronan inquired.

"She would tell me to destroy this building or take out that person. I never asked about a greater goal. I did what I was told. I was her champion. Her instrument in this world. She told me to jump, and I asked how high."

"You just blindly took commands from her. You never questioned why?" Ronan found this hard to believe. He felt like he had questioned everything the Justice of Death had told him. Maybe he was just a bad champion, but he didn't trust the Justice. There was just too much secrecy and too many unknowns.

Mishkawl shook his spectral head. *"The Justice gave me unbelievable powers. I was not about to anger her and ignore her commands. Why would I risk what I was given? Think about it. The closest thing to an Eidolon is an Ethalladros.*

232

Their connection to the Ether is limited to the control of one element. They are not able to change how that element functions at its core. But us Eidolon, we can change the laws of reality. We can rewrite them for our own benefit. I could tell gravity to stop and start. I could lift buildings into the air and walk on ceilings and walls like they were flat ground. No one could stand against me. That was until you killed me, I suppose. Now I am just a spirit, stuck under your control. I should have listened to the stories about you. I thought they were all exaggerations."

Ronan felt a level of guilt rising up inside himself. He suppressed it by reminding himself that Mishkawl had been trying to bring him into the Council to collect a bounty. Then he registered what the spirit had just said.

"Stories?" Ronan asked curiously, a level of excitement blossoming in his chest at the mention others were talking about his deeds.

The spirit's laugh reverberated through Ronan's mind. *"You really are dense if you thought your antics had gone unnoticed. You left quite a path of destruction behind you. Word reached my ears about you pretty quickly after you attacked that infirmary."*

Ronan countered, *"I didn't attack the infirmary! That was an accident."*

Mishkawl shrugged, *"Whatever helps you sleep at night, spirit man. The good old Council definitely saw it as an attack. That's why they hired me to hunt you down. With a price tag as pretty as they were offering, how could I refuse. I have been following you for a few days. You were all the buzz in the Apollymi camp, killing that old woman and everything. The guards on the south bridge reported a deformed version of you when I inquired. Then there was the prison. After I saw the destruction and learned that half of the guards and all the Ether Crafters were killed, I started wondering if I really wanted to tangle with you. The Justice had told me that you were the Eidolon of Death. I should have recognized your blood lust and left you alone."*

Ronan couldn't believe his ears. *'Blood lust? I don't have a blood lust.'* His mind was racing with everything the Eidolon had said. Ronan hadn't killed an old woman in the Apollymi camp. Then, with a sickening dread, he realized what his interaction with the Kitmazi must have looked like to an outsider. The caravan had been destroyed after he had been attacked by the spirit, and the old woman had vanished after they had made a deal. Someone must have witnessed him leaving the wagon and concluded he murdered the old woman. Then his mind jumped to the prison. He had not been the one who had killed all those guards. That had been Leo's Ether Crafting. Not that it mattered. He wondered how far these stories had spread.

Ronan sat on the ground and put his face in his hands. He didn't know what to think. How had things escalated so drastically in only a few days? He thought about what Vallia had said about him changing. Was there truth behind her words? Nizomotus' legacy rose in his mind as he thought about the stories Mishkawl had talked about. People of old must have whispered about the lord of the dead with much fear and trembling. He must have been a terrifying fantom of a man with his armies of the dead following in his wake. That wasn't the sort of persona that Ronan wanted to be linked to, was it? If people were going to look up to him, he didn't want it to be from a position of cowering.

"*Mate, don't be so hard on yourself,*" Arkeen's voice penetrated Ronan's mind.

Raising his head, he looked at Arkeen. His stomach felt like it was filled with cold stones. "*Do you think I have changed?*" Ronan mentally demanded more harshly than he had intended.

"*Everyone changes at some point. Change is not always a bad thing.*"

"*What do you mean by 'not always?' What are you saying?*" Ronan's temper flared up. "*Let me guess, you are siding with Vallia. Of course you are. You don't think I have my priorities straight, do you? Is that what you two talked about when I generously gave you a chance to say goodbye?*"

"*What are you talking about, mate? We didn't...*"

Ronan cut him off. "*Look! I know what my priorities are. And maybe I have changed. I'm not the helpless kid you took under your wing when I joined the Carpenters. I am stronger. More powerful. I am the Prince of the Dead, for crying out loud. I have been blessed with these unbelievable powers. Am I just supposed to not use them? Ignore my connection to the Nether and hope my Justice stops haunting my dreams. I'm on a path that I don't want to be on but what other choice do I have?"*

Ta Rhe floated forward. *"Young Ronan, calm your anxious heart. You speak of paths and choices. You worry that you are lost to the woes of this world. I will confirm, you are not too far gone down a path that you cannot come back from. In my spare time as I have been tethered to you, I have constructed a poem in your tongue about this very thing. I wish to share it with you now in hopes that it will aid you in your distress.*

There is a long, solitary path that winds far out of site.
Darkness fully envelopes this trail except at the end there is Light.
No one has ever mapped this path for there is no page that can contain it.
It winds deep through valley passes and over mountain summit.
There is nothing easy about this trail and by no means is it safe.
At every twist and turn, countless challenges await.
Travelers are beckoned off the thoroughfare to wonder in the darkness.
But when their feet leave the road, they find the shadows heartless.
So, when the world seems dark and hopelessness presses in.
Turn your eyes back to the path of the Light, the one that is sovereign.

Ronan blinked several times, not knowing what to say. He scowled as the words' meaning seemed to hang just out of reach. This only made him more upset. What was Ta Rhe trying to say about the path he was on? Was he implying that Ronan was lost in darkness? Where did this spirit get the nerve to give him life advice? Ronan didn't need some dead warrior to tell him that he was lost. But he didn't have a choice in the matter. That is what none of the spirits understood. No one understood. This is where he was and he was doing his best to not die, let alone make better choices.

"I can't do this right now. I am not done with you," he pointed at Mishkawl, *"But I will deal with you later."* He dropped his connection to the Nether and sat in the darkness, listening to the sounds of the night that had been muffled by his powers. He tried to clear his mind but all he could do was think about the last line of the poem. *'So, when the world seems dark and hopelessness presses in. Turn your eyes back to the path of the Light, the one that is sovereign.'*

What did that mean?

Lost in his thoughts, Ronan jumped when he heard Maya's voice from behind him.

"You good?"

"What! Oh hey, yeah, I'm fine," he stammered. He didn't want to talk about it right now.

She gave him a quizzical look, clearly seeing through his fake contentment. "I can take the watch if you want. I checked the carriage and Osmodius was curled up on the floor. I'll make sure he stays there."

Ronan nodded and stood up. "Thanks, that would be great." He began walking to his tent.

"You sure you're good?"

"Yeah, I just need some sleep," he said and turned away before she could press more. He crawled into his tent and laid down, falling asleep almost instantly.

Ronan found himself in Osmodius' laboratory. He was kneeling on the ground: cradling Mishkawl's body which had the ruby knife sticking out of his chest. Mishkawl was blinking up at Ronan. He asked, "Why did you stab me? We could have been friends. Why did you kill me?"

Ronan was trying to stop the bleeding. He kept apologizing but he could not stop the flow of crimson gushing out. The Eidolon of Gravity breathed his last breath and closed his eyes. Ronan beat on his chest saying "Don't die. You can't die!" He knew there was no hope. He had killed this man.

Then Mishkawl's eyes opened. His blue eyes were now entirely black. Mishkawl's body spoke but it was not his voice. It was the deep voice of the Justice of Death.

"Eidolon. Why do you mourn the dead? By this man's death, you grew in strength."

Ronan shoved the body off of himself and scrambled back on the floor.

The body of the dead Eidolon pushed itself off of the ground. He looked at Ronan with empty voids. **"Today you killed a man. Because of this, you feel sorrow and regret. I do not understand. Was this man not trying to capture and or kill you?"**

"That does not mean that I wanted him dead. I didn't have another

236

option."

"**Oh, there were other options. However, you chose the option that saved your life and gave you another servant to command. This was the option that most accurately matched who you are. The Eidolon of Death.**"

Ronan shook his head. That was not true. "My friends would have died if I had not killed Mishkawl."

The deep voice chortled from the body of the dead Eidolon. "**You can lie to yourself all you want, but you do not fool me. I didn't see you let the spirit depart in peace. You actively tethered him to yourself. You embraced your abilities. Your new nature. I am proud to see it. Soon you will realize that a spirit is no more than a tool to be utilized while you have access to it.**"

Ronan stood up from the ground and challenged, "You are the Justice of Death. You are not a human. You don't see any value in human life."

"**No, I am no human. Far from it. However, you are incorrect in your assumption that I do not see value in life. You will find that I highly value human lives.**"

"Yeah, sure you do."

The Justice contorted the dream Mishkawl's face into a wide smile. "**Spirits are wonderful instruments to master. However, our control of them is but a blip in time. Our influence over them is regulated and allotted during the instance between death and the beyond. You and I may hold a spirit in your world, but we cannot stop their inevitable transition into judgment. My sentence as Justice of Death, has only grown my understanding of the power that can be gained from the living.**"

Ronan couldn't help but wonder at the logic of the Justice. What was it he said, 'regulated and allotted.' By what? 'Sentenced'? By whom?

The Justice waved his hand and green flames appeared between him and Ronan. The flames transformed into silhouettes of people.

"**You see, humans are malleable and full of potential.**" The silhouettes mimed different tasks; farming and chopping wood. "**If you can win over** a human, you do not just gain their service, you gain the service of their children and their children's children." More green silhouettes split from the originals until the room was filled.

"They naturally seek to follow those who are stronger than them. How easily they turn to cower at the feet of power."

The silhouettes all turned, knelt, and genuflect before the Justice inside Mishkawl's body.

Ronan was transfixed by the silhouettes. As he watched, he ruminated about how this contradicted what the voice had said in the past.

"You told me you want to be anonymous. Now you want humans to bow before you, which is it?"

The Mishkawl's head nodded at the question. "Both, my champion. I desire both. Just like you, I want to be respected and in a place of power that I deserve. We both want to be lifted up and recognized for who we are. We want to be feared for our power, and obeyed for fear of our wrath."

The shadows in the room seemed to grow and darken as he spoke. "This elevation is impossible, however, if the existing powers are present to stop us. They know who we are, and they know us to be a threat to their control. That is where anonymity comes in. If no one knows who we are, the seat of power is ours for the taking. People will be lining up to kneel before us after they see what we do to the Council. Me as king and you as my prince."

All of the silhouettes stood and looked at Ronan. Then they all saluted him, hand to their hearts. Ronan could not ignore the feeling of ecstasy that came with the gesture. What would it be like to be second in command over the Zwellian Empire he contemplated?

The Justice of Death looked at him across the multitude of salutes. "This anonymity is why I have intervened in your dreams tonight. Your recent escapades for knowledge have identified a problem that I had previously overlooked: the Arch Archivist you now travel with. He is full of information about the Eidolon and the Nether. I am sure his knowledge extends to the Justices as well. I believe you are taking him

to a Bridge Point that leads to the Nether. I task you with this. Gain what information you desire from him. Hear him, for his research is thorough. Then take your sword and run it through his chest. He is too large of a liability to be left alive. This is your new task."

The shadows increased and began to force the dream to darken.

"Oh, and by the way, give Mophantatha my regards," the deep voice echoed, and everything went completely black.

Chapter 32

Ronan opened his eyes and was immediately forced to curl his body around his arm as it once again exploded in a blast of searing pain. He did not scream despite his deep desire to call out. Just as quickly as it had started, the pain stopped completely.

Ronan began to gingerly lift his sleeve to see the damage. It was at this moment he remembered this pain had occurred after he had accidentally left the ruby knife behind. How bad had the charring gotten?

He took in a sharp breath when he saw his forearm. It would have been easy to assume he was wearing a wrist guard at first glance. The blackened charcoal skin had now encircled his arm. It was only a few inches from his hand and his elbow. The red flame symbol glowed in the midst of the fire-ravaged flesh. Ronan put his sleeve back down. He found the fingers of his unburnt hand shaking.

He took several long breaths trying to slow his breathing. There was obviously a limited amount of time to complete the Kitmazi's mission. Was this burning going to happen every morning, he wondered? Should he tell everyone that they needed to go to the Ether Scar before they went to the Bridge Point? He rolled over in his tent and grabbed the map from his backpack. Carefully rolling it out, he triangulated their current location, the Scar, and the Bridge Point. From where he assumed they were, it was the same distance to both locations. He estimated two and a half days to either.

That would mean five days of the burning if they went to the Bridge Point first. What condition would his arm be in after five days of this? But just yesterday he had told Osmodius that they were going to the Bridge Point. That was what was keeping him at bay. Would the Ether Scar be of similar appeal to the Archivist?

'I was told to kill the Archivist,' he reminded himself. *'Does it matter what I tell him?'* He put the map away and sat up on his bedroll. He had no love for Osmodius and knew the man to be vile. That didn't mean that he should die. Ronan didn't even know if he would physically be able to kill him in cold blood. The persistent dark rumination rose in his mind. *'All I would have to do is say the word and one of the spirits would kill him for me.'* He pushed this thought down and got up out of his tent. He needed to stop thinking things like that.

Vallia was walking back to their camp. It appeared that she had gone on a morning stroll. When she was closer, Ronan saw that she had some goods under her arm.

"I walked to the main road to find some traders. I got lucky and met some just up a mile. I thought it was best not to make business transactions with our captive present. He may say something to them," she said as she handed Ronan some rations and some new clothes. "I also thought we might want to ditch our old clothes. Between the prison and the laboratory, mine were pretty nasty."

Ronan accepted the new clothes and nodded in agreement. He was watching her, trying to get a read on her, but her emotional walls had been built back up. He debated if he should say something to her. He decided to wait and see. They would be in close proximity over the next few days and if he had an opportunity, he would talk to her. This may have been a more cowardly route, but it was also a safer one.

Vallia walked over to Leo who was picking some flowers and tossed him a bundle of clothes and a cloth sack of food. He looked at the gifts and said, "I have nothing to pay you back with. I can't accept these."

Vallia scoffed, "Not my money. It is your dad's. You can owe him. I figured those may fit you a little better. Make it so your whole ankle is not showing." Leo nodded at this and accepted the items. Ronan was honestly surprised Vallia had said anything to Leo at all. He wondered if Vallia's final interaction with Arkeen had involved the topic of Leo. He knew it was none of his business, but he was still curious about what he had said to get her to stay.

Vallia then opened Maya's tent flap and threw a similar bundle in. Maya, who was obviously still sleeping after her watch, shouted, "What was that for?!"

Vallia, with a satisfied look on her face, replied, "New clothes and food. Sorry the merchant didn't have any princess dresses or tiaras." The bag of clothes flew back out at Vallia's head. She caught the bundle and shrugged. "Whatever, wear your old robe and leathers. When you get a rash from those filthy rags, I don't want to hear you complain." She dropped the bag at the tent flap and walked away.

Ronan saw Maya's hand slowly come out and grab the bag, pulling it within again. Ronan smiled to himself. She was definitely not a morning person.

They all dressed and packed up the camp. Ronan ditched his soot covered tunic to put on a deep green cloak over a long-sleeved, black tunic and black pants. Green paisley embroidery decorated his shirt's cuffs. He appreciated Vallia's choice of style for him and the fact that his burnt wrist was hidden.

Vallia had changed into a long sleeved dark blue shirt with a black leather corset on top. She had also bought a new black-hooded cloak with a blue inlay.

Leo had been given a colorful poncho arrayed with oranges, reds, and browns. He wore it over a white shirt and brown pants that fit him much better than Ronan's. Vallia had also gotten him a wide brimmed woven hat that hung on a string around his neck. Ronan assumed her logic was it may help him hide his face from passers by. While wearing the hat, both his Elven and UN'kra features were mostly hidden.

Maya still wore her old medical robe. While the robe made an odd style choice, Ronan had to admit it had come in handy before. Under the robe she had put on a deep burgundy shirt and men's carpenter pants. At first Ronan thought this was another jab from Vallia; then he realized the practicality behind the purchase. The carpenter's pants had countless pockets in which he saw Maya fill full of her knives, ball bearings, and other small objects to throw. She had braided her hair back on both sides of her head into one long ponytail. Ronan liked her look. It suited her personality well and he thought the ponytail helped bring out the features of her face. *'She is a pretty girl'*, he admitted to himself. Then he shook his head, once again surprised at the thought.

Leo, being the most empathetic, let Osmodius out of the carriage to relieve himself. The old man did not make a run for it. Ronan assumed that he knew he would never make it far between Vallia's sharpshooting and Maya's impeccable aim. Ronan watched the old clamber back into the carriage begrudgingly and felt a renewed dread in his chest. The old man had no idea that a kill contract had been issued by the Justice of Death. How could Ronan kill this man? He was despicable and a swindler through and through, but executing him?

Leo and Maya took the first round of driving the carriage while Ronan and Vallia sat in the seats on the back. Ronan had given Leo his map for the time being to help them navigate toward the location of the Bridge Point. He knew the main road would only take them so close before they had to leave the path.

Ronan was lost in his own thoughts for most of the first day of travel. He kept going over his dream from the night before. Everything he had learned about the Justice of Death swam in his mind as if the facts were fish in murky waters. Difficult to see and impossible to grasp. Ronan felt like he was not able to really focus on the individual items he had discussed with his Justice. Maybe it was the lack of specifics, or maybe it was the fact his mind kept wandering off to other topics like the Bridge Point, fighting the Eidolon of Entropy, and being asked to kill Osmodius.

As they traveled to the northwest, the landscape slowly transitioned to short clay-filled cliffs. This northern road was less traveled than the southern as there were fewer settlements up here. The groups they did pass on the road were given a wide berth, partly to avoid recognition, and partly to prevent Osmodius an opportunity to tip someone off about his situation.

While it was Ronan's turn to drive the horses, he spotted a nook of four trees in the distance and decided it would make a good spot to stop for the night. Not enough cover for a bandit ambush, but enough to pull the carriage behind. A small babbling brook ran near the trees which was good for watering the horses.

As an attempt at extending an olive branch, Ronan invited Osmodius to join them for dinner. He refused, so Ronan locked him up again for the night. The stubbornness of the Arch Archivist annoyed Ronan and led him to dislike the man all the more.

After dinner, Ronan considered talking to the spirits again but didn't think he was ready to open himself up to more criticism from them. He told himself that they would be there when he was ready to speak with them again. Instead, he went to sleep early in the evening. The Justice did not visit his dreams tonight. Rather they were filled with terrible visions of people Ronan knew being disintegrated by a giant masked man.

He woke again to the now familiar burning on his arm. With difficulty, he elected not to check the size of the scorched skin as he knew it would only lead to more anxiety. He forced himself to not think about the imminent spread of the fire or the possibility that it would consume him before he accomplished the Kitmazi's mission. It was too much to think about himself as a shambling charcoal monster with only one motivation.

Their second day of travel began as they got back on the road. Ronan started out on the back of the carriage. He sat hunched on the uncomfortable seat. His arms crossed and his face set into as neutral of an expression as the storm inside him would allow. He glared up front at Maya and Leo as they chatted away. Ronan envied their ability to relax and enjoy the ride while he rode wrapped in anxious fears.

He heard Maya ask, "Do your people live up by the Ether Scar?"

Leo replied. "My mother's people do. They are the UN'kra who live closest to the Scar."

"What's it like up there?"

"Unfortunately, I do not remember much of the area. I was young when my mother sent me away to live with my father. I do remember that it is not just humanoids who are Ether touched up there. Animals often give birth to babies with dramatic Ether connections. Squirrels that can expel great blasts of air to sail through the sky and birds who zip around the forest shrouded in lightning. The Ether causes the land to change up there as well. I do remember that. Magma sometimes boils up from the ground and rare metals can be located in spires of rock that appear overnight."

Ronan understood the awe that crossed over Maya's face. He had to admit that he was excited that if all went well, they would get to see these things soon enough.

Maya then asked, "Do you miss your mom? Have you not seen her since you were a child?"

Leo recalled, "I have seen my mother twice since she sent me away. Once with my father on a business trip, and once before I joined up with the other UN'kra that taught me about my crafting. She tried to get me to stay with her the second time by telling me she would appeal to the elders about my expulsion. I told her that it was not my place to ask that of the elders. I needed to find people who could help me with my abilities. Truly, it was very sad to have to leave her again. It was for everyone's good but still difficult. It has been far too long since I have seen her."

"You should see your mom, Leo. You never know how long you will have her around," Maya said in a quiet voice. Ronan knew she was speaking from the experience of her mother.

Ronan felt a pit in his stomach as his own mother filled his thoughts. Every one of the few memories he had of her, she was wearing that blue flowered apron. He thought about her smile and her hugs and how they always made him feel safe. She had a demeanor about her that filled his old home with warmth. Even amongst his father's sporadic outbursts of anger.

I was so young when I lost you,' he thought as sadness swelled up in his chest. '*If only I had my powers that night the house burnt down. I could have done something. I could have stopped dad from yelling at you. I could have saved you and Sabastian.*'

He couldn't think like that. He had only been five. If nothing else, maybe he could have at least said goodbye to their spirits.

Suddenly, Ronan's eyes narrowed, and his mouth thinned. He may have been five, but he definitely had the tattoo of the skull on his arm. It was there when he was born. Had he not been chosen at birth? Wasn't that what the Justice had said? He has been the Eidolon of Death even back then. But his powers had not activated. 'So, it was the Justices fault,' Ronan contemplated. 'He could have activated my powers, and I could have saved them.' He felt his fists ball up and begin to shake. 'So, it wasn't just a fantasy of a lonely child.'

His Justice had a lot to answer for.

Ronan realized he was crying and quickly wiped his face. He looked around to see if anyone had noticed. Vallia was staring off in the distance and Maya had moved onto another topic with Leo.

Ronan let out a short whistle and his Ether Hawk appeared out of nowhere with a pop. Sabastian landed on Ronan's lap. Ronan nuzzled the bird and thought about his pet's namesake, about his brother. He did not have many memories of him. But the few he did, he cherished.

"I have heard stories about the UN'kra people," Ronan heard Maya say. "I heard that they have temples where they kill animals. What is that about? When we go up to the Ether Scar, will you need to go to some kind of temple and kill something?"

Leo mulled over the comment. He seemed to choose his words very intentionally. "I can see why this would be a question you would have. This practice is one of the pieces of propaganda that the Council uses to cast UN'kra in a dark light. The truth is the sacrifices of animals are not done out of savagery. They are the way the UN'kra seek forgiveness for the transgressions they have committed against the Great and Holy Light."

Maya gave Leo a blank stare.

Leo explained, "The Great Light created everything, from the rocks to the sky, to you and me. The Light is perfect and holy, without blame. As a people of the Light, UN'kra are called to live our lives, holy and blameless."

"How is that going for you?" Maya jested.

Leo accepted this statement. "No one is perfect, for all fall short of the glory of the Light. We are sinful creatures who seek to do what is right in our own eyes, as opposed to trusting the way that the Light sets before us. That is why we are separated from the perfect Light. That is why everyone deserves death. The Light is the opposite of sin. That is where the sacrifices come in. A pure, clean animal is taken and offered up to the Light as a sin offering. The animal dies the death that is due for the one who sacrifices it."

Maya looked confused. "Why do you believe in this Light if it means you are under constant scrutiny?"

Ronan thought this was a fair question. He contemplated jumping into the conversation but wanted to hear Leo's response.

Leo thought about how to best answer her question. "If I stand outside in the sunlight, close my eyes, and believe the sun is gone, does that mean I am safe from its scorching heat?"

Maya shook her head.

Leo nodded. "Correct. The sun is there whether or not I believe in it. And it will burn me regardless of my thoughts about it. The same goes for the Light. But unlike the sun and its unrelenting power, the Light graciously provides opportunities for our repentance."

"Like what?" Maya challenged.

"You see, we know that there is a day of salvation and hope apart from judgment. A day that all those who trust in the Light can look forward to. The recorded promises of the Light tell of One to Come who will take the place of the sacrifices we make. They call him the Child of Light. From the pure love of the Light, the Child of Light will come and live a perfect life of humbleness and sinlessness. He will walk this very ground. The Child of Light is from the Light and of the Light. He is promised as a coming redeemer. The Child of Light will offer salvation to those who believe."

Maya squinted her eyes trying to understand what Leo was explaining. "What is the Child of Light going to do, go around the world and tell everyone they are not good? And that will change people?"

Leo shook his head. "The Child of Light is prophesied to die. After living a perfect life, he will willingly sacrifice himself for all races and groups everywhere."

"Why would he do that? How would that help?"

Leo seemed to be excited by her interest. "Because that is the only way to bridge the divide between broken sinners and the righteous, holy Light. From the very beginning of creation, the Light has always wanted us to live and walk in righteousness, to praise the Light and grow in wisdom under the Light's instruction. And for a time, people did. But then the powers of darkness deceived people and led them to turn away from the Light and from righteousness. This betrayal of the Light led to the corruption of creation. The perfect, sinless Child of Light, the One to Come, is to die to mend the divide between creation and creator."

Maya shrugged, "I don't understand how one guy dying makes the whole world stop its selfish, corrupted ways. No matter how good of a person he is."

Leo smiled in a genuine, warm way. "That is the best part. The promise does not stop with the Child of Light dying for us. He will die, but he will be resurrected through the glory of the Light. And this resuscitation will not be like the abilities of our friend here," he gestured at Ronan.

Ronan pretended to not be eavesdropping.

Leo explained, "Not spooky spirits filling dead bodies. But a true resurrection from death to life. If anyone believes in the One to Come, The One will become an intercessor between them and the Light. A reunification between the Light and the people of faith who seek true repentance. I realized this truth and accepted that I needed to stop defining what is good and bad for myself. Instead, I needed to trust in what the Light defined as good and bad. I needed to stop being the master of my life and invite the Light to be the Lord of my life; I needed to repent. The Light saved me from myself and my sin. I am no longer a slave to sin but a son to righteousness."

Maya crinkled up her nose at the word repent. "Not everyone needs to seek repentance. What do I have to repent for? Everything that I do, I do it to survive. Why would I be convicted? I don't need repentance for just living my life."

Leo stated, "For someone with nothing to repent for, you sure seem awfully defensive."

Maya sputtered as she tried to come up with a retort. She ended up mumbling something about repentance but seemed to have lost her desire for conversation.

Petting Sabastian, Ronan sat listening to the conversation. He contemplated both Leo's and Ta Rhe's dedication to this Great Light. What a different path from that in which Ronan found himself. Ta Rhe's words from the night before rose up in Ronan's head: 'I will confirm, you are not too far gone down a path that you cannot come back from.'

Ronan wondered how that could be true. Between his contract with the Kitmazi and his obligation as champion to The Justice of Death, he felt like his path was well set before him. He entertained the idea of one day settling down and devoting himself to something wholesome like the Light. He wondered what it would look like for him. Maybe if he was alive in a few weeks, it would be something to investigate.

With this thought, the conversation about the Light sank out of his mind and was replaced by the swirling vortex of anxieties that had been fighting for his attention. He determined that if he survived the next few weeks, it would be a miracle.

Chapter 33

Ronan opted to take the whole watch that night. He fended off the others' disapproval of this with an insistence that he would not be able to sleep anyway.

While this was partly true, the real motivation behind this was a desperation to avoid the continued burning of his skin around the fire emblem on his arm.

To stay awake, Ronan sparred with Ta Rhe and Arkeen. He elected not to spar with Mishkawl out of a slight fear that the spirit would try and take the opportunity to exact revenge. Ronan didn't have the willpower to hold a deep conversation with any of the spirits. He kept his mind focused on the training. None of the spirits pushed him to talk. He assumed this was a result of them being able to read his thoughts and emotions.

The sparring was difficult as Ronan only owned one sword. They made it work by using sticks that they found. By morning, Ronan's muscles were sore, and his skin was bruised in many places.

The sun rose into the sky and cast the world into a technicolor display of pinks and oranges among the swirling clouds. Ronan sat on a rock watching the globe of warmth rise in the sky and chase off the cool of the evening. Just as he thought about waking his friends to get an early start to the day, his arm exploded in pain. He gritted his teeth and rode the wave of burning until it finally subsided.

He lay on the ground and cried for a few minutes, letting his frustrations seep out of him. *'Of course the burning is not dependent on my sleep,'* he chastised himself. *'Great, now I am exhausted for no reason.'*

He grumbled through the morning as the party got ready. The others didn't bother him, which he was grateful for. The anticipation of the Bridge Point was starting to get to him. A fear kept plaguing his thoughts that the cave on the Kitmazi map was going to lead to an empty field. He didn't know what to do if that was the case.

It was not long before they had to depart from the main road. Ronan's map did not show a path to follow, but they found a small game trail that allowed the use of the horse and carriage for a little longer. Ronan smiled to himself as he felt the carriage rock violently over the rough terrain, imagining Osmodius being thrown around with every lurch.

The game trail ended in a thicket of trees, and they had to make the concession that they would have to walk the rest of the way.

Osmodius protested this with an annoying amount of defiance. "I will not be walking though some strange forest with a bunch of murderers!"

"We could always just murder you outside the forest if you would prefer," Vallia threatened.

Osmodius grumbled under his breath but protested no more.

Ronan stared at the ground, desperate to find another way around the murder of the Archivist. There had to be another way.

"What are we going to do about the horses?" Maya asked with genuine concern in her voice.

Vallia cut the horses free from their restraints. "We'll send them to the north, and they can roam free up there."

Ronan didn't voice his assumption that it was more likely the horses would be captured by a very happy farmer or some lucky bandits. Maya seemed to have become attached to the horses and he didn't think it was worth it to worry her. Once cut free, the horses did not bolt or run. They were too well trained for that. After a few attempts, the group decided that the horses would eventually wander off on their own.

They then began to make their trek through the trees. Vallia led, using her wind blades to cut through the underbrush. Ronan followed with the map. Osmodius trailed behind Ronan with a resentful look on his face. He flinched at the sound of every bug that buzzed through the air. He was flanked by Maya and Leo. They hiked for a few hours. Ronan kept his focus on the map and his compass to make sure they kept heading the right way. But he kept losing focus. His mind would wander to the Bridge Point up ahead and what mysteries it would house or the fight he had with the spirits the other night. Without fail, his thoughts kept drifting back to Osmodius with every huff and grumble from the old man. Why was he even contemplating killing him? What did he gain? After thinking on this, the question that worried him was, what would he lose if he disobeyed?

The undergrowth continued to thicken making travel slow while the day blossomed in an unfortunate heat. Ronan assumed this was the last warm day of the year before winter began to creep in. He had already soaked his new shirt with sweat, and he felt he had killed over one hundred gnats that kept attacking his eyes and nose. He was relieved when Vallia stopped and said, "I see something up ahead."

Sure enough, off to the right was a stone structure. It appeared to be some form of ancient obelisk. Osmodius pushed past her and walked forward with a captivated look on his face. He reached the stone spire and ran his hands over it.

Ronan was also transfixed by the stone. Upon closer inspection, it was covered with faded symbols and pictographs. Looking around, he was able to make out several other stone structures. All encased in moss and seemingly untouched for centuries. Then his eye caught the symbol at the top of the obelisk. It was a goblet encircled by seven spider legs.

"This is the location." Ronan confirmed. He turned to Osmodius, "Which means you owe us some answers."

The Archivist sat on the ground and wiped his brow with a handkerchief. "Not even going to give the old man a chance to catch his breath. Typical youth, no respect for their elders. Just care about themselves."

"Stalling will not help you."

Osmodius put away the cloth and gave Ronan a venomous look. "What is it that you think that I owe you? What information do you want to squeeze out of me?"

"Let's start with the Nether. This place has some kind of connection to that, right?" Ronan felt the familiar excitement begin to rise up in himself.

Osmodius rolled his eyes and said, "I forgot that you were blessed with the powers of an Eidolon but know nothing." He bent over and grabbed a stick from the ground. He then began to draw in the dirt.

He drew a wavy oval and said, "This represents the Ether. It flows and ebbs and is chaotic and unpredictable." He then drew a rectangle that intersected the top of the wavy oval. This represents the Nether. It is a realm of rigid law and order. Just as the Ether teems with elemental energy, the Nether is filled with energies of reality." Then he pointed at the intersection between the two shapes. "This is the Prime Plane. I believe that the Prime Plane is a result of the two planes colliding together. Chaos and order coming together to form our world."

Leo let out a chuckle at this. Ronan gave him a curious look. Leo shook his head and mouthed the word "later".

Ronan looked back at Osmodius. "What do you define as 'energies of reality?'"

Osmodius sighed and said, "I mean the rules that dictate how reality functions. Let me make it simple for you." He pointed to Vallia. "She is an archer. When she pulls back her bow string, her arrow is filled with an abundant amount of potential energy. When she releases the string, the energy becomes kinetic and the arrow moves, the arrow flies through the air until it is pulled to the earth by gravity. Then the arrow hits the ground which results in a noise as well as heat from friction. If the arrow is left in the ground, it will eventually experience weathering and decay. And of course, the archer herself will be subject to all these forces until she is claimed by the final law of reality. The archer is guaranteed to die like every other living thing. Do those forces sound familiar?" Osmodius asked with a belittling expression.

"The Eidolon. You are describing their powers." Ronan said in a realization.

"There you have it, your explanation of the Nether. Congratulations. You are now one of the few people alive who understand this."

"So, why is the Nether a secret again?" Maya asked.

"Because, as I said in my lab, the Council wants the populace to be ignorant about how they came into power. It's much simpler to remove teachings of the Nether than to let people know about the plane but not talk about the Eidolon. People know of the Ether and that is confusing enough for most common folks."

In these words, Ronan was reminded of the Justice of Death's desire for anonymity. The same desire that had resulted in charging Ronan to kill the Archivist. This knowledge that Osmodius had just shared was the same knowledge that had put a target on his back. The Justice had said, 'He is too large of a liability to be left alive.'

"What do you know about the Justices?" Ronan asked to distract his mind from the thought of killing this man.

Osmodius' eyes widened at the question. "Only what I have read from Nizomotus' journal. How do you know of the Justices?"

Now it was Ronan's turn to let out a laugh. "Because every few nights one of them haunts my dreams."

Osmodius stood up, something close to elation covered his face. "So, you have spoken to one? You have conversed with a Justice?"

Vallia also gave Ronan a curious look. He remembered at this moment that he had not shared that information with anyone else.

Ronan crossed his arms in a defensive stance. He did not like the looks he was getting from the whole group. "So, what if I have? What do you know about them?"

Osmodius pointed at the goblet with the circle of spider legs. "I know that we stand in a historic temple of a Justice. I know that they are the fathers of the Eidolon. That they are beings of unimaginable power from the Nether. Nizomotus sought the Justices out. His journal recorded him finding two of them. The way he talked about them; the Justices were worshiped by people. If I had to guess, we stand in a temple to the Justice of Rest."

Vallia let out a disbelieving noise. "Did they name themselves?"

"They have names." Osmodius explained. "But those who worshiped them only referred to them by their titles. These titles are similar to the ones I showed you in my lab. For example, there is a Justice of Rest and an Eidolon of Rest. The same is true for all the Eidolon as far as I can tell. Nizomotus names the two that he met. But the other five names have been lost to history."

Ronan wondered what the name of the Justice of Death was. Why had he been hiding it from Ronan?

Osmodius looked at Ronan with a gleam in his eye and said, "The Justices are heavily protected. Nizomotus had to seek them alone. He was unable to take any of his spirit army with him as he transitioned into the Nether."

Ronan smirked. He bet that the Archivist would like nothing better than to get rid of Ronan's spirits. One less obstacle to overcome when he tried to weasel his way out of his situation. "Yeah, sure he did. Nice try."

Osmodius smiled at Ronan. "I do not lie. Nizomotus wrote that some form of barrier prevented his spirits from coming with him. As a result, he sucked the energy out of the spirits and ventured in alone."

The thought of sucking energy from the spirits sickened Ronan. His reaction to this statement was more violent than he would have expected. He felt anger at the Eidolon of Death. It seemed wrong and an abuse of the spirits to siphon their energy. It was dark, perverted, and unnatural. He didn't want to think about it more, so he asked, "What did Nizomotus say in the journal about controlling spirits? How did he get so strong to control so many?"

Osmodius said, in a casual voice, "I would imagine that a lot of his power came from striking deals with Justices and other powerful beings. In terms of what the journal said about controlling spirits, I think a large part of the control he had came from his lack of care for the spirits he enslaved. Not only would he leach power from them, but he would also force them to stay in this plane until the spirits were changed. He described them as becoming 'deformed and hollow.'"

The words struck Ronan with the force of an avalanche. His forearm tingled where the flame emblem rested. The deal he had made with the Kitmazi had been made to gain information and inevitably power. He then thought about the three spirits that followed him at this moment. *How long did it take a spirit to become hollow?* He wondered. He felt a wave of nausea

255

as he compared himself to the cruel Nizomotus. He looked around at the others to see their reactions to this statement. Vallia refused to make eye contact with him. Maya and Leo shared a look of uncomfortable concern. Ronan closed his eyes and focused on catching his breath.

"Watch him," Ronan instructed his friends. "Don't let him out of your sight. I will be right back." He walked off knowing what he had to do.

Chapter 34

He walked a few hundred feet away from the others and activated his connection to the Nether. He looked at the three spirits with fresh eyes. Taking the moment to truly scrutinize the apparitions, he noticed that the spirits of Ta Rhe and Arkeen did look different from his first conversation. They were not as crisp and clear, maybe even more hazed around the edges. Their spectral faces were also slightly blurred. Ronan's heart sank. So, it was true after all. They were not meant to remain on this plane. It pained him to his core knowing that he was the reason they were still here. If these changes had begun to happen in a few days, how quickly would their personalities fade? The thought of Arkeen being 'hollow' stung his eyes with tears. He needed these spirits but how could he keep them here, knowing what he now did? They had protected him and given him control that he could have only ever dreamed of, but at what cost?

He projected his thoughts to the three spirits. *"I want to apologize for how I acted over the last week. For keeping you here against your will. For stopping you from seeing your family,"* he said, looking at Ta Rhe. *"I am sorry that I killed you and then forced you to follow me,"* he said to Mishkawl. *"And I am sorry that I was not strong enough to let a friend die in peace."* He looked at Arkeen. *"After what I just heard, I am appalled at what I have done. I do not deserve your forgiveness. You all have the right to be so mad at me."*

A smile appeared across Arkeen's spectral face. *"I guess it is a good thing that you are the Prince of the Dead and not the prince of judgmental, grudge-holding preteens. Turns out that we spirits don't really do the whole ill will, resentment thing. We don't have it in our bones."* His deep laughter filled Ronan's head.

257

Ronan would have appreciated this joke any other time but right now, he was too angry at himself.

Mishkawl shrugged his green flaming shoulders. *"I am new to the whole spirit thing. I mean, obviously I would prefer to be alive, but that ship has sailed. Now that I am dead, I surprisingly don't have a lot of resentment for you, which confuses me to be honest. I can say with confidence, if you had tried to shackle me up when I was alive, I would have crushed you into the dirt with my powers. Right now, I don't seem to have that desire, which I find odd."*

Ronan gave him a cautious look. *"Do you think that is because you are dead or because you are tethered to me?"*

Mishkawl crossed his arms. *"I don't know, untether me and let's see if I want to kill you."*

Ronan bowed his head. *"I will untether all of you. I should not have tethered you in the first place."*

Arkeen projected into Ronan's head, *"You really are too hard on yourself, mate. Sure, you could have let us go sooner, but you gave me a chance to say goodbye to the woman I loved. You gave Ta Rhe here someone to share his wisdom with and he loves spewing off random proverbs and stuff. You even were able to talk to someone with similar life experiences as yourself."* Arkeen looked at Mishkawl. *"I don't know, you haven't been here that long. I don't know if you really got anything out of this but two out of three is not bad."*

Ronan listened to the words and felt a little better. Arkeen always had that effect on people. He shared his father's charisma, but he also had an empathy for others that his father lacked. Ronan looked at his friend. *"I guess I can start with you."*

Ronan swallowed as a lump appeared in his throat. He knew he was not ready for this. How could he be? Arkeen's death had been so sudden. But it had been completely out of anyone's control. Then he reminded himself of what Vallia had said about never being ready to let someone go. Ronan felt as if he was sentencing Arkeen to die. Closing his eyes, he reminded himself that Arkeen was already dead. That all he was doing was setting him free.

Ronan fished out the ring on the necklace that Arkeen had given him the day he died. *"I never thanked you for this. For trying to help me out and for believing that I could be worth something as a scavenger. I guess, looking back, I never really thanked you for being my friend."*

Arkeen gave Ronan his signature sly grin. *"That's the best part about a good friend. You don't have to thank them. Because odds are, you mean just as much to them as they do to you. As for believing in you, of course I did. I could see your effort and how much you tried to succeed. You were never really given anything in life, mate. I knew that from the first time I met you. You were a fighter and you worked for everything you had. That's what I liked about you. You never gave up. That can be a good quality if you are headed in the right direction. It can also be dangerous if you're headed off a cliff. You need to remember that. Take it from me, it's important to look where you are headed. Otherwise, an UN'kra may jump out of a bush and stab you."* He smiled at Ta Rhe. Ta Rhe gave a rare smile back.

Arkeen looked back to Ronan; his face now serious. *"Take care of Vallia. She has a good head on her shoulders, but she needs a friend in her life. She pretends to be all self-sufficient. I know better. She can't do everything alone. Stick with her and you will have a loyal ally to the end. She will probably never admit it, but she does appreciate your friendship. Oh, and keep an eye on Leo. It seems he has gotten his life together, but he still needs someone to look out for him. Don't let the powerful Ether Crafting fool you. He needs help just as much as you do."*

Ronan accepted Arkeen's last wishes and committed them to memory. Be a friend to Vallia and help Leo. He could do those things.

Arkeen smiled again, *"I am ready if you are my friend."* Ronan felt tears start to fall down his face. He nodded and held the ring tight in his hand. The tethering energy was thin but powerful. He focused on that tether and willed it to break. Like a lute string wound too tight, he felt the tether snap and the energy dissipate.

The green flames of Arkeen's spirit began to dissolve. The flames flicked higher and small chunks of his visage floated upward as green sparks. In a few seconds, there was nothing left but open air. Ronan felt the void in his chest. This was the second time he had dealt with losing Arkeen. His death would be something that Ronan was going to deal with for the rest of his life.

"You don't have to have a whole heartfelt moment to let me go. You can just do it," Mishkawl interrupted Ronan's thoughts.

Ronan glared at the spirit and his insensitive nature. *"You have to earn that right. I still have questions for you. If you answer them, I will let you go."*

Mishkawl raised his hands in mock surrender. *"Ask your questions. I am an open book."*

Ronan doubted that but asked anyway, *"You said the Council hired you to track me down. Did you ever meet any of the Legislators?"*

"I met one, yeah. Creepy bloke with yellow eyes."

Ronan couldn't believe his ears as anger flooded his thoughts. *"You met the Eidolon on Entropy!? Why didn't you tell me!"*

The spirit shrugged. *"You never asked."*

"I need to know everything you know about him. If I am supposed to fight him, I need every advantage I can get."

"Like I said he was a creepy bloke. He interrupted one of my bounties. I had the scum dead to rights, cornered in an alley in Ristiven. *Suddenly the poor schmuck started writhing and screaming. I watched as the man shriveled up and fell to the ground as a smoking pile of bones. His skin and muscle were turned to ash. Most disturbing thing I ever saw, and that's saying something. I turned around and recognized the Legislator by the mask. I was about to crush in his chest for interfering when he offered to pay me double the man's bounty for my troubles. Obviously, that got my attention."*

"What did you talk about?" Ronan demanded, his heart pounding in his throat.

"He told me that your capture was of utmost importance. An issue of imperial security. That I would be well compensated for your capture."

"Did he say why it was so important?"

"It's bad business practice in my line of work to stick my nose in the affairs of my clientele. All he told me was that you were another Eidolon. That your allegiances were unknown, but you had already shown a proclivity towards violence."

"That is it? He didn't say anything else?"

Mishkawl thought for an infuriatingly long moment. *"He did mention he had a proposition for me when I returned with you. Something about an alliance. I think he wanted to offer us some kind of partnership or something. I told him I worked alone. He hinted that I may be singing a different tune once I saw the culmination of his plan."*

Ronan was taken aback. The Eidolon of Entropy wanted to form an alliance with other Eidolon? He was trying to destroy the world. Why would he think others would want to help with that? *'Was there more to the plan than Maya's vision had revealed? Or more that she was not sharing? What if the Eidolon was not crazy? What if he knows something that I don't?'*

Ronan couldn't start questioning his mission this far in. He had to stop the Eidolon from destroying everything. *'What if he still offers an alliance?'*

Ronan shook his head. It was not even a consideration. To distract himself from the strange notions that kept arising at the back of his subconscious, he asked, *"What can you tell me about the Justices? If we can figure out how to cross over the Nether from the Bridge Point, we may be meeting one soon. I want to be prepared for that."*

"I only ever spoke with my Justice, so I don't know about the others. Based on those interactions, the best advice I can give you is to not make them angry."

Ronan rolled his eyes at this. *"Yeah, I have gotten that much from my own Justice."* The memory of the spirit smashing him into cupboards of the Kitmazi's wagon was still all too vivid.

Mishkawl nodded at this. *"That doesn't surprise me. You seem like the kind of person that would irritate any authority figure."*

"So, you have no other helpful information," Ronan asked, annoyed.

Mishkawl thought again and said, *"This isn't about Justices per say, but it may help you. Find out what makes them tick and use that to their advantage. That is what I would do with my bounties."*

Ronan heard this as a useless cliche before he took a second and thought about the statement. He considered what the spirit said. *'I was your bounty, what made me tick?"* He was curious to hear what the Eidolon may say.

"You are very self motivated," Mishkawl answered simply. *"Nothing would stop you or get in your way of getting what you wanted. Not that poor old Apollymi woman, not the prison guards. You couldn't even keep watch outside*

the laboratory for ten minutes. I watched you from a distant roof. You were so eager to get inside you never even saw me. I figured that was the perfect time to strike when you were so distracted by your own selfish desires."

Ronan was speechless. He could not believe his ears. Anger bubbled up inside his chest. The effort to not shout was difficult. Instead, he clenched his jaw and thought, *"I'm not going to miss you."* Then his guilty conscience provoked him to not let those be the last words to this spirit. *"I am sorry that I killed you,"* was the best thing he could come up with. With that, Ronan focused on the thin strand of energy linking the spirit to himself. He released the energy comprising the strand and felt it break, like a rope under too much weight. Mishkawl's spirit faded away before his eyes.

Ronan closed his eyes for a moment to try and clear his head for his last conversation. *'Stupid Eidolon of Gravity,'* he thought. What does he know?

Opening his eyes he saw Ta Rhe floating all alone. Ronan looked over his shoulder at his living party. Vallia, Leo and Maya were where he had left them, close together pointing at different features of the old temple. Osmodius was about fifty feet away from Ronan, deeply engrossed in some writing on a stone wall. Ronan turned back to Ta Rhe to send him off. *"It's time I fulfilled my word to you and let you go. I just have one question for you before I send you off to your ancestors and your Light."*

Ta Rhe nodded his head, *"Ask that I may answer and be set free."*

"The other night you told me that I was not too far gone down a path that I could not come back from. How do you know?"

Ta Rhe inclined his head in recognition. *"As long as you draw breath, there is an opportunity to seek repentance. For every breath you breathe is given by the Light."*

Ronan's confusion must have been apparent over their connection. Ta Rhe went on to explain, *"To understand the gift of grace, you must understand the character of the Light. The Light is merciful, patient, and forgiving. But The Light will not let the guilty go unpunished for the Light is also just and righteous, demanding obedience that is well deserved. No different from a King who demands respect and obedience of their kingdom.*

Ronan looked at the spirit trying to unravel the mystery behind his words.

"So, I guess I don't have much hope because I feel guilty."

The spirit shook his head as if Ronan did not understand. *"Of course you are guilty, no one is good, not even one. But you ignore the positive characteristics of the Light."*

Ronan countered, *"I do not know the Light of your people. Why would the Light grant me any mercy or grace? I don't deserve anything like that. I'm not even a follower of the Light. I'm the champion of the Justice of Death."*

The spirit laughed at this. *"No one deserves anything from the Light. Who can say they deserved to live before they were created? It is not a matter of deserving anything. Rather, it is by the mercy and grace of the Light that we have anything. As for not knowing the Light, consider the fact that the Light knows you. For the Light made your innermost parts. You were woven together by the Light inside your mother's womb where all your hairs were counted by the Light. It matters not who you serve right now. The Justice of Death may have lured you into his grasp, but the chains that tether you to him are easily broken by the Light."*

Ronan knew Ta Rhe didn't understand. Ronan was not an UN'kra. He had not lived his life following any path but his own. Then the Justice had chosen Ronan to be the Eidolon of Death and to do his bidding. The power that he now had was a result of his service to the Justice. It was not something he could just walk away from.

Ta Rhe, clearly reading Ronan's thoughts, said in a voice of a patient teacher, *"A man may only serve one master. If he is a slave to death, he cannot also serve life. If he is a slave to sin, he cannot also serve righteousness. I believe Leo fa Kemin mentioned the Child of Light?"*

Ronan nodded, recalling the conversation from the day before.

Ta Rhe explained, *"Then you have heard the good news! The Child of Light, the One to Come, will set the captives of sin free. Believe in this promise and look forward to that day. Until it arrives, we are to seek repentance from the Light. We are to admit our sin every day, and its deadly effects. Then, by the power of the Light and not your own strength, walk away from that sin. Let it die in its corruption. Accept a new life where you strive for righteousness and holiness for the glory of the Light."*

Ronan didn't know what to think about this. Everything the Ta Rhe said sounded too good to be true. But what did this spirit know about the power of the Justice of Death? How could he know that Ronan could be set free? This was something that would take a long time to process. He felt a desire in his heart to not let the UN'kra spirit go. What if he had more questions? What if he wanted to learn more about the Light? Then he recognized his selfishness and threw it off. *'Let my yesses be yes and my nos be no,' he reminded himself. This is the lesson Ta Rhe had taught him about promises.,*

Ronan pushed himself to say, *"You have given me much to consider. Thank you for everything you have done for me. I am sorry that Vallia killed you but in a weird way, I am grateful to have had this opportunity to get to know you."*

Ta Rhe floated forward. *"Vallia intended to harm me, but the Light intended it for good to accomplish what is now being done. I see that now. Is this goodbye then? You are letting me go?"*

Ronan *"I told you I would."* He began to focus on the energy tethering the spirit to him.

Ta Rhe said, *"As humans go, you are not the worst of them. You have a long way to grow but I see hope for you. Remember young Ronan, you can only serve one master."*

Ronan nodded and then thought of one more thing. *"I don't know where spirits go when they depart from this world, but if you can, keep an eye on Arkeen."*

Ta Rhe gave Ronan a sad look. *"I will not see Arkeen where I am going. He never knew the Light and thus Arkeen will go..."*

But Ronan never heard where Arkeen would go. The spirit never finished his sentence. Instead, he looked behind Ronan and yelled *"Look out!"*

Ronan didn't understand until there was a tug at his waist. The weight of his sword was suddenly lifted off his hip; pulled free from behind him. Ta Rhe's warning allowed Ronan a split second to pivot as a response. If it was not for the warning, the following stab would have pierced straight through his core. Instead, the blade sank through the side of his abdomen.

The excruciating pain from the wound radiated through his body with every breath. Ronan, who had still been focusing on the energy of the tether unintentionally let the energy go. There was an ethereal snap as Ta Rhe's tether was severed.

A warm sensation spread over Ronan's side and down his leg. It took several seconds for him to realize the warmth was from his own blood. Every thought came to him like it was pulled through a murky bog. He saw Osmodius dropping the sword and watched in bewilderment as the old man ran away, disappearing into a small doorway in a wall that Ronan had previously not noticed. Ronan looked to the ground and slowly registered his sword was covered in a dark liquid. It took him another moment to realize the liquid should have been crimson had it not been for his active powers.

'He stabbed me...'

With pure malevolence as his only driving force, the shouts from Ronan's friends fell on deaf ears. He clumsily grabbed his sword from the ground in one hand and, holding his bleeding side in the other, ran after the Archivist. The adrenaline coursing through him was the only thing keeping him on his feet. Osmodius had just made Ronan's mission from the Justice vastly less complicated. Ronan was going to kill the Arch Archivist.

Chapter 35

Heart pounding in his ears, every breath agonizing, Ronan stumbled through the narrow stone doorway, He found himself in a long room decorated with elaborate pillars of mosaic stones. The room was lit by the sun as a section of the roof had crumbled in. The opening had resulted in a verdant explosion as nature attempted to reclaim the manmade structure by deteriorating what was once surely a beautiful place.

Ronan hunted for the orange glow of Osmodius' life energy. He spotted it on the other end of the room, disappearing down a staircase. Ronan didn't know where it went, and he didn't care. He ran after his target, pain aching through his side with every footfall.

Ronan pelted down the steps two at a time. He barely registered the tool carved walls transition into natural cave walls. The stairs had been eroded away by water over the years. He almost tripped on a particularly weathered section. At the bottom of the landing, he was out of breath and his side was making it almost impossible to move. He didn't see the Archivist in the darkness. He knew that he had to be down here. There was nowhere else he could have escaped. Ronan moved forward more slowly, relying on his Nether vision. His own life force cast a green, orange glow on the walls. Ronan felt a grin tug at his cheeks when he saw a glow up ahead. The old man had cornered himself.

He slowly rounded a bend in the cave and stopped dead in his tracks. The glow was not in fact Osmodius. It was a shimmering veil that filled the entire cave before him. The wall seemed to flow like silk curtains in a slight breeze. Ronan stared transfixed at the phenomenon before him. He

266

almost forgot about his pursuit of the man who had attacked him. Then he noticed a number of skeletons on the floor of the cave before the veil. It looked like they had been there a long time.

He deactivated his Nether connection and was surprised to not see anything before him. The cave was pitch black. No veil or glow. His senses no longer dimmed by his powers, he heard several footsteps behind him. Vallia, rounded the corner holding a torch. Leo and Maya appeared a second later.

"Ronan, you're hurt," Vallia exclaimed as she saw him. He looked down to find his pant leg soaked with his own blood.

"Where is the snake?" Leo asked.

"I don't know, I think he went through the veil." Ronan said suddenly feeling queasy.

"What veil?" Leo looked down the tunnel.

Vallia handed the torch to Leo and pulled her pack off. She extracted a small mending kit and hoisted up Ronan's shirt. A pained look crossed her face.

Ronan couldn't bring himself to look. "We don't have time for this. We need to stop the Archivist. He is getting away. We need to go through the veil."

Vallia forced Ronan against the stone wall and said, "You won't make it if we don't stop." She produced a small glass bottle of a clear liquid with a cork. She pulled the cork with her teeth and said, "Brace yourself." Ronan knew what was coming. The bottle was full of pure, distilled alcohol. He closed his eyes and scrunched up his face. A scream escaped his lips as the liquid touched his wound. Not able to hold himself up, he collapsed down the wall. Vallia began wrapping white cloth around Ronan's abdomen.

Leo asked again, "What veil Ronan?"

Not opening his eyes, he pointed at the location the shimmer wall had been.

Maya said, "I see it. It must be something to do with the Nether. It looks like a weird version of one of your rifts Leo. I think that must be the Bridge Point."

"We need to go through and kill Osmodius," Ronan urged.

Maya bent down. "I don't know if that is the best idea. Look at these Legionnaires. It doesn't look like they were able to make it through." Ronan slowly opened his eyes and looked her way. She was stooped down next to one of the bodies. "Looks like he was dissolved or something." She touched the skeleton's face and Ronan saw what she meant. The bones were not normally decayed. The skull looked as if it had been taken to a grinding stone. Eroded away in specific spots.

Leo knelt down as well, holding the torch close to the bodies. "Something is wrong, these breastplates all have the symbol of the Legion on them. But that didn't exist until nine years ago. There is no way the skeletons should have deteriorated this much."

"What does it matter," Ronan said, exacerbated, using his sword as a cane to help himself stand. "Osmodius made it through, so we can too."

"Ronan, he is not worth getting disintegrated over." Vallia warned. "Plus, you need to rest. The more you move the more you bleed."

Ronan shook his head. "I am going to kill him." He activated his powers to see the veil again. After two shaky steps, his strength gave out and fell forward, passing through the shimmering barrier. He fell on his good side but was still rocked by the impact causing him to curl into a ball on the floor. Not a rough cave floor. A smooth stone floor. The cave had vanished around him. The shimmering glow of the veil at his feet illuminated a perfectly square, hewn, stone hallway.

Vallia materialized out of thin air next to him holding her torch again. She helped him up and then she looked around in amazement. Maya and Leo materialized next to her and shared in her stunned reaction.

Leaning on Vallia for support, Ronan looked at the walls around them, illuminated by the torch. They were covered in detailed paintings depicting many people bearing large slates of gold and food and valuable objects. All of the painted people were headed in the same direction. They all faced an image of a floating goblet surrounded by seven spider legs.

"So, this is how you see when your eyes flash green," Vallia said in a small voice. She rubbed her eyes and blinked a few times. Confused, Ronan deactivated his powers and saw that color did not come back. Everything around them was black and white.

"You get used to the colors being gone." Maya announced. "I am not an Arch Archivist of planar research, but if I had to guess, I would say we are in the Nether. I bet you Osmodius could read the hieroglyphs up above and knew exactly where to go."

Vallia looked at Ronan, "There is no way to convince you to stay here is there?"

"Not a chance," he confirmed. "Osmodius is somewhere up there and so is the Justice of Rest."

"What are you going to do if I refuse to support you?" she asked with a raised eyebrow.

"I guess I'll slump against the wall and let that support me." He retorted.

Vallia let out a stubborn, angry sound and said, "Fine, come here." She threw his arm over her shoulders. Between her and his sword, he was able to move forward. Ronan doubted that he would have actually been able to use the wall as a support and was thankful for her help.

Leo took point as he grabbed the torch from Vallia. "We should not stay here long. I don't know about the Nether but when Ether Crafters have experimented in the past with entering the Ether, they either never came back or appeared months later, driven totally mad. I have heard of people who attempted it and came back without the ability to speak. They would just mumble nonsense."

"You are just mentioning this now?" Maya asked as she looked around cautiously. This would have concerned Ronan too if it were not for his current drive to end Osmodius.

They proceeded down the stone hallway. The sound of their steps echoing all around. Stealth was out of the question with Ronan in his state.

After a few moments, he looked to Vallia and said, "I let him go. After Osmodius talked about the old Eidolon of Death, I couldn't hold Arkeen here any longer. I let them all go."

Vallia did not say anything for a moment. Her voice came out quiet and small. "Did it hurt?"

269

Ronan didn't know how to answer the question. He eventually responded, "Me? Yes. Ten times more than this cut in my side. Arkeen? No. It was his time to go, and he knew that. He faded away with a smile on his face."

Neither of them said anything more on this. They didn't need to. Ronan was once again grateful for Vallia's friendship. Like a big sister by his side.

The hallway opened up into a vast expanse of a room. Ronan looked around at the vast expanse. The torch only illuminated a small portion of the space before them. From what he could see, there were several decorative columns stretched up to a vast, domed ceiling. This room was also not a natural cave. It resembled drawings Ronan had seen at the Carpenters that depicted the inside of the Watch Tower. Amazingly, the architecture was not the most captivating feature in this room. The floor was littered with copious piles of treasure. Stacks of coins and currencies from all over, large busts of people long lost in history, fine wooden furniture, bejeweled goblets and crowns, dazzling works of metal craft and glasswork, paintings in old ornate frames, and much more that was unidentifiable given the light source.

The four stood, mouths agape at the collection of wealth before them. This was not at all what Ronan had expected. He didn't really know what to anticipate but he didn't assume to find a hoard of immeasurable wealth.

"This must be the treasure trove of the Justice like in the wall paintings back there," Maya whispered. "I have a bad feeling about this place." Despite her low tone, her voice was amplified by the domed structure.

"Does anyone see the Archivist?" Ronan asked quietly. He scanned the piles of treasure. Osmodius could be hiding anywhere behind any number of objects.

Vallia whispered "He is not interested in riches. He wants knowledge and probably hopes the Justice will protect him from us. He is going to be wherever the Justice of Rest is."

"Did someone say my name?" A slow, high-pitched voice called out, reverberating around the space. The four looked around for the source of the voice. Ronan didn't see anyone.

"Show yourself," Ronan called to the vast room. His voice echoed through the chamber in a haunting way.

"You must be the Eidolon that I am smelling," the voice echoed. "No one else would be so bold to command a Justice."

A skittering, clawing sound filled the air. The noise of metal scraping against stone that made Ronan's teeth hurt. Out of the shadows above came the face of a man that just penetrated the upper darkness. The torch barely illuminated his features.

Leo lifted the torch a little higher revealing the figure's bare shoulders. "Are you the Justice of Rest?"

The face smiled. It was too smooth. Like a porcelain doll.

"Yes. I am the Justice of Rest. And who might you four be? I have not had guests in so long. Then, to my surprise, I was woken by the sounds of a pleading human. He was begging for help. Said something about someone trying to kill him."

"My name is Ronan. I am the Eidolon of Death, and I was the one looking to kill that man. Where is he?"

The face of the Justice curled into a smile that was far too large. All of his teeth were pointed. "Ah, see now that is a fair transaction. A name for a name. Oh, how I missed a good trade. But I did ask who you four are. Not just one." The statement was not a threat, but Ronan felt there was a hint of menace behind his words.

Maya spoke up. "I am Maya Alithan. Eidolon of Kinetic Energy. This is Vallia, Ethalladros of wind, and this is Leo Fa Kemin, a powerful Ether Crafter."

The Justice looked at each as they were introduced. "I thought I smelled the stench of the Ether. Why is it that two Eidolon and two Ether scum have come to my sanctum? You are not my chosen Eidolon. And I have not called you here. So that means you have come here by your own will. How interesting."

Ronan continued his role as the spokesperson for the party, ignoring the Ether scum comment. "I told you; we are here to kill the pleading man. I ask again, where is he?"

"He came seeking my protection, but he had nothing to trade for

271

his safety. Nothing to give me that was worth his life. That wouldn't do. Not at all. He told me he could give me wisdom and knowledge." The Justice laughed high above them, as he continued to seemingly float above their heads. The high pitch sound of his mirth was ghastly. **"Look around you. Does it look like I have a place to put knowledge and wisdom? These are useless commodities. No value in them at all."**

"Did you let him run away?" Ronan said, looking around again.

"Oh no. I took all that he had to give me. It has been a while since someone came to me with nothing. I had to make an example of him. See for yourselves my new trophy?"

The Justice pointed to a nearby pile of valuables collected around one of the columns. Leo shifted the torch and they all saw the trophy the Justice referred to. A chandelier of elk antlers hung on a bracket that was mounted to the column. Impaled on several of the antlers hung the limp body of the Arch Archivist Nimin Osmodius. Blood still dripped from his chest where one of the antlers stuck through his heart.

Ronan averted his eyes from the gruesome sight. He looked back up at the Justice with a new understanding of who he was talking with. Mishkawl's words came to Ronan's mind, *'Find what makes them tick.'* Ronan didn't have to try very hard to imagine what motivated this Justice. He liked to make trades.

Ronan thought for a moment and then said to the Justice, "You have killed my enemy and I must thank you for that. However, you deprived me of doing it myself. Seeing as you took something that was mine, I feel it only fair that you give me something in return."

The Justice thought about this for a moment, clearly weighing what Ronan said. **"What would you say one old human death is worth to you?"** he asked, full of curiosity.

"Seeing as I am the Eidolon of Death, it matters a great deal to me. But I will trade you for something simple. If you tell me about your powers and how they relate to the Eidolon, we will call it a fair deal." He knew he was taking a leap asking for this when he had no real claim on the life of Osmodius.

272

The smooth face of the Justice of Rest split into a wide grin. **"Typical Eidolon. Always trying to learn about themselves and their creators. But I have to admit that this does seem like an equally weighted deal. And who am I to reject a little bird asking its mother where it came from and how to fly. It is just nature. Now, where to begin? Hmmm... I am Mophantatha, the Justice of Rest. I am the shepherd of the Law of Rest."**

Ronan was surprised by the name. He had heard the name before. He racked his brain. Then he recalled that in his last encounter the Justice of Death had said, *'say hello to Mophantatha for me.'*

Mophantatha surveyed the four. **"Judging by the blank expressions on your faces you do not understand what that means. Let me put it this way. An object at rest will stay at rest, until that rest is interrupted by something. Everything is an equal trade in this world. For something to move it must first be pushed or pulled. Otherwise, everything wants to stay exactly where it is. If there is not a trade, then nothing happens. That's the deal. I am the father of that deal. I am the one who wrote the law of that deal."**

Ronan listened intently. This Justice spoke so differently than the Justice of Death. He claimed to be the creator of the law whereas Ronan's Justice made it sound like a job or punishment. This made Ronan question which Justice was telling the truth.

Mophantatha continued to explain, **"As for Eidolon, you are children of the Justices. Not by birth and blood but by generosity and choice. The planes shift and flow like water. When they shift just right, the Justices are able to impart their powers onto a developing spirit in your plane. They mark that spirit and claim them as their champion. I, of course, reference the mark on the top of your left forearms."**

Ronan subconsciously felt his left arm where the skull résumé mark rested.

Mophantatha asked, **"Where do you think your people developed the idea of marking their arms? What once was a symbol of esteemed power is now seen by your people as an identification of trivial**

occupation. But I digress. Eidolon are the chosen champions of the Justices. Born to serve their Justices. Born to do the bidding of their creator."

"This creature spits lies covered in venom," Leo spoke out in a sudden, loud voice. "He did not create any law, nor did he create any Eidolon. Maybe some of his power seeped into the Prime Plane and affected a poor innocent developing baby, but he has no power of creation. The Light created all and set all in motion. The Light is the father to all life. This creature can be nothing more than a pawn of the Light. But if I had to guess, he envies the Great Light. He claims to have the power of the Light, but he is dim in comparison. Everything is dim in comparison."

"You dare to bring the name of the Light in my hall! You dare to challenge my powers in my realm!" Ronan flinched as the Justice yelled.

The Justice advanced forward in a flash, coming face to face with Leo. The details of his body were revealed as he did. A human head, torso, arms, and hands atop a carapace of dark black plates. A massive body of a centipede protruded from where his waist should have been. His visage extended upwards into darkness. Rows and rows of a segmented carapace with razor sharp legs jutting out in all directions. The grotesque body clung onto at least two of the room's pillars. His exoskeleton glistened in the gray light of the colorless fire.

Leo stood his ground; staring into the smooth face that challenged him. "If my words are lies, why did they create such a violent reaction out of you? It seems that a reaction of that size would need a powerful initiation. There is always a trade, correct?"

At this challenge, the Justice stared into Leo's eyes and smiled. **"There is always a trade."** With the skuttle of countless skittering legs, he slowly backed up. **"But do not question my power, boy."** He scooped up two large handfuls of coins and threw them into the air. The coins hit the top of their arch in the air and froze. A glistening frozen rain of circular metal. **"I control movement or lack thereof. I can stop anything from moving. Say for instance your heart."** He waved a hand over Leo's chest threateningly.

274

Leo's eyes followed the movement. Taking in the threat.

Ronan addressed Mophantatha again, hoping to distract him "Maybe we can interest you in another deal. We have things to trade if you can give us what we want."

Ronan's ploy worked. The Justice turned his head from Leo. **"You want to make more deals? Oh, how wonderful. What is it you have to give me?"**

Ronan pushed, "Well, first we need to know if you have what we want."

"Look around you. Does it seem like I lack anything? What is it that you want that I might not have?"

"We don't want trinkets or treasures. We want information about the Eidolon of Entropy."

"Speak for yourself," Ronan heard Maya say behind him. "Maybe we do want some trinkets or treasures." He glared at her. She was staring intently at a nearby pile of gemstones. She caught his eye and said, "Or just information is fine."

Mophantatha gave them a pondering expression. **"What a coincidence that you would be seeking information on my last guest."**

Ronan's eyes widened at the statement. "The Eidolon of Entropy came here?" *'Of course he had been!'* Ronan felt so stupid. He thought back to the Legion skeletons in front of the rift. It was just like Mishkawl had said when he met the Eidolon. 'The skin and muscle were turned to ash.' A shiver ran down Ronan's back as he realized the implications of the skeletons. The Eidolon of Entropy had killed his own men, likely his own royal guards, before entering the rift. He really was demented *'But why? What had the maniac talked about with the Justice of Rest that was such a secret?* Ronan had to know. Which meant he had to figure out what he had to trade. "Why was he here?" he stalled.

"To make a deal of course." Mophantatha smiled, some of his razor-sharp legs shifted as he said it. Ronan took in the details of the smooth face, a knot growing in his stomach. **"Now what could you give me that would be worth information about this Eidolon? What is worth divulging the intent of another Justice?"**

"So, his plan is not his own but his Justice's?" Vallia asked, interpreting the slight slip of information.

Mophantatha frowned at this. **"What do you have to offer me?"**

Maya inquired, "You have so much wealth. What could we possibly offer you that you don't have?"

"There is always more wealth and always more power. But you are right. I require something I don't have. Something rare and unique, or powerful."

Ronan's forearm tingled and seemed to grow warm as the Nether being spoke to Maya. He rubbed it hoping it would stop. Did time pass differently down here? Was it already morning on the Prime Plane? The last thing he needed right now was his arm to burn. Then he remembered the ruby dagger. The dagger that he could not leave behind. Wheels started turning in his head. A proverb from Mr. Kemin ran through his mind. *'If you are going to make enemies, get what you need from them first and then make sure you have an exit strategy.'*

"I have something to trade you for your information," Ronan called out. Mophantatha turned to face him, eyes gleaming with interest. "A being as powerful as you must be aware of other powerful beings of the other planes. So, I would assume you know of the Kitmazi?"

"Of course."

Ronan continued, "Have you ever had the privilege of meeting one such entity?"

Ronan could tell that he had the Justice's attention. **"No, I have never had the... pleasure as you say. Ether beings tend to avoid the Nether and Nether beings the Ether. It is the way things are. Are you telling me you met with a Kitmazi and lived to tell the tale?"**

Ronan nodded; his suspicions confirmed. This would only work if Mophantatha had a limited understanding of the Ether creatures. He gave a small shrug to show it was no big deal despite the pounding of his head in his chest. "He has never met a Kitmazi," Ronan said to his friends, hoping to see if they understood where he was going. He caught a glimpse of Vallia's eyes. They were wide and foreboding. She knew exactly what he was thinking but was not about to say anything.

Ronan looked back at Mophantatha. "Not only have I met a Kitmazi, but I have brokered a deal with one and, as a result, have acquired this beautiful dagger." He slowly withdrew the dagger. He held it flat on his palm for the Justice to examine. In the colorless environment it appeared to be a ghostly white.

"It ripples with strong Ether energy. I can feel it... I can smell it." He was drawing closer to the dagger and began reaching out his hand.

"So, you are interested," Ronan said as he pulled the dagger away.

Mophantatha's concentration snapped back to Ronan. **"Very."**

"I ask for three pieces of information in exchange for the dagger." Ronan wanted to make sure he was very careful with his wording of his requests. "First, I want to know what information was exchanged between you and the Eidolon of Entropy. Second, I want to know where that Eidolon is currently. And Third, I want to know the path to get out of this cave and back to our home plane."

Mophantatha considered each item as it was said. Visually weighing it in his mind. **"Three items for one item is a steep trade. But I will make this bargain because two of the questions have the same answer. Let's make a deal, little Eidolon."**

He extended his arm out, palm up, toward Ronan. At this proximity, Ronan could see that his arms were covered in small cracks that leaked a shadowy glow.

Before Ronan could hand over the dagger, Vallia called out, "How do we know that we will be allowed to leave safely? That was not part of the deal." She glared at Ronan and his negotiations.

Mophantatha gave a mischievous grin. **"No, it was not part of the deal. You are correct. But the trade off of killing you would not be worth the resulting complications. I do not want to have to deal with their Justices as a result of their death. So no, I will not kill you."**

Ronan looked at Vallia with an apologetic expression. Vallia eyed Ronan and thinned her lips. "I guess that is as good as we are going to get. Are you sure we don't have anything else to trade, Ronan? That dagger is really valuable, and it would be so difficult to lose."

Ronan nodded at the comment. "I am sure. This is the best thing we have to give. Trust me." He held out his hand to her, palm facing her. To anyone else it would have looked like he was telling her to stand down. But, just as Arkeen had done, he was asking for her trust. She looked at his hand and contemplated it. He knew this was a big ask.

"Ronan, I thought that the dagger..." Maya started to say but Vallia stomped on her foot. She seemed to register what was happening and recovered with her superb ability to lie. "I thought that the dagger was your most prized possession."

"It is," Ronan agreed. "And if I am going to give it up, I need everyone's approval." Vallia took a deep breath and reached out and grabbed Ronan's hand. He nodded at her, a silent thank you. He looked at Leo who seemed lost. He hoped that he would catch on.

Ronan slowly handed over the dagger to the eager Mophantatha. It was snatched away from his grip in a flash. Mophantatha then retracted his segmented body back up into the heights of the chamber. Once again leaving only his face visible in the torch lite, his nightmarish body was obscured by the darkness. Ronan felt a tingle in his arm and took several steps forward looking up at the Justice. The tingling stopped.

"A deal is a deal. The Eidolon that came before you brought me many questions. Similar to you, he wanted to know what I would tell him about the Eidolon and about their powers. So, we made some deals. He seemed to have a better understanding of his inheritance than you, but still wanted to know more. He also sought information about amplification of his powers."

Ronan began to wonder if Leo's stories were right. Maybe all Eidolon just wanted more power. That had been his driving force to meet this Justice after all.

Mophantatha carried on, **"So I gave him a history lesson about the first Eidolon. I told him about how two hundred years ago, the Eidolon of old sought the same increase in their powers. During the briefest of times when they were working together, they discovered their access**

to the Nether was limited, which meant their powers were limited. Together, the seven traveled into the heart of the Nether where they found a rare crystal. The mineral was filled with the same energy as the Bridge Point you crossed through when you came to meet me. Naturally in their limited creativity, they named it bridgestone. When held by the Eidolon, they were able to channel power directly connected to the laws of this plane."

Ronan listened with an intense curiosity. This crystal directly connected the wielder to the Nether. Images and aspirations flashed through his mind with all the things he could do with that sort of power.

"What did the old Eidolon do with the bridgestone?" Maya asked. Ronan nodded, eager to hear the outcome.

"They did what people always do. They envied each other's power and began to divide and fight amongst themselves. The bridgestone was weaponized as the Eidolon mounted it onto their swords or staffs or armor. Then they used their enhanced powers to conquer your world. This is what I shared with the Eidolon of Entropy."

"Did you tell him where to find some of this bridgestone?" Ronan asked, dreading the answer.

"No," Mophantatha answered.

Ronan let out a breath of relief.

Mophantatha smiled. **"I gave him some. I gave him a sword with the bridgestone set into the hilt that was wielded by his predecessor. He made me an offer I could not refuse."**

"What did he give you?" Maya asked, her curiosity clearly matching Ronan's.

Mophantatha waved his finger at Maya and made a tsk tsk noise. **"Our deal was for the information exchanged, not the goods and services."**

Ronan cursed himself for his own specificity. He realized his muscles were all tense after hearing the information. He had to force himself to take several slow breaths to relax even a little. So, the Eidolon of Entropy was vastly more experienced and he also possessed an amplified connection to the Nether. Ronan shuddered as he processed this. He had previously questioned if even a powerful Eidolon could accomplish what the Legislator of War was planning. Now it seemed like more of a possibility. "Did you talk about his plans?" He asked hopefully.

"Not in the slightest." Mophantatha said in a lazy voice. **"His Justice's plans are of no concern to me. Just as I don't care about your plans."**

"Do you have more of the bridgestone?" Maya asked with a glint in her eye.

"Are you looking to make another trade?" Mophantatha asked her with a grin.

Ronan was very interested in getting his hands on some bridgestone. He was actively thinking what else they could trade when he reminded himself that his first trade was temporary and could backfire at any moment. The fear of this led him to say, "I think we have made enough deals today. Don't you?"

Maya scowled at him. "We have made deals for your future but not for mine."

He was taken aback by her answer. *'What did she mean by that?'* He didn't have the time to ask right now, however. His head was already spinning from everything the Justice had said. Or maybe that was his blood loss. He looked back at Mophantatha and knew he had pushed his luck far enough.

"I don't think we will be making any more deals today," he said. "Let's finish up the one we have going.

Mophantatha's eyes sparked. **"Very well, you know where to find me when you decide you need something else. I will be here, waiting to make another trade."**

"Just tell us where the Eidolon of Entropy is," Ronan prompted, feeling a sense of urgency as the possibility of his collapse seemed to be growing. Vallia had wrapped his wound but he feared he had bled through the bandages by now.

"All business business business. I respect that," Mophantatha extended one of his arms and pointed back into the cavern and said, **"If you take the cave exit under the double arch, that path will take you within five miles of your prey. Your exit, as bargained, and his location."**

Vallia challenged, "Within five miles, that is a pretty large area. How do we know where he is in that space?"

Mophantatha's grin grew even more unnatural. **"Trust me Ether girl, you will know where he is. Just listen for the screams of the warriors being turned to ash. He should be close by."**

Chapter 36

Ronan's forearm tingled. He had no idea how long the dagger would stay in Mophantatha's hands. They had the information they were going to get at this point. Ronan pushed their farewell by saying, "Mophantatha, we are very grateful for an opportunity to make a trade with you. We must go and confront that Eidolon. Thank you for your hospitality. Can we just walk to those arches this way?"

"Leaving so soon? You don't want to stay and offer me anything else. No more artifacts? Or possibly you want to pledge your eternal servitude to me?"

Ronan's heart was pounding in his chest. His vision started to split so he was seeing two of the smooth faces up above. "As nice as that sounds, we really have to be going." He hoped that the Justice of Rest could not sense his heartbeat.

"Well, if you must go, then follow the path between my spoils. But I warn you. If you touch any of my riches at rest, there will be a reaction. A violent reaction."

Ronan leaned on Vallia and whispered, "We need to leave. Now." She obliged and they began to move forward. Leo followed with the light source. Maya brought up the rear.

They had to pass underneath Mophantatha as they walked. His torso slowly turned as they passed. The sound of his many legs shifting in the darkness echoed over their heads. As the light revealed more of the room, Ronan saw riches that an individual could not even fathom. Piles and piles of things. Just on the outside of the torches glow, Ronan swore he saw the

282

hull of a large galleon ship. But he couldn't make out the details in the dim light.

The torch illuminated a set of double stone arches with pictographs covering the surfaces. As they pass through it. Mophantatha's voice rang out throughout the cavern.

"Eidolon!"

Ronan immediately panicked. His forearm was tingling and growing warm, but the blade had not returned yet. He turned to face the Nether being.

"Equal trades are all that keeps this world from chaos. So, I will give you one more piece of information to keep things equal. In the future when you cross paths with my Eidolon, they will not be as generous as I have been. They have their mission. If you get in their way, they will stop you, permanently." As he said the last sentence, he smiled as he tossed the ruby dagger up into the air.

Ronan felt a surge of pain in his arm and knew in that moment the dagger had surpassed its distance limitations. To his horror, the dagger burst into flames, midair and vanished. Flames engulfed Ronan's hand along with a searing pain and the dagger appeared in his fist.

Ronan yelled, "RUN!"

The echoing scream of Mophantatha filled the cavern. The walls shook with the sound and dust fell from the ceiling. **"I gave you so much and you would steal from me! You will pay for this! I will hang your lifeless corpses on my wall as trophies!"**

The scratching sound of hundreds of armor-plated legs against stone tortured Ronan's ears. Ronan glanced over his shoulder as Vallia practically dragged him along. He regretted looking back when he saw the immense form of the Justice careening toward the group.

Mophantatha extended his hands forward.

Ronan's body froze mid step. Every muscle came to a sudden, screeching halt. He should have toppled over as he was not balanced at all on his one foot. But he was even denied the ability to fall. Out of his peripheral vision he could see Leo's arm extended forward mid-swing. He could still feel

Vallia holding him, but she too was frozen. His friends were all going to die, and it was his fault. He would have screamed if his mouth had been allowed to move.

Mophantatha's face came into Ronan's view. His long carapace encircled the group. Plates ground against each other. Legs criss crossing in front of them. Ronan felt helpless. He needed to swing the dagger in his hand. Needed to fight back but he could not move.

"You broke our trade! You violated a fair deal! What was your plan, little Eidolon? Give me your dagger and flee only to summon it back once you had left? Did you think you could run from me? I can stop mountains from falling into the sea. I can halt stars falling from the heavens! And you tried to run from me?"

Ronan tried to respond but his mouth would not open. The body of the Justice continued to squeeze the group. Tightening and compressing like a giant snake. Mophantatha's face hovered inches from Ronan's. Fear overwhelmed Ronan's thoughts. This was it. This was how he died. Staring into this Justice's wide grin.

Then out of the corner of his eye he saw a small spark of light, but it vanished immediately.

"Eidolon are all the same. They squander the blessings given to them. They have no respect for what power they come from. The first Eidolon were no different. All they cared about was their own power, their own abilities. Let's be honest. Once you Eidolon start thinking for yourselves, your value plummets. That's when we Justices need to look into trading up to a newer, better model. I have no use for a slave who questions their master."

Ronan saw another tiny spark of light out of the corner of his eye. Then another. The lights were coming from Leo's hand. Ronan felt a glimmer of hope. Leo was trying to open a rift. Another larger spark appeared. Mophantatha didn't see Leo's attempts. He was too focused on Ronan.

'Light that Leo serves, if you can hear me, please help him now,' Ronan desperately thought, not knowing what he expected.

One last flash led to a consistent glow. A small rift the size of Ronan's head flickered into existence. Something blurred out of the planar hole immediately after it had opened. It darted directly at Mophantatha and collided with his face. Ronan's heart leapt as he recognized the feathers and wisps of his faithful companion Sabastian, bursting forth from the Ether rift, as if he was waiting for his opportunity.

Sabastian's talons raked across Mophantatha's face. His beak pecked at Mophantatha's left eye. The Justice screamed and his whole body recoiled backward. Ronan's muscles unfroze. His foot found the ground and without hesitation, filled with a renewed adrenaline, he darted forward and ducked underneath Mophantatha's thrashing body. He dodged two legs that slammed down in front of him. Leo and Vallia followed suit, dipping and ducking the razor-sharp appendages that were flailing about as Sabastian continued his assault. Maya jumped up and vaulted off one leg onto another and then somersaulted over the armored body. She pushed off the plate and flipped in the air, landing next to Ronan as he hobbled under the archway.

Ronan looked back and saw Mophantatha's smooth face was now covered in dark, oily blood. Sabastian had definitely destroyed one of the Justice's eyes. Sabastian was looping around for another assault. Ronan watched the Justice as he reached out his hand. Sabastian froze. A beautiful bird mid-flight, motionless, as if painted onto a black canvas.

Ronan watched in horror as Mophantatha stooped down and picked up a metallic harpoon from a pile of weapons that lay nearby. Mophantatha rose and drew his arm back.

"Nooooo!" Ronan's scream filled the chamber.

The harpoon flew through the air. Its trajectory was impeccable. The sharp barbed point impaled Sabastian's breast. The frozen effect ended suddenly, and the bird and harpoon fell to the ground with thud and a small wisp.

Ronan lost all sense of everything except the blinding rage that filled him. He forgot about escaping, about the power of the Justice, even about his ever-increasing blood loss. All he cared about was destroying this Justice for what he just did to Sabastian. Maya tried to stop him, but he shoved her off. Ronan ran forward, ready to end Mophantatha.

Then pain exploded in the back of his leg. He collapsed and smashed into a pile of treasure. Looking down, he saw one of Maya's knives sticking out of his calf. He couldn't comprehend how it got there. Then he saw her running forward, toward him.

She yelled, "Oye, Justice of Greed!" as she spun around and launched another dagger high into the air.

Mophantatha turned away from the body of Sabastian toward Maya's call, just as the knife reached him. The blade sunk into his remaining eye. His scream rattled the domed chamber. He writhed and thrashed about. His centipede body collided with one of the columns supporting the roof and shattered through the stone. The column teetered and then fell backward impacting the double archway and demolishing the whole structure.

Ronan stared at the rubble where the exit had just been. Where Vallia and Leo had just been. Did they get out? Or were they crushed? There was no chance of getting through the rubble to see if they were okay. The column had eradicated the archways and the passage. Maya came beside him and tried to help him up.

"Stay quiet and help me, I can't lift you by myself," Maya whispered.

"You stabbed me," Ronan said in disbelief.

Maya tried again to heave him to his feet. "No, I saved your neck. You were going to get yourself killed. My vision showed you turning back but I didn't know why."

"What vision?" Ronan asked.

"Not now you idiot," Maya protested. "Get up, so we can get out of here."

Mophantatha's tortured scream filled the room. **"Eidolon! Where are you? I will end both of you. You have taken my vision. But I will find you and I will tear your eyes out, chain you to my wall and repeatedly stop your heart until it fails."**

Maya put her finger to her lips and gave another heave.

Ronan didn't know if he could trust her. If the other option was anything other than getting found by the now blind and enraged Justice, he might have resisted more. He helped her pull himself up so she could support him.

286

Together they hobbled off as the Justice searched for them. Mophantatha skittered his body over the piles of treasures and trinkets, trying to locate them. Ronan and Maya struggled around the outside of the round room until they found another opening in the wall. Without thinking Maya half carried, half dragged Ronan into that entrance. They limped blindly down the small stone hallway.

Ronan lost track of their progress in the darkness. He wanted to collapse and cry but Maya kept moving him along. She seemed to know where she was going, and Ronan had no energy to question her. They finally halted their retreat under an odd glow that filtered through a crack in the ceiling. Maya slumped Ronan against a wall. Then she sat across the narrow hall and faced him. Both breathed heavily and stared at each other.

"Do you want to tell me why you stabbed me?" Ronan said between wheezing breaths.

Maya rolled her eyes, "I already told you, I had to save you from your stupidity."

"That monster killed Sabastian. I was going to kill him," Ronan insisted.

Maya shook her head, "Even with both his eyes gone, he was still unbelievably powerful. Look, I saw this was going to happen. There was one way out of there and it was not with you as the victorious conqueror over the Justice of Rest."

"You had a vision about Mophantatha killing Sabastian and you didn't warn me? When was this?"

"I had a vision the first night after we kidnapped Osmodius. I watched you walk away into your tent and was suddenly racked by a vision. I have told you before, sometimes my future glimpses are hard to interpret until the circumstances are in front of me."

"What did you see?" Ronan asked, not sure if he even cared to know at this point.

"My vision showed the four of us running through piles of gold and silver. Obviously, that didn't make sense until I got into that room. I told you I had a bad feeling about the place. All I knew was that we were trying to escape but I had no idea what we were running from. Then I saw a flash of your bird frozen in time. How was I supposed to know he was going to die?"

At her words Ronan felt the reality of the statement and closed his eyes. Maya continued, "Then I saw you, wounded and weak, running into a dark shadow. I knew if you reached it that you would die. But I stopped you in my vision." She paused and Ronan knew there was something else. Something she didn't want to say.

He opened his eyes and narrowed his brow. "What else did you see Maya?"

After a moment of not meeting his eyes, she said, "I saw you here under this light... alone."

"So, your vision was wrong?" he asked, confused.

She stood up with something clutched in her hands. It took Ronan a moment to realize she was holding the Kitmazi's map case. He stared at her perplexed. Then he understood why she had been reluctant to say the last part of her vision. She was going to leave him here. She had played him. Probably played him from the beginning. Of course she had. How had he not seen it before? She was such a good liar. This realization hurt more than all his wounds together.

"You're just going to leave me here to die?" He asked. His trust for her shattered in that moment.

"You won't die. You still have to face the Eidolon of Entropy. I don't know how you live through this, but my visions have never been wrong before."

Ronan's head throbbed. How could she do this? "What about the one where we fight the Eidolon together? If you leave me, that vision won't come true."

"I told you from the very beginning, that vision showed you, Vallia, and Leo fighting the Eidolon. Never me."

Ronan questioned this. Hadn't she said the four of them? Did she not mention herself? He tried to push himself up but had no strength. He wanted to try to stop her. "If you don't help us and we fail, the Eidolon will dissolve the barrier between the Ether and the Prime Plane and destroy everything. That is what you said. If that happens, it will be on your conscience."

Maya laughed and fastened the map case on her belt. "Well, I'll probably be dead if that happens, so I am not too worried. Look, I thought you would understand this. Your future is directly tied to fighting and stopping this Eidolon. Mine is not. I am on a path to avenge the death of my mother; I always have been. The Council made the laws that led to our encampment in Latis. They are the reason that she died, and they will pay for that in kind with their own lives."

"Then why don't you help me kill the Legislator of War?"

Maya sighed, "Ronan, I would help you but it's not in my vision. I don't choose what the visions show me."

"You said it yourself; your visions are vague and hard to interpret. What if you were not in the vision because you were mounting a sneak attack or because you were helping hold back Legionnaire? There may be something your visions didn't show you."

She shook her head. "This map shows the location of the Bridge Point that links to my Justice. I think it is time that their silence is addressed. Mophantatha told us about the bridgestone and the weapons of the old Eidolon. If my Justice can tell me where to find one of those, that would give me the power that I need to dismantle the Council. I really think you can stop the Legislator of War. But if you kill him, they will just replace him with some other corrupt person. I need to burn them out at their roots."

Ronan couldn't believe his ears. "My Justice wants me to destroy the Council as well. That is what he wants me to do once I kill off the Eidolon of Entropy."

Maya gave him a sad look. "You don't have to lie to me, Ronan. You can't stop me. We have different fates and that is okay. If you live through the upcoming battle, I feel we will see each other again. If you don't... Well, I hope to see you again."

Ronan's anger bubbled over. He swore and tried to kick Maya. She dodged it with ease but the hurt expression on her face grew. Without another word, she walked off into the darkness.

Ronan watched her go. How could she be so lost and deceived by her own personal agenda? It took him a long time seething under the glowing crack before he compared Maya's motives to his own.

He sat, propped up against the wall of the dark hallway and contemplated what his pursuit of knowledge and power had led to. Just days ago, he had felt more powerful than ever. He had three spirits following his every command, a party of powerful friends looking to him for direction, and his powers were growing with every day. Now his spirits were all gone, his friends were either back on the Prime Plane or crushed under several tons of rubble, Maya had betrayed him to die, and even his trusty hawk was gone. Now his body would lay here forever, like one of Mophantatha trophies. Lost in some forsaken hallway of the Nether. If he had any strength left in his broken body, he would have sobbed. But even tears seemed to be beyond him at this point.

There was no way to tell the passage of time in this hallway. The crack of light above was unwavering. He didn't know if he laid there for hours or maybe even days. At some point his exhaustion took over and he passed out on the floor.

Ronan dreamt of the caravan of the old Apollymi woman whom he had discovered to be the Kitmazi. The old woman sat across the table from him. The ruby dagger lay on the table. The Kitmazi stared at Ronan. "Eidolon..." her raspy voice cooed.

Defeat filled Ronan and dread crashed through him. This was it. She was here to collect his body. He had failed his end of the bargain, and she was about to claim him as her charcoal minion, empty and wandering the land trying to complete his task. He was tired and beaten down. There didn't seem to be any hope. He could grovel at her feet but what was the point? He looked at her wrinkled face that was covered with small glowing cracks. A sadness slowly washed over Ronan. He had been so focused on himself the last few days he had never taken the time to consider her situation.

"When you were pulled from your world, you must have felt all alone."

Pain flashed across her face at the statement.

"I know what that's like. I have seen the world you come from. To me it is terrifying. But to you it's home." Ronan saw longing in her eyes. "If I

290

stab the dagger into the Ether Scar, do you get to go home?"

The old woman nodded slowly before she had to stifle an ash filled cough.

He looked down at the knife. Maybe there was an option for one more deal to be made.

"You healed my arm back in the camp. I don't know if you had an ulterior motive or if you were just being generous. But maybe you could heal me again if I am not too far gone. I think we can still help each other. If you heal me, I will fulfill my end of our bargain. I don't care if I have to recruit an army of spirits to stop the Eidolon of Entropy at the Scar, I'll get you home.

She watched him for a long while, considering. She then slowly extended her hand.

Ronan let out a deep breath he had been holding. This time he understood what he was committing to. He reached out and clasped her hand.

Flames engulfed the caravan, burning it away until all that was left was the Kitmazi and Ronan, clasping hands amongst a burning inferno.

Ronan woke up screaming and writhing. His entire body felt like it was being cooked in a furnace while his vision flashed in and out until the pain finally subsided. It took him a long while of heavy breathing to realize that he was not lying on the floor. The sensation of him being upright confused him. Then he realized that his legs were not supporting him. They were sliding behind him along a stone floor. He squinted to his left. Through the haze of his vision, he saw a skeleton with glowing green, flaming eyes dragging him. He looked to the right and saw another skeleton.

He struggled against his captors but found their grip unyielding. The skeletons rounded a bend and Ronan saw a large double door at the end of the hallway made of solid metal. Torch sconces filled with bright green flames were fastened on either side of the door. The flickering emerald light cast shadows along the ancient gateway as well as the ominous embossed emblem set into the door. It was the mark that had been on Ronan's arm as long as he could remember. The skull split in half. One half on each door coming together at the seam to form the familiar mark. The left skull looked to be made of chiseled marble. The right skull's smokey visage consisted of glowing green crystalline material that ebbed and pulsed. The mark of the Justice of Death.

Chapter 37

The metal doors swung open without the skeletons touching them, revealing the room within. Ronan shivered as he was hoisted over the threshold. He was not sure if this was his nerves or the drastic drop in temperature that accompanied the new space.

Ronan let out a gasp as he entered into a spectacular rotunda. Around the circumference of the room, small stone pillars supported the eerie green ceiling. Ronan's breath quickened when he looked up and saw that above him was a shifting sea of green flames behind some kind of thick glass. As he watched the writhing mass of flame, several faces appeared, pressing against the transparent material and then vanished. The sight made him uneasy as he remembered the infirmary and the spirits pressing against his mental shield.

Then his eyes fell to the center of the room where an intimidating throne composed of sharp, glossy, black and green rocks sat. Ronan swallowed hard as his gaze made contact with the black eyes of the being sitting on the throne.

Ronan was suddenly released by the skeletons, causing him to smack into the stone floor. He moaned and only lifted his head when the being spoke from the throne.

"Welcome Ronan, my Eidolon. I am Mawveth. Justice of Death. How are you, my champion?"

With a strained heave, Ronan shakily stood up. His knees wobbled but he was able to stand. He looked upon his Justice with trepidation. Mawveth. Ronan finally had a name for the shadowy benefactor.

293

Fascination and fright filled him at the same time. The black voids that were his eyes bore into Ronan making him feel small. The flare of the Justice's nostrils, or more accurately skeletal slits, added to the foreboding appearance as much as the wide grin filled with several rows of pearly white, razor-sharp teeth.

Ronan took a breath to steady himself and called out, "I feel sore, stiff, and exhausted but I'm still breathing so I am guessing I am not dead."

"You are not dead, despite your best efforts. Though I must admit that I feel no sympathy for your condition. Were your wounds not a result of your own incompetence? Turning your back on an enemy, trusting another Eidolon?"

Ronan's fear began to turn into irritation at the accusation. He could admit he was stupid to turn his back on Osmodius. But he had thought Maya was his friend. Even thinking of her now caused a wave of sadness and anger to wash over him. His instinct was to snip back, but he resisted. *'I need Mawveth.'* He told himself. *'I need what he can give me.'*

"Yeah, I went through a lot to get here. But I would also say I've proven myself in the process. I think I have earned some of your respect."

Mawveth inclined his head. **"What you say is true. You have been through a lot. Look at how much you have survived in order to stand before me. How many people can say they fought a Justice and walked away, not only breathing but with the Justice mutilated and blind?"**

"Mophantatha got what he deserved." Ronan balled his fist at the thought of Sabastian.

"I do not deny it."

Ronan raised his eyebrows in surprise. He had thought his Justice would have been furious about what had happened.

"What an ironic punishment for the junk collector. Now he is trapped among a fortune that he will never be able to see. Forced to feel every artifact that he has."

'Trapped?' Ronan caught the curious word but did not have time to process it before Mawveth continued.

"Not only is the Justice of Rest blind. Before you took out his

294

eyesight, you tricked him into killing The Arch Archivist. I did not think you would accomplish this task, but I commend you."

Ronan's surprise only grew. He wasn't in trouble? In fact, he was being praised? Part of himself felt emboldened by the recognition. The other part knew the praise was unearned. While Ronan had been filled with anger at Osmodius after he had stabbed him, Ronan had not killed him. Mophantatha had. Ronan had also not blinded the Justice. That had been Sabastian and Maya. But if Mawveth was applauding Ronan, who was he to tell him otherwise. Hadn't he spent the last few days working to appease his Justice? Didn't he need his clandestine benefactor to help to stop the Eidolon of Entropy?

"Yes, Osmodius is dead. I did what you commanded. Now, I think it is time that we talk about the future." A knot in his stomach began to tighten with anticipation. "I still need to face the Eidolon of Entropy. But I have no spirits, no friends, and I am stuck in the Nether with no escape."

"You do seem to be in quite the predicament."

Ronan furrowed his brow. Was Mawveth playing coy with him? He chose his words carefully. "Like I said, I don't have any of the… resources that I need to fight the Eidolon of Entropy. He is a Legislator of War, and he has a standing army at his command, not to mention he possesses bridgestone."

Mawveth smiled a wicked grin and nodded. **"What is it that you would request of me?"**

This was it. Ronan bit the inside of his cheek contemplating what he wanted to propose. He had told the Kitmazi that he would fulfill their bargain without any idea of how he was going to accomplish that. But now he was standing in front of the Justice of Death. Mawveth had given him his powers. Now he could give him a chance to stop the Eidolon. An opportunity to shed the helplessness that Ronan felt had encased him.

He had given the problem of the Eidolon of Entropy a fair bit of thought on his journey north from Ristiven. Thinking about the information he had gained from Mophantatha, he knew what he thought would be most helpful if he was going to have a chance to stop the Legislator of War and his plan for destruction.

"I have heard a lot of disturbing facts over the last few days about the Eidolon of Entropy. He is powerful and has had his abilities half the time I have been alive. If I am going to face him, I want to make it as even a fight as possible. The Legislator has an army of Legionnaires. I am going to need an army of spirits. He has an amplified connection to the Nether. I need bridgestone to have a chance to fight him."

Mawveth folded his hands and leaned back onto his throne. He stared at Ronan as if evaluating him. After a long silence, Mawveth said, "**An army I can do. In fact, I had anticipated this need. Bridgestone is another story.**"

Ronan frowned, "You don't have any? Or know where I can get it? Mophantatha said the Eidolon of old came into the Nether and found the bridgestone. Why can't I find more?"

"**The Eidolon searched for weeks into the deepest parts of the Nether to find the few fragments of bridgestone that they did. You don't have that kind of time and even if you did, the things down there would eat you alive.**"

Ronan swallowed hard, a disheartened ache growing inside him. Without the bridgestone what was the point of an army? He had struggled to solidify two spirits in a fight for an extended amount of time. How was he supposed to command a squadron of spirit soldiers? Then he began to question what the Justice had just said.

"Wait, if you have an army of spirits at your command, why don't you just kill the Eidolon of Entropy and then attack the rest of the Council?"

"**If that was an option, what would I need you for?**"

Ronan recognized the acknowledgement of the Justice's predicament. He understood this meant he had some level of negotiating power. He watched as Mawveth tilted his head to size up Ronan. Ronan wondered if the Justice was gauging how much to reveal. This annoyed Ronan after all he had done for Mawveth.

Eventually Mawveth explained, "**In my current position, I am not allowed to control spirits in your plane. I can get away with one or two here and there, but an army is out of the question.**"

Ronan squinted as he took in this information. *'Not allowed?' Who was able to restrict the Justice?'*

"Then how do you have an army?"

"When you met the Eidolon of Kinetic Energy, she informed you about the Eidolon of Entropy's plan. From that point, I have been preparing. I may not have command over the spirits, but I can delay their transition for a time. The Eidolon of Entropy has left quite an impressive trail of corpses in his wake. These casualties will be his inevitable downfall. I have gathered the spirits. Called them to the Scar, like moths to a flame. They stand ready for their commander. They wait for you."

Ronan's heart started pounding in his chest. He had not expected the Justice to accept his need for an army. Let alone, have troops ready to be deployed.

An army of spirits, under Ronan's command. He thought back to the dreams of the spirits saluting him bowing to him. With an army he may be able to actually stop the Legislator of War. A prospect that he had never really had full confidence in. Then he began to think about what else he could do with an army. He could march on the gates of various labor camps like Latis and free the captives. The walls of Ristiven would not stand a chance against the flood of corpses that he could release through the secret aqueduct tunnel. The Council would be defeated within the day. Ronan could have powers that matched those of Nizomotus, but with morals and respect for the spirits.

This thought brought his plotting to a halt. The army was composed of spirits. He could not hold them on the Prime Plane too long or they would become hollow. Which meant his time to use them was limited. He reasoned that fighting the Eidolon should not be an issue assuming he could get out of the Nether soon. But marching an army, even an army of spirits puppeting corpses, would take time.

Then his hopes were dashed even further as he recalled his initial problem. He was nowhere near strong enough to command an army and had no way to get bridgestone. There was no choice. Despite his pride he had to tell this to Mawveth.

"Without bridgestone, I don't know how I would be able to command your army. I am still figuring out my powers. Give me a few years and maybe, but right now, I don't think that is an option." He hated saying this, but all he could think about was the spirits trying to overwhelm him at the infirmary. That was less than one hundred spirits. He could not even imagine the scene if there had been thousands.

To Ronan's surprise, Mawveth let out a deep laugh at this.

"Of course you are not able to command the army by yourself. I never thought that you could."

Ronan balled his fists, anger blazing up inside him. Before he could lash out, the Justice said, **"Don't look so surprised. If you had the ability to command that many spirits, I would be calling you the Justice of Death. No, I would never have made an Eidolon if they could become powerful enough to rival my own prowess."**

"Then why even mention the spirits in the north? Why bring me here at all if you knew I couldn't command an army?" Ronan's voice echoed off the sickly green walls. He had not meant to shout but his anger was now well provoked.

"Watch yourself Champion. I have my reasons for bringing you to my domain. Do not question my motives." This was said in a threatening tone, but Ronan was not in the mood to care at this point. What did he have to lose?

"There is a way for you to control the army I have procured. I can make a pact with you like I did with Nizomotus years ago. A pact of power and control. I gave you your powers. I can also open the floodgates of your Nether connection."

Ronan's anger was suddenly stifled at the prospect. He had thought his powers were already strong. What would it be like if he made this deal? *Is another deal really what I want?* He was suddenly racked with flashes of all the deals he had made since gaining his powers. Mr. Kemin's deal to get Leo out of prison had almost killed him and his friends. The Kitmazi's deal had resulted in his slow transformation into a charcoal monster. Osmodius' deal to take him to the Bridge Point had resulted in him getting stabbed. Mophantatha's deal for information had resulted in him losing his friends and Sabastian. Now he was staring at his shadowy benefactor, looking to make another deal? At what cost?

"You give me power to command an army. What do you get out of it?" Ronan asked, trying not to let his voice portray his hesitancy.

"Your boon of power would come with a more... permanent commitment to my plans for the future. I branded you as a babe with my mark in order to claim you as my champion. This pact would interweave that mark with a binding life contract under my service."

A life contract under the Justice of Death. The thought constricted Ronan's chest, making it difficult to breathe. So far, he had done as he was directed by the Justice but oftentimes with reluctance and much debate. What if the Justice told him to do something he didn't want to do? The instance in the Kitmazi's caravan came back to him as he was beaten to a pulp by the Justice's spirit. He could only imagine what would happen if he disobeyed or said no under the pact. How could he possibly accept this?

A battle was raging in his head as he debated with himself. *"If I don't have an army, I stand no chance against the Legislator of War. If I don't stop him, he will destroy Celcus. But that only matters if I am on Celcus. If I stay in the Nether, what does it matter?"* He shook his head at this selfish thought. Of course it mattered. He may be alone right now, but the destruction would affect everyone. Mr. Kemin, the Carpenters, the people oppressed by the Council that he felt an obligation to help. *'I need that army to stop the Eidolon of Entropy.'*

Trying to buy time to think through the flood of conflicting thoughts, he asked, "If you are able to do that, why have the other Eidolon not made these pacts with their Justices? The Eidolon of Gravity would have made that deal in a heartbeat. But I don't think he was ever offered that. Or the Eidolon of Entropy. All he wants is more power. Why would he not take that deal?"

"Because it can only be done in person. I doubt that the Eidolon of Gravity ever met his Justice. It is prohibited to tell our Eidolon how

299

to find us. If the Eidolon is not looking for their Justice, they won't find them. As for the Eidolon on Entropy, who's to say he has not made a pact deal."

The look on the Justice's face told Ronan he knew more than he was letting on. Ronan couldn't believe his ears. He realized his mouth was open, so he shut it. Then he opened it again exclaiming, "He has bridgestone and a pact with his Justice? That's not fair! That's unbelievable. That's... that's..."

"That is the reason you will need to make a pact with me." Mawveth's mouth curled up ever so slightly. "I have only seen the combination of a pact and bridgestone once. Nizomotus made a pact with me and received his boon. Then, the selfish fiend determined that was not enough, so he led the other Eidolon on the expedition into the Nether. Trust me, if the Eidolon of Entropy has made a pact with his Justice and has bridgestone, the Ether barrier will break like glass before him."

"If what you say is true, I have no hope with or without your pact." Ronan knew he had already been defeated. He had failed. There was no chance he could fight the Eidolon. There was no point going to the Ether Scar, which meant he had failed the Kitmazi twice. It did not matter what he did. He could go to the Ether Scar and die, or he could be burnt alive from the inside out by the Kitmazi.

"You forget one thing. He may have the power to dissolve the bonds holding back the Ether and any warrior that faces him will be ash in seconds. But he has no power to touch their spirits. I am not even given the ability to destroy a spirit."

Was there really a chance if he attacked with spirits? Mishkawl had been able to fling Arkeen and Ta Rhe out of the laboratory, but thinking back, they were not harmed despite being smashed into a wall. Ronan had felt the impact through his connection, but they were fine. If that was true, then maybe he could stand against the Eidolon of Entropy.

Then he registered the last thing Mawveth had said. 'I am not given the ability.' Who gives abilities to a Justice? It was not the first odd thing he had said. Before he had said he was 'not allowed' and something about

300

Mophantatha being 'trapped.' These things didn't add up. If Ronan was going to even contemplate accepting this pact, and it boggled his mind that he was considering it, he needed to know where this language was coming from.

"If I am going to accept this pact with you, I need to know where your allegiances lie. You keep making it sound like someone is putting rules and regulations over you. Honestly, I am amazed you follow them."

Mawveth's face elongated in a deep frown. He did not look pleased with the statement.

"I serve no one. Others serve me and my will."

"But who is allowing you to do things and setting your rules?"

The Justice glared at Ronan, working his jaw furiously.

Ronan was fearful of the murderous look he was receiving but forced himself to say, "You want me to make this pact. I can tell. But if I am going to, I need to know this."

Finally, through a clenched jaw, the Justice said, "I serve no one. But like everyone and everything, I am subject to the laws of the Light."

"The Light?" Ronan was surprised by this. Mawveth was the second Justice to mention the Light. The same one Leo and Ta Rhe faithfully served. The same Light that Leo had stood behind when calling out Mophantatha on his lies.

Mawveth spat on the ground at the name. **"Do you really think that if I was not forced into my position as a Justice of Death, I would gleefully help spirits transition into judgment? Do you really think Mophantatha would officiate over the latent energies of your world if his hand was not forced?"**

Ronan had considered their dedication to their roles odd. As he thought about this truth, it made sense. If the Light made the world and everything in it as Ta Rhe had said, it would make sense the Light would also have made the Justices.

"So why are you a Justice if you don't want to be one?"

"Foolish boy, all the Justices are confined to their individual roles as punishments. Trapped in their own enclosures to work our tasks.

We are all unrightfully being penalized. We are in these positions as a supposed retribution for our actions against the Light."

"This is a punishment?" Ronan found this difficult to understand. "You have unimaginable power and control over spirits, and you see this as being victimized? What did you do to be punished in this way?"

Mawveth looked up in the air as if recalling an event. **"We tried to overthrow the Light near the beginning. You see, we recognized the weaknesses of the Light, where others did not. We saw that the Light was too merciful and gracious. Too slow to anger and filled with love. What a terrible combination of attributes for a supposed king of kings."**

Ronan considered the list of attributes. Oddly enough he was not unfamiliar with the list. He thought back to when Ta Rhe had spoken the very same list. But hadn't the UN'kra spoken of them as unequivocally good?

"What makes those things negative?" Ronan probed. "My friend told me that this Light was the creator of all life. That those attributes were what informed us about the goodness of the Light."

Mawveth grimaced at this and clawed at the stone of his throne. **"The Light may have given you life but ponder this. Before the foundation of the world, the Light knew all who would live as the Light created all that live. The Light also knew when all will die. That means the Light condemned all to death. Is that not cruel?"**

Ronan thought about the statement. The Justice seemed correct at first. Then Ronan started to see holes in the logic.

"My knowledge of this Light comes from my UN'kra friends, so I don't know much. But one said that the Light is good, pure, and just. He believed that after death, he will go to be in the Light's kingdom where he will praise and worship the Light for all eternity. That does not seem cruel to me."

Mawveth made a guttural noise of indignation **"Do you believe him? Do you believe that in the kingdom of the Light, mortals are welcome? For the Light's own law condemns all for it says that all have sinned and fall short of the glory of the Light. You have been lied to about**

302

the Light. If all fall short in glory, who would be granted access to the Light's kingdom?"

Ronan recalled Leo saying this same statement to Maya. *'All have sinned and fall short of the glory of the Light.'* And what was it Ta Rhe had said? *'No one is good, not even one.'* But that was not where either had left the statement.

"I didn't think that it is based on the goodness of any individual. My friends made it seem like it is based on the goodness of the Light. Everyone may fall short, but I thought the Light offers forgiveness. My friends said forgiveness can be attained by those who repent of their walk along the path of darkness and turn to walk the narrow path the Light sets before them."

Ronan had the realization of the oddity of the conversation. This seemed like a strange choice of person to be having this discussion with. But something in Ronan had awakened and he had to understand this. He didn't know why, but it was inexplicably an imperative at this moment.

Mawveth cackled at this, **"More evidence of cruelty. The Light offers forgiveness for only those who repent? How gracious is the Light to withhold glory eternal from everyone?"**

This statement kindled the fire of Ronan's anger. Should the Eidolon of Entropy be rewarded for trying to kill everyone? Should the Council Legislators be blessed once they die for all the darkness they have pursued and created? It would be one thing if they possessed even a spoonful of remorse for their actions. But, to Ronan, it seemed fair that those that chose to walk in darkness were destined to stumble and fall and be penalized. Ronan's stomach sank as he thought about his own walk. It had definitely been one of darkness. He had only ever lived for himself and his own desires. Seeking power over his life, and respect from those around him. Even now he was trying to save face with Mawveth because of what he offered. This realization led him to say what he was really thinking.

"If the Light created all and gave life to all, who can blame the Light for setting an end to all life? That seems like the privilege of the one who makes the rules. If the Light offers life after death and forgiveness for trespasses to those who truly repent of their path in darkness, then that is gracious. Those who walk in darkness don't get to be blessed for ignoring or breaking the rules. I think you're just upset that you are being punished for your actions."

Mawveth snarled at this. **"You speak of things you have no understanding of, and you are testing my patience. You don't want to do that, I promise you. If you know what is good for you, you will shut your mouth and you will submit to me. I offer you a path to power and victory and you have the nerve to challenge me?"**

A path to victory… Something about this statement brought up Ta Rhe's poem about a path. One of the lines had said something about travelers being beckoned off the right path by darkness. But when they left the path, the shadows were heartless. Ronan scrunched his nose trying to remember the last part of the poem. Something about hopelessness and turning back to the path of the Light because the Light is sovereign.

Ronan stared at the Justice with disdain. He felt he was trapped in this decision. If he turned down the pact, he would not be able to fight the unbelievably powerful Eidolon of Entropy, and everything would be destroyed. But if he said yes, he would be committing to leaping into the darkness with no promise that he would ever emerge. Ta Rhe had told him that he was not too far down a path that he could not repent of. But why even test the line? Ronan's experiences in his life had shown him that corruption leads to more corruption. Not to repentance. There is always one more reason to justify the nefarious and crooked things. Why tempt that when there was an option to pick a better path. 'A better path.' Was there an option for Ronan to pick a better path? For him to pick the path of the Light? It would mean refusing the Justice, but the Justice was under the subject of the Light. Maybe there was a chance that the Light could help him stop the Eidolon.

He looked directly into the Justice's eyes and asked, "What if I say no?"

At Ronan's challenge, Mawveth looked surprised. Recovering quickly, the Justice slowly stood up from his throne. While sitting, he looked small and diminutive. But standing, he became fiercely imposing. He flexed his back, and inky black feathered wings unfurled. Two sets of them. One set was high on his shoulders and the other set extended out of his mid back. The wings had somehow been hidden when he sat but now, they filled the chamber. He was easily ten feet tall and with the shadow of the wings, he looked massive.

"What do you mean no? You are faced up against impossible odds and want to refuse your only chance to succeed? If you turn down this deal, you are refusing my aid. And if that is the case, I have to question your loyalty to me. If I have to question your loyalty, then what use are you to me? And after all I have done for you."

Any other time in his life, Ronan would have been petrified with fear. But the same desire that had inspired him to learn more about the Light rose up in him as a blazing courage. Mawveth did not respect Ronan. He didn't even care about him. Why would Ronan make a pact with him? Why would he even want to be his champion? He was just as vile as the Council that Ronan was dedicated to fighting. Mawveth had proven himself to be selfish and only concerned about himself. Then again, so had Ronan.

The thought made him think about Ta Rhe's account of 'the good news.' About how he could seek repentance for his actions in the Light. How by the strength of the Light he could walk away from the darkness. Away from what Ta Rhe had called his sinfulness. Ta Rhe had said, 'Let it die in its corruption. Accept a new life where you strive for righteousness and holiness for the glory of the Light.'

Ronan didn't want to follow the path of darkness he had been on. He had thought it would lead him to happiness, but it had only led to pain. It was at this moment that he realized that the path of the Light seemed unequivocally better than the path of Death. Hadn't Ta Rhe said that he could not serve death and life at the same time? So that could only mean one thing.

Ronan's confidence, bolstered by the sourceless determination, led Ronan to stand tall and say, "After all you have done for me? Really, is that what you think? Let's walk through that, shall we?" Ronan could feel the tension in his chest and neck. "You claimed me as a baby. But where were my powers when my house burnt to the ground?" Ronan gritted his teeth. "Where was my command of spirits as I was beaten every day in the orphanage. Where was my benefactor when I was starving in the streets? You activated my power only when it benefited you." He felt his anger flowing like a breaking dam. "You gave me these powers that I thought were a blessing, but if it means being enslaved to you and your schemes, then it is not worth having them. You could give me the power I need to save thousands of lives but that doesn't matter to you! Why would it! You claim to care about the living but all you want is their worship. But why would they worship you? You are a chained-up dog. You say you serve no one but you can't pick your teeth without consulting the Light? You are.."

"**Enough!**" The Justice's voice boomed through the chamber. He bent over, grabbing his throne by the armrests and heaved, hoisting it over his head. With a snarl, he hurled it through the air at Ronan. Ronan dove out of the way and rolled on the stone floor. His body screamed in pain with the effort. The throne smashed into thousands of pieces.

Ronan got to his feet and stared into the rage filled voids of Mawveth's eyes. Despite being almost crushed, Ronan felt a strange calm wash over him in that instant. Mawveth was furious but Ronan didn't care. The flood of Ronan's emotions that had just poured out had been a confirmation that he could not serve the Justice of Death.

"I never asked to be your champion. I can't lie, at first, I thought it was a blessing, but now I realize it was a curse. Maybe it could have been something good without the strings attached. I don't know. What I do know is that I'm cutting those strings. I am no longer going to be your marionette. I'm done."

"**You think you can just quit? You think that I will let you leave? You will either walk out of here as my champion, or you will not walk out of here at all. Bow before me Eidolon. Or prepare to serve me forever as an enslaved spirit.**'

Ronan almost pitied the Justice in that moment. "You and I both know you don't have that power. You're just the gatekeeper. All the authority you have was given to you by the Light. You may take my powers or break my

306

body. But come what may, I am choosing to serve the Light."

As he said this, a gust of wind ruffled Ronan's hair.

Mawveth became visually concerned. The breeze suddenly picked up speed and became like a hurricane. Mawveth called out over the gale, **"What is this? What are you doing? What is happening?"** His focus suddenly shifted from a piercing intensity directed at Ronan, to an almost fearful caution directed above Ronan's head. Ronan looked up. He saw a small particle of light suspended ten feet over his head. Just floating in mid air. It drifted unaffected by the wind. Ronan blinked several times, but it did not fade. There was a strange beauty about the globule of light.

The globe of light began to wobble. Ronan watched as it fluctuated shape and then began to shift through brilliant colors until it produced a small tendril of flaming light.

Mawveth narrowed his black eyes. He said in a low, slow voice, **"How is this possible?"**

The flaming tendril of light wiggled in the air. It slowly flowed back and forth. Then it began to grow longer. As it grew, it started flowing down toward Ronan. He just stared up at it, captivated by its splendor. A chroma of living color in a black and white world.

Mawveth shouted over the wind, **"You... cannot... do this... He is mine!"** Ronan looked at the Justice as he yelled. Mawveth fully unfurled his four black wings and flapped them all at once catapulting himself forward; clawed hands outstretched toward Ronan's throat.

A flash blinded Ronan for a second accompanied by the crack of thunder. The sound was clearly audible even over the forceful winds. Mawveth was launched in the opposite direction, where he collided with one of the columns, shattering it on impact. The room shook as he hit the ground. Ronan saw a second tendril of flaming light retract slowly back into the particle. The particle had protected Ronan by smacking Mawveth across the room with no effort at all.

The first tendril of light continued its slow journey down. As it did, Mawveth began to push himself off the ground. Black blood ran down his face from a cut just above his eye. He looked at Ronan with a savage wildness about him and bellowed. **"You are my champion! Not some follower of the Light. This is not your path. You are nothing without me. You have no army, no hope for a future. I will destroy you and all that you hold dear for this betrayal!"** Mawveth flapped his wings again, bringing himself upright and into a full sprint toward Ronan. As he bounded forward with a bloodthirsty visage, the tendril of light touched Ronan on the forehead. Ronan was blinded immediately, his vision going white.

Chapter 38

Ronan's eyes fluttered open. Then he bolted upright as the memory of Mawveth's attempted assault materialized in his mind. But Mawveth was nowhere to be seen. Ronan was alone. He took in his surroundings to find that he was lying on a grass mat inside a tented structure. The tent around him was not made of cloth but animal pelts sewn together. The space was bare except for an empty metal pot hung over a cold fire pit made of stones. Sunlight streamed in through the tent flap.

He had no idea where he was. How long had he been out? How had he gotten out of the Nether?

Then he realized all his clothes except for his undergarments and the chain holding Arkeen's ring had been taken off of him. The cool air chilled his skin. Or at least what was left of his skin. Looking down at his chest, he was overwhelmed by the sight. Half of his torso and all of his arm was blackened and burnt. The burning seemed to have radiated from the location where he had been stabbed by Osmodius.

He flexed the charcoal fingers and found they worked without issue. His skin felt like it had been covered in wet clay and left to dry. No pain came from the burnt sections of his body which possibly unnerved him more. Looking at the chard body parts made him woozy. His leg, where Maya's knife had stabbed him, was similarly a charcoal mess. With his unburnt, flesh-covered hand he felt the charred areas. They were hard like the bark of a tree and left a black residue on his fingers. The glowing fire rune of the Kitmazi caught his attention and he stared at it with a feeling of hopelessness. It appeared that the sealing of his wounds had come at a great cost to his body. How could he have been so stupid to make that deal?

"Why are you so sad? Today is a day for rejoicing," a voice announced to Ronan's right.

Ronan shouted in sheer surprise. A second ago, he had been alone in the tent. He looked up and saw a human man in a simple white robe sitting on the floor next to the fire pit. The fire was somehow lit, and stew was boiling in the pot.

The stranger said, "Do not be afraid, Beloved, for you have found favor on this day." He spoke slowly with a drawl in his voice.

"What?" Ronan blearily asked, blinking his eyes several times to make sure he was not hallucinating the man and the food.

The stranger stirred his stew and then smiled at Ronan. "Look at you, exiting the chamber of death more alive than when you went in."

Ronan looked around, hoping for some context to the situation. "I'm sorry, who are you? And where am I?"

The stranger pulled out two bowls and started ladling the stew into them. He offered one to Ronan.

Ronan took the stew cautiously. His stomach growled at the sweet aroma of the broth. 'How long had it been since I had eaten?' he wondered. "Thank you," he said, but refrained from eating. The Carpenters had taught him to never be the first person to eat any food offered by a stranger.

The stranger took a spoonful of the stew and slurped it up, smacking his lips. Having seen him eat, Ronan assumed it was not poisoned and began to devour the wonderfully flavored mixture.

The stranger watched him for a moment and said, "Getting saved from death to life can build up quite the appetite, can't it, Beloved?"

"How do you know about me being rescued from Mawveth?" Ronan managed to ask through a mouthful of hot soup. "Who are you?"

"I am just a messenger of good news and glad tidings," the stranger explained. "As for how I know about your rescue from death, I was the one who carried you out, Beloved."

"You were that particle of light?" Ronan asked, surprised.

"Oh no," the stranger exclaimed. "No Beloved, that was not me. I told you; I am just a messenger. What you saw is far beyond and above me. I merely did as I was told and carried you out from the darkness. I did not save you from death."

"I don't understand. Who saved me if it was not you? What happened to Mawveth?" Ronan asked after he had drunk the last of the stew. He was sad that it was gone as it had been so good. He eyed the pot but didn't want to be rude and ask for more.

The stranger smiled and reached over, filling his bowl again. "Beloved, you are saved by the only one who can save. The Justice was stopped by the only one who can command darkness and death."

Ronan stared at him, clearly missing something. Why was this man talking in riddles? Who was he and where had he brought Ronan? So many questions, but the one that he asked was, "Why do you keep calling me that?"

"Calling you what? Beloved? That is who you are." The stranger said this with an odd certainty about him.

"My name is Ronan, not Beloved," Ronan corrected him.

"Your name is Ronan but that is not who you are. You are Beloved," The stranger corrected back. Then the stranger casually looked out of the tent flap. "It looks like it is time for you to put your armor on, Beloved."

"I don't have any armor," Ronan said, trying to make sense of the sudden topic change.

The stranger nodded at Ronan's feet. Sure enough, a pile of armor sat on the ground. Ronan had not noticed the armament when he had inspected his leg. Had it been there the whole time? He picked up a pair of black studded leather pants and a black belt. They looked to be about his size. The stranger gave him a nod in reassurance. Ronan had no idea what had happened to his blood-stained clothes, and his backpack was nowhere to be seen. What other option did he have than the strangers clothes? He put on the pants and was surprised at the tailored fit to his waist. He fastened the belt despite the fit of the pants.

The stranger sighed, "Ah, the Belt of Truth. It is so important to know the truths that you tie around your waist so that the lies of the world don't pull down your pants and trip you up."

Ronan stared at the stranger, not understanding. "The belt has a name?" he asked. He didn't know if it was the fact that he was still groggy from waking up, or if this was just one of the strangest conversations he had ever had.

"That belt does not. I merely thought you could use a walk through about the protection your newfound faith grants you. Would you like to hear about the spiritual armor and what it means to stand in faith?"

"What do you mean I am protected in my new faith?" Ronan wondered, not fully sure what the stranger referred to. He felt like all he had done since waking up was ask questions.

The stranger sipped his stew and let Ronan think about it for a moment. Seeing he was not comprehending, the stranger sat his bowl down and said, "Consider for instance the breastplate of righteousness," he gestured to a chainmail shirt that lay on top of the pile at Ronan's feet. Ronan picked it up and saw the metal rings were stained orange and found the mail was lighter than it should have been. The front had a design of white ribbon interwoven into the links that made up an eight-pointed star. Ronan did not know the symbol but something about it seemed sturdy and steadfast. The stranger continued, "In the past, you believed in your own goodness to protect you from this world. You tried to protect your heart by your own abilities. The breastplate of righteousness helps you remember you cannot rely on your own goodness. Only the goodness of the Child of Light who is to come."

Looking at the stranger in surprise, things he had said started clicking in place. Ronan remembered his decision in the chamber with Mawveth. His decision to reject serving the Justice of Death and his leap of faith in the Light. 'The only one who can save.' He now understood the basis for the riddles. "You are a follower of the Light?"

The stranger beamed at him. "Since before you were born, Beloved. Not a day goes by without me relishing in the glory of the Light. The spiritual armor I speak of is a result of your new faith in the Light. Please finish putting on your physical armor and I will explain your spiritual armor."

Ronan did not question the stranger. The knowledge that he, too, was a follower of the Light excited him. So, it was the Light who had saved Ronan from the clutches of Mawveth. If that was the case, he wanted to know everything he could about the Light. He slid the chain shirt over his head and found it also fit him well.

The stranger inspected the armor and nodded his approval. "You put your faith in the Light and asked the Light to be the Lord of your life. As a result, you must stand firm in the readiness that comes with the good news of peace. Put on the boots of peace, for peace is your new foundation," again he gestured at the pile.

Ronan saw a pair of metal greaves that matched the color of the chain shirt. Ronan sat down to pull them on. Each one strapped on as if hand made for him. The material was unyielding yet not cumbersome.

The stranger explained, "You will never find peace on your own. But stand firm in the knowledge that there is peace in the Child of Light for he is the Prince of Peace. You must also put on the helmet of salvation," he pointed to a brilliant shiny metallic helmet with the eight-pointed star emblazoned in the center of the brow.

Ronan saw his warped reflection in the metal. *'I look so different than I did a week ago. So much has changed.'*

"When the enemy comes swinging at your head with disbelief and deception, your assurance of your salvation is what protects your way of thinking. Your salvation is something that cannot be taken away from you. You will be attacked, and the attacks will hurt but they will not cripple or kill."

Ronan knew he didn't understand the wisdom the stranger was saying. At least not a true understanding. That did not stop him from repeating the words in his head. The belt of truth, the breastplate of righteousness, the boots of peace, the helmet of salvation. He knew this wisdom was for his benefit and was grateful to hear it as he owed the Light his life. While he didn't know this stranger, the stranger knew of the Light and that was good enough for Ronan who found himself craving more information.

The stranger stood up and walked over. He bent down and picked up a

313

silver shield that was leaning against a tent post and gave it to Ronan. He said in a firm voice, "Along with the rest of the spiritual armor, you need your shield of faith to protect yourself from the flaming arrows of darkness. Let me tell you, those arrows come at you constantly. Putting down your shield of faith is dangerous and costly. But it's important to remember the only saving faith is in the Child of Light who will come to eradicate the darkness forever."

Ronan took the shield on his charcoaled arm and felt the weight of it. Then he considered the weight of the words of the stranger. *Flaming arrows of darkness will come at you constantly.'* This was not a mystery to him. He knew these words to be true. But according to the stranger, he was no longer unprotected. Ronan didn't know what that meant fully but he felt reassured by the shield. It reminded him of his memories of his mother's hugs.

The stranger appeared to mentally check off the pieces of armor. Once he was certain he had not missed one, he presented, "Lastly, you need a sword, Beloved." He removed a sheath from his own waist and handed it to Ronan. Ronan recognized the simple sheath immediately and knew it to be his own sword, the one that Osmodius had stabbed him with.

Ronan looked at the blade. "My friend gave me that sword," he stated. But it was not special. Arkeen just pulled it out of a dead centurion."

"This is not the sword of truth. None of the physical armor I have given you has any power. It is just metal, leather and steel. You must understand, I speak of spiritual armor that cannot be held but is what you believe." The stranger sat back down at his stew and said, "The sword of truth is a spiritual sword that is forged from the sacred words and texts that all point to the One to Come. This sword is both offensive and defensive. You will need to parry the blows from the darkness while also being able to cut through the darkness's lies."

Ronan wished he could comprehend the depths of the wisdom the stranger was telling him."

The stranger smiled at Ronan. "This is your spiritual armor which you are to never take off, for the enemy is always ready to attack you. This physical armor I gave you will tarnish and fail but as long as you stand fast in your spiritual armor, darkness has no power over you. Not anymore, thanks to the glory of the Light. Beloved Ronan, you will need to remember that in the battles to come."

Ronan was about to ask more questions when he heard loud voices from outside the tent. He looked up as Vallia burst in through the flap with Leo right behind her. They were both heavily armored in thick, dark leathers and furs.

"...don't care if you have to carry him to the battlefield, we need..." Vallia stopped yelling and stared at Ronan.

Relief and sorrow washed over him, and he moved forward hugging her.

"You're alive! I can't believe you're alive." She was stunned for a second and then to his surprise hugged him back. He relished the embrace before she pushed him off. "You're awake?" she exclaimed. Then looking down at him she asked, "Where in the Ether did you get that armor?"

Ronan, with tears in his eyes, beamed and said, "From this stranger here..." He gestured to the cooking pot, only to see that the fire was gone, the pot was empty, and the stranger had vanished.

Chapter 39

Vallia and Leo looked at each other and back to Ronan, not knowing what to think. Vallia spoke up, "It doesn't really matter where you got it, are you able to fight?"

"Fight?" Ronan asked.

Vallia nodded, "Yeah, we need you and your spooky powers. The Eidolon of Entropy decided that the war was going too slow and stepped in. He is about to break through the defensive line and that is all that stops him from getting to the Ether Scar."

The urgency of this statement confused Ronan.

Vallia stated again, "The Eidolon of Entropy is coming. Are you able to fight?"

Ronan felt a crushing weight as he realized what she was asking. It seemed the time had come for the battle against the Eidolon of Entropy that Maya had predicted. This conflict had always seemed so far away. Now that it was actually upon him, Ronan was all but helpless. He had forsaken the Justice of Death and for all he knew, he was no longer the Eidolon of Death. How was he to fight the Eidolon of Entropy without his powers?

Before he could voice any of this, Vallia said, "Come on. I will explain everything on the way to the command tent." Then she left.

Leo did not follow. He was simply staring at Ronan's chest. He opened his mouth to say something but was prevented by Vallia sticking her head back in the tent. "Come on you idiots, command is expecting us."

Leo closed his mouth and gestured for Ronan to follow. Ronan obliged, thinking about how grateful he was to see both of his friends alive. As he exited the tent into the blinding sunlight, he saw his tent was surrounded by hundreds of others of a similar nature. The pelt covered tents populated a grassy field. Ronan was surprised to see UN'kra moving about the camp. Everywhere he looked, he saw the hulking hairy UN'kra hastily hurrying about.

Vallia was walking through the sea of tents and UN'kra without a second thought. Ronan jogged to catch up. "Where are we?" he asked as he watched an UN'kra woman beat a glowing iron sword on an anvil at a blacksmith tent.

"We are exactly where little Miss Foresight predicted we would be. We are about a half mile from the Ether Scar." She pointed off into the distance. "We are standing with the UN'kra against the onslaught of the Legion invasion, trying and failing to prevent them from getting to the Scar."

Ronan's head swam as he took in the crazy explanation. *We made it to the Scare after all. We really are fighting off the Legion.'* a tremble ran up his back. *'We really are going to have to face the Eidolon of Entropy.'*

With great effort, he took a breath and asked, "How did we get here?"

Vallia ducked under a wooden beam that two UN'kra men were carrying. They grunted at her in UN'kran but continued on with their task. "Leo and I escaped the Nether about three days ago just like the creepy centipede man said," Vallia explained. "We crawled out of a cave and found ourselves looking down on a war zone. UN'kra on one side and Legion on the other. Legion scouts appeared out of nowhere, and we dispatched them. I guess some UN'kra guards saw the fight. They encircled us and demanded we surrender. Leo spoke with them in UN'kran and somehow convinced them to take us as prisoners before the war chiefs. They chained us up and brought us here. We lucked out because as it turns out, Leo's wonderful mother is one of the war chiefs. They listened to our account of the Eidolon of Entropy, and we have been fighting with them since."

Ronan had to jog to keep up with her pace. It was difficult to take in so much information while dodging through an encampment preparing for battle. "What about me?" he asked, desperate to hear all that had happened

317

since they had been separated.

"We thought you were dead for sure. You and Maya ran back after… well, you two ran back and then everything collapsed. We tried to move the rubble, but there was too much. So, we had to leave the only way we could. Then to our amazement, a day ago, you were found by some UN'kra children in tall grass not too far from here. We just happened to be in the war tent when you were brought in. You looked… rough."

She didn't elaborate and there was no need to. She had seen the same thing that Ronan had when he had woken up.

She continued, "We identified you as the Eidolon of Death and the UN'kra seemed to know what that meant. Seems like the Council has not been able to cover up the Eidolon among the UN'kra. Anyway, we set you up in a tent and checked on you occasionally, hoping you would wake up before we lost the fight."

Ronan was amazed by the account. He had been found in a patch of grass. The stranger said that he had carried Ronan out of the darkness. Had he been the one to leave him in some random weeds? Then again, the children had found him so maybe it was intentional. Vallia was clearly in a rush, so he didn't want to ask too many questions. He did however force himself to ask, "I'm guessing there has been no sight of Maya?"

Leo, who had been quietly keeping pace next to Ronan, spoke. "I am sorry, my friend. But we have no reason to believe she made it out of the Ether."

Ronan pursed his lips and acknowledged, "Oh, she made it out alright. But I don't think we will be seeing her any time soon." He paused, finding it hard to admit what had happened. But they needed to know. "She sort of rescued me from Mophantatha. Then she left me bleeding out in some hallway and she stole my map so she could find her Justice."

At this Vallia stopped in her tracks and looked back at Ronan in disbelief. "I knew that girl was trouble from the beginning. If I ever see her again, I'll…"

Ronan shook his head, "It doesn't matter. She is gone."

"That is unfortunate to hear." Leo expressed. Then he looked at Ronan.

His eyes were wide, and a smile filled his face. "What I want to know is how you survived?"

Horns sounded in the distance. Vallia looked to the sky and shook her head. "Yeah, I want to know that too, but we don't have time right now. The war chiefs are meeting for the last stand. We need to let them know we have the Eidolon of Death."

"Vallia..." Ronan tried to explain about his decision in the Nether.

"Later Ronan," she directed. "If we are alive later, we can hear about it then."

She began her jog again and Ronan had no choice but to follow. In a minute they reached a tent, larger than the rest. It was a hive of activity, with UN'kra shouting commands and following orders. Tables and chairs had been set up in various corners with maps and battle plans strewn across them. Vallia led Ronan to a large circular table with an odd assortment of individuals around it.

There was an old UN'kra whose body hair was gray and patchy. He wore large, cracked spectacles.

A female UN'kra stood next to him. Her hair was a deep chestnut brown. Ronan saw a lot of Leo's features in the woman's kind, slightly wrinkled face and knew this to be Leo's mother. She was not as old as the bespectacled UN'kra next to her but was entering into the later half of her life.

A behemoth of an Ether touched UN'kra woman stood next to Leo's mother. Ronan guessed she was easily seven and a half feet. He couldn't help but stare at her muscular arms that were covered in red veins of what looked like magma just under her skin. She was definitely an intimidating person. The shaved sides of her hair and braided dreadlocks sticking out the top and running down her back added to the commanding presence. As he looked at her, he swore he could see heat waves radiating off her.

Then Ronan registered that the fourth person at the table was a human man with a shoulder length gray ponytail. He was marked with scars and had a haggard look about him.

Seeing Vallia, the oldest UN'kra nodded and spoke in a slow high pitched, heavily accented common tongue, "I see you have woken the Eidolon of

Death, Wind Walker." He looked at Ronan. "I am BoRa Fa Glee Vos Kortha. Chieftain of the Kortha people. We are pleased to see you healthy and alive." Then his eyes traveled over Ronan's armor and his gray eyebrows rose. "Where did you get your armor, Eidolon of Death?"

Ronan looked down. "It was a gift from a strange man back in my tent. He wore a white robe and spoke with great wisdom about the Light. He said he was the one who pulled me out of the Nether?"

The three UN'kra war chiefs all looked at each other and mumbled among themselves in UN'kran. Then the large woman walked up to him and inspected the armor. She smelled of sulfur and brimstone. Poking the chain shirt and running the rings through her calloused hands, she scrutinized every link. He was most surprised when she leaned in and gave the armor a sniff.

BoRa asked, "Smog Sul, what do you think?"

Smog Sul, gave Ronan a curious look. She said in a low gravelly voice, "I've been forging for forty years and I ain't ever seen no armor made like dat. Dis is good stuff here. Ya said a strange man gave it to ya?"

Ronan took a deep breath and told them about waking up to an empty tent and then the presence of the stranger and the lecture he had given about the Light and the spiritual armor. When he had finished, the war chiefs all stared at him in shared wonder and amazement.

BoRa spoke first. "By your account, I don't think you understand who that stranger was. If I am not mistaken, you met a messenger of the Light today. If this is true, then I have no doubt that you are our deliverance from these dark times of war. The Light has given us a judge to free us from the devastation of the coming battle. Legends of old tell about the strength of the Eidolon of Death. Now the new Eidolon of Death is here by the grace of the Light to save us."

At this praise and dedication, Ronan felt the bottom of his stomach drop out. They not only thought he was as strong as the old Eidolon of Death, but they also believed him to be some judge sent by the Light. He had only truly learned about the Light the other day. In terms of putting his trust in the Light, it had only been about an hour of consciousness for Ronan. He was working out how to explain how he had rejected the Justice of Death when another blast from distant horns sounded.

All the chieftains turned to the noise with grave faces. The human man standing among the UN'kra chieftains spoke up for the first time. "It seems we only have minutes to discuss our plans." He looked at Ronan. "I may be one of the most informed people about what it is you can do as the Eidolon of Death. After the death of Osmodius," Ronan assumed Vallia and Leo had reported the events of the Nether to the chieftains.

Ronan gave him a curious look. How would this random human know anything about the Eidolon?

Seeing his reaction, the man elaborated, "My name is Dezden Thonbrough. In the past you may have known me by a different name. Nine years ago, I was the High Arbiter of the Council of the Zwellian Empire. At that time, it was my job to make sure that people never learned about the Eidolon and how the Zwellian Empire came to power. I have spent years of my life studying the Eidolon. The only way I was able to keep them covered up was to know everything I could about them."

Ronan's eyes raised in surprise. He looked to Leo who nodded in affirmation of the man's identity. Ronan found himself baffled. "How does a man of your stature end up at an UN'kra war meeting standing against an impending attack from the Zwellian Legion?"

Dezden shrugged, "A man condemned by his own has nowhere to go but his supposed enemies. I fled the Empire and sought shelter up north where I was graciously accepted as a refugee. But that is a tale for another day. What we must focus on now is that the enemy approaches and we need your help if we are to stand a chance. The Eidolon of Death of the past was famous for controlling entire armies of the dead. We need you to do that now."

Ronan felt the eyes of everyone on him. It was as if iron chains were being wrapped around him and he was being told to jump into deep waters. He looked around and quietly said, "I don't even know if I am the Eidolon of Death anymore."

The stares bore into him. Leo's soft-spoken reply sounded behind Ronan,

"What do you mean?"

Ronan's cheeks began to burn from his embarrassment. "I was trying to tell you on the way over here. My powers came from the Justice of Death. I was his champion, and that pact was the foundation of my abilities over the spirits. But when I was speaking with him in the Nether, I realized that I could not in good conscience serve him. So, I rejected him and denounced my role as Eidolon of Death. That is why the Light saved me. I chose the Light as my master over the Justice. That seems like the sort of thing that would lose me my powers."

Dezden squinted at Ronan. "I have never heard of an Eidolon losing their abilities. In the past, some of the Eidolon disobeyed their Justices but never lost their powers. You have no connection to the Nether at all?"

A feeling of stupidity smacked Ronan over the head as he realized he had not thought to check before saying something. He closed his eyes and felt a familiar pressure behind his lids. The Nether blink activated, and he found the world before him black and white. He blinked the powers off again and sheepishly disclosed, "I have my powers, somehow."

Dezden nodded, "It is my understanding that the Justices put all their eggs in one basket when making an Eidolon. I do not think it is something that can be reversed no matter the desire of the Justice."

Ronan wished he could celebrate the preservation of his powers but knew there was little reason to rejoice. "I may have my powers, but I don't know what good they will be. In the past, I have struggled to fight with just two spirits under my control. How can I command an army? I really don't think I am this judge you speak about."

BoRa smiled at this. "That was when you were under the influence of a Justice. Now you are doing the work of the Light. Our enemy comes against us with sword and spear and javelin, but you come against them in the name of the Light Almighty. Take heart, young Eidolon. When the storm has swept by, the wicked are gone, but the righteous stand firm forever."

Ronan looked at the group. They all expected so much from him. Then he checked himself. BoRa did not have faith in him. He had faith in the

Light Almighty. This was a model of how Ronan should trust the Light.

Ronan swallowed his pride and said, "I will trust in the provision of the Light." He looked around the group, feeling inspired.

"I hate to ask, but where do you keep your wounded and dead?"

Chapter 40

Ronan, Vallia, Leo, and Dezden Thonbrough, entered into the makeshift medical tent. UN'kra warriors lay on the ground. Some were missing limbs or wrapped in bandages that hid their face. It struck Ronan how similar this scene was to the infirmary in Shem. He supposed that it didn't matter which side of a war you were on; Casualties were casualties. He felt his nerves rising up as he remembered his last venture into a similar space. *'This time is different,'* he reassured himself.

Mawveth had told him that he had been holding an army of spirits in the north for Ronan. There was no hope that those spirits remained, not after the way Ronan had left. With those spirits gone, Ronan sought those who may have died fairly recently. Even a handful of spirits was better than nothing.

He took a deep breath and Nether blinked. At least ten green spirits floated about the space. As he activated his powers, the spirits all turned to him like moths to a flame. *'I'm doing the work of the Light now,'* he repeated to himself. *'I no longer am restricted by the weakness of the Justice.'* He thought about how the stranger had described the belt of truth. Ronan then understood that the truth he needed around his waist was the provision of the Light.

Ronan cleared his throat. Then he felt silly as he remembered that he spoke telepathically to the spirits. He addressed the room mentally. *"You all have lost your lives in this tragic battle."* He knew that this was a stupid thing to say. They all knew they were dead and why. If only he was as eloquent of a speaker as Mr. Kemin.

324

But this self blame was not about to win over any soldiers to his cause. He reminded himself of the breastplate of righteousness. It was not his own abilities or attributes that mattered. It was those of the Light. He started again, *"If you trusted in the promises of the Light when you were alive, you are now looking to move on to that glory. But, if you will allow me, I would ask for a few more hours of your time in this world. With your help and the sacrifice of your former bodies, we may have a chance to stop the attack that is endangering your friends and family that still live as well as the land that was your home. Will you stand with me in this fight?"*

Ronan waited with bated breath as the spirits looked at each other. His heart lurched as one floated forward.

The spirit projected, *"We would be honored to serve the Light by your side. Do not worry about the sacrifices of our bodies. Our enemy is limited in their power. The worst they can do to us is destroy our flesh. They have no power over our souls. We trust in the One who can crush both body and soul."*

The other UN'kra spirits nodded in communal agreement. Ronan was impressed by his devotion. What a trust in the power of the Light's salvation. Ronan understood that this is what it meant to put on the helmet of salvation. No enemy sword could take away the faith of these warriors. Ronan mentally projected, *"Find your bodies and let's go. We don't have much time."*

He focused on the energy of each spirit as they floated over to their bodies which were covered in woven fabrics. "By the power of the Almighty Light, **rise and follow me**," *he* commanded.

The energy that left him seemed significantly less taxing than what he was used to. *'Was it the simple command? Or was it that the command was coming from a deeper well of power outside of himself?'* The spirits sank into their cloth covered bodies and Ronan felt their energy lock into place inside the corpses. He heard shrieks behind him from the nearby menders as the ten bodies all sat up. *'Probably should have warned them that I was going to do this.'* Ronan assessed his new recruits. He counted two missing arms, several severe lacerations, but no missing legs. This was a positive as there should not be any mobility issues.

Registering that none of the corpses were armed, Ronan turned to a young UN'kra boy who looked absolutely terrified of what he had just witnessed.

"Do you speak common?"

The young boy nodded, wide eyed.

"I need ten weapons and I need them now."

Clearly scared senseless by the human that had just raised ten dead warriors, the boy ran off to complete his assigned mission.

"That was absolutely terrifying to watch." Vallia muttered as they exited the structure. Flanked by the bodies. "I am really happy that you are my friend. I can deal with a guy who dissolves things and withers them away. But I don't think I could mentally fight a bunch of walking corpses."

Ronan looked at his new soldiers and appreciated the fear these walking corpses could invoke on his opponents. *What would it be like to be a Legion soldier who has to fight these dead warriors,'* Ronan wondered.

He looked back at his living friends. "I am ready for the battle if everyone else is."

Vallia nodded, "I just need a moment to confirm our tactics with Dezden." She turned to the older man to converse.

Leo looked at Ronan and said, "I am grateful to fight by your side, Ronan."

Ronan looked at him and felt the moment called for a rare opening of his heart. "Thank you for being bold enough to talk about the Light with Maya. It was some of your words that helped me choose the Light in the Nether."

Leo shook his head. "All praise goes to the Light for that. I did not tell Maya those things on my own accord. I just pray to the Light that she was similarly convinced."

Ronan tilted his head. "Pray?"

Leo looked surprised but then understood. "Yes, prayer. It is how we speak to the Light. We lift up our adorations, our confessions, supplications, and thanksgiving to the Light from our hearts. The Light listens to the prayers of those that walk the path of the Light. From our trivial needs to the requests from the bottom of our broken hearts, the Light listens."

This amazed Ronan. The mere idea of talking to the creator of the world was mystifying. "The Light answers all prayers?" Ronan inquired.

Leo thought about this for a moment. "The Light answers but it is not always a yes. When our hearts are attuned to the will of the Light, and we ask for things that align with that will, that is when prayers are truly answered."

Ronan marveled at this truth. What wonderful news this was. The stranger had told Ronan to stand firm in the readiness that comes with the good news of peace. Ronan understood that he was to stand on the foundation of news like this. If he was able to do that, he would never slip.

Dezden turned back to Ronan and said, "Eidolon, Vallia has informed me of the information you have gleaned about the Eidolon of Entropy. I don't have to tell you how dangerous he is."

Ronan nodded. "When I was in the Nether, speaking to the Justice of Death, he hinted that the Legislator of War could possibly be even more powerful than we originally suspected. We know he has bridgestone but there is a chance he has also made a pact with his Justice to further amplify his powers."

A misty look crossed over the face of Dezden. In a soft voice Ronan heard him say, "Yawbashé, what have you done?"

"Yawbashé?" Ronan inquired. "Is that the name of the Eidolon of Entropy?"

"Yes, at least that is what he was called as a boy. Who knows what name he goes by now that he is a Legislator.

Ronan had forgotten Leo's mention of the Eidolon of Entropy being a boy in the courts of the Council in his youth. "You did know him?"

"Yes, I knew him as the son of a brutal politician. I felt bad for the boy back then. He was always in the shadow of his father, never able to appease the cold-blooded man. I watched him lash out for attention and in desperate plots for approval. I was not surprised when I discovered his father had orchestrated a coup against me. Nor was I surprised when I heard the young man had been established as the Legislator of War."

Ronan took in this information. It didn't change anything or give him any advantage in the fight to come. But it couldn't hurt to understand the enemy better. "Thank you for the information. If we survive this, I would be very interested in talking to you about what else you know of the Council."

Dezden nodded. "If we survive, I would be happy to share my knowledge with you. You will have to forgive me, but I am not much of a fighter. My skills lay back in command. It was an honor to meet you, Eidolon." With that he bowed and then left.

Vallia looked at Ronan. "I guess we are really doing this."

"Don't let Maya's vision tie you to any commitment. I would completely understand if you didn't come to battle with me." Ronan said to her.

She laughed. "Her stupid vision is not the reason I am by your side. We are in this together. Sure, your powers are pretty odd and you can be a selfish jerk. But most of the time your heart is in the right place, and I can trust you. That is rare. There is a reason Arkeen was your friend. It is the same reason I am your friend."

Leo clasped Ronan's shoulder. "My brother had some questionable attributes, but his judgment of character was always rock solid. I too will follow your lead."

Ronan smiled at the two. He looked off to the fields where the battle was taking place. "Let's go stop a maniac from destroying everything and maybe end a war."

Chapter 41

The battle was a small hike away from the UN'kra encampment. Far closer than Ronan felt comfortable with. He was able to hear the clash of weapons before he saw the conflict. The ting of metal on metal permeated the air as they crested a low hill. Ronan looked out over the carnage laid out before him, feeling a sickness in his stomach. He had seen battlefields when scavenging. However, something about seeing the fighting soldiers and warriors was drastically different than seeing a meadow of corpses. This was real, in his face, war. When someone fell to the ground bleeding and unmoving, Ronan did not just see a dead body. He saw a person, with a life and family. He felt bile in the back of his throat. This needed to stop. Not just the Eidolon and his plans. But this war.

The Council behind these needless deaths needed to be disbanded. Ronan vowed in that moment, if he lived through the next few hours, he would find a way to stop the Council and their tyranny.

Looking around, Ronan observed the UN'kra defensive line. Several barriers were built out of rocks and spikes of wood. The line stretched for a good way along the field. Behind the line, Ronan could make out a large chasm that seemed to be filled with shifting colorful lights. It was breathtaking to behold. The chasm was massive, even at this distance. It looked as if the world had spit open in some kind of primordial elemental explosion. All around the fissure he noticed black onyx pillars and pockets of steaming, boiling liquid. The air itself was dense with the smell of sulfur and metallic fumes. Ronan was amazed to even see several pools of molten Lava bubbling and gurgling. This place was truly a wonder to behold.

'What a contrast to the destruction of the war.'

There was no time to take in the scenery anymore. Ronan surveyed the scene before him as two vastly different armies collided head-to-head. The shiny armored bodies of the Legion were easily identifiable contrasted to the leather clad army of the UN'kra.

The desire to pray came to him at that moment. He didn't know how to pray, but he felt the need to try. Tilting his head to the sky, he declared, "Great Light. It is me, Ronan Riviera. I don't know how this works, but I was told that I can come to you from the depths of my heart and you will hear me. This is my prayer. End this fight. Please. Use me to do so if that is what you want. However, it happens, end this fighting. Thank you."

He looked at Leo to see if he had done it right. Leo had bowed his head as Ronan had spoken. When he finished, Leo smiled at him. "That was immeasurably special to be here for your first prayer. That was good. Now we get to see how the Light will answer."

Ronan looked at Vallia. "Will you stay back and provide us with cover fire?"

Vallia shook her head. "No. I have never been that kind of archer. I prefer to be closer to my targets when I bury my arrows in their necks. I'll be right behind you. Don't worry Prince of the Dead. I got your back."

He could not express how much her company meant to him. If it had not been for Vallia, he would not have been able to make it this far. Ronan glanced over at his half UN'kra friend.

"Will you stay by my side? There is no judgment if you choose to back out. But do it now because once we enter this battlefield, there is no going back."

Leo smiled. "I pray by your side just as I will die by your side if that is the Light's will. I am not going anywhere."

Ronan was immeasurably warmed by the sentiment. Arkeen's departing words could not have been more correct. He was very fortunate to have both of these individuals by his side. He felt tears in the corner of his eyes.

Blinking them away, he looked at the corpses. Activating his Nether connection he commanded, ***Protect us.*** They formed a circle around

Ronan and his friends. Ronan nodded, drew his sword, and then began moving forward before he second-guessed what he was doing.

He couldn't help but think that they were the most peculiar platoon on the battlefield. Ten corpses, an Ethalladros archer, an Ether Crafter, and an Eidolon in golden armor.

Eight Legion soldiers came at them from their left. Ronan braced himself for an explosion of pain as the Legion soldiers attacked. However, even when steel cut the skin of the corpses, he did not feel it. *'I'm not tethered to them,'* he breathed a sigh of relief.

The ten dead warriors took brutal attacks without so much as a wince. Ronan watched the fear grow in the eyes of the soldiers under their helmets as they realized something was very wrong. When one of the UN'kra corpses was stabbed through the chest, the prevailing soldier looked triumphant until the corpse retaliated by stabbing the Legionnaire in return.

Vallia's bow twanged behind Ronan as two arrows skillfully found their mark in the helmets of two other soldiers. Leo sliced his hand through the air and opened a rift that vented a superheated blast of steam, catching three more Legionnaires unaware. They were downed immediately before they could even scream. The smell of scolded flesh made Ronan want to gag.

Ronan could tell the last two soldiers were desperate by their frantic attacks. The UN'kra corpses took more hits without so much as a grunt. An UN'kra corpse smashed the helmet of a soldier with a club, and another stabbed the remaining soldier with a spear.

As their bodies fell, Ronan acknowledged that the bloody assault had lasted only a matter of seconds. The bodies on the ground were a gruesome sight of blood and sweat. If there was any other way to find the Eidolon, he would have taken it in a heartbeat.

Ronan activated his Nether connection to see the green flames of the freshly diseased soldiers. Knowing his work was far from done, he said in a solemn voice, "For the glory of the Light, **join us in our fight.**"

Eight Legionnaires stood up from the ground, bloody, crushed or severely scalded from the blast of heat. Again, Ronan was amazed at the ease of the command. There might be something about commanding spirits inside of bodies. He supposed it was a more natural state then free-floating spirits.

They continued deeper into the battle; Ronan craned his neck in search of telltale indicators of the Eidolon of Entropy. But he was distracted as another squad of Legionnaires came at them from the right. Shouts of confusion rang out when the soldiers saw their comrades standing with UN'kra. Ronan flinched at the sound of crossbow bolts smacking into the wall of corpses.

The animated dead reached the living and another short, brutal battle ensued. Ronan knew as he watched the last soldier fall, that he was not made for war. He was doing everything he could to not look at the new bodies as he issued another command. This group of spirits also reunited with their bodies and stood. Ronan averted his eyes from the platoon of bloodied bodies and scanned the field. Bouts of combat were all around them but no sign of the Eidolon of Entropy. What was he even looking for? Disintegrated bodies? Shriveled corpses? He had no idea. But he needed to find him. *He is supposed to be here. I don't want to have to kill every Legionnaire out here to find him. But I will if he doesn't show himself.*

They pushed deeper into the conflict. The Legionnaires with crossbows provided the growing hoard of corpses a new, deadly range. Ronan raised several more corpses off the ground, not sure who had killed the soldiers but willing to add them to his numbers. Their group was now easily the largest unanimous unit on the field. A menacing mass of mutilated members.

Ronan couldn't help but think about how this sort of power had been his motivation and purpose the last week. It was not hard to imagine how this power could fill him and consume him. With one command these spirits would do whatever he wanted without question. He had to remind himself of the teaching of the stranger about the shield of faith. His faith was in the Light, not himself or his own power. The desire for power was one of the fiery darts the stranger had warned him about. How easily they found a way into his heart if he was not focusing on the Light.

It was at that moment that Ronan saw what he had been looking for. A black horse galloping across the field with a cloaked rider on its back. The rider swung their sword through the air and a blast of yellow energy struck a group of UN'kra warriors. The UN'kra were turned to dust the second the energy made contact with them. The rider then turned the horse and pointed it straight at the army of corpses.

"Take cover!" Ronan yelled and dove behind a small, gnarled tree. Vallia and Leo jumped behind a moss-covered rock. The corpses did not react to Ronan's statement as it was not a command to them. He watched as the rider swung his sword and sent another blast of yellow energy into the army of the corpses. The bodies that were in the direct blast instantly became dust. The ones that were caught on the outside of the attack withered away to smoking skeletons as if they had been subjected to ten years of decay in the matter of a second. Ronan's tree took the blast. All of the leaves fell off as the branches withered and dried out. Ronan's heart felt like it was attempting to escape his chest. How was he supposed to fight that kind of power?

Ronan watched from behind the tree as the cloaked rider pelted forward. Just when he thought the Eidolon intended to fight, the black horse was prompted to bolt past him. Ronan watched as the black beast dashed away straight at the UN'kra line of defense. *Why is he not fighting me?*

Ronan watched in bewilderment as the Eidolon of Entropy dismounted the galloping horse, rolled once along the ground, before leaping up. A volley of arrows flew through the air at the Eidolon. When the projectiles got within fifteen feet, they all seemed to fall apart. From this distance, Ronan couldn't tell exactly what happened, but it looked like the feathered fletchings fell off and the arrows all fell short as if they were a pile of sticks.

The Eidolon of Entropy sliced his sword through the air and the barricades before him shattered and fell into disrepair. Ronan watched in horror as UN'kra guarding the defenses made an attempt to fight until they too were dispatched by a wave of yellow energy. Now nothing stood in the path of the Eidolon. He mounted his horse to jump the pile of broken barricades and he rode directly toward the Ether Scar.

Ronan checked on Vallia and Leo. Their rock had protected them. Some of the corpses had survived but were in no shape to fight. Ronan released all of the spirits except one to solidify. The rest faded away, leaving only what remained of their bodies behind.

'I need you for just a little longer.' He informed the spirit.

The spirit nodded and saluted. *'It is an honor to serve the Light by your side.'*

"How are we going to fight that guy?" Vallia asked as she surveyed the scene around them.

Ronan felt a similar discouragement. "I don't know but we have to follow him. There is no point in fighting this battle if he makes it to the Scar and dissolves the barriers holding back the Ether. Let's just hope the Ether barriers hold up longer than the wood ones or we are doomed."

They ran in the direction of the Ether Scar. It would take them longer on foot than horseback, but that was okay with Ronan. It gave him a little time to think.

As they neared the giant fissure in the ground, Ronan could make out a multicolored glow coming from its depths. Yawbashé was nowhere to be seen. Only his horse remained up top. Ronan used that as a waypoint to where the Eidolon must have descended.

When they were about two hundred feet from the black horse, the ground violently shook almost making Ronan lose balance.

"Don't worry, that happens here occasionally," Leo called out.

Just as Ronan was accepting that the chasm of elemental energy could be erratic in nature, the ground shook again. The black horse began to run away from the tremors. It only got twenty feet away before the ground shook a third time and suddenly split. A small fissure appeared, and a green glow seeped out. Seconds later, Ronan watched as four acid green spiders, the size of large dogs, leaped out of the ground and attacked the horse. One of the spiders spewed a jet of glowing liquid at the steed. Upon impact, the horse whinnied and collapsed on the ground twitching.

"Is that normal around here?" Ronan called out, terrified of what he had just seen.

Leo looked wide eyed at the scene. "No, that is not normal," he confessed. "I have never seen Ether creatures escape their plane like that."

All Ronan could think about was how the Ether was truly a nightmarish place. Just as he was processing how to get around the spiders, continued shaking of the ground produced another fissure near the acid arachnids. A tall, six-legged creature emerged from the newest fissure. It looked like a lizard with a long snake-like neck and tail. It stood on thin, spiky legs. Its grotesque scaly body was covered in flesh sacks that looked as if they were full of lava. This creature began attacking the spiders over the body of the horse.

Ronan thanked the Light that he didn't have to fight the spiders or the lizard and ran the rest of the way to the edge of the Scar. Looking down, he saw a vast river of multicolored energy that flowed in large swirling patterns under some form of translucent glass looking barrier that rested on the surface. He then saw a small black sand beach on the edge of the energy. The figure of the Eidolon of Entropy knelt on the bank with his sword sank into the molten sand. Pulses of yellow energy radiated from the blade. With each pulse more hairline fractures formed on the surface of the translucent barrier.

"Come on. We have to stop him," Ronan called, and without thinking about how he was going to accomplish this, he began hopping down the rock wall of the fissure.

Vallia and Leo followed after him, descending as quickly as the loose rock would let them. Leo stumbled once and sent several large rocks toppling down the side, only to smash on the surface of the river below. If Vallia had not grabbed the back of his armor, Leo would have fallen as well. Ronan saw the Eidolon look up at them when this happened. His face was obscured by a black metal mask. His eyes glowed yellow through small slits. Ronan knew there was no hope of surprise at this point. They reached the bottom of the climb, finding themselves standing thirty feet from the kneeling Eidolon. He made no effort to remove the sword and attack them.

The masked figure called out to them. In a calm unassuming voice. "Eidolon of Death. I thought that might have been your army of the dead I dissolved up top. It is my pleasure to finally meet you. Something tells me your presence here is not a coincidence."

"Not a chance," Ronan said. "I am here to stop your insane plan, but this does not have to escalate to violence. I am asking you to be reasonable and stop what you are doing." As he shifted toward the Eidolon, Ronan felt the fire emblem on his arm tingle as if it could sense his proximity to the Ether Scar.

The Eidolon of Entropy tilted his head. "And what is it that you think I am doing here?"

"You're dissolving the Ether's connection to this world," Ronan stated. "You are putting thousands of lives in jeopardy because you have been persuaded by your Justice that this is what needs to be done."

The Eidolon of Entropy looked at the sword stuck in the ground and then at the Ether River, as if to confirm that was what he was doing. "I do believe I have greatly underestimated you. Your understanding of the current state of affairs is impeccable. I must ask, do you know why I am pursuing the course of action? Do you believe that I am oblivious to the implications of my actions here today?"

Vallia drew back her bow and called out, "Unfortunately, crazy doesn't usually need a good reason."

The Eidolon of Entropy narrowed his eyes behind his black mask. "Are you going to stand there and pretend you are innocent with a clean conscience? The fact that you are currently not in the chains of Mishkawl is a testament to your transgressions. Tell me, Eidolon of Death, did he die at your hands?

The image of the spirit of Arkeen stabbing Mishkawl in the chest on Ronan's orders flashed before Ronan's eyes. He grit his teeth.

Yawbashé continued without waiting for an answer, "How is it that you came to know about my plans for the Scar? Which of my subordinates do I need to punish for betraying my trust?"

Ronan offered, "Pull the sword out of the ground and we can talk about it. I would love it if this did not end in violence, but if you don't stop what you're doing, we'll have no choice but to stop you."

The ground shook and the sound of cracking glass echoed in the chasm. Slightly larger fractures formed on the surface of the Ether barrier. Ronan's desperation to stop the Eidolon grew.

Yawbashé calmly said, "I'm afraid I can't do that. This is the only way to fix our world. My actions here have been calculated and determined as the only course of action."

"How is mass destruction the only path forward?" Vallia challenged. "What backward world do you live in where this solves anything?"

As the Legislator looked at Vallia, Ronan tried to shift to the left in order to split his attention.

Yawbashé pointed a finger at Ronan. "Move one more step and I'll dissolve all three of you into ash. You'll make a wonderful addition to the molten sand. And if you do anything with your spirit friend," he gestured to the remaining spirit, "I'll erode all your bones, so they snap under your weight. As a matter of fact, remove the spirit. You said we're just talking right?"

Ronan glared at the Legislator. *'He must have an understanding that he can't affect the spirits.'* Ronan knew he had no choice if he hoped to not provoke the wrath of the Eidolon. He let the energy holding the spirit dissipate. The green flame slowly faded away.

"Good, now to answer your question," Yawbashé looked back to Vallia, "Unleashing the Ether solves every problem. My actions here are the only way that true change will happen. The only way to fix our broken world."

"That is not true," Leo said. "I don't know what will happen when this barrier is gone, but I can tell you firsthand that people almost always get hurt when I free even small amounts of the energy from the Ether."

Vallia followed by saying, "Yawbashé, we know who you are. You are a member of the Zwellian Council, which makes you one of the nine most powerful and influential people in the Zwellian Empire. And you're telling me you couldn't change the world from that seat of power?"

The Eidolon tensed as she said the name. He spoke calmly but Ronan picked up on a slight twinge to his words. "I am intrigued to learn how you came to know my name."

Ronan answered, "Let's be honest, it doesn't matter how we know your name. What matters is the number of people that are going to die if you don't stop dissolving the Ether barrier."

Yawbashé stated, "The numbers that will die are an unfortunate side effect

337

of enacting the change that needs to happen. The change that I can enact as Legislation is short lived and easily undone. But here, in this chasm, the change that will take place when I release the powers of the Ether are irrevocable."

Leo said in a somber tone, "I of all people understand the thrall of the Ether, its power and its beauty. I have opened more rifts than I can count, and I have witnessed first hand the amazing energies within. Please listen to me, for I speak with experience. If what you seek is more power, what you will find is an infinite supply that is absolutely uncontrollable. Ask any Ether Crafter. If what you seek is change, know that the only change this will bring is the complete and total devastation of the Prime Plane."

Yawbashé nodded at Leo's warning. "Your words mean more to me than you realize, friend of Eidolon. If my plan is to work, I need absolute devastation."

The ground gave a seismic shudder and more cracks appeared along the translucent barrier and up the rock walls. Flaming birds escaped out from the new opening in the wall and then lava poured out after them.

Ronan, feeling frantic, shouted, "What can you possibly gain from this?"

Yawbashé looked out across the river of Ether energy. Then back to Ronan. "We currently live in a world divided by hatred, jealousy, and bitterness. Some people possess much wealth while others have very little. Some hate others because of what they have or don't have or even how they look or live. I have seen this firsthand in every city and town in the Zwellian Empire. So, I asked myself, what could stop this division? I knew governing policies would not work. Some people would see this as oppression and that would only cause further division. I knew that this could not happen through freedom of the people. When people get freedom, they feel entitled and again increase division."

Ronan found it hard to deny the things that the Legislator said. Regardless, he knew that this man's logic, wherever it came from, was corrupted.

Yawbashé exclaimed, "It was my Justice who gave me the answer to this problem. She informed me that the only way to truly remove division from this world was to start anew. When the Ether is set free, I am counting on

338

the devastation that will come with it. I know many people will die. But they will not die in vain. Their passing will be a door into a new world. A world where there is no division. Everyone who survives will start in the exact same place. In an elemental wasteland where people can either work together to survive or die by the harsh forces of the Ether."

Ronan was not at all surprised to hear this madman's plan had come from his Justice. If only the other Eidolon would question their Justices instead of being their mindless puppets.

"This plan will not solve the division of the world," Leo exclaimed. He stood tall and declared, "The world is divided because the world is full of sinners. If you kill ninety percent of the sinners in, you are left with ten percent of sinners. The world without division that you are talking about is only possible through the Light's provision of the Child of Light. Believe me; the world you seek is a world that will one day come to pass. When the Child of Light comes and frees us from our bondage to sin."

Yawbashé laughed. "I have heard of your Light. I have been warned about the falsehoods and misdirection of this Great Light. Look around you. We live in a broken world. Your Light is not doing anything to change that. That is why people like me must take a stand, why my mission is necessary."

Leo shook his head. "The only reason there is any good at all in our world is because of the Light. Without the Light we are all trapped in unrelenting darkness."

Ronan thought back to the darkness of his life before accepting the Light. Before the Nether, he would never have believed he could have his heart changed so radically. Was there a chance that Yawbashé's heart could change as well?

Vallia tried a different line of logic. "If you cut the restraints holding the Ether back, you're going to die just like everyone else. Is that worth it to you?"

"I have no intention of dying today. My Justice has promised to pull me into the Nether where I will be safe from the events that will take place. Then, once the Ether has thoroughly altered this land, I will come back to the Prime Plane and help rebuild the new world. With my Justice to back me, I will rebuild everything from chaos. That is what entropy is all about. Deconstructing order until there is no more order. That is when a new order can grow and blossom. That is why I wanted to meet with you Eidolon of Death. With all the death, you could stand by my side as my lieutenant. Helping me to rebuild the world with an unstoppable spirit army. It is not too late to join me."

Ronan couldn't believe the Eidolon was trying to recruit him into his insane plan. Even before trusting in the Light, Ronan would not have even considered this. But he had to remind himself of how convinced he had been that more power would solve his problems.

Ronan needed to come up with a plan right now. The Ether barrier could break at any time. He needed to focus but his Kitmazi mark was throbbing so intensely he could barely think.

This man was delusional. He not only believed that he could rebuild society, but that his Justice would save him from dying. But Ronan couldn't convince this man of anything. He was too caught up in the schemes of darkness and the Ether barrier could break at any time. Ronan then remembered the last piece of spiritual armor that the stranger had told him about. A spiritual sword forged from the word, given by the Light. The stranger had told him that this sword is necessary to both parry the blows from the darkness while also cutting through the lies of darkness. Ronan needed this spiritual sword right now. He desperately wished he was more versed in the word of the Light. He thought about the limited things he had heard about the Light. It had been enough to convince him to say no right to a Justice's face. There must be something that he could use now. At the thought, the throbbing in his arm grew to an excruciating level.

Ronan knew the mark was a symptom of his sinful heart. But why did it have to act up right now? He needed to find a solution. Unless... Ronan remembered some of Ta Rhe's final words. *Vallia intended to harm me, but the Light intended it for good to accomplish what is now being done.'* The Light was powerful enough to use the sins of Ronan's past for good. There was a way to glorify the Light with the scars from his former life. He thought about the fire elemental that had given him his mark. She had asked him to stab the ruby knife into the Ether. Here he was, thirty feet from the Ether River.

Thinking quickly, Ronan caught sight of the lava flowing from the wall and thought of the flaming birds that had escaped. If things could escape, could they also enter the same way? Hadn't Leo sent thousands of gallons of water in and out of the Ether? But how to convey what he needed to Leo?

Ronan attempted to inform him of his plan. He made eye contact with Leo and said, "If the world was not so divided, Sabastian may still be alive."

Leo gave him a baffled look.

Ronan continued; he lived between two worlds. Always popping between them. Now he is dead but maybe there is a way of honoring his memory.

Leo narrowed his eyes. Ronan could tell he was close to understanding but not quite there yet.

Yawbashé said, "It sounds like your friend died because of the division in our world. Think about a world where everyone was forced into equal positions. Do you think your friend would have been singled out then?"

Ronan gave Leo a stern look, praying he understood. "Sabastian would have understood. He would have transitioned to stand next to Yawbashé. Will you help me honor his memory?"

Leo stared at Ronan for a long agonizing second. Then recognition crossed his face. He flexed his fingers. Ronan gave the slightest of nods. Leo looked at the Eidolon and then back to Ronan calculating. The ground gave the largest shake yet and Ronan took that as his opportunity.

"Now!" he called out. Leo opened a large rift next to Ronan. Thankfully no superheated steam came out. Instead flames erupted from the mouth of the rift blasting Ronan with a wave of heat. Closing his eyes and covering his face with his charcoal hand he ran into the rift.

In a second, the chasm around him vanished and so did the ground below Ronan's feet. He went from running to slowly falling through an open void of flames and rocks. Ronan could barely open his eyes from the intensity of the air temperature. Through his squinted lids, Ronan saw a second glowing rift open in the middle of the air. It was below him but off to the side, far enough away that his current floating trajectory would miss the opening. Ronan immediately regretted his plan. Why had he thought that the landscape inside would be predictable? Why had he assumed that gravity would work here? That was a force from the Nether. His heart pounded as he contemplated the idea that he could be trapped in this inferno until he was cooked from the outside in.

Frantically trying to correct his path, he saw a flaming rock passing by in the opposite direction. With a well-timed kick, he was able to push himself just enough that his path met up with the second rift.

Ronan passed through the glowing opening. He appeared behind the Eidolon of Entropy right next to the shore of the Ether River. Yawbashé's yellow eyes flashed to Ronan's appearance. They were wide behind his mask. Ronan was close enough to attack the Eidolon but knew that would only result in his disintegration. Instead, he grabbed the ruby dagger from his belt and knelt, plunging the blade into a crack in the translucent barrier hovering above the glowing Ether River.

The world exploded. Ronan flew back ten feet, smashing into the ground. Yawbashé was thrown to the ground and his sword was dislodged. Leo and Vallia must have seen the blast coming as they both dove for the ground. From his position laying on his back, Ronan watched a giant flame sprout from the Ether River. Burning arms stretched out above them. A face bloomed in the inferno. A deep chortle echoed throughout the chasm.

The Kitmazi towered twenty feet over the scene. She surveyed the gathering of people before her. Her eyes landed on the comparatively diminutive Legislator. Yawbashé looked up at the flaming Ether being. His eyes had lost their yellow glow behind his mask and were now filled with fear.

The deep voice of the Kitmazi called out. "Eidolon!" She pointed at him. "Attack. Ether. Punish."

The Eidolon of Entropy pointed his sword at the Kitmazi. A yellow beam of energy blasted from the tip of the sword. It passed through the flame and collided with the stone behind her, turning it to dust.

The Kitmazi laughed. She raised her arm. The flames formed into a fist shape, and she brought it down onto the Eidolon of Entropy. The fire poured onto the rock, as if it were a waterfall. The heat was so intense, Ronan had to look away and protect his face. The fire blasted the rock where Yawbashé had been for several sweltering seconds.

When the Kitmazi stopped her assault, the rock glowed red like an ember. As it cooled, Ronan could see that there were not even bones left from the blast. All that laid on the ground was the Eidolon's sword and his black metal mask.

Chapter 42

The towering figure of fire began to shrink. When her giant visage had dwindled to a human size, she glided to the shore. Ronan stood up from the ground and walked to where the black sand met the river of energy.

Ronan couldn't believe his eyes when the Kitmazi bowed before him.

She said in a low crackle, "Eidolon. Thank you." She pointed to the river around her. "Home. Safe."

Ronan pointed to the mask and sword. "No, thank you. Thank you for stopping the Eidolon of Entropy and for saving my life in the catacombs." He didn't know what else to say to her. He felt torn between gratitude and disdain. If it had not been for her, he would have bled to death in the Nether. But she was also the reason half his body was a charcoal mess. His eyes unintentionally glanced down at his charred arm.

She looked at his arm as well and smiled. "I. Will. Remember."

Ronan didn't know what to do with that. He nodded at her. "Yeah, I will remember as well. It will be hard to forget."

The Kitmazi bowed again. Then she backed away from the shore, sinking into the Ether River and was gone.

Ronan stood on the edge of the river, staring into the pulsing colors under the cracked translucent barrier. Vallia walked up beside him.

She asked, "Was that Kitmazi living inside of you?"

Ronan looked down at his charcoal arm. The fire emblem no longer glowed red. "Yeah, I assume she was burning me to a crisp from the inside."

Leo walked up on his other side. "Sometimes, our sins leave scars. We can either let the scars tell our story. Or we can tell the story of those scars

344

to help others avoid the same fate."

'Could I use my burned arms to tell a story of how the Light delivered me from a path of darkness?' Ronan contemplated as he stared into the swirling energy before him. Vallia and Leo stood silently by his sides. There was an odd peace standing just feet away from elemental chaos under the translucent barrier.

Eventually, Ronan shook his head to clear it and walked over to where Yawbashé had been. As he knelt to pick up the mask, he found it still hot to the touch. It was hard to imagine the dark things this mask had seen. He decided to keep the mask as a reminder that the path he now walked was narrow and that it was surrounded by darkness.

His foot brushed against the jagged broadsword as he stood. His eyes locked onto the black crystal that was crudely set into the hilt. *'Bridgestone.'*

Ronan found himself mesmerized by the way the crystal glittered in the chromatic light. Or maybe it was the power that he knew dwelt within the stone. A direct connection to the Nether. *'What could I do with that kind of power?'*

Ronan took a deep breath. *'The only thing that this power would bring me is sorrow,'* he told himself.

"Do either of you want this sword?" Ronan asked his companions.

Vallia smirked. "Not really my style. But thanks. Although, if we are going to keep meeting up with other Eidolon, I may need to find an alternative weapon because it seems like you all are immune to arrows."

"I don't think I am immune to arrows," Ronan jested.

"Good, because if you ever go crazy with power like the Eidolon of Entropy, I am going to empty my quiver into you."

Leo picked up the sword. He gave it several swings. "I think I know where to put this where it cannot be used for future dark deeds." He tossed the sword into the air and flexed his fingers. A rift ripped open, and the blade was consumed into the Ether.

Ronan felt a pang of regret, but he pushed it away, knowing Leo had done the right thing.

Without saying another word, they all turned and began to climb up the now cracked stone wall. As they crested the top, they saw in the fading light of the sunset, the four spiders and the large lizard creature all dead on the ground. It appeared they had killed each other off. The spiders looked melted, and the lizard was covered in acid burns.

Off in the distance, it seemed like the fighting had ended. Ronan was perplexed by this. There was no way the Legion soldiers could have known the Legislator of War was dead. They walked over to the location of the barricades and saw what had ended the battle.

A large fissure had split the field in half and enormous, luminescent snakes the size of tree trunks had slithered out and now covered the ground. The hatred of the two groups had not been great enough to fight through the invasion of the massive Ether snakes. Ronan, Leo, and Vallia slowly backed away from the hissing monstrosities. Ronan wondered how far out the fissures had spread from the Ether Scar.

They reached the encampment and saw several tents had been destroyed. At first, Ronan thought the Legion had broken into the UN'kra camp. Then he saw what had caused the damage.

A large mound of fur and flesh was lying on the ground, surrounded by UN'kra. The creature's body dwarfed the nearby warriors, even on its side. Black spears stuck out of its blue fur. Ronan saw the head of the creature had four large sapphire tusks jutting out of its mouth.

One of the UN'kra around the creature was Smog Sul. Ronan walked up to her and nodded at the creature. "I think this might have been our fault. We stopped the Eidolon of Entropy but not before he did some serious damage to the barrier over the Ether."

Smog Sul clapped him on the back, almost buckling his knees. "Look at ya. Ya didn't die and ya stopped da maniac. Praise da Light on high. Ya done good Eidolon. Ya done good." She turned to the furry mound. "And don't worry about dis beastie. We took 'em down and now we got some good eatin. We're gonna celebrate da retreat of da Legion dogs."

Leo chimed in, "The Light delivered us in the battle and gave us victory." The crowd cheered at the news.

Smog Sul asked, "So ya saw more of dese brutes, did ya?"

Ronan explained about the spiders and lizard and snakes. She listened and nodded.

"Last I knew, da odder chiefs were deep in prayer. BoRa is gonna wanna hear dis from ya lips. Imma gonna go find dem. Let 'em know ya back. I magin BoRa will find ya. Go in rest for now before another creature goes and sticks its head out a hole in da ground or dem Legion come back, angry 'cause you killed da leader. I'll send BoRa ya way."

Rest sounded so good to Ronan. He did not need any more convincing. Vallia led him to the tent they had been allocated. There were only two mats on the ground. Ronan smiled to himself at the idea of Vallia and Leo having to share a tent. If it had not been for the battle, he imagined this would have caused a lot of conflict. He flopped to the ground exhausted. Vallia shared a potato looking thing with him. It tasted salty but was surprisingly filling.

Ronan laid his head back against the canvas and belt as if his eyes were made of lead. He couldn't keep them open. He was alive. The Eidolon of Entropy had failed to unleash the Ether. *'Great Light. Thank you for delivering me through this trial.'* That was all he could think of before he passed out.

Chapter 43

Ronan awoke to Chief BoRa Fa Glee gently shaking his shoulder. He had no idea what time it was. A sharp pain in his neck indicated he had fallen asleep in a terribly awkward position. He pushed himself off the floor and wiped the spittle from his mouth.

"You have had a very busy day, Eidolon." BoRa said quietly. He handed Ronan a smoking ceramic mug.

Ronan was taken aback by a warm, bitter chocolate taste that tingled across his young.

BoRa smiled. "The Ether Scar provides some very unique opportunities to grow some exotic things. Now Eidolon, tell me everything that happened yesterday in the Scar."

Ronan took a deep breath. "I may need another cup to get through that."

BoRa smiled and nodded.

Ronan then recounted all that had transpired the previous day. From waking up to the stranger to the Kitmazi decimating the Eidolon. It felt surprisingly cathartic. BoRa was silent during the explanation. He was easy to talk to. Ronan understood why he was a chief ten of this UN'kra clan.

Once Ronan was finished, BoRa joyfully explained, "The Legion forces were reported to begin their retreat last night after numerous Ether rifts opened up near the Legion encampment. Ether creatures began to emerge from the ground and terrorize the troops. It would appear that the loss of their leader and the aggressive assault of the planar creatures was enough to send them running. We cannot thank you enough for all that you have done for us."

Ronan did not know what to do with the praise as he felt it was mostly unearned. Instead, he diverted, "What happens now?"

BoRa said, "Life goes on. We will rebuild what is gone and repair what is broken. The three of you are, of course, welcome to stay in the village as long as you wish. But I should not presume anything. Would it please you to stay in our village and recover from your long journey? Our scribes would be enthused to write down the story of the latest judge of the Light that saved our people."

A judge. Ronan liked the title. He had helped not only the UN'kra people but everyone in Celcus. This was a form of respect that he never could have dreamed of. Hero of the people. Sent by some incomprehensible master plan of the Light. He had always thought that if he worked hard enough, he would gain respect. But this respect came from doing the right thing and obeying the Light.

Ronan looked at his friends. Vallia shrugged. "I'm not gonna lie, I have been wanting to take a vacation for a while."

Leo nodded. "I would enjoy spending time with my mother's people."

Ronan looked at BoRa. "Sounds like we'll stay."

BoRa stood up and exclaimed, "Splendid, in that case, Eidolon, would you do me the honor of walking with me?"

"Of course," Ronan replied, surprised by the request.

They walked out of the city of tents up a winding path. The road led to a village of houses made out of a plethora of materials ranging from wood to stone, slabs of marble, and metal plates. One building even looked as if it was made from black onyx.

BoRa must have noticed Ronan's interest in the buildings as he explained, "The Ether Scar has always provided for us. Materials for buildings and tools. Minerals not found anywhere else on the continent. It has proven to be a wonderful blessing of the Light."

Ronan could imagine this to be true. The minerals were one of the reasons the Council coveted this land so much.

They continued to follow a trail out of the village and into the forest. BoRa did not talk for a long time. Rather, he seemed to just take in the beauty of the trees around him. When he eventually spoke, he said, "You said that you saw a particle of light? I wish to know everything about that encounter and the one with the stranger who gave you your armor."

Ronan did as he asked and recounted his trip to the Nether. He provided context about the Nether as another plane of energy but built on the rigid laws of the world. BoRa did not question this or challenge the idea. He seemed to grasp the concept quickly. Ronan told BoRa about Mophantatha and Mawveth and about how he had discovered their individual corruptions. Then he identified Leo's conversation with Maya about salvation and repentance. He accompanied this with the parting words from Ta Rhe to fully paint the picture.

All the time Ronan spoke, they continued to slowly walk through the woods. BoRa simply nodded and listened, offering only the occasional question for clarification. Ronan found himself unintentionally divulging the entire account of the last week. There was something about this older UN'kra that invited trust and openness. Ronan found it freeing to tell someone else about the trials and struggles that he had been dealing with. He talked for what seemed like hours.

When Ronan finally finished his story, BoRa stopped walking.

BoRa concluded, "You have certainly been through much young Eidolon. Through it all, the Light used you to do some amazing things."

Ronan nodded, knowing this to be true but wishing he understood why. "I want to know more about the Light. I feel like I haven't even scratched the surface in terms of what there is to know."

BoRa gave him a soft smile. "Young Eidolon, I have lived for eighty-three summers and have been under tutelage about the Light for most of those years. I feel that I have not even scratched the surface of knowledge about the Light." He paused and looked around. Spotting something on the ground he sat down and motioned for Ronan to do the same.

BoRa pointed at a line of leaf cutter ants that marched across the path. "The way of the Light is much like these ants. There is but one path forward for those who follow the Light. We all have our own burdens to carry along the path. Some are small and some are large. Sometimes we need help carrying our burdens."

He pointed to an ant that was helping another carry a particularly large piece of leaf. "Life does not always make it easy to walk this straight path." BoRa picked up a small stick and placed it in the path of the ants. Several of the insects stopped and others bumped into them. "It is important that no matter what roadblock or destruction tries to take us from the path of the Light, we always find our way back."

As he said this, Ronan was fascinated to see several of the ants begin to walk around the stick and rejoin the line. All the other ants followed their lead.

BoRa continued, "Once these ants were larva. They were small and weak, and they did not walk the path. But one day, they changed forever, becoming the insects you see here today. They will never be larva again. So are we changed forever when we give our life to the Light. I assure you that there is no force of darkness or scheme of evil that can separate us from the love of the Light."

"You speak with such wisdom. I wish to be as wise as you one day."

BoRa replied, "There is no better pursuit than wisdom of the Light. Fortunately for us, we are surrounded by the creation of the Light. Every tree, every rock, and even every ant is a bold testimony about the character of the Light. Such beautiful intricacies of detail have no other explanation but a sovereign divine creator. This is why we are starting here. This is how we teach the young UN'kra. Ronan Riviera, your desire to know everything about the Light is admirable. Never lose that excitement and hunger. For the Light will meet you where you are at and will continually fill you as you will allow."

Ronan's excitement filled his chest at this statement. For so long, he had felt that no matter how much effort he put in, life would continually demand more from him. But to hear that the Light gave as he sought was intimately comforting. "Teach me. I need to know more."

BoRa happily obliged. He began to teach Ronan about the very beginning of the world when chaotic elements had come under order and law by the Light's sovereign command. It was such a different outlook compared to that of Osmodius, claiming that by chance, the Ether and Nether collided and the Prime Plane was spontaneously formed. Ronan remembered Leo's reaction to Osmodius' primordial outlook. Now it made sense. Ronan found that Osmodius' concept of random haphazard creation took more faith and hope than the idea of a sovereign design.

BoRa followed up this account with ancestral UN'kra submission under the Light and resulting blessings as well as times of hard-heartedness and subsequent punishments. Ronan was captivated by the recollections of past battles and victories mirrored with laments of tragedies and failures.

BoRa talked until the evening had begun to creep and he could not talk any more. Ronan's head swam with all the information. Once they had finally returned to camp after nightfall, Ronan found that he was not able to sleep at all with everything swirling around in his head.

The next morning, Leo found Ronan and Vallia and informed them that Dezden wanted to speak with him. Ronan had not expected the previous High Arbiter of the Council to keep his word about having a conversation. As Leo led them into the heart of the Kortha village, Ronan found he was strangely anxious to speak with Dezden.

Leo led them to a simple wooden longhouse where Dezden sat on the porch in a finely crafted rocking chair, waiting for them.

Dezden acknowledged them and said, "Hail and well met. I hope I am not interrupting your time of rest. This conversation will not take up much of your time. I wanted to talk with you as you are the first people from the Zwellian Empire that I have met in a long while. How is the Empire?"

Ronan was taken back by the question. "In what regards?"

"How are the people? How are the civilians? What does the oppression of the Legion look like nowadays?" Dezden folded his hands in his lap and leaned back.

Somehow Ronan found it hard to process the fact that this man, who had once occupied the most powerful seat of the nation, was now asking three strangers about the political atmosphere. "Well, everyone is still struggling under the oppression of the Council. In the years you have been gone, things have gotten worse. People are scared to go outside for fear of invoking the wrath of the Legion that now prowl the city streets. Tax collectors commonly break down doors and steal every possession worth 2 pieces of silver that they can find, leaving people with nothing left for the next month. Labor camps are constantly needing to expand because they're at capacity. No one has anything in plenty except for fear and loathing of the Council. I think people have become used to the circumstances. But by no means is anyone but the wealthiest doing anything but surviving. But, the oppression is not something new. It was there when you were in office. I would love to hear your justification for that."

Ronan had not meant to get so heated but found he could not help himself. This man was just as responsible for the state of the empire as the current Legislators.

Dezden gave him a sad look. "When I was the High Arbiter, I did not take my position as reverently as I should have. I was selfish and all I cared about was maintaining the status quo of the nation. I cared only for the control, not for the people. I was not a kind and benevolent leader. My time with the UN'kra has shown me that. Their community thrives even in this time of war because of their deep devotion to their beliefs and values. Every day I wish that I could right the wrongs I have committed against the people of the Zwellian Empire."

Ronan was about to make a snide remark before he recognized that Dezden was showing remorse and a desire for repentance. He had to remind himself that he had made a lot of poor choices in his life. He was just fortunate that those choices had all been made when he had no authority. Dezden was not so fortunate.

Vallia inquired, "Why do you hide and lament about the past? Why not do something to right some of those wrongs?"

Dezden perked up. "What do you mean?"

Vallia looked at Ronan and Leo. "We happen to know of an organization that operates counter to the efforts of the Council. They are not necessarily attempting to overthrow the empire, but everything they do is in direct opposition to the current government. You would be very provocative to the leader of the group. Maybe you could convince the group that it would be worth their while to make more of an active stance against the Council. Who knows, with your knowledge and their influence, you may be able to start some kind of revolution or something."

Dezden nodded intently as he thought about what she said. "And you would be willing to introduce me to this group?"

Ronan looked at Vallia with a questioning glance. She was not the type to mention the Carpenters to strangers let alone offer to make an introduction.

Vallia caught his eye. "After seeing what I have in the last week, I think it is about time that someone does something about the unchecked power of the Council." She looked at Leo. "Can he be trusted?"

Leo smiled. "I will vouch for him. I have heard much about his growth from my mother. Besides, he can't possibly be more detrimental to travel with than our previous companions."

Vallia accepted this statement with a stern nod. "Dezden, when we leave here, you can come with us. We can make an introduction, but the rest will be up to you. Understand? I can't promise you anything beside that."

Dezden stood from his chair. "I understand the risks of leaving this place. I do not do it lightly, but I think it is high time for a change in my life. I can no longer sit by and watch as the Council crushes the life out of the Zwellian Empire. Please let me know when you are ready to leave. I will pack right now and be ready for our departure. Thank you."

"Before you go," Ronan said. "I was wondering if, in your study of the Eidolon and Justices, you knew their symbols. It may be helpful to know them all considering I have tangled with three of them in the last week and each one almost killed me. There are only three more, but if I know the symbols, it might help me to not die in the future."

Dezden nodded. He produced a piece of paper and scratched out the symbols. Then he handed the paper to Ronan.

Ronan scanned over the shapes recognizing the half smoke skull, the goblet with legs, and the triangle with the three moon phases on top. When he saw Maya's mark, he wondered about her. Where had she gone? What was her plan? He reminded himself that she had left him to die, and he should not care about what happened to her. Regardless of this truth, he found it difficult to shake her from his mind.

Chapter 44

Ronan spent the next few days learning about the Light and the UN'kra way of life. Leo took him and Vallia on several hikes around the mountains to see breathtaking views. Along the way, they were able to see some exotic Ether-touched creatures like the lightning birds Leo had mentioned and large bullfrogs with diamond-studded skin.

Ronan was glad to see Leo spend a lot of his time in the village with his mother. Ronan learned quickly that she was a wonderful woman with a fantastic knack for cooking. He found his preconceptions about the UN'kra being changed. He had never believed them to be monsters, but he was honestly surprised at how similar their lives were to those back in the Zwellian Empire.

When he was not with his mother, Leo was in the temple reading ancient texts of the Light and teaching Ronan a small amount of UN'kran.

Ronan noticed several occasions when Vallia trained with the UN'kra archers. Apparently, they were very skilled bowmen. He had never seen her prouder than the night she returned from a hunt with the archers. Apparently, she had managed to score the killing blow on a large elk with massive antlers.

Ronan was wondering how she was dealing with the fact that some of the archers were Ether Crafters like Leo.

When he asked her, she shrugged. "They definitely are different from the Crafters of the Legion. They respect the Ether. They still force it to come into our plane, but when they do they have a reverence for the elements. They taught me some breathing techniques they use that they think could help with my wind abilities."

Ronan was grateful for this downtime. He saw that it was good for his companions and knew it was good for himself. He felt he had been through a lot and needed to rest and process everything that had happened. Just when he was feeling relaxed and optimistic, the village received news via messenger eagle from a nearby UN'kra settlement.

Ronan heard about the eagle but did not know what the message encompassed until a town meeting was called that night.

At the meeting, BoRa read the letter to the gathered crowd. He spoke in UN'kran, so Leo quietly translated for Ronan and Vallia.

"To the Kortha tribe, our sister under the sovereign Light. From the KeeHosha tribe. Peace and prosperity be yours. We write to report that Ether fissures have opened up all over the mountains. Energy has poured out, followed by various Ether creatures. Some were docile but others were dangerous and destructive. We have also heard rumors of similar events happening south, within the Zwellian Empire."

Chatter ran through the crowd at the news. BoRa read on, but Ronan couldn't focus after hearing that Ether creatures were being spotted in the south. *'How far south?'*

Ronan whispered to Vallia and Leo, "It seems that whatever the Eidolon of Entropy did, it is causing a ripple effect across the land."

Vallia seemed pensive. Eventually she said, "I want to investigate these claims in the Zwellian Empire. I need to see for myself how bad it is." She paused and processed how to say her next statement. She sighed, "Would you two be willing to come with me? I know you are both happy here so I don't want to pull you away from that, but I think you could both be very helpful."

Ronan was surprised by this request. He was even more addled by the fact she had invited Leo along.

She saw the look they both gave her, and she rolled her eyes. "Look, if we run into an Ether creature, it would be nice to have someone with some experience with the Ether and the ability to put it back where it came from if that is possible."

357

Leo smiled at her. "I consider you both as friends. I have not had friends for a long time. I would be honored to come with you."

They both looked at Ronan. Ronan wanted to stay with the UN'kra people. But he could not shake the nagging self-blame that he felt for the appearance of the Ether creatures. Had he stopped the Eidolon of Entropy sooner, these anomalies may have been avoided. Vallia was right. They may be able to help clean up the mess that he felt partially responsible for.

Ronan said, "You have never led me astray before. Of course I'll come with you."

Vallia nodded. "Then I don't see a need to delay. I think we should leave tomorrow morning. We can let Dezden know and see if he wants to come with us."

Ronan sadly agreed that time was of the essence. He decided to wait after the town meeting to catch BoRa. He wanted to say goodbye and thank him for everything.

After BoRa was done speaking and the other UN'kra started to dissipate, Ronan caught up with the elder. "We heard the news. I fear this was my fault."

BoRa shook his head, "There is no way you could have known how the actions of the Eidolon were going to ripple outward. You stopped things from getting worse."

Ronan felt comforted by the reassurance. "Either way, my friends and I have decided to leave and investigate the Ether anomalies in the South. We think we may be able to help in some way."

BoRa smiled in a way that accentuated the wrinkles by his eye. "Something told me that you would feel called back to the south. It is unfortunate because I have enjoyed your time here. But I understand that you must go. The Light does not call you to stay here forever. Thank you for your dedication to knowledge and the truth. I don't have much to give you except some parting wisdom. Having faith in the Light is imperative. Hoping in the Light is indispensable. But most importantly, love as the Light loves you."

Ronan took in the advice. He said, "Thank you. For mentoring me and helping me these last few days. I have learned much. Maybe one day I can return and learn more."

BoRa nodded and patted Ronan on the back. "Maybe we will see each other again, young Eidolon. Safe travels and fair blessings."

As Ronan began to walk away, BoRa called after him, "Remember your powers are a gift, but they are not who you are. Your power does not come from yourself. Do not get lost in your powers."

The words echoed in Ronan's mind as he looked for his friends. He found Vallia saying her goodbyes to the hunters. He watched as they surprised her with a gift of a modified UN'kra bow. The bow was made from a light-colored wood and had beautiful antlers carved all around it. They had even crafted prongs from the antler of the elk she had killed, into the top and bottom of the bow.

Ronan looked over and saw Leo hugging his mother. He heard Leo say, "If the Light wills it, I will return."

His mother told him, "The Light be with you always my son. It was so wonderful to see you again. Even for a short while." She then gave him a pack of sweets that she had baked, and a long hug. The sight of the embrace brought a tear to his eye. In that moment, he was happy for his friend as much as he was mournful for his own mother.

They exited the town meeting and headed back to their cabin. Ronan went to sleep that night with a new excitement kindling inside for the future adventure.

That night he had a dream.

He was on a large ship in the middle of a violent storm. Ropes criss crossed all around, running up the three different masts that bore torn black sails. Waves crashed up against the boat, causing it to list and sway. Ronan looked around but saw no sailors aboard.

Ronan then heard the cold voice of Mawveth.

"Hello, Traitor."

Ronan responded to the open air, "Have you come to beg me to come back to you? Was I unclear clear enough that I am not going to be your slave?"

Mawveth laughed, "**You think I would beg you? You think that you are better off following the Light than you are with me? You will come crawling back to me, begging me to accept you. When the Light fails you, I will be here. You can come to me and grovel at my feet. Maybe I will be generous and let you live your life out as a prisoner in the deepest depths of the Nether.**"

Now it was Ronan's turn to laugh. "I can tell you are hopelessly lost without me. What is your plan now? Wait for me to die and in two hundred years, see if you can pick an ignorant Eidolon to do your will?"

"**Two hundred years to me is nothing. Though I will not have to wait. I have another that will do my will. I made you in an attempt to double my influence. You were never my only pawn. Look to the helm of the ship and see my true champion.**"

This statement smacked Ronan like the waves colliding against the hull of the ship. He walked toward the back of the ship and climbed the wooden stairs. A crack of lightning flashed in the sky. The sudden light illuminated a figure dressed in a black leather tailcoat that was pulled over an iron breastplate with black glittering crystal set into the chest piece. Ronan recognized it as bridgestone. The figure wore an old tricorne hat adorned with a long weathered black feather. Green burning eyes glowed out of the darkness under the hat.

The clouds above shifted, and rays of moonlight filtered through the air. The shadowed face of the figure looked up at the moon, revealing his grotesque features.

Ronan almost fell down the stairs. The man that stood before him was missing half of the skin and muscle on his face. The bone of his jaw was exposed on one side of his mouth revealing a bony smile. The other side was covered in a gray bushy beard. His right eye sat vacant. All that could be seen was the revealed bone of his skull and flaming green socket next to a flaming green eye.

Mawveth said in a low threatening voice, "**Say hello to Nizomotus, The first Eidolon of the Dead.**"

The air caught in Ronan's chest. Panic filled him with the haunted vision

360

that stood before him. All he could muster was, "How is he alive?"

Mawveth responded, **"It's amazing what can be accomplished when you are willing to push the boundaries of what is possible. If that means siphoning the energy from spirits to keep himself alive, he is willing to do that. Willing to loyally serve me for two hundred years. He is ready to take up his crown. The crown that you could have shared with him."**

Ronan's heart was hammering in his chest. Lightning flashed again, illuminating the surrounding ocean. To Ronan's horror, he saw two other ships with black sails to the left side. He looked right and a lightning strike illuminated another two ships. Ronan turned around and looked toward the bow of the ship. What had been an empty deck just moments before, now teamed with motion. Skeletons covered the ship. They crawled up the rigging and tied off ropes. Some bailed water and others pushed crates and moved supplies. The countless army of skeletons moved about as if there was not a raging storm assaulting the ship. Each skeletal sailor possessed a set of burning green eyes.

Ronan turned back to the captain, panic overwhelming his mind. All he could think about was the destruction and chaos that the Justice of Death could cause with a spirit fueled armada controlled by an undying Eidolon.

As he came to this conclusion, Mawveth's laugh filled the night. **"I promise you this, you made a grievous mistake when you walked away from me. Prepare yourself Prince of the Dead. There is a storm coming, and it is about to make landfall."**

Authors Note

Thank you for taking the time to read this book. This story was four years in the making. Starting from a particularly low point in my life, I found that writing this novel was oddly cathartic. Building up a fantasy world of elemental chaos and rigid order was a blessing every time I sat down and wrote. But I wanted you as my dedicated reader to know that not every element of this book is fictional.

The Prince of the Dead features Ronan coming to terms with the dark path he has been walking and his journey that leads him to put his faith in the Light who is the sovereign creator of all things. This theme is not one of fiction. We live in a world created by a loving God. A perfect God. A God that we are immeasurably separated from due to our indisputable pride and our habitual selfishness. In short, we define what is good for ourselves and thus walk a path of darkness.

The Bible, which is the word of God written down by men who were inspired by God, attests to the separation from God when we walk this path of darkness.

"This is the message we have heard from him and proclaim to you, that God is light, and in him is no darkness at all. If we say we have fellowship with him while we walk in darkness, we lie and do not practice the truth." (1 John 1:5-6 (English Standard Version)).

This proclivity to walk the path of darkness is in all humans. It is called sin.

"All have turned aside; together they have become worthless; no one does

362

good, not even one.""" (Romans 3:12).

So if everyone walks a path of darkness, and that separates us from God for all eternity, what hope is there?

Please look at another true theme in this book. The Child of Light. The One to come.

In this book, the UN'kra look to a future savior who will become a bridge that spans the separation between them and the Light.

We can praise God because in our world, the One to Come has already came.

"For God so loved the world, that he gave his only Son, that whoever believes in him should not perish but have eternal life." (John 3:16).

The son of God called Jesus the Christ, came and did the impossible. He lived a perfect life walking only the path of light and never straying from the path. Never sinning.

"Again Jesus spoke to them, saying, "I am the light of the world. Whoever follows me will not walk in darkness, but will have the light of life."" (John 8:12).

Jesus lived a perfect life but his story did not stop there. If it did there would be no home for us. But Jesus willingly was crucified and died. In his death, he took on all the sin and darkness of every person. God condemned Jesus on the cross so that we could be seen as righteous in God's eyes. Jesus sacrificed himself so we could walk the path of light with God. He took the punishment that was reserved for us because of our sin.

"There is therefore now no condemnation for those who are in Christ Jesus. For the law of the Spirit of life has set you free in Christ Jesus from the law of sin and death. For God has done what the law, weakened by the flesh, could not do. By sending his own Son in the likeness of sinful flesh and for sin, he condemned sin in the flesh," (Romans 8:1-3).

If Jesus was just a good person that died for the benefit of others, there would still be no merit to his story. But the final element of his coming was that three days after he died, Jesus Christ rose himself from the dead.

"For if we have been united with him in a death like his, we shall certainly be united with him in a resurrection like his. We know that our old self was crucified with him in order that the body of sin might be brought to nothing, so that we would no longer be enslaved to sin. For one who has died has been set free from sin. Now if we have died with Christ, we believe that we will also live with him. We know that Christ, being raised from the dead, will never die again; death no longer has dominion over him. For the death he died he died to sin, once for all, but the life he lives he lives to God. So you also must consider yourselves dead to sin and alive to God in Christ Jesus." (Romans 6:5-11).

There is hope for you today. You are not forced to walk the path of darkness that only leads to eternal sorrow and separation from God. But through trusting Christ's life, death and resurrection, we can walk the path of light. There will still be darkness along the path. Life will still have its trials, but they have no lasting power over those who trust in Christ.

"because, if you confess with your mouth that Jesus is Lord and believe in your heart that God raised him from the dead, you will be saved. For with the heart one believes and is justified, and with the mouth one confesses and is saved. For the Scripture says, "Everyone who believes in him will not be put to shame."" (Romans 10:9-11).

Consider your life today. Are you like Ronan, trying to get by in this world, walking a path of darkness? If so, think about that path. Is it worth it? Does the pain and sorrow that comes with the darkness ever seem too much to handle? You are not trapped on the path of darkness. Think about these words.

"No, in all these things we are more than conquerors through him who loved us. For I am sure that neither death nor life, nor angels nor rulers, nor things present nor things to come, nor powers, nor height nor depth, nor anything else in all creation, will be able to separate us from the love of God in Christ Jesus our Lord." (Romans 8:37-39).

Take some time to reflect on your life. Look into these scriptures. Look into Jesus. Ask what is stopping you from accepting him into your life? If you have questions about what I have said in this note, reach out to me. I would be happy to talk with you about these things.

I pray that this note has helped you in some way, to come closer to knowing and loving the Lord of Light.

Contact me at pagesbyajmitchell@gmail.com